NO FEAR

NO SHAME SERIES BOOK 3

NORA PHOENIX

Love,
Nora

No Fear (No Shame Series Book 3) by Nora Phoenix

www.noraphoenix.com

PUBLISHER'S NOTE

This novel depicts mature situations and themes that are not suitable for underage readers. Reader discretion is advised. Please note there's a trigger warning for mentions of domestic abuse, sexual abuse, and sexual violence in this series, including rape.

1

The yellow sticky note on the kitchen counter left little room for misinterpretation.

"Aaron: clean your shit up. Now."

Aaron Gordon didn't need a name to know who wrote it. Blake. Aka Professor Kent, the Brazilian-jiujitsu teacher who'd kindly taken Aaron into his home, a home he shared at the moment with two women and an older guy—all victims of domestic abuse. And apparently, Aaron had repaid his kindness by making a mess. Again.

He looked around the well-used kitchen and winced. His stuff was everywhere. He'd left his backpack on the floor, his shoes next to the back door, and his dirty dishes on the counter. He'd even forgotten to throw the carton and plastic from the microwave meal he'd devoured for dinner yesterday in the trash.

A check of the living room revealed the same. The sleeve of the Xbox game he'd played was still on the table, as was the magazine he'd been reading, and the wrapper of his candy bar. He'd even discarded his dirty socks on the floor, right under the coffee table.

The kitchen and living room were common areas, meaning everyone could use them. It also meant you weren't supposed to leave personal stuff lying around. Aaron had his own cabinet in the kitchen where he could store food and china—if he'd had any. His room also had a large closet for his stuff. It wasn't even half-full. All he had left were his clothes. He'd sold his furniture and everything else when he'd lost his job and had to cancel the lease on his apartment in a DC suburb. His clothes and his car were all that remained from the up-and-coming lifestyle he'd once had.

He needed a job. Desperately.

But first, he needed to clean up his stuff. His shit, as Blake had put it, though words like that still did not come easily to Aaron. It was the result of a conservative Christian upbringing, strict parents who did not tolerate that kind of language. He'd never even uttered curse words till a few months ago.

He cleaned up the kitchen first, making the extra effort of wiping down the entire counter after doing his dishes. The living room was little work, which made him feel even guiltier he'd left his stuff there.

It was hard to think of things like that when he'd never had to. His mom had always cleaned up after him, and when he'd lived on his own, nobody else had been around to see. He'd cleaned up maybe once a week, once every other week if he'd been busy. He couldn't do that here, not in a house he shared with others—as Blake had explained to him multiple times in the last couple of weeks. He felt like such a kid when the guy did that, even though they were only ten years apart. And the fact that Aaron had forgotten again, had received this publicly visible reminder from Blake, man, it made him feel like a total loser. A fuck-up, was the better word.

He tasted the foreign, rude word on his tongue. Fuck-up. Yup, that was exactly what he was. An utter and complete fuck-up. And he'd managed to disappoint Blake once again, the man who'd taken him in weeks ago and had asked for nothing in return. Not even rent—which Aaron wouldn't have been able to pay anyway, but that was beside the point. Blake deserved better.

Aaron looked around the living room. It could do with a bit of cleaning, actually. The kitchen too. It wasn't gross, but there was dust, and both the tile floor in the kitchen and the hardwood floors in the living room could use a good mopping. Should he? Yeah, that would make up for his slovenliness.

It took him two hours, but by the time he was done, the kitchen was sparkling and smelling of the lemon-scented cleaner he'd used, and the living room was dust-free. He'd even vacuumed the couch cushions, finding a condom packet when he did. Was it Blake's? He'd never seen the guy with a woman so far, but who knew.

He admired his cleaning work, satisfied he'd done a good job. At least Blake would be happy with him now. He checked his watch. Two o'clock. That late already? Huh, he must have slept in again.

Oh, crap! He was supposed to meet Blake at the jiujitsu studio at two to help him with some stuff. He'd completely forgotten.

He got changed in a hurry and ran out the door. The studio was close, but he still didn't arrive till fifteen minutes past the agreed time.

"You're late," Blake greeted him when Aaron hurried in.

He was dressed in tight gray training pants and a form-fitting black shirt, looking good as always.

Aaron's shoulders slouched. "I'm sorry. I lost track of time. I cleaned the living room and the kitchen?"

Blake's face softened. "I appreciate that, Aaron, but we had an agreement you'd be here at two."

"I know. I'm sorry." He stared at the floor. Even when he wanted to do the right thing, he still messed up. Yup, total fuck-up.

"Look, I know things haven't been easy for you, and I get that you needed some time to figure things out. Time's up. You need to get your shit together, Aaron, because I have no patience for people who don't keep their promises. I need to able to count on you, trust that your word means something, you feel me?"

Much to his embarrassment, Aaron felt hot tears burning in his eyes. Life sucked so very badly at the moment. Would it ever stop? He swallowed, determined to fight back the tears. "You're right. I'm trying, but I don't know where to start. It's all so overwhelming."

"Do you want my help?"

His head jerked up. "Of course, I do!" What kind of question was that?

Blake's expression was kind. "You haven't asked for it, so far."

Aaron frowned. Why would he have to ask for help? Couldn't Blake see he needed it? Why would he make Aaron go through the humiliation of having to explicitly ask for it? "I didn't realize I had to," he said.

"And there is arrogant Aaron again." Blake shook his head. "Boy, you know how to push my buttons, don't you?"

Aaron shoved his hands in the pockets of his jeans,

feeling infinitesimally small. "I don't mean to," he said softly.

"I know, which is the only reason I let you get away with it. What you need more than anything is an attitude adjustment. You have this sense of entitlement that rears its ugly head all the time. Until you get rid of that, you're not gonna get far, boy."

"I'm not a boy. I'm twenty-four." It was all he could say when his soul felt like it had been cut to shreds. He'd never realized how much Blake didn't like him.

Blake's eyes narrowed. "Then fucking act like it. You're entitled to shit, and the sooner you realize that, the better. If you want something, anything, you're gonna have to work hard for it. And you'd better learn how to ask for help, because people aren't lining up to help you."

He would not cry. He clenched his fists, biting back his tears with all he had. "I need help. Please." It didn't come out as nicely as Blake might have wanted, but it was the best Aaron could do right now. He even managed to look Blake in the eye, saw a flicker of something he couldn't identify.

"All right, then. Let's get to work. Since you seem to enjoy cleaning, why don't you start by dusting and vacuuming the entire studio? After that, you can clean the big blue mat with a special cleaning product you'll find in the cupboard below the kitchen faucet. Make sure it's all done and dry before five because that's when the kids' lesson starts."

Aaron's mouth dropped slightly open. When Blake had said he could use Aaron's help, this was not what he had in mind. He'd thought it was a quick job, like hanging up a picture or something. Not hours and hours of cleaning, and especially not after he'd already done the kitchen and living room at home. Besides, he'd asked the guy for help. How did cleaning help him?

"I don't get it. How does this help me?"

Blake sighed. "Remember what I said about you not being entitled to shit? You've lived in my home for almost a month now, without paying rent. Think that's what you're entitled to? Think again. Until you're able to pay rent, you can work it off. Now, get your ass to work, because I have more to do."

As HE SAT in his tiny office, updating the financial data for the previous month, Blake wondered if he'd been too hard on Aaron. It was always a tricky line between confronting the folks he tried to help with a truth they needed to see and hurting them so much it rendered them passive. He could only hope he'd gotten it right with Aaron. He wasn't a bad kid, not by any means. Simply spoiled, as far as Blake could tell.

It was hard because Aaron often behaved in contradicting ways. Self-assured and cocky one second, insecure and hurt the next. Entitlement and arrogance were followed by confusion, helplessness, and social ineptitude.

Blake wondered what the story was with Aaron and his brother Josh. As far as Blake knew, they hadn't seen each other since Aaron moved in. Aaron hadn't even seen him for Christmas, had spent it alone as far as Blake could tell.

It could be because of personal stuff. Blake still hadn't been able to figure out what Noah and Josh were to Indy, and to each other, let alone what that cop's role was, but they were obviously tight. Noah had been in the hospital, and Indy had been on the run for some reason, so Josh likely had more on his mind than hanging out with his brother. Plus, from the little interaction he'd witnessed, they weren't close. Josh had seemed happy to be rid of him.

A soft buzzer alerted him someone had come in. Aaron was vacuuming the main floor, so he couldn't have heard it. Blake got up and walked into the hallway.

"Indy!" he said, surprised to see the young man by himself. "How are you?"

Indy was dressed in his gi, proudly wearing his brown belt. He was a natural, like the letter from Matt Fox had said. Blake had no idea what Indy's story was, but if Matt Fox requested you'd train him for free and keep his identity a secret, that's what you did. The guy was the highest-ranking Brazilian-jiujitsu professor in the country, a true guru of the sport. Blake had met the man twice, had seen him fight once, and was still in awe of his skills.

"Good. Thank you again for being a go-between for me and Connor."

Blake nodded. "No problem. You here to train?"

Indy looked apologetic. "If possible. I wasn't sure I would be able to come, so I didn't call."

"You here by yourself?"

"Yeah. Noah is still recuperating from his surgery, and Josh is taking care of him. Connor's at work."

Blake marveled at the casual way Indy suggested the four of them were together. They couldn't be, could they? Fuck, what did he care? He'd seen stranger things, and if they loved each other and it made them happy, it was fine with him. He honestly didn't care as long as it was all consensual.

"No problem. I need to finish something in the office, so why don't you get warmed up?"

Indy nodded. "Thanks, Professor."

Blake smiled as he went back to his office. He loved grappling with Indy, as he was so ridiculously talented. He was at most five foot six, so Blake had a good five or six inches on him and at least fifty pounds, but the guy simply never gave up. Indy didn't know the word defeat, and Blake respected the hell out of him for that alone.

It didn't happen often to Blake that he misjudged people, but he'd been wrong about the interaction between Noah and Indy. When the boy had shown up for the first time with that big guy in tow, his body language had been uncomfortable. Blake was a trained observer, and he'd spotted tiny moments of hesitation and flinching on Indy's part, followed by deliberate contact initiated by Indy. Blake had concluded Indy wasn't comfortable with Noah, was afraid of him on some level.

He'd been wrong.

Indy was uncomfortable with anyone touching him, though he tolerated it during grapples and practice and it was getting better. Blake could only guess the cause, but he didn't want to. It wasn't his place, and by now he was confident that whatever the relationship was between Indy, Noah, Josh and even Connor, Indy was safe and loved.

It had been unfortunate that Josh had concluded Blake had an issue with gays. He didn't, not even close. How could he when he himself was gay? Not that he was broadcasting it. Brazilian jiujitsu was still a bit of a macho sport, and he didn't want to deal with the inevitable homophobic reactions from some people. Also, not all parents were okay with a gay man teaching their kids.

But his brothers knew and so did his close friends, and of course the one-night stands he fucked at a gay club twenty miles away. He only went once a month, but he rarely left without finding a suitable guy willing to bottom for him. It wasn't ideal but it worked. For now, at least.

He quickly finished his bookkeeping so he could move on to more fun stuff. He changed into his gi, preferring to be on equal terms with Indy. It could be a disadvantage when one person was wearing one and the other wasn't since it made gripping and pulling your opponent down easier.

When he walked into the main room, Aaron had shut off the vacuum cleaner and was talking to Indy. Oh, fuck. He'd forgotten Aaron was there. Damn. He'd wanted to keep him away from Indy, not sure if Indy wanted Josh's brother to know him. Well, too late now.

Aaron had his back toward Blake, but Blake had no trouble picking up his words.

"Maybe we could go out some time?"

Blake's eyes went big. What the fuck? Aaron was asking Indy out? Shit, the kid really had no self-preservation instinct, did he? Anger rose up in him. What the hell did Aaron think he was doing, asking strangers out like that? Fucking moron.

Indy found his eyes over Aaron's shoulder and shot him an apologetic look. Blake sent him a reassuring smile back. Nothing to apologize for. Definitely not his fault. There was not a sliver of doubt who had initiated this. The concept of Indy flirting was too absurd to even consider.

"Look, I'm sure you're nice, but you're skipping a few steps."

Aaron jammed his hands into his pockets, which seemed to be his go-to thing when he was insecure. "I just want to get to know you better."

"You could've started by asking my name. Then I would've told you that my name is Indy, and I am Noah's boyfriend. It would've saved us both this highly uncomfort-able conversation."

Aaron's posture froze. "How did you know who I was?"

"Dude, you look enough like Josh to make it obvious. You guys have the same build, the same eyes, and you even sound the same. I know you recently came out as gay, but Aaron, you really need to learn how to do this. You cannot walk up to men you've barely met and ask them out. Some-body will take offense and beat the shit out of you."

Blake stepped in. "They already have, and I'm starting to see why."

Aaron blushed. "Can't blame a guy for trying."

"Actually, I can," Indy said. "It's offensive to be asked out simply because you can tell I'm gay. It reeks of you wanting to lose your gay V-card, and while I'm sure there are guys more than happy to help you out, it doesn't appeal to me at all. You're not even close to being my type, as any gay man would've been able to tell you, and I'm damn sure I'm not yours, either."

Indy wasn't pulling any punches, and Blake almost felt sorry for Aaron. Almost, because Blake's anger was still bubbling below the surface, and there was no doubt in his mind Aaron needed to hear this. He might not realize it now, but Indy was doing him a massive service. "Why would I not be your type?"

Indy deserved credit for not rolling his eyes at that ques-tion. Blake would have, no doubt in his mind. "You've met Noah, right? That's my type. Big, strong, bossy as fuck. Which would be your type as well if I had to hazard a guess."

Aaron's face grew even redder. Blake suppressed a chuckle. It looked like Indy's guess had been spot-on.

"How the f-f-fuck would you know what my type is?"

Aaron sputtered, clearly embarrassed as hell. It would have come out a lot stronger if he hadn't stuttered on the word "fuck."

Indy laughed. "Experience. Now, that's 'How to Be Gay 101' for today. I have a training I want to get back to."

He turned around, but Aaron, clearly frustrated by something, stepped forward and put a hand on his shoulder. Blake winced, knowing what was coming. Within a second, Indy grabbed that hand and put his foot back, twisting his hips and slinging Aaron over his hip, flat on the ground. The air left Aaron's lungs with an audible whoosh. That had to hurt since his previous injuries weren't completely healed. Well, he shouldn't have touched Indy.

Lesson learned. Hopefully.

Aaron groaned in pain. "What the heck did you do that for?"

Indy looked at him calmly, not even breaking a sweat. "Don't ever, ever put your hands on me again." He turned around and went back to his warm-up exercises as if nothing had happened.

Blake reached out a hand to Aaron, letting him pull himself up. Aaron grimaced in pain. Good. He'd remember this for the next time. "Can he do that? Isn't there like a code for jiujitsu or something that you can't use it to harm others?"

Blake mentally counted to ten. For some reason, this boy exasperated him. "Did you put your hands on him?" he asked.

"I was only touching his shoulder!"

Blake was done being patient. Apparently, the message had not been clear enough yet. He stepped in, bringing their faces close. They were the same height, so he stared hard into Aaron's eyes. "You put your hands on him without his permission. He defended himself, as is his right. The next time I see you do that with him or with anyone else, I will kick you out on your ass. Do you feel me?"

Aaron nodded, looking intimidated. Good. Maybe a solid dose of fear would help him develop some common sense. Fuck knew he needed it.

2

There had to be a more accurate word than embarrassed to describe how Aaron felt.

Mortified.

Completely and utterly humiliated.

He cleaned the restrooms and changing rooms in the front of the studio, making sure to sanitize everything. People always forgot to clean the door handles in his experience, so he wiped them down with antibacterial spray. He mopped the floors next, leaving them looking shiny and smelling clean. All the while his brain was spinning with how badly he'd messed up.

He vacuumed the hallway, shooting a look over his shoulder every now and then to watch Blake and Indy fight, or whatever it was called. He would have thought the much smaller and lighter Indy wouldn't stand a chance, but he made Blake work for it. Judging by the big grin on his face, Blake didn't mind.

This was the happiest Aaron had ever seen him. Not that that was saying a lot because Blake was always strict and sour with him. For some reason, Aaron seemed to exasperate Blake, which made him feel hopeless. He wasn't doing it on purpose. He felt lost, clueless about what to say, what to do—especially around Blake who seemed to be perfect, put together, always in control.

It was unfair, how Indy had called him out. How was he to know this slender guy with the gorgeous eyes was the elusive Indy? He'd only overheard Josh and Connor talk about him, without a clue what he looked like. All he'd done was meet a cute guy, deduce he was gay, and ask him out. What was so wrong with that?

Well, it had been kinda awkward, he had to admit that. And Indy did have a point that he wasn't Aaron's type. Aaron could objectively say Indy was cute, but he wasn't, like, attracted to him. Still, he figured maybe attraction came later? He knew nothing about this anyway as he'd demonstrated.

He'd googled some stuff, had discovered that gays were either a top, a bottom, or versatile. The terms were pretty self-explanatory he presumed. He'd tried to find out how you knew which you were, but the advice hadn't been very helpful. Experimenting had come up—which had been his motivation to ask Indy out. He'd figured an obviously gay guy like Indy would have been up for a little experimenting. Not so much, as it turned out. His mistake.

Why was this so hard? First he'd tried at that bar and had gotten a solid beating as a reward. He'd worked up the guts to ask someone out again, and Indy had put him flat on the floor. What was wrong with him that he couldn't make this work? He'd done it exactly as he'd read online: flirt a little, then be self-confident and ask. Like everything else in his life, he sucked at this, too. Fuck-up, all over again.

He opened the door to Blake's office to vacuum in there. Everything was ridiculously neat. Almost OCD-tidy. His eyes fell on some pictures on the wall, and he stepped closer to examine them. Blake, holding up a trophy he'd won. Blake with two other men handing him a black belt, all dressed in the same white uniforms. Blake with a group of kid students.

His favorite was Blake during a match of some kind, wearing only tight shorts. His face was covered in small droplets of sweat, his dark hair even longer back then and tied back into a ponytail, his piercing blue eyes completely focused. He was sexy, Aaron thought, not for the first time. And his body was...well, perfect. Not the bulky, almost fake build bodybuilders displayed so often, but lean and muscled all over.

Aaron stepped closer. The guy had an actual six-pack in that picture. An eight-pack, more accurately. Not an ounce of fat on his body. How had Indy put it? Big, strong, bossy as fuck. It sure as heck applied to Blake, and Aaron couldn't deny that looking at this picture made his stomach swirl.

He forced himself to look away. It was useless. Even if Blake were gay, he'd never give Aaron a second look. The man was annoyed by him, an effect he seemed to have on people. Josh and Connor sure had gotten rid of him as fast as they could. Then again, he couldn't blame Josh. Not after what he'd done to him. It was just... He'd hoped to be able to mend fences with him and get his brother back. Without his parents, his brother, and without any friends as well, Aaron was so lonely. Lost. Drifting.

There was another picture on the wall, a little to the side from the others. Blake with three other men who had to be his brothers since all four shared the same black hair and that Mediterranean look. Younger brothers, by the looks of it. Blake wasn't smiling, but it was close enough, and two of the others were sporting big grins. It was the fourth brother, the one who appeared the youngest, that made Aaron pause. His focus was slightly off, instead of at the camera, and his face was blank, for lack of a better word. Like he wasn't entirely present for what was happening.

The floor behind him creaked, and he startled, looking over his shoulder. Blake stared at him, arms crossed. "You snooping around?" he asked.

Aaron shook his head vehemently. "No. I came in to vacuum and got distracted by the pictures on the wall, that's all." Had he disappointed him again? Would there ever come a day when he got it right with this man?

Blake's face softened. "Okay. Sorry. Didn't mean to accuse you, but I'm a rather private person."

"That's interesting, considering you have strangers living in your house," Aaron remarked.

Blake shrugged. "I don't mind sharing quarters with others, as long as I have a room to myself. You may have noticed my bedroom is always locked."

Aaron hadn't, but the mere thought of Blake's bedroom was enough to unnerve him. What would it look like? Would he ever bring anyone home?

"Speaking of bedrooms, you and I need to have a conversation about sexual boundaries," Blake said sternly. He lowered himself on the edge of his desk, gestured for Aaron to take a seat in the desk chair.

Please, no. He wanted to sink into a large hole, right now. "Do we really?"

It was meant as a plea, but for some reason it came out the wrong way, like he didn't think he needed any help. He winced. Was this why Blake thought he was arrogant, because he meant one thing, but communicated something else entirely?

"Aaron, what you did with Indy, it was wrong on so

many levels. That kind of behavior may be acceptable in a gay club, but not in everyday life. You cannot walk up to someone you don't even know and ask him out. It's the kind of thing that will get you in trouble, do you understand what I'm saying?"

They were really going to talk about this? It seemed his humiliation knew no end this day. "I get it, okay? No more asking strangers out, noted."

Blake's posture changed, softened. "I know this is all new for you, but surely the same rules applied when you were dating girls?"

"I never dated girls," Aaron blurted out, then wanted to curl up and die. Why did he confess that embarrassing truth? As if he wasn't enough of a loser already.

Blake's eyes widened for a second before he had himself under control again. "Hmm. I guess the whole thing is new to you then, huh? How come, if I may ask?"

Aaron cleared his throat. If Blake had even displayed a trace of judgment in his voice, he would have taken off, but the man seemed truly interested. He was a good listener, Aaron had discovered before.

"I grew up in a conservative Christian home. The no-sex-before-marriage kind, so you can imagine what happened when Josh came out as gay. My parents were livid. After that, all the attention was on me. I'm not kidding: they were watching me like a hawk to make sure I wouldn't end up like my brother. I was supposed to be the perfect son who would marry a nice virgin girl and have three kids and a Golden Retriever."

"I take it they didn't show much understanding when you, too, came out."

Aaron sighed. "No. Which showed how superficial their love was. They only loved me as long as I was their perfect son. When I stopped conforming to the ideal they had of me, when I wanted to be myself, they threw me out. I lost my parents, my job, my apartment, all because I came out."

"And maybe your identity, too?" Blake offered.

Aaron's brow furrowed. "What do you mean?"

"You had an identity as a Christian, a son, a congressional aide, a professional, and a heterosexual man. All of that is gone, correct? So who are you now?"

Aaron opened his mouth to answer, then closed it again. Who was he? Who was Aaron Gordon? He couldn't come up with a single word, other than gay, and surely he was more than that. His heart painfully constricted. How had his life crumbled right before his eyes? And more importantly: where the heck did he start to rebuild it?

"I don't know," he said, Blake waiting for him to answer all that time. "I honestly don't know."

"That's a good place to start, by admitting that you don't know," Blake assured him.

"You told me I needed to get my shit together, and that I had to learn to ask for help. I'm asking, Blake. Where do I start? How do I find out who I am, now that I'm no longer who I thought I was or pretended to be?"

Somehow, his chest felt lighter saying that. Maybe there was something to be said for the statement that asking for help was the biggest hurdle in getting better.

Blake smiled, an honest-to-God smile, and Aaron's insides reacted with fervor. "I'm proud of you, Aaron. That was not an easy thing to say. Well done."

Oh, boy, that smile in combination with those words had a funny effect on Aaron. His stomach was doing a happy dance, and his hands were getting all clammy. "Thank you," he managed.

"Look, here's what you do. Write down ten things that

you want to be, do, or have. Like a job, or new friends, or whatever. Then write down ten things that you don't want to be, do, or have anymore. Maybe you could include that snotty, self-entitled attitude. Then we'll start tackling those things, one at a time."

"We?" It was the word that had jumped out to him. Was Blake really offering to help him?

"Yes, we. I'll help you, Aaron. You're not alone in this."

For some reason, those words broke him. He'd been on his own ever since his parents had kicked him out. He'd lost all his friends—well, maybe they had never been friends in the first place. Josh had been lost to him long before that, which he only had himself to blame for. He'd felt so incredibly lonely, like he was drowning and no one was even trying to save him. And here was Blake, throwing him not just a lifejacket, but jumping in to swim him to shore.

Tears started streaming down his face. "I'm sorry," he said, his voice tight with emotion. "I can't seem to..." A sob escaped, and he buried his head in his hands. The next sob was powerful, racking his body. He gave up, unable to stop the flood that was coming. He put his arms on the desk, cradled his head, and let go.

Seconds later, Blake's hand came to rest on his shoulder, squeezing him gently. "It's okay, Aaron. You've been holding a lot in. Let it out."

Aaron cried and cried, while Blake's hand moved from his shoulder to his hair, rubbing his hair, his head, his scalp. It was a soothing gesture that made him feel protected and safe. After what seemed like half an hour, the tears stopped and the sobs subsided. He hiccupped and released a long breath. Blake's hand stilled but remained on his head.

"You okay now?" he asked.

"Yeah. Thank you."

"No problem. I'll let you collect yourself. Finish here afterward and then go home. You can do the mat tomorrow after your first lesson."

Aaron's head came up, and Blake's hand slid off. "Lesson?"

"Yeah. Rebuilding your identity means realigning body, mind, and soul. We'll start with your body. You need rhythm and exercise, and you're gonna get both when you show up here tomorrow morning at eight."

"At eight?"

Blake laughed softly. "By then I've already finished an hour-long workout. Eight o'clock sharp, Aaron. Don't let me down."

Aaron nodded automatically. Blake gave his head an affectionate little pat and walked out, leaving Aaron behind. He was exhausted from the crying spell and self-conscious that Blake had seen him break down like that, but in his heart a strange excitement burned. Tomorrow, Blake would start training him. He would not let him down.

BLAKE LOOKED AT THE CLOCK, wiping the sweat off his face with a towel. Seven forty-five. Would Aaron be on time? More importantly, would he even show up? Blake had not explained anything to him about the training he had in mind. That would have been impossible, since it had been an impulse decision—in itself an extraordinary event, since he rarely gave in to his impulses. He'd seen firsthand what happened if you didn't have your temper and impulses under control, so he had a tight rein on his.

It's why his offer to Aaron had been so surprising. Something about the kid got to him. Well, at twenty-four Aaron was anything but a kid, but with his incredible naïveté he might as well have been. Life had dealt him a nasty curve ball, and it would be interesting to see what Aaron was made of.

Blake threw the towel in the laundry basket. He stretched, allowing all his muscles to tighten, then relax. With complete focus, he went through an extensive routine to stretch all of his big muscles. As he was stretching his hamstrings, the doorbell buzzed. Seven fifty-nine. He smiled. Cutting it close.

Aaron walked in, dressed in training pants and a simple white T-shirt, his dirty blond hair looking like he'd rolled straight out of bed. It was kind of adorable.

"Good morning," Blake said in a friendly manner.

"Hi. Erm, I wasn't sure what to wear, so I hope this is okay?" He pointed to his pants.

"You're fine. Ditch the shoes and socks, though. Bare feet only in this room."

Aaron looked at his shoes. "Oh. Sorry," he said sheepishly. He walked back to the hallway, came back a minute later barefoot and walked to the mat. "So, erm, what are you going to teach me?"

"Brazilian jiujitsu, obviously."

"Aren't I a little old to learn?"

"Not at all. I have many adults who come in for beginner's classes. We'll start easy, okay? You have any experience at all in martial arts?"

Aaron shook his head. "No. Only sport I played was baseball."

Blake didn't count that a sport, considering how little physical activity most recreational baseball players got, but he didn't say that. "Have you worked out recently?"

"It wasn't a priority. And when I still lived in DC I barely had time. I went to the gym every now and then, but…" He didn't finish his sentence, blushing.

Blake had no trouble filling in the rest. He'd gotten distracted by ogling men, no doubt. Not something he would tease Aaron about. He'd been through that phase himself, short-lived as it had been. "Okay, that means we're starting from scratch. I'll put you on a couch to 5k program that will help you build up your endurance in running, and we'll work on core and strength training as well."

"Why?"

Five minutes in and he already wanted to smack him. This was not gonna end well. "Are you gonna question everything I say?"

"No. Sorry. Didn't mean to imply you don't know what you're doing. I was surprised because I thought you would teach me jiujitsu, not make me do all kinds of other stuff."

Blake sighed. "Three things. First, jiujitsu is a full-body sport. You won't get far if you only work on your moves. You need to get yourself in solid shape. Second, your life is in shambles, and you've lost a sense of who you are. It's wise to start with rebuilding your body, then the mind will follow. A strong mind in a strong body, that's kind of our mantra here. And last, you don't have anything else to do, so what the fuck are you whining about?"

Aaron shuffled his bare feet, his ears turning red. "Sorry," he mumbled.

"You know what, let's make a deal. If you do exactly what I tell you for the next hour without asking any more questions, you'll get a reward. How's that?"

Aaron's eyes widened, and a smile spread across his face. He looked like an eager puppy who was promised a dog treat if he plopped his little butt down. "What kind of reward?"

"I'll think of something. Do we have a deal?"

Aaron nodded enthusiastically. "You're on."

He stepped onto the mat but Blake pulled him off. "First, let's teach you the proper etiquette. This room is not to be stepped in with anything else but bare feet. Before stepping onto the mat, you bow toward the wall." He demonstrated a bow. "Since we are starting together, you wait for me to step on the mat first, since I'm your professor."

Aaron gave a clumsy bow, but he wasn't making fun of it. If he had, Blake would have gotten on his case. He demanded respect for this sport. He stepped on the mat and Aaron waited a second or two before following him. Good.

"Start with jogging around the mat for a few minutes. I'll tell you when to stop."

Aaron took off too fast and promptly ran out of breath after a minute, then settled on a much slower tempo. His reaction to Blake's spontaneous reward idea was interesting. It meant he had the instinct to please, wanted Blake to like him. The truth was that Blake did like him, though fuck knew why. The kid had an uncanny ability to push buttons Blake would rather not see pushed, but something about him tickled Blake's attention.

Aaron had begun to pant, and he subtly held his right side. "Walk two laps," Blake called out. Aaron slowed down, a look of gratitude on his face. After that, Blake took him through some more warm-up exercises. "Let's do push-ups," he said.

Aaron bit his lip. "I suck at those," he admitted.

"All the more reason to start training them. Show me one."

He did about the sloppiest excuse for a push-up Blake had ever seen. He lowered himself on the mat next to Aaron. "Your form and posture is all wrong. Watch me do one. I'll do it slowly." He lowered himself on his arms, keeping his body perfectly straight, then pushed up again.

"If I do it like that, I can only do one," Aaron admitted.

Blake smiled. "Not much use in doing them wrong so you can do more. It's cheating. We'll keep at it until you can do one hundred."

Aaron's eyes grew big. "A hundred? Are you serious? That would take like a year."

"You'd be surprised at how much you can achieve when you set your mind to it. Now, stop talking and show me a good push-up."

Aaron's position improved slightly, but he still arched his back, and his hands were too far forward. Blake put a hand on Aaron's lower back. "Pull your stomach in, tighten your abdominal core. Yeah, like that. Now, bring your arms farther back. They should be in line with your shoulders. A little wider. Yes, perfect. Now lower yourself and push back up."

Aaron's muscles strained as he did one push-up. A small tremor indicated his muscles were getting tired. "One more," Blake told him. He almost held his breath, waiting for Aaron to protest. He didn't. Instead, he closed his eyes tight, lowered himself again and pushed back up, his whole body rippling with the effort.

"Good job. Stand back up." Aaron climbed to his feet, beaming with pride. "When you're up to ten push-ups, we're gonna start doing burpees."

"What are those?" Aaron didn't sound too enthusiastic, but Blake didn't blame him. The guy was out of shape, so this had to be pretty intimidating.

"They're a combination of sort-of squat, then a push-up and a jump. Watch," he said and executed two perfect burpees.

"Those look like torture," Aaron said.

"We'll get you there, I promise. Now, let's start with the most important jiujitsu move of all: the break fall. Stand and let yourself fall backward on the mat. As you fall, you slap both your hands and forearms on the mat to break your fall and tighten your core to the max to avoid hitting your head. Your head should stay off the mat, letting the rest of your body take the impact."

He showed the move a few times, Aaron studying him with concentration. Then he gestured for Aaron to try it. It took him about twenty turns until he had the hang of it.

"Okay, good. We'll start with practicing from wrist grips." He grabbed Aaron by his right wrist and held it with a tight grip. "If someone were to grab you like this, how would you get out?"

Aaron tried, Blake had to grant him that. For almost a minute, he tried different pulls and pushes, the only result being that his wrist got warm and red. He even tried to kick Blake, but the move was so predictable Blake simply stepped out of reach, while still holding on to the wrist.

"Okay, I give up," Aaron finally said.

"Let's use your other wrist, because this one is getting angry with me," Blake said, releasing Aaron's right wrist and latching onto the left one. "Look at how I'm holding you. Where would my weakest point be?"

Aaron shrugged. "No idea."

"Use your brain. What's the weakest point in a connection? Which muscles that I'm using have the most strength and which are the weakest in comparison?"

"I didn't think you had weak muscles," Aaron mumbled. The statement was factual, but the undertone of admiration was clear.

"Relatively, remember?" Blake made light of it. He had

no idea what Aaron meant with that statement, but it did strange things to his body. He pushed it down. "Grab your left hand with your right hand. Now quickly move both your hands upward. I'll have no choice but to let you go."

They practiced the move twenty times until Aaron could do it automatically. It would take a lot more repetitions before it was ingrained, but it was a start.

"Here's another technique," Blake said. He grabbed Aaron's wrist again, which was warm under his touch. "When someone is holding you, the weakest point is always where the thumb and fingers meet. If you move your arm in that direction, fast, you're often able to break free. It doesn't work as well when someone's hand is bigger than your wrist, because if they can completely span it, the weakest point isn't as weak. Try it."

Aaron tried it, with Blake correcting the move of his hand until he got it right. The first few times he let his grip go easily, but after that he made Aaron work for it. By the time he'd escaped about twenty times, both his wrists were red from irritation.

"Okay, we'll practice one more thing. What would you do if someone came at you like this?" He reached out and went for Aaron's throat with both hands. As expected, Aaron reacted too slowly. He gave a half-assed slap against Blake's arm that did nothing to deter him.

His strong fingers circled Aaron's neck. His skin was ridiculously soft for a man. The kid barely had any beard growth, either. Blake was pretty sure that he hadn't shaved this morning, considering how early he'd had to be at the studio, but there was not a trace of stubble on his chin.

He cleared his throat. Right. "The best thing is to prevent someone from being able to choke you. Let me show you. try to choke me."

He let go of Aaron's neck, stepped back a little. Aaron came at him hesitantly.

"Do it like you mean it," Blake snapped.

Aaron tried again with more determination. Blake brought his arms up lightning fast and did a move as if he were swimming. "Did you see what I did?" He repeated the move, slowly this time. "When I teach kids this move, I call it the Dory move. Just keep swimming. If you keep doing this, you'll break off the hold before someone's hands can ever reach your neck. Do it to me a few more times."

Aaron came at him again, and Blake showed his move, repeating it three more times to make sure Aaron had gotten it.

"Now you."

He didn't wait but came at Aaron, and he reacted too slowly. Blake's hands were on his neck before he'd brought his arms up. "Faster. Do it like you mean it."

He attacked him again. This time Aaron's hands came up, but he didn't put enough strength behind it. His arms were loose, not tightened enough to push Blake's arms away.

"Again. Put some force behind it. You won't hurt me, you know."

After that, Aaron got into it. After practicing it a time or ten, Blake was happy he knew the basics of that move.

"Time for the cooling down. Let's do some stretches. Follow my example." He showed him a simple arm stretch. "Do you see why working on your overall strength could help you?"

Aaron nodded, copying his move. "Do you have the highest belt in this?"

"No. Not by far. I have a black belt, but there are grada-tions within the black belts. I have what's called a second-degree black belt, but there are many more like me. But once you have a black belt, you are to be addressed as professor."

Blake gestured to Aaron to follow him to the mat as he sat down to demonstrate a back stretch.

"I need to call you professor?" There wasn't indignation in Aaron's voice, more like surprise.

"Not when it's the two of us. But should you ever join in a class, yes." Blake had never been formal, unlike some of his colleagues across the country. The kids didn't call him professor, simply Blake, and even with the adults he wasn't too strict about it. For some reason he was strangely looking forward to Aaron calling him professor, though.

He worked him through some more stretches, commenting on Aaron's form to make sure he got it right. As they got up, he noticed Aaron's wrists had gotten even redder. He reached out without thinking and grabbed his hand. "Your wrists are swelling up. Do you bruise easily?"

Aaron shrugged. "Yeah. My PE teacher even asked me once if someone was abusing me, 'cause I had bruises so often."

Blake's eyes narrowed. "Were you?" Strict religious folks, wouldn't be the first time he'd encountered an abuse victim from a background like that.

"Nah," Aaron said. "I was the golden boy, remember?"

"And Josh?"

Aaron looked away, fidgeting with the hem of his shirt. Blake was still holding on to his hand and he let go with reluctance. "They weren't exactly understanding when he came out, but they never touched him."

What was the story there? If his brother had been treated like that in front of him, what had Aaron's reaction been? Something Blake intended to find out. "When you get home, pull two cooling packs from the freezer and put those on your wrists for at least ten minutes, a couple of times today."

Aaron nodded. "Yes, Professor."

It might have been said half-jokingly, but Blake had been right. He did like it when Aaron called him that. In fact, he liked it very much.

3

He hadn't missed a lesson for two weeks straight. Every morning, week or weekend, rain or shine, Aaron had shown up at the studio at eight sharp. And every morning, Blake had been there to teach him.

They'd gone through tons of exercises, most leaving Aaron out of breath and hurting afterward. He was sporting bruises all over his body now, courtesy of what Blake called grappling. It meant Blake would hold him down in a certain way and Aaron had to escape. Blake let him, provided Aaron did the moves correctly.

He could do a break fall in his sleep by now, but Blake still had him practice it at least twenty times each session. It was the most essential move, he'd explained, because once you hit your head and were knocked out cold, you were done for.

Aaron hadn't asked for his reward after the first session, had figured he'd been enough of a nuisance to Blake. The second session, Blake had made him a deal: he'd get an even bigger reward if he stuck with it for two weeks. He had, and he couldn't wait to see what his reward was.

Would Blake maybe buy him something? New clothes would be nice, though not awe-inspiring. That was true for many things he needed. He hoped his reward wasn't something he needed but something he wanted. More than anything, he wanted to do something with Blake. For some reason his presence steadied him. Blake made him want to do better, be better, and it was an unfamiliar feeling.

He stepped into the studio. Rhythmic thuds told him Blake was punching one of the huge boxing bags with fervor. He'd come to understand why the guy was so toned. He not only worked out every single morning but also demonstrated exercises throughout the day and participated in every single lesson. Aaron still struggled to do more than five push-ups in a row, but at least he was improving.

He'd taken up running, as Blake had suggested. Ordered, more accurately. He was building up endurance, but he still couldn't make it past five minutes of running before he had to take a break and walk for a minute or two.

He took off his shoes and socks, neatly put them in one of the lockers in the locker room and hung his coat. When he stepped into the main room, Blake was indeed pounding hard on a punching bag, naked from the waist up, his hands wrapped in some kind of protective bandages. His toned legs were hugged by a pair of tight shorts, much like biker shorts, that outlined every muscle. His body was drenched in sweat, his black hair slick with perspiration.

Aaron swallowed. He grew hard instantly.

Blake's body was...perfect. His abdomen was a frigging eight-pack, each muscle perfectly defined on his stomach. And his chest, those arms, that ass. It was the stuff of dreams, of the porn that Aaron had starting watching since he came out, though he still felt guilty about it every single time.

Blake spotted Aaron before he could announce himself, and he gestured Aaron over. Luckily, he went right back to pounding the bag, so Aaron could discreetly rearrange himself. His training pants were not as tight as those things Blake was wearing, but his erection still showed. He pulled his shirt out of his waistband, hoping it would cover him well enough.

"Morning," Blake said, chipper as ever. Clearly a morning person.

"Good morning." His voice was hoarse, but hopefully Blake would chalk that up to it still being early.

"I laid out a pair of training gloves for you. Put them on."

Aaron found the shiny black gloves, clumsily put his hands in them. They felt strange, big.

"Why aren't you wearing these?" he asked.

"You and your infernal questions," Blake sighed. He stopped punching the bag and turned to face Aaron. "My hands are used to it, plus I'm wearing wraps."

"Oh, okay."

"We're adding boxing to your workout program. It's a great way to build up strength in your arms and core while working on your reflexes. Plus, if you need to let out some aggression a punching bag is your best friend."

He gestured for Aaron to step closer to the bag, and he obeyed. At least his erection was settling down. Couldn't Blake put on a shirt or something and stop teasing him with that perfect body?

Blake took position next to him. The musky smell of his sweat was strangely intoxicating. "Let's start with the most basic of punches, a jab. We'll do twenty on each side, okay? Step in with the same foot as you're punching with. Tighten your core and keep your arms tight as well."

He demonstrated a few jabs with his right hand, then with his left. "You're up," he said.

Aaron did his best to punch the bag hard, but it barely moved. He tried again, but looked at his feet to get the position right and half-missed the bag. After a few tries he seemed to have the basic coordination down. He did another jab. This was kinda fun.

Blake stepped in behind him, putting his hands on Aaron's stomach. "Engage your core," he said.

Aaron froze. All his nerves seemed to suddenly end on his stomach, where Blake's hot, sweaty hand was touching him. His dick loved it, that much was clear. What if Blake noticed? Would he be offended? He was straight after all.

"What are you waiting for?" Blake snapped. "Jab again with your right hand, but keep your core tight."

He couldn't think, let alone move. Not with that hand on him. Not with Blake's smell assaulting his senses. Not with his hot breath tickling his neck.

"What's the matter?" Blake asked.

"Stop touching me," Aaron blurted out. The hand disappeared immediately. And of course, he already missed it.

Blake stepped up to his side. "What's wrong?" he asked. "Why do you suddenly have an issue with me touching you?"

Aaron bit his lip, his eyes trained to the floor. He couldn't say it. Blake would never look at him again, let alone train him.

"Aaron, look at me when I talk to you. What the hell is wrong?"

"You're...I'm..." The words wouldn't come. A fierce blush crept over his cheeks. He kept his eyes lowered, refusing to look at Blake. "I have an erection, okay," he finally said. He looked up from underneath his lashes.

Blake's gaze traveled lower to Aaron's crotch where his hard cock was clearly visible, perfectly outlined under the shirt and pants.

"Oh," Blake said.

This was it. Surely Blake would walk away now, kick him out, even.

"Is that all? Who cares?"

In complete disbelief, Aaron raised his head. Was Blake joking? Was he somehow, in some sick way, making fun of him? Blake's expression was relaxed, though.

"Are you serious?" Aaron asked.

Blake shrugged. "Normal reaction, nothing to be ashamed of."

"It's just that you were...you don't have a shirt on, and you smell, and now you were touching me." Oh, crap, he should've stopped talking.

Blake smiled, a smile unlike anything Aaron had ever seen on him. One corner of his mouth curled up while the other pulled back. It was sexy, sinful, and absolutely breathtaking.

"You didn't need to explain, but it's okay."

"You're not offended?" Aaron asked.

Blake arched his brows. "Why would I be?"

"Because I'm gay."

"Yeah, so?"

Aaron sighed. Wasn't it obvious, even to him, a complete novice at this? "I thought most straight guys took offense when a gay dude, you know, notices them."

Blake seemed to hesitate a little before he answered. "I'm not straight, Aaron. But even if I had been, I understand that you're still coming to terms with this part of you. You're new at this, and it must all be rather overwhelming, so I can understand why you get easily excited, so to speak."

Aaron's mouth dropped open. "You're gay?"

"Yes. But I'd appreciate it if you kept this to yourself. It's not a big secret, but I try to keep that part of my life personal."

Aaron's mind went crazy. Blake was gay. How the heck had he missed that? "Clearly my gaydar needs work," he said.

Blake smiled. "Don't blame yourself. Not many people notice. Not even Indy or your brother."

That made him feel better. At least it wasn't so obvious everyone noticed but him. "Do you have a boyfriend?" he asked before he realized how personal that question was. What if Blake took it the wrong way, like Aaron was coming on to him? Oh, God.

Something flashed in Blake's eyes. "No."

Aaron blushed all over again. "I wasn't implying anything," he blurted out. Blake raised his eyebrows. "That I wanted to be your boyfriend," Aaron added. Stop talking, he told himself. Holy moly, how deep a hole could he talk himself into? A very, very deep one, apparently. Like, Grand Canyon deep.

Blake's lips curled. "That's good to know. Aaron, you're fine. It's all good. I know you're new at this, so ask away."

"Really?"

"Why does that surprise you?"

Aaron bit his lip. "'Cause you're usually not too fond of my questions," he offered.

"True. I guess you're growing on me," Blake teased. "You're like a little lost puppy, looking for an owner who will teach you how to be a dog."

It was a playful side of him Aaron had never seen before. He liked it. Correct that, he loved it.

"No, Aaron, I mean it. When we met, you'd been beaten

up for getting a signal wrong. If I can prevent that by helping you navigate a culture that's new to you, I'm willing to do that. So if you have any questions, fire away."

"Really?"

"Why do you keep asking that?"

"Because I have so many questions and I can't believe you'd be willing to answer all of them. Or even a few of them. I mean, this is pretty personal stuff." Did Blake not guess the type of questions he had? He hated to admit it, but a lot of them were sex-related. He'd googled stuff, but it was hard to find honest, real answers instead of either sexual bragging or porn.

"I tell you what, consider it your reward for showing up for two weeks. You finish today's workout and I'll sit down afterward with you to answer any and all questions you have. Sound good?"

It sounded perfect. Too good to be true, actually. But Blake had proven to be trustworthy so far, so Aaron would take him at his word. He'd better come up with a mother load of questions, because this was an opportunity that wasn't gonna present itself again any time soon.

AARON WAS BROODING ON QUESTIONS, that much was clear. He followed Blake's instructions, but his mind was elsewhere half the time. Blake understood.

When he'd first realized he was gay, he'd had a thousand questions. His mom had been too busy surviving, his father already dead—not that he'd ever breathe a word about himself to that asshole. It had been his school counselor who'd stepped up. A gay man himself, Mr. Faulks had been

Blake's lifesaver. He'd answered all of Blake's questions as best as he could, had signed him up for jiujitsu so he'd be able to defend himself if someone took offense to him being gay. The man had even paid for it, knowing Blake's mom couldn't afford it. Blake had vowed to pay it forward. He'd helped dozens of abuse victims over the years, but here was his chance to repay the kindness Mr. Faulks had shown him.

He was curious what questions Aaron would ask. His guess was that he'd start easy, safe, before moving on to what he really wanted to know. Sex. The kid had sex on his mind, for sure. Blake still made him finish the lesson, though. As much as he wanted Aaron to have the chance to ask questions, he wanted him to learn discipline first. It was what would help him succeed in life.

"Okay, that's it for today," he announced. Aaron looked relieved. "You're doing well," Blake added. "I can already see you're making progress."

"I am?" Aaron looked happy with his praise.

"Absolutely. Your arms are getting stronger, you're not out of breath anymore after the warming up, and you did six push-ups today. Plus, you're starting to master the basic escape techniques."

Aaron beamed. There was no other word for it. His face lit up and it transformed his face completely. The kid was cute, Blake mused. If he changed his hairstyle a little and found his groove and place in the gay scene, he'd have no trouble getting attention. He wasn't a twink—too tall, for one—but at least he didn't look like he'd break when you fucked him. Blake never went for the fragile types, too afraid they couldn't take his pounding.

"Blake?" Aaron asked, insecure.

"Sorry, daydreaming for a second. I'm gonna grab a

quick shower." On impulse, he added, "You can ask questions while I'm at it."

Aaron swallowed. "You want me to join you while you shower?"

"Not in the actual shower but yeah, you can sit in the locker room."

"But...you're gonna undress in front of me?"

Blake bit down his amusement. This kid had wanted to ask Indy out but was embarrassed to be in a men's locker room? Holy fuck, he had a learning curve to overcome. "Yeah. Is that a problem?"

When Aaron swallowed again, he said, "Look, Aaron, I know it's awkward and uncomfortable for you. But as a gay man, you're gonna have to get used to stepping into a locker room and seeing other men naked. It's something you'll have to learn to navigate if you're out publicly. Others will be watching you, so you need to know the etiquette. Come on, I promise I won't bite."

He walked away, confident Aaron would follow him. He did, though slowly. Blake waited for him to step into the room before he started undressing.

"Fire away," he said casually.

Aaron sat down, studiously avoiding looking at him. "I don't know where to start."

"Start with asking me about locker room etiquette for gay men."

"Oh, okay. How are you supposed to behave and not draw attention to yourself?"

Blake nodded. It was a start. He stripped to his underwear. "You avoid looking at body parts, especially guys' junk. Straight men do it, but they get away with it. Gay men won't. If someone talks to you, you look them in the eye." He waited for Aaron to look up, but apparently the tile floor was way more interesting. "Aaron, look at me. Keep your eyes on my face."

Slowly, Aaron raised his eyes, his face beet red. So fucking adorable. "Ask me the next question and keep looking at my face."

"Erm, okay. I read that gay men are more promiscuous than straight men. Is that true?"

It was a good question, though his formal language showed self-distancing. Blake pondered how to answer while taking his boxers off.

Aaron's eyes were glued to his face. Why was Blake disappointed in that? He'd love to see Aaron blush even more when ogling his cock. It sure was nice enough, if he said so himself.

"Yes, according to the statistics. But men tend to lie when self-reporting sex, both gay and straight. So I don't know. I have straight friends who fuck way more than I do, but that's anecdotal evidence."

He grabbed his towel and shower gel, walked over to the shower. Right before stepping into the shower area he looked back over his shoulder. Aaron was totally checking out his ass. He couldn't resist it and shook his ass. "Eyes off my ass, Aaron."

He didn't need to look again to know how red the guy would be. He smiled as he turned the shower on as hot as it would go.

"Ask me the next question," he shouted out. Aaron would have to come close to be able to communicate. For some sick reason, Blake delighted in making the boy squirm a little.

It took a while, but finally Aaron's voice rang out. "How do you know what your type is?"

Blake soaped his hair. "Close your eyes. Imagine yourself

having sex with someone. What does this person look like? Or another way: what porn gets you off the most? Do you like two twinks? A daddy-twink relationship? Two muscled guys, or maybe a bit of spanking and bondage?"

He rinsed his hair out while Aaron apparently needed time to mull that over. As he was soaping his body with shower gel, the next question came. "What's your type?"

"Strong, but not too buff. Not too dainty either, though. I don't want to be scared of breaking someone when we fuck."

"Do you...fuck someone regularly?"

Blake suppressed a smile. The kid still couldn't say the f-bomb without stuttering. It was too cute. "Depending on your definition, but yeah, about once a month or so."

He rinsed off, turned off the shower.

"How do you find someone willing to have sex with you?"

Fuck, how did he answer that one without sounding either like a complete braggart, or making it way too easy? "I go to a gay club nearby. There's a sort of code, a game, if you know what you're looking for. It's all subtle signals, or in some cases pretty blatant ones, until one of you makes a move and the other accepts. Then it's on."

He slung the towel around his hips before stepping out. He'd surmised Aaron was sitting on the bench right around the corner. No need to swing his junk in the kid's face when he stepped out.

"Do you think... Would I be... Would somebody be interested in me?"

Blake's eyes found Aaron's, the boy looking heartwarmingly vulnerable. "Kid, they'd eat you alive if you gave them the chance." He hesitated. Was Aaron ready yet for the next bit? "You have to be yourself first, though. You can't step into a gay club as you are now. You'll attract the wrong kind of men."

Aaron dutifully followed him again as he made his way back to the lockers. "What am I doing wrong?"

Blake flinched. Guess it was time to tell the truth. "Aaron, you're trying too hard to be someone you're not. You're aggressive, for instance, when that's not your nature. It's like you're an omega trying to pretend you're an alpha wolf. You're not. You're a puppy, a pleaser, born to be conquered."

He dropped the towel, grabbed a fresh pair of boxers. This time, Aaron's eyes did drop to Blake's cock. They widened as they took in Blake's length and girth, both above average. Aaron swallowed and that movement shot straight to Blake's balls. His mind created a vision of Aaron sucking his cock, swallowing his cum. So perfect. So right. What was this kid doing to him? That innocence was so damn alluring.

His cock stirred, grew rigid. "It likes your attention," Blake said, his voice hoarse. He wasn't ashamed of his erection. Why would he be? Any gay man would get hard when a cute guy like Aaron checked him out so adorably. Aaron still didn't peel away his eyes, so Blake kept standing, his cock growing erect till it proudly jutted forward.

"How do I know if I'm a top or a bottom?"

Aaron's voice was slightly more than a whisper, but Blake gave him credit for even asking that question. It was so crucial to a gay man's identity, and at least he'd informed himself of the right terminology.

"If you look at me, if you see my cock all hard and ready for action, what do you imagine doing with it?"

Aaron's blush was fierce and instant, giving Blake the confirmation he never needed in the first place. "Ah, I see.

Nice little fantasy of my cock filling you up, huh? That's your answer, right there."

"Isn't a bottom less than a top?"

"Absolutely not. Straight people see it that way, because they consider being fucked as gayer than doing the fucking, but that's bullshit. It's not about more or less, or status. It's about what brings you pleasure. For some gay men, anal sex isn't pleasurable at all. There are gay couples that never go beyond blow jobs and hand jobs. Others are strictly top or bottom, and there are also those that enjoy both. It's all good, Aaron, trust me."

"Do you..."

Aaron didn't finish the question, but Blake knew what he was asking. "I usually top. Bottoming is a trust issue for me, and with one-night stands I don't have that level of trust, so topping is easier."

He was still rock hard, his cock more than interested in the conversation. Not much sense in putting on his underwear if it was gonna get stained with pre-cum. "Aaron, do me a favor, and lock the front door, would you? I don't mind answering all these personal questions, but I'd rather not get disturbed."

No questions this time, merely quiet obedience. Fuck, he loved it when Aaron did what he told him.

When Aaron came back into the locker room, his eyes were once again drawn toward Blake's cock. A thought occurred to Blake. "Have you ever touched another dick than your own? Or seen one up close and personal?"

Aaron shook his head. "No. And you're circumcised, which looks different, too."

Blake stepped close to him, bringing his cock within reach for Aaron—and on eye level. "Wanna study me up close?" Aaron's eyes flew upward, probably to check if Blake wasn't joking in some crude way. "I'm serious. Go ahead, take your fill."

He could rationalize why he was doing it. Aaron needed to learn from someone safe, needed to gain knowledge and experience without getting hurt. That was one aspect and it definitely came into play. But on a whole different level, Blake loved being watched by the kid. His reactions were so pure, so adorable. And such a damn turn-on.

Aaron bit his lip as he let his eyes trail down. He seemed to take in every detail, as if he was getting ready to draw a nude picture of Blake.

"Are you big?" he asked.

Yup, damn turn-on. "Bigger than average. And thicker, too. But not as big as some guys."

"Wouldn't it hurt?"

"For someone like me to fuck you, you mean? No, not if your partner does it right. There's often some burning, a little discomfort, but it's overshadowed by the pleasure it brings. Your hole is sensitive as I'm sure you've discovered by now."

Aaron looked at him quizzically.

"You've never put anything in your hole? Ever?" Blake asked in surprise. "Not even a finger? Hot damn, we need to buy you a little anal dildo so you can fuck yourself. I guarantee you, you're gonna erupt like a fucking volcano."

Aaron looked at him in disbelief. Fuck, the kid was missing out. What was holding him back from exploring his own body?

"Can I touch you?"

The question was so unexpected that Blake almost took a step back, but he held his ground. He did not see that one coming. Should he let the kid touch him? Might as well, since they'd gone this far already.

Why was Aaron getting under his skin so much? Blake had iron self-control, but something about Aaron made his self-discipline crumble.

"Sure."

He mentally braced himself as Aaron hesitantly reached out. His touch was feather light, just his index finger caressing the skin of Blake's cock. He drew his finger forward, all the way to the tip.

"The head is less sensitive than with uncut men. With uncut men, even a little nail will make them wince, whereas I love being scratched a little," Blake said, trying to keep it educational. Yeah, right.

It was as if he'd given Aaron a command. He shifted his finger and drew his nail over Blake's crown. He bit back a moan. This innocent touch was completely turning him on. Aaron turned his finger again and rubbed it over Blake's slit, eliciting drops of precum. He rubbed back and forth a few times until the entire crown was slick. Blake clenched his hands behind his back to keep from fisting himself. He was so damn hard, his muscles trembling with held-back need.

All of a sudden, Aaron's head came forward, and his tongue peeped out of his mouth to lick Blake's crown. This time, he couldn't hold back a moan. Aaron licked him again, his hot, wet tongue lapping up new drops on his dick. Liquid heat rushed through Blake's veins, making him sway a little. Aaron was destroying him, one lick and touch at a time.

"I wondered what it would taste like," Aaron whispered.

"And? What does it taste like?"

"Salty. Creamy. A little bitter. But like you."

The innocent words made Blake wobble, but he regained his balance. Aaron was showing more of his true nature than he'd ever done before. "Don't stop on my account," he said with a low voice.

Aaron peeked at him from underneath those ridiculously long eyelashes. Girls would kill for eyelashes like that, Blake couldn't help thinking. "Are you sure this is okay?"

"It's all good, Aaron. I get your need to explore. Besides, it's not like it's unpleasant." Now there was an understatement.

Reassured, Aaron's attention turned back to Blake's cock. He touched it again, first with one finger, then circling his hand around it, giving an experimental squeeze. Blake let out a sigh of contentment. It felt so right to have Aaron touch him like this. Those hesitant, awkward touches were way sexier than many experienced, sophisticated bottoms he'd encountered.

Aaron's hand dropped to his balls, weighed one, then the other. "Are they sensitive to touch?" he asked.

"Mine are, but it differs. I love having my balls licked and sucked during a blowjob or sex, but others care little for it. Then again, I don't get excited if someone plays with my hole while I've had partners who can come from that alone."

Aaron's face was so serious, as if he was trying to remember it all to pass a test later. His left hand dropped to his crotch, where he needed to rearrange something.

"You wanna maybe take off your clothes, too?"

Aaron shook his head.

"Why not? It's okay, Aaron. Look, I'm buck naked. The door is locked. There's no reason for you to be afraid."

He mumbled something that Blake didn't catch. It was clear, though, that he was afraid of something. "What was that, Aaron?"

"Nobody has ever seen me naked," Aaron managed, still soft and somewhat muffled but at least audible.

Blake understood at once. "You're scared something is off about your body, that you'll be different in some way. Am I correct?"

Aaron nodded. "What if my penis is weird or my balls are lopsided, or something?"

Penis. The fact that he still used such a clinical term after what he'd done to Blake was so telling. "Strip. I promise I'll be both honest and kind, okay? Nothing to fear here."

Reluctantly, Aaron pulled off his shirt first. He was lean, but his muscles could use some definition. His pants came off next. He was wearing white briefs, and Blake suppressed a shudder. "Those briefs have got to go. We'll go shopping to buy some nice, tight boxers for you, the kind that make your ass pop."

Aaron stopped with his hands on the waistband of his briefs. "Why my ass?" he wondered.

Blake grinned. "Because you're a bottom and, as such, your ass is your selling point."

His eyes were focused on Aaron's hands as they slowly, finally, pulled down his briefs and revealed his junk. "Hot damn, that's a nice surprise!"

Aaron's head jerked up. "What do you mean?"

Blake pointed. "Your cock. It's perfect. Nothing to be ashamed of, on the contrary. Step closer."

Again, Aaron obeyed immediately and it touched something deep inside Blake. Why did he like it so much when the boy did as he told him?

He studied the gorgeous, uncut cock in front of him, which had to be about the same length as his, only less thick. But it had a perfect curve, and Aaron's balls were full and round. His pubic hair was blond and irregular in appearance, the only thing that stood out. "Nice length, perfect upwards curve. All you need to do is some manscaping, and you're good to go."

"Manscaping?"

Blake pointed toward his own neatly trimmed pubic hair. "You gotta trim it back a little. Maybe go completely hairless? Wouldn't look bad on you."

Aaron crumpled his nose. "Wouldn't that be too feminine?"

It wasn't the first time Aaron had mentioned something like that, so Blake's curiosity was piqued. "Why would that matter?"

Aaron stepped back, then lowered himself on one of the benches. Blake did the same across from him to encourage Aaron to talk. Something was bothering him.

"I don't know. I've heard so many times that it's important for a man to be masculine that I kinda figured it was the gospel truth."

"Look, for straight men it's still more important than for gay men, especially if they have a negative connotation with being gay. People tend to call effeminate men fags, and to avoid that label, men will go over the top in their masculinity. Within the gay community, few people care. There's all kinds of gays and they range from masculine to effeminate, to the point of crossdressing or a being transvestite. It's who you are and how you want to express yourself. Me, I'm kinda boring, also because I'm not that open about my sexuality."

"But would gay men still be attracted to a person who's more feminine?"

Something clicked in Blake's head. Aaron's perceived arrogance. His over-the-top behavior toward Indy. His insecurity. These questions. It was all starting to make sense. "Aaron, do you like dressing and appearing more girly?"

The blush appearing on the kid's face was unlike anything before, and his head hung low. He was softly shaking his head, his mouth opening and closing. Was there more? Blake switched benches to sit down next to him. "Aaron, it's okay. Who you are is okay. You don't need to be afraid."

All Aaron did was sit there, shaking his head. Blake had to tread lightly here, the emotion in Aaron's posture thick. "Do you feel like you are a woman on the inside?" Aaron wouldn't be the first transgender person he'd met, but somehow with the others it had been different.

"No. I wondered that, too. Googled a bit on experiences from transgender people, but I don't recognize myself in that. I feel like a guy. I just like girly stuff, too. Like pink and glitters, and I don't know, maybe makeup?"

Blake let out a breath. It wouldn't have mattered to him if Aaron had been transgender, but his road would have been even more difficult than it already was. "That's fine, Aaron. I guarantee you: it's absolutely fine. If you feel comfortable and happy as a gay man who is more effeminate, that's fine. Nobody gives a shit and the people who do, shouldn't mean anything to you."

Aaron looked at him sideways. "My parents?"

Blake put a hand on his shoulder. "From what you've told me they're not accepting you anyway, and they never will as long as you're gay. So the choices you make now won't make a difference, as harsh as it may sound."

Aaron's shoulders slumped, but he nodded. "I know. But it's hard to let go of that voice in my head that tells me that if I simply give up all this gay nonsense, I can have their love back."

"You have to wonder," Blake said kindly, "if love that has strings attached, that requires you to be a certain way, is truly love."

"I can't wrap my mind around it, that their religion means more to them than their two sons. That's not what parents are supposed to be like."

Blake knew all about what parents were not supposed to be like. He'd had a prime example himself in his father, who'd made their lives a living hell till the day he died. "I know. And I'm truly sorry for you. It sucks. Your parents suck. There's no other way to say it. They suck. But not you, Aaron. This is not your fault. It's squarely on them."

They were quiet for a bit, two naked, gay men sitting in a locker room. The sexual tension was gone for now, Blake's cock going soft.

"Would men still find me attractive?" Aaron said softly.

"If you would wear makeup for instance? Sure, men who are attracted to that or men who don't mind."

He wondered what Aaron would look like with makeup on. It would certainly bring out those gorgeous eyelashes. An idea popped into his head. "You know what, I should introduce you to one of my adult students. His name is Charlie, and he does a drag show in the gay club I mentioned earlier. I bet he could help you out with figuring out clothes and makeup and stuff."

Aaron looked up, a sparkle returning to his eyes. "Do you think he'd be willing to help me?"

"Fuck, he'd love it. He lives for that kind of thing. I'll text him afterward. Charlie is one of the few who know I'm gay. He got harassed at school and my brother Brad noticed. He asked me to teach Charlie self-defense. He's one of my most motivated students and moreover, he's a real sweetheart."

"Blake, why are you helping me? Why are you being so nice and patient?"

"Because a long time ago, someone was kind and nice and patient to me when I needed it, and it changed my life. Now, I don't know about you, but I'm freezing my ass off here, so let's get moving."

He stood up and stretched, not caring that Aaron checked out his body again.

"Where are we going?" the boy asked.

"Shopping. You need sexy underwear, and we need to buy you some sex toys. After that, we'll work on your manscaping. I have till five before my first class of the day starts, so let's go."

4

I f someone had told him a year ago he'd be at Macy's shopping for sexy underwear with another guy, Aaron would have laughed hard. Yet here he was, following Blake as he made his way toward the men's underwear section.

"So, erm, tell me again what's wrong with my underwear?" Aaron asked.

Blake shot him a look over his shoulder. "They're white briefs. If you're eighty and senile, you can wear those. Until then, you need something else. That is, if you ever want to get laid."

He nodded when they'd reached the right section and pointed toward the first display. "These are nice, but they're a little loose after a bit. You want something that stretches tight around your ass. Like these." He held up a package of black boxers from another display. The model on the box was ripped, of course. Aaron wouldn't even come close to looking like that with those boxers on. Then his eyes fell on the price sticker.

"Those are way too expensive," Aaron protested. "I can't afford to pay that much for underwear."

Blake smiled. "My treat. Trust me, investing in underwear always pays off."

"Hi. Can I help you guys find anything?" a male voice said.

A sales guy, impeccably dressed in suit pants, a pink shirt and a darker pink tie, smiled at them. Colin, his nametag read. Blake gave him a once-over, his smile broadening. "Yes, I think you can. My man Aaron here needs some sexy underwear."

Aaron wanted to crawl under the display table in embarrassment, but Colin's eyes sparkled. "Is that so? You've come to the right place. And if I may be so bold, are we aiming to attract boys, girls, or both?"

Aaron's throat was so dry he couldn't have spoken if his life depended on it. Luckily, Blake had his back.

"Guys. Big, strong, sexy guys."

Gay. Colin has to be gay, otherwise Blake would've never said something like that. That knowledge released some tension in Aaron's shoulders. At least the guy wouldn't laugh at him.

"All righty then," Colin said, then winked at Blake. "Like you, then?"

Blake grinned at the shameless flirting, then his eyes narrowed. "You look kinda familiar."

Colin shot Blake a look Aaron didn't understand but didn't say anything.

"Oh," Blake said.

What was going on? They seemed to speak some kind of code he wasn't privy to. "What?" Aaron asked Blake.

Blake shrugged. "I think Colin wasn't sure if he should

mention in front of you that he and I hooked up. Very discreet of him."

Aaron's eyes went big. "You didn't remember him?" he blurted out to Blake.

Blake chuckled. "He's new at this," he explained to Colin, who seemed amused as well, for some reason. What was so funny? Surely you'd remember someone you had sex with, right?

Colin stepped in close, lowering his voice. "Honey, I go to that gay club about every weekend, looking to score me a hot man. I love being fucked and I'm not ashamed of it. Blake here fucked me twice, but my feelings aren't hurt that he doesn't remember it. I do. He fucked me so good the first time that I let him do it again a few months later. Doesn't mean I want to marry him and have his babies."

Aaron nodded as if he understood, but he didn't. The concept of such casual sex was so foreign to him he couldn't even wrap his mind around it.

"Anyway, let's score you some sexy undies. Considering your skin tone, I'm thinking black. Stretch. And very, very tight."

Blake nodded in approval. "Sounds good."

Aaron had assumed he'd choose a pair and take them home, but Colin and Blake insisted he try them on. "I thought you weren't supposed to try on underwear?" Aaron protested.

"He's adorable," Colin laughed at Blake. "Honey, you need to try them on. With boxers this tight, the fit has to be exactly right. We want to showcase your assets without choking off the blood supply to your essential parts."

Aaron was pushed into the dressing room with a pair of the boxers in his hand. They were black stretch with a simple black elastic waistband and white letters that said "sexy and I know it." He took off his clothes and put them on. Dang, they were tight. He looked at himself in the full-length mirror and had to admit they looked good on him.

"Okay, they fit," he shouted to Blake.

Before he realized what was happening, Blake yanked the door of his dressing room open. "Let me have a look," he announced.

"Blake," Aaron said in protest, but Blake ignored him.

"Turn around."

Why did he have this instinctive urge to obey Blake? It was infuriating at times, and so confusing.

"Hot damn, these look good on you. Colin, come have a look."

Seriously? He was gonna let a stranger ogle him in his underwear? Aaron quickly turned again, resisting the urge to cover his crotch with his hands. He might as well been naked for all the tight boxers were showing. Colin stepped inside the dressing room as well before Aaron could even utter a word.

"Wow, nice," he complimented Aaron. "Turn around for me, honey." He hummed. "Oh, yeah, these will do the trick. Make sure to wear low-cut, tight jeans so the waistband shows."

"You have any you can recommend for him?"

"Hell, yeah. Give me a few minutes, okay? What size are you, a thirty-one in the waist?"

Aaron nodded, too stupefied to say anything.

Colin walked out, whistling. Blake remained in the dressing room with Aaron, getting another look at him in his new underwear. "Blake, this is inappropriate," he whispered.

"You're kinda uptight," Blake said.

"I'm not uptight!" How could Blake even say that? The

fact that he'd been instilled with a decent set of manners and a sense of propriety, didn't mean he was uptight.

"You're constantly in your head, worrying about everything and everyone else instead of listening to yourself. Stop analyzing everything. Feel."

Aaron scoffed. "I can't turn my brain off like that."

Blake shot him a sexy smile, letting out a soft growl as he studied Aaron's backside again. "Your ass looks hot in those boxers."

Aaron stilled. He checked himself in the mirror again. "It does?"

Blake stepped in behind him, so close his body heat warmed Aaron's skin. "Can I touch you?" he asked.

Aaron nodded, breathless. Blake put his hands on Aaron's hips and slowly pressed his cock into Aaron's ass. His mouth came close to Aaron's ear, his hot breath causing goose bumps all over Aaron's skin. "You're an uptight, stubborn little shit, but your ass is delicious. Feel this?"

Blake's erection was hard to miss as it pressed against Aaron. "Yeah," Aaron whispered. His cock grew hard.

"Watching you with that cute butt of yours in those damn tight boxers has made me horny. Can I touch your cock?"

Another breathless nod. What was Blake doing to him?

Blake's hand snaked around Aaron's waist. Aaron almost stopped breathing. He watched in the mirror as Blake palmed his cock through his underwear, then increased the pressure. Oh, so good. Tingles were racing up his spine.

"You like that?" Blake breathed in his ear.

Completely foreign sensations were assaulting Aaron's body. Before, when he'd touched Blake, he'd been aroused. He'd been aware of his flushed skin, his hard dick, and a slight tremble. But this, this was on a whole different level.

His body didn't even feel familiar anymore. It was like someone else had taken over, someone who wanted to beg Blake to please, don't stop. Someone who wanted to bend over and offer himself to Blake.

"Yeah," he whispered.

"You're so responsive." Blake's voice was low, hoarse. He blew a hot breath over Aaron's ear, making him shiver. "Your body reacts to every little thing I do. Where do you feel it most, Aaron...your cock? Your belly?"

He didn't think. The answer came automatically. "My hole. It's twitching." As strange and somewhat humiliating as this admission was, admitting the truth brought freedom.

Blake rubbed his erection against Aaron's ass again. "It longs for more, huh?"

Aaron dropped his head back against Blake's shoulder, barely able to stand anymore. "What are you doing to me?"

"Showing you your body knows what it wants. What it needs. Stop overthinking everything. What do you want?"

A knock on the door prevented Aaron from answering. Blake was slow to step back, making no secret of his obvious arousal. Colin stepped back in, took one look at the two of them and grinned. "Getting your dirty on in the dressing room? Lock the door next time, okay?"

He held up two pairs of tight jeans. "I think these will look awesome on you. Why don't you try them on? Do you need a shirt or something to go with it?"

Aaron's head spun.

"Yes. Something pretty. Sexy. Feminine colors," Blake said. "What would look good on him?"

"With his eyes and complexion? Pastels. Baby blue, soft pink. Not yellow. Hardly anyone looks good in soft yellow. Lavender, maybe."

Blake nodded. "Sounds good. Can you find him something like that while we try on the jeans?"

"Your wish is my command," Colin said. He handed Aaron the jeans, winking, before stepping out again. "Lock the damn door," he called out.

Aaron's eyes found Blake's. Would he continue with what he'd been doing?

"Try them on," Blake said. His voice was low, sexy.

Aaron bit his lip. He dropped one pair of jeans on the faux-leather bench in the dressing room, then held up the other, eyeing it critically. "They're really tight."

Blake's eyes sparkled. "That's the whole idea. With your long legs and your perfect ass, you're gonna have everyone drooling over you."

Aaron doubted the accuracy of that statement, but he wasn't about to argue with Blake. He stepped into the jeans, then inched them over his legs bit by bit. He had to hold his breath to drag them over his hips. Was he supposed to be able to breathe in these? He sucked his stomach in even farther and managed to pop them shut.

Blake let out a sound that came close to a growl. "Perfect," he said. "Look at yourself, Aaron."

He faced himself in the mirror. The jeans were indeed riding low on his hips, showing his boxer's waistband which he assumed was sexy. They hugged his body, leaving nothing to the imagination. "They're too tight," he protested.

"That's because you're still hard."

"Yeah, well, nothing I can do about that," he muttered. For a second he'd hoped Blake would finish what he'd started before, but of course he wouldn't. They were in a dressing room. The whole thing was already highly inappropriate.

In a flash Blake was behind him again, pressing his hard

body against Aaron's. "Do you want to do something about it?" he breathed in Aaron's ear.

Aaron watched them in the mirror. They were the same height, yet Blake was so obviously the stronger one. The dominant one. And it felt right. It felt absolutely right to not try and be the aggressor. Blake had been right. It wasn't who he was, what he felt deep inside. He wanted to be something else. He wanted to be conquered, wooed, cherished.

He raised his arms, looped his hands backward behind Blake's neck, and pushed his ass back until it ground against Blake's cock. He was still hard as well. "What do you suggest we do about it?"

"Fuck, yes, Aaron, this is who you are, what you are," Blake whispered in his ear. His hand found Aaron's cock again and pressed against it. Aaron closed his eyes and leaned back his head. "Look at you, surrendering to me. You've been craving to do that all along, haven't you? Stop fighting it, puppy."

The unexpected term of endearment did him in. "Please, Blake."

"Please, what?"

"Whatever you want."

Blake let go of him, and for a second Aaron feared he was about to get massively rejected, humiliated. Instead, Blake locked the dressing room. Making eye contact with Aaron, he sank to his knees. With effort, he popped open Aaron's ridiculously tight jeans, managing to drag them down far enough to free his dick from his underwear.

"There are all kinds of things I want, but right now, as a reward for giving in, I'm gonna take care of you, okay? Don't make any noise."

It was all the warning Aaron got before Blake lowered his mouth and took his cock in. The hot, wet sensation of

Blake's mouth made him cry out, but a stern look from Blake caused Aaron to stuff his fist into his mouth to keep the noises in.

Blake licked, nibbled, sucked. Aaron's head swarmed, trying to process all the sensations, but his knees buckled. Blake's hand grabbed his hips and held him steady as he continued his glorious assault on Aaron's cock. How was it possible that this perfect man was on his knees, giving Aaron his first blow job?

His balls pulled up, so tight it bordered on painful. He was gonna come in Blake's mouth. Seconds later, his orgasm barreled through him, tears forming in his eyes at the force of it. He clamped down hard on his fist, managed to keep the noises in as rope after rope of cum ejaculated from his cock. Blake swallowed again and again. Aaron shuddered, his body going slack. If Blake hadn't held on to him, he was pretty sure he'd collapse to the ground. Blake licked Aaron's cock clean, then let his tongue dart around his own mouth to take in the last remnants.

"You taste damn good," he said. He tucked Aaron's cock back into his underwear and rose. "How did you like your reward?"

Aaron removed his fist from his mouth, noticed he'd bitten down so hard there were teeth marks on it. "Yeah. Good. Perfect, I mean. Shit, I can't find the words."

Blake grinned. "You said 'shit,'" he pointed out. "I think that says enough."

Aaron blushed. He had, hadn't he? Blake was right; it was a telling sign. Oh, well. He'd just gotten his cock sucked in a dressing room at Macy's. In comparison, swearing seemed mild.

"Try on the other jeans."

Aaron raised a brow. "I thought you liked these on me?"

He stuck his lower lip out, peeking at Blake from underneath his lashes.

Blake shook his head and smiled. "Boy, when you embrace your true nature, you're gonna be deadly. There won't be an alpha male able to resist you, not when you pout like that. Now, try on the damn jeans. I want to see how they look on you. Colin has an eye for this kind of thing."

Colin. Aaron's somewhat giddy mood sobered. He was naïve to think all of this flirting meant something to Blake, even the sexual act they'd engaged in, or him using nicknames for Aaron. Blake did this all the time and with so many guys he couldn't even remember all of them. Aaron would do well to see things in the right perspective. It didn't mean anything at all.

AARON shimmied out of his jeans, his back turned toward Blake. Still, Blake had no trouble picking up on his mood change. What had happened?

He couldn't believe he'd sucked Aaron off. In a dressing room, of all places. First of all, he never got involved with his students on principle. It was asking for trouble, most likely in the form of a sexual harassment lawsuit.

Second, he didn't do blowjobs that often. He hated doing it when the guy was wearing a condom, but doing it bare meant risking an undisclosed STD. It was one advantage Aaron had: being a virgin, Blake was pretty damn sure he wouldn't contract anything from him.

And why the hell had he blown him in a dressing room, an almost public place? Aaron had tugged at his heartstrings for some reason. The constant fight between what he wanted, what he desired, and what his head was telling him was appropriate and acceptable was crystal clear to Blake. Aaron was so lost, looking for guidance. Blake wanted to help him find his true nature, embrace it. The fact that he'd been so damn sexy in those tight boxers had changed Blake's more or less honorable desire to help into something a little more basal. Like a desperate need to fuck him.

Years and years of training had ensured Blake had a tight grip on himself. He rarely gave in to impulses. The force of his want for Aaron had taken him aback. He hadn't merely wanted him like he'd been sexually interested in the guys he'd fucked at the club. A deep, primal need to claim him had pulsed through him. His vision had blurred for a second, replaced by the image of fucking Aaron's hole until it was overflowing with his juices.

He'd held back, knowing Aaron wasn't ready for any of that, and even if he was, Blake wasn't gonna allow his first time to be in a dressing room. The guy deserved more. Blake wasn't even sure if he should have sex with him in the first place, if Aaron asked him or showed signs he wanted that.

He reasoned with himself about it, telling himself it was what Aaron wanted. He wanted to experiment, right? Doing it with Blake was safe. Fuck knew who he'd run into otherwise. There were a lot of sick dudes out there who would love nothing more than to have a chance at a virgin boy's ass.

Blake winced. If he was honest with himself, the thought excited him, too. Aaron made him horny in general, but the thought of being the first to claim him? It triggered all kinds of caveman-like feelings Blake hardly recognized in himself.

"What do you think?"

Aaron's voice was soft, hesitant. No wonder, Blake had

ignored him for minutes, lost in his own thoughts. He pulled himself back to the present.

The second pair of jeans was equally skinny but rode even lower on Aaron's hips. He should wear those commando. If he did, the top of his crack would be visible. Hot damn, no one would be able to keep their hands off him, Blake included.

"We're definitely getting these," Blake said. "The other pair, too."

Colin knocked on the dressing room door. "You decent?" he asked, a laugh in his voice.

Blake opened the door for him. "Yeah. Look at my boy here, being all sexy."

Colin whistled through his teeth. "You're gonna have to swat the men off you if you wear that. Look, I picked a few tops that would suit you, I think."

He held up a simple, ribbed tank top in pink. "This would look great on you by itself. If it's too cold—which it won't be in a club—you can wear an open white shirt with it."

Aaron's eyes latched on to it, Blake noticed. They widened slightly, and he almost imperceptibly licked his lips, then nodded. Colin held it out to him and he took it, caressing it for a second before pulling it over his head. It reached his waistband but not more, which was perfect.

Aaron turned to look at himself in the mirror. The small sigh he let out said it all. "Perfect," Blake decided. "What else do you have for him?"

Colin had also brought a baby blue, tight-fitting polo shirt that brought Aaron's eyes out, and a lilac short-sleeved button-down that showed his lean body.

"I wasn't sure about this last one, but I think it would look fantastic on you," Colin said. He held up a flowery, sleeveless top in all shades of pink and purple, made from a sheer, fluid fabric.

"It's a girl's top," Aaron said.

Colin seemed to sense he needed to tread lightly. "So is that pink tank top, but it looks amazing on you. Forget about the labels, honey. Wear what you love and what you feel beautiful in."

He held out the top to Aaron. For a few seconds, Aaron studied it, and Blake was sure Aaron was gonna reject it, when he accepted it. He put it on with slow movements, as if he still needed time to think about it.

Blake's breath caught when he took Aaron in. He was beautiful. The soft colors made his skin glow, and the top danced and swung around his hips. His nipples were visible through the sheer fabric, offering a tantalizing glimpse of his body. Blake swallowed. "We'll take it. You'll go commando under the jeans, and we'll wax all your body hair off. You'll look absolutely stunning, Aaron."

Aaron made a tiny move with his hips, causing the top to swirl. He didn't even look at Blake, his eyes glued to the mirror to watch himself.

"You like it, honey?" Colin asked, his voice warm and soft.

"I love it," Aaron finally admitted.

"Blake is right. You look stunning." Colin smiled, putting a hand on Aaron's shoulder. "Welcome to the light side where we love pretty clothes."

Aaron nodded but still couldn't take his eyes off himself. That told Blake more than anything else. He'd done a good thing here, helping Aaron find a piece of his identity.

"Thanks for all your help, Colin," Blake said.

"You're welcome. Look," Colin lowered his voice at the sound of others coming into the dressing area. "I also work as a personal shopper and stylist. If you need anything else for Aaron, or for yourself, give me a call. I can find more amazing clothes for him, but it's easier if I'm not limited to what we sell here."

Blake's decision was instant. "You have a three-hundred-dollar budget. He needs everything, so make it match."

Colin beamed and handed him a business card. "On it. You're gonna love the new you, honey," he said to Aaron.

Even after Colin had left them, Aaron kept looking at himself. Blake stood next to him. "You like what you see?"

Aaron nodded. "I'm pretty," he said, emotion thick in his voice.

"You are."

"Not handsome, or masculine sexy, or hot. Pretty."

Blake could argue with him about the sexy part, since Aaron looked damn sexy, but he got the underlying message. "How does that make you feel?"

Aaron sighed. "I like looking pretty," he said. "It makes me feel good about myself."

"But you're still worrying," Blake said.

Aaron turned to look at him. "What will Josh think when he sees me like this?"

"You're talking about the guy who shares his house and I'm pretty sure his body with three other men?"

Aaron's eyes almost popped out of his head. "What?"

Blake grinned. "You never noticed?"

"Josh is with Connor," Aaron protested.

"Sure, but he's had sex with Noah, and I'm pretty sure about Indy, too. You can tell by their body language. I've watched all four of them interact with each other, at some point, and there's a casual familiarity with each other's bodies that stems from sex."

"But how would he... You can't have sex with three other guys at the same time!"

Aaron was whispering, but his indignation was clear. Blake kept his face neutral. "Haven't you heard about double stuffing or double penetration?"

The look on Aaron's face was a mix of horror and fascination as he shook his head.

"Some guys like their holes full. Really full. One way is to have two guys fuck you at the same time, double stuff you with two cocks."

"That has to hurt," Aaron said, shock still on his face.

"Can't say I've ever tried it, but then again, I'm not a natural bottom. Clearly it has to bring pleasure to some, otherwise they wouldn't do it. And it's nowhere as much as anal fisting. I've seen videos where guys take up a man's arm all the way to his elbow."

"Hell, no," Aaron said.

He was looking pale, and Blake took mercy on him. "You can start with plain vanilla sex, work your way up to the kinky stuff," he said with a laugh.

"You make it sound boring," Aaron complained.

Blake sobered. "No, and I'm sorry for teasing you. You set the pace, Aaron. If you're not ready for sex, you wait. If you are, you find someone who will respect you enough to take it slow, okay?"

Aaron reached out for his hand and held it tight. "Will you do it?" he asked.

Blake's heart jumped in his chest. Was Aaron asking what he thought he was? "What do you mean?" He needed to be certain.

"I want you to be my first."

He looked so cute and pretty and sexy, still in that gorgeous top and the tight jeans. But his words were cute and pretty, too, like a schoolgirl on prom night. Blake needed to manage expectations. "Aaron, I don't do relationships. I like you, I really do, but don't read more into this. I don't date or hold hands or do romantic dinners."

"That's okay. I don't need that. What I need is a safe place to gain some experience. You said it yourself, I need someone who respects me enough to take it slow. I want my first time to be good. I trust you. Please, Blake?"

Blake couldn't help himself. He pulled Aaron close and brought their mouths together. At first, Aaron kept his mouth closed. Blake increased the pressure, licked his lips and pushed with his tongue until Aaron let him in. He angled his head a bit more, dove in deep. Aaron's movements were slow, insecure, but he wound his arms around Blake's neck and held on.

His mouth was sweet, hot. Blake tasted the peppermint Aaron so often suckled on, those white-and-red-striped ones. He teased Aaron's tongue with his, until it responded and they were doing a slick dance of push and pull. He was a fast learner, copying Blake's moves at first, then coming up with a few of his own.

He was everything Blake usually avoided. Inexperienced, vulnerable, insecure. Yet kissing him did something to Blake's body that he didn't recognize. It triggered a hunger in him, a fierce need to possess, to own.

His hands lowered till they reached Aaron's ass. He put one hand on each butt cheek, pulled Aaron close to him and ground his hips into him. The kid was hard again, and he himself had barely been soft since they had gotten into the dressing room. What was Aaron doing to him?

He broke off the kiss, swearing softly at the sight of Aaron's dazed look, his swollen lips. Fuck, Blake didn't want to stop, not even close. He kissed him once more, the gentlest of kisses. "Not here. Not now."

Aaron blinked. "But you'll do it?"

"Tomorrow. I want you to have time to think about this, sleep on it. If tomorrow in the cold light of day you decide this is what you want, I'm your man."

5

H e'd barely slept. Aaron kept playing the events of the day in his head. Blake inviting him to ask questions, then stripping naked in front of him. Watching Blake, touching him, tasting him. That glorious body, that perfect cock. Blake teasing him and pushing him in that dressing room until Aaron had surrendered. And Blake on his knees, sucking him off.

Aaron's thoughts were all over the place, trying to make sense of it. He'd even gotten up in the middle of the night to put the flowery top back on, with the skinny jeans. He'd studied himself in the mirror, wondering if the shame would always be there when he looked at himself in the mirror.

The shame of being gay.

The shame of wearing something so feminine.

The shame of betraying everything his parents had ever taught him.

The shame of wanting Blake, needing him with a fierceness that was foreign to him.

He would've let Blake take him, right then and there in that dressing room. That's how much he'd wanted him. Blake had been right. It wasn't the place, nor the time. He'd proved once again that he was an honorable man.

If Aaron still wanted him in the cold light of day, Blake would take him up on his offer, he'd promised. Aaron doubted there was anything that could make his need disappear, but the night did bring uncertainty and indecision. Not so much about wanting Blake—that ship had sailed. It was more doubt about the wisdom of having sex with him.

He was ready to have sex. Sort of. He wanted to, despite that voice inside his head that kept telling him it was wrong.

Shameful. Sinful. Deviant.

He didn't believe that, yet it was tiresome that he still hadn't gotten rid of that judgmental voice. He wanted to start this part of his life. The part where he could be himself, where he could embrace who he was. And sex was a part of that, a crucial part, or so he figured. Being gay and having sex were sort of synonyms, from what he'd discovered. Every blog post he'd read, every article in gay magazines had talked about sex in some way.

Blake had been right about Aaron not being himself. He wanted to, but he still struggled with who he was. Would he ever have the guts to accept himself, to love himself exactly the way he was?

He wondered if it was a reason to postpone sex. With anyone, but above all with Blake. If he was still struggling to find himself, would sex hurt or help? And what if he disappointed him, humiliated himself all over again? Blake already saw him as a kid. The last thing he needed was for the man to start to feel sorry for him.

They'd gone home after their trip to Macy's, despite
Blake's earlier plans to buy him sex toys and do manscaping.
Aaron wasn't sure if he was disappointed they'd skipped
those two things. Both had intimidated and thrilled him in
equal measures. He'd wanted Blake to touch him again,
which he would have had to if he'd helped Aaron trim his
pubic hairs. And the thought of him and Blake shopping for
an anal dildo made him blush, even now, lying in bed.

He sighed. He was hard. Again. It happened every time
he thought of Blake, especially about the flirting and the
sucking off and all the sexual stuff they'd talked about. At
least Blake had said Aaron's dick was nice. That had been a
huge relief, to know he wasn't some outlier in that department. He had enough weird tendencies to compensate, but
that was one less thing to worry about.

His hand traveled to his cock, and he gripped it through
the boxers he was wearing. The boxers Blake had bought for
him, that, according to him, made Aaron's ass pop. Man, he
was so hard.

He jacked himself off almost every day, but it was more
mechanical than anything else. It was something that
needed to be done, as far as he was concerned, if only to
avoid embarrassing erections throughout the day. Plus, his
balls tended to get sore when he didn't masturbate.

He'd started watching porn since he came out, had all
but spontaneously erupted the first few times he'd seen men
on screen fuck. It had been everything he'd dreamed of,
everything he'd wanted. Yet he'd never managed to get rid of
the guilt while watching. It was why he'd never dared to
play with himself too much. He'd jack off, twice if he was
excited, and that was it.

He dragged his boxers down. Blake had handed him a
bottle of lubricant before they'd gone to bed. He'd winked,

told him to experiment a little. Aaron had blushed, of
course, and put it in his night table drawer. He reached for it
now and squeezed out a little, the gel cold in his hand. He
laid back on his back and coated his cock with the lubricant
until it was slick everywhere. Aaron fisted himself a few
times, biting back a groan. The lubricant made it so much
more pleasant, so slick.

He brought his right hand to his ass. Should he? He
squirmed until he'd found a position where he could use his
left hand on his cock and his right hand on his ass. He made
sure his index finger was lubricated before pushing against
his own entrance.

He'd expected to push through with ease, but his ass
seemed intent on keeping the intruder out. Push back, he'd
read on the sites he'd visited to educate himself about gay
sex. He forced himself to relax and pushed against his finger
at the same time. It slipped inside, and he let out a little yelp
of surprise.

With some effort and a little panting, he managed to get
his entire finger in. He wanted to groan at the sensation. It
was a delicious mix of burning and fullness, of pleasure
with a hint of pain. He moved his finger back and forth,
slowly sliding in and out of his ass. His left hand resumed
jacking off, if somewhat uncoordinated because he was
right-handed. Within a minute he came, an orgasm that
barreled through him and had his vision go white for a
second.

He removed his finger from his ass with regret. If he
came this hard from fingering himself with one digit, he
couldn't even imagine what it would feel like when Blake's
cock was inside him. It would be so full. So perfect.

With that, his decision was made.

He checked his alarm clock. Six o'clock. Blake would

almost be awake, the early riser that he was. It was Saturday, but even on the weekend he didn't sleep in. He was at the studio at seven, every day, rain or shine, as far as Aaron could tell.

Aaron grabbed a few tissues to clean himself up, then washed his hands, and put his boxers back on. He'd have to be quiet to not wake up the others, but the chances were slim. Their bedrooms were at the other end of the hallway, plus they were all late sleepers. He rarely saw them before eight-thirty.

He quietly opened his door and tiptoed through the hallway till he reached Blake's door, opposite his. The handle didn't make a sound as he pushed it down and opened the door. The lights were still out, but he had no trouble making out Blake's form in the king-size bed. He'd never even set foot in this room, yet here he was, sneaking in at six in the morning. He closed the door behind him. Still no sound or movement from the bed. What should he do?

He stepped closer to the bed. Was he overstepping his boundaries here? He bit his lip, suddenly insecure of his plan. Was this a good idea?

"Are you gonna stand there and watch me, or was there a reason you snuck into my room?" Blake's voice was low but surprisingly awake. Aaron practically jumped out of his skin.

He put his hand on his heart, which threatened to beat out of his chest. "You scared me."

Blake's reaction was a soft chuckle. He held back the covers. "Come here, puppy."

Aaron snuck into the bed beside him without even thinking about it. As soon as Blake's arms came around him, he relaxed. Blake's presence always steadied him for some reason. Touching him, feeling his skin against his own, it calmed him. Even the sound of his name rolling off those perfect lips comforted him.

"To what do I owe this surprise?" Blake asked when Aaron's heart rate had normalized again.

He said the words before he could change his mind, or chicken out. "I want to have sex with you."

His head was on Blake's shoulder, Blake's right arm around him. He turned on his side, putting his right hand on Blake's chest.

Naked.

Blake was naked.

It hadn't registered with Aaron before, but everywhere they touched, he came into contact with hot, naked skin. It sent his heart back in overdrive.

"On three conditions," Blake said.

Conditions? He was attaching conditions? Aaron frowned. He'd thought Blake would be happy, honored even.

"One, you come with me to the club tonight. I want you to see what's out there before you make your final decision. You may run into someone there that you like more."

"I trust you," Aaron protested. "I want you to do it."

"It can't be me only because I'm the first gay man you encountered. You need to see you have options."

Aaron pouted. "Okay. What else?"

"You can get rid of that snotty tone, Aaron, or there will be no fucking at all." Blake's voice was stern, and it did funny things to Aaron's belly.

"Okay. Sorry."

"Second, we'll buy you that dildo, and I want to see you fuck yourself with it before we do anything else."

"Why?"

Blake growled, and a second later Aaron was flipped on

his back with Blake on top of him. His hard body pressed into Aaron everywhere. Blake's mouth descended on his, kissed him till he ran out of breath. It was rough, hard, dominant, and all Aaron wanted to do was take, take, and take more. He wanted everything Blake was dishing out, submit to anything the man brought.

Finally, Blake tore his mouth off. Their panting breaths mingled. His hard cock was poking against Aaron's belly, smearing fluids all over him. Aaron's skin was flushed, his dick as hard as Blake's. "I swear to God, Aaron, you drive me insane with your questions. It was either kissing you or spanking you."

"Connor spanks Josh," Aaron whispered.

"What?" Incredulity laced Blake's voice.

"I overheard them talking about it. They even went to some guy to get lessons."

Blake circled his hips, grinding against Aaron. "You sound intrigued, Aaron. Does the idea of spanking turn you on?"

"I don't know." Aaron was honest. His mind was such a confusing mess.

"That's a good answer. Honest. It's okay if it does, you know."

"I mean no disrespect, Blake, I swear, but why are you making me do the thing with the dildo?"

"You can't even say it."

"Say what?"

Blake rolled off him with a sigh and Aaron felt cold. He hesitated but turned on his side and snuggled close to Blake again. To his relief, the man didn't push him away, though he wasn't holding him, either.

"I'm not making you do a thing, Aaron. I'm telling you I want to see you fuck yourself with a dildo. The fact that you can't even get the word fuck over your lips is the exact reason why. You're a virgin, in every way, and I won't have you blame me if we do something you end up hating or regretting. You need to learn to walk before asking me to teach you how to fucking sprint."

Aaron bit his lip. "I f-fucked myself with my finger this morning," he whispered.

Blake pushed himself up on one arm to look at Aaron. Electricity crackled between them. "How did that make you feel?"

"Good. So good. My orgasm was... I came so hard."

"Show me." Blake's voice was commanding.

"S-s-show you?" Aaron stuttered. Did Blake really expect him to do that in front of him? Wasn't that way too personal?

Not as personal as sticking his dick in Aaron's ass. Blake did have a point about him still being squeamish and prudish about all this. If he wanted Blake to do this with him... If he wanted Blake to fuck him, he corrected himself, he'd have to show him he was ready for it.

"Okay," he said.

Daylight was breaking outside, filtering through the curtains in Blake's room. It was light enough for him to see Blake's eyes looking at him in disbelief. Clearly, he'd expected Aaron to say no.

"Do you have lubricant?" he asked.

Wordlessly, Blake leaned over the side of the bed, opened his drawer and handed Aaron a bottle. Aaron nodded, his face determined. He yanked down his boxers, finding himself still hard. Or hard again. Same difference. Where and how should he sit?

"On your knees in front of me, ass toward me," Blake commanded.

Aaron did as he asked, pushing down the incredible amount of embarrassment at being so exposed. He squeezed some gel out, lubed his cock and his fingers. He fisted himself a few times first and moaned softly. His dick was a tad sensitive from his previous orgasm. His eyes drifted shut as his hand traveled between his ass cheeks, to his hole. He knew what to do now and pushed inside with ease.

"Oh," he grunted. If it already felt this good with a mere finger, how would that dildo feel? Or Blake's thick cock? He'd be so full, so complete. His finger slid in and out, his other hand going up and down on his cock.

"You like that, Aaron?" Blake's voice was low, seductive.

"Yes."

"You like playing with your hole, putting your finger inside?"

"Yeah."

"Add your middle finger."

Aaron hesitated.

"Do it, Aaron."

He took a deep breath, overcoming his fear. He slicked up his middle finger, then kept his two fingers close together and pressed. His hole was too tense, and he couldn't move past his own barrier of muscles.

Relax. He had to relax. He breathed out, focusing on relaxing his muscles as he did. Bearing down, his fingers slid inside and he gasped at the new intrusion. It stung but not in a bad way. Aaron relaxed his muscles again and pushed his fingers in deeper. A soft sound escaped from his lips.

The bed moved, and he opened his eyes, looked over his shoulder. Blake had pushed himself up against the head-board. That beautiful cock was jutting upward, completely hard. Blake stroked his cock slowly, his eyes fixed on Aaron.

"Your little show has gotten me so damn hard. Fuck yourself, Aaron. I want to see those fingers move in and out of that perfect ass of yours."

He obeyed, closing his eyes again as the sensations overwhelmed him. Slick noises filled the room. His hand on his cock, his fingers in and out of his hole, Blake jacking himself off, all mixed with his own panting breath. His balls tingled and pulled up. He shoved his fingers in harder, deeper, desperate for more. Why did he still feel so empty?

His entire body convulsed as he came all over his hand and Blake's sheets. Ears buzzing, vision white with release, he let go and plopped his face down on the bed, barely managing to withdraw his fingers in time. His ass was still sticking up in the air, facing Blake, but he couldn't muster the energy to move.

"Damn, look at that sweet little hole of yours. It's still quivering, begging for more. You have a hungry little pucker, Aaron. It wants more."

The filthy words washed over him, strangely comforting. His ass twitched again, signaling the truth of Blake's remarks. "It craves your cock," he whispered.

Blake grunted in approval. "My cock wants your ass, too, baby. Look how damn hard I am."

Aaron found the strength to move, smearing his cum all over himself as he sat up. Blake was leaning against the headboard, still fisting himself. Aaron's stomach swirled at the sight of him, every muscle tight and clearly defined. He was so beautiful, so sexy. How could this man be interested in him, even if only for sex?

He crawled toward him, filled with a sudden need to prove himself worthy. He sat between Blake's widespread legs, lowering himself on his stomach so his face was in Blake's crotch. Blake removed his hand, probably guessing where Aaron was going with this. Blake's cock stood straight up, clamoring for attention. Aaron took an experimental lick, rolling the salty taste over his tongue. It tasted like Blake, somehow. Dominant, sexy.

He licked again, then remembered what Blake had said, how he loved to be scratched. He scraped his teeth over Blake's head and was rewarded with a low moan. He licked and scraped again, Blake's hands coming to his shoulders, then his head to caress him. Encourage him, maybe?

He took a deep breath, then took the head of Blake's cock in his mouth. He sucked, remembering how good it had felt when Blake had done that to him. His mouth was stuffed with Blake's cock in it, and he started to drool. He swallowed, but that wasn't easy. Logistically, this was a tad more difficult than he had anticipated.

He used his tongue to lick around Blake's cock, teasing his slit and doing it again when Blake groaned in pleasure. At least he was doing something right. More precum flowed from the head and Aaron happily lapped it up. What else could he do to make Blake happy?

His balls. Blake had said he loved having his balls licked and sucked.

He let the man's dick plop out of his mouth, which made a deeply erotic sound that shot straight to Aaron's own balls. He nuzzled Blake's balls first, inhaling deeply. They smelled like sweat mixed with a musky smell that was purely Blake.

Blake kept his pubic hairs trimmed—the manscaping he'd mentioned to Aaron. His balls were hairless, however, making them smooth and silky under Aaron's tongue. He licked, tasted, lapped. Blake gave his consent by spreading his legs even wider, allowing Aaron full access.

Gently he took one of the balls in his mouth, sucked it carefully, not sure how much pressure he should use.

"Fuck, puppy, you're good at this," Blake groaned.

Aaron smiled. He loved Blake's nickname for him, stupid as it was. He sucked on the ball some more before moving on to the other testicle. He couldn't leave that one out, now could he? It was slightly bigger than the left nut, but it still fit into his mouth. He teased it with his tongue, lapping all around and sucking. Blake's ass came off the mattress as he bucked in pleasure.

What other areas would be sensitive for Blake? Aaron decided to experiment a little. He pushed against Blake's knees till the man got the message and pulled them up, exposing more of his ass. Aaron dug in, licking his way from Blake's balls backward. Blake had said he didn't care much if someone played with his hole, but maybe he'd appreciate it more when it was a tongue instead of fingers? Aaron had seen it done in porn movies—had even looked up what it was called: rimming—and it had excited him to no end. The strange thing was that he'd always imagined himself as the one doing the rimming, not the one receiving it. Here he was, living out his fantasy.

The rough area between Blake's balls and his hole was sensitive, too, Aaron discovered. He nibbled and sucked, Blake's legs coming around him to rest on his shoulders and back. He dug in deeper, wanting more. Finally, he reached that puckered hole that fascinated him so much. He'd never imagined how good it would feel to play with himself there, but now he had the chance to see if he could make Blake enjoy it as well. Aaron licked it first, then used his teeth to scrape, eliciting goose bumps on Blake's skin. He liked that, huh?

He lapped his tongue around it. It should completely gross him out by all standards, but it didn't. Instead, it felt so right, so natural to be doing this. Aaron pushed his self-criticizing thoughts back and focused on Blake. He licked again, reveling in the foreign taste, then decided to go all the way. He pushed against Blake's entrance and slipped in with ease. Blake's legs tightened around him, pulling him closer. Aaron started sliding his tongue in and out of that little hole.

Fucking. It was time to use the right words, instead of hiding behind euphemisms. He was fucking Blake's asshole with his tongue, and judging by the now almost constant stream of grunts and moans Blake was producing, he liked it as much as Aaron did.

Blake moved, reaching for his cock with his right hand. He started jacking himself off for real, his big hand fisting his cock with little finesse. Aaron matched his rhythm with his tongue, fucking that asshole until Blake was thrashing on the bed.

"Aaron, I'm coming," Blake warned, his voice tight.

Aaron let go, not wanting to miss Blake's finale. Blake's legs fell aside and Aaron sat up. Blake's eyes were pinched shut, his head thrown back in abandon. Slick noises of his hand on his cock reverberated through the room.

"Come on me," Aaron said impulsively. Again, it was something he'd seen in porn and had wanted to experience. To make a man lose control like that, allow him to paint you with his cum, had looked so sexy to him.

Blake's eyes flew open, and he adjusted his cock a flash of a second before he erupted. Thick ropes of semen landed on Aaron's face and chest, another jet on his belly. Blake let out a deep growl as he spurted one more time, his eyes never leaving Aaron's.

Panting, he lowered his gaze to take in Aaron. "Holy fuck, you have a talent for rimming. That's the single best rimming I've ever had. And I gotta admit, I really appreciate the sight of you covered in my cum."

Aaron beamed, crazy pleased with Blake's praise. It felt like a fire had been lit inside of him, warm enough to chase away the cold of all his self-condemning thoughts.

He looked down at himself. The creamy, white ropes slowly dripped downwards. He dipped his index finger in it, sucked it off with a slow move.

"Next time I want to taste you," he said.

Blake's eyes darkened. "You're starting to discover your sexy side, aren't you? I like Sexy Aaron. In fact, I like him a lot, way more than Prude Aaron. Sexy Aaron should come out to play more often."

Aaron acted on instinct. He crawled toward Blake and lowered himself on top of him, stickiness and all. Blake's eyes widened in surprise. Aaron hovered above his mouth. "Sexy Aaron wants you to fuck him," he breathed.

Blake lifted his head to close the distance. This time the kiss was slow and scorching hot. Blake flipped him on his back with ease, taking the top position again, his mouth never leaving Aaron's. Aaron loved being handled like that. The display of pure masculine strength and dominance had him all gooey in his belly.

Finally they ended the kiss, Blake staring at him with blazing eyes.

"What's the third condition?" Aaron whispered.

Blake sent him a sexy smile that spread slowly across his lips. "You already did it. I wanted you to take initiative for once. It can't come from me. You have to show me you want this."

"I rimmed you," Aaron said with pride.

The sexy smile spread even farther. "You sure did,

puppy. And you did a helluva job. Didn't expect that from you. Not many newbies like rimming."

"I loved it."

Blake's eyes burnt even hotter. "Make sure to bring Sexy Aaron to the club tonight. We're gonna have fun, you and me."

6

Josh woke up to the sounds of soft slurping noises coming from right beside him. He blinked a few times, his brain slow to start the day. What was making the noises? He turned his head sideways.

Ah. Right.

Connor was at work pulling a night shift, and so Josh had crawled in bed with Noah and Indy, who now started the day in the most delicious way. Indy was sprawled on top of Noah, kissing him as if his life depended on it, while Noah's hands gently kneaded his ass.

Josh's hand traveled to his morning wood which presented itself with extra fervor, it seemed. No wonder, with the titillating scene next to him. He scratched his balls, gave himself an experimental tug.

Wait, what? Connor had forgotten to put his cage back on. They'd sixty-nined each other the evening before, Connor eating Josh's ass out while he sucked the Beast. A highly satisfactory session, but his body was itching for more.

They hadn't had a Dom/sub session in four weeks.

They'd gone to Master Mark twice, but that was weeks ago. He wasn't sure what the issue was. Noah and Indy knew about their...preferences, so that had nothing to do with it. Connor had started work again, so time had been a factor, and he'd been busy with the paperwork for the house. The contract was signed, and if everything went according to plan, they were moving in next month. Noah had put the house up for sale, and they'd had some interested viewers already. It was all moving fast, but it felt so right. Josh couldn't wait to make a home with the three men he loved the most.

Noah's finger slipped inside Indy, fingering his hole. Judging by the soft moans, Indy didn't mind at all. Should he leave? Josh slid his hand on his shaft again, fisting it gently a few times. Fuck, he needed a release. He needed more than that. He needed Connor to work him over good. Both his body and his mind craved the peace it would bring.

"Noah, we need to stop," Indy whispered. "Josh..."

"Josh woke up minutes ago. If he wants to leave, he's more than welcome to. He'd better do it fast, because I'm burying myself in your sweet ass in about a minute."

Both heads turned to him and Josh smiled. "Having fun over there?"

"You gonna leave?" Noah asked.

Josh considered it. "Nah. We forgot to put my cage back on, so I'm gonna enjoy the show."

Noah nodded, but Indy's eyes narrowed. "Will Connor be okay with that?"

"I hope not. I hope he's gonna punish me real bad," Josh said, his eyes sparkling. There was no doubt in his mind that he could trick Connor into working him over. If he caught him in bed with these two, all bets were off. Damn, Josh couldn't wait. "He should be home in about twenty minutes, so if you could stretch it out so you're not done before he arrives, that would be much appreciated."

Noah look horrified for a second, then started laughing. "Fuck, you're bad. Whatever makes you happy. We'll do our part, right, baby?"

Indy grinned. "Fucking for at least twenty minutes... Jeez, Noah, I'm not sure if you can last that long."

"You little shit. I'll show you how long I can fuck you. Hand me the damn lube," Noah growled.

Josh smiled as he watched them. They were so fucking perfect together, these two. Indy dutifully reached out for the lube and dropped it in Noah's hand. He squeezed out some on his hand, coated his cock, then added more on his fingers. He dropped the lube while mashing their mouths back together. His finger slid inside Indy without preamble. Indy spread his legs wider, pushing his ass back. Yeah, he wasn't exactly protesting.

Josh angled for the lube himself. He wanted a little so he could jack off easier. He sat up against the headboard with a pillow behind his back—perfect position to watch his own personal porn show. This had to be weird for most people, watching an ex—two exes, technically—have sex, but he loved it. Watching Noah and Indy turned him on as evidenced by his rock-hard cock. His hole twitched, wanting to be filled.

Noah had Indy prepped in a heartbeat. Josh had expected Indy to ride Noah, but Noah flipped the boy on his back, taking the top position. It showed how well his leg was healing, that the stump was already recovered enough to carry weight. Indy pulled up his legs, opened wide. His soft sigh as Noah filled him touched Josh. It was only months ago that the boy had flinched from every touch, not sure if he'd ever be ready to be fucked again. Yet here he was, taking Noah with ease. And the man wasn't small, either, with his thick cock.

Noah slid in and out of Indy, his mouth never leaving Indy's. That was the big difference in the sex between Noah and Indy and Noah and him, Josh mused while he fisted himself. He and Noah had rarely kissed, not even during sex. It hadn't been part of their routine, for lack of a better word. Their sex had been functional and dysfunctional at the same time, aimed at providing them both with an outlet, but never granting either of them what they truly craved.

He jacked himself at a leisurely pace, wanting to time it so he'd come seconds before Connor walked in. The man would come looking for him if he didn't see them downstairs. Hopefully, he'd be so fired up he'd start fucking Josh right away. Because damn, he needed to be filled and fucked hard. Maybe he should prep himself?

He kept on fisting himself with one hand while the other traveled south. Not the easiest angle, with him sitting. He let himself fall on his side, pulled his legs up so he could reach his hole easier. Much better. He didn't even bother with one finger, but shoved in two. His ass burned in protest, and he sighed with pleasure.

"Harder," Indy begged. "Dammit, Noah, fuck me harder."

Noah raised himself up on his hands, his upper body sweating. "Fuck," he said between pants. "I'll never, ever get my fill of you. Ever."

He deepened his thrusts, moving his hips with more force. Indy closed his eyes, throwing his head back. The moan from his lips was low and long. "Like that...so good... Don't stop, Noah, don't stop," he babbled.

"I have zero intention of stopping," Noah promised him.

Noah was stunning when he fucked. His strong arms

never protested against carrying his weight, his perfect ass contracting powerfully every time he surged forward inside Indy. Noah's eyes were fixed on Indy's, his face painted with a mix of deep want and pure love. As if Indy was his sun, moon, and everything.

Josh fucked himself with three fingers, slowing down on jacking his dick so he'd last a little longer. He watched as Noah ravished Indy's ass, keeping it up longer than Josh had expected. Indy thrashed on the bed, his restless hands grabbing his own cock and furiously jacking himself off.

The garage door opened with a soft whirl. Connor was home. Perfect, because Josh couldn't keep himself from coming much longer. He added a fourth finger, teased his slit with his other hand to stay on the edge a second or two longer.

Indy came first, crying out as he spilled his load all over his hand and Noah's stomach. Noah followed on his heels, firing off a few hyper-fast thrusts before his body froze, all his muscles coming to a standstill as he came with an obscene moan.

Josh clamped down hard until Connor's heavy footsteps sounded on the stairs. He jacked himself hard, and as the door opened, he came all over the sheets.

"Joshua!"

Connor's voice was stern, but he wasn't mad. The steely edge in his voice when he was pissed off was missing. A shiver tore through Josh's body, and he trembled with the aftershocks of his orgasm as much as in anticipation of what was coming.

"Fucking hell, I leave you with these two for one night and you're having an orgy."

Josh's skin prickled. Hell, yes. He retracted the four fingers from his ass. Since his back was toward the door, he was sure Connor would pick up on his not-quite-subtle clue. What would Connor do next? Would he dare to fuck him in front of Noah and Indy? He'd proven to be a bit of an exhibitionist when he'd let Josh suck him off in front of Noah a few weeks back, but this would take it to a whole new level.

His hands were jerked back, cold metal encircling his wrists. Josh looked over his shoulder. Handcuffs. Connor had handcuffed him. He was still in full uniform and boy, was that a turn-on. The crisp blue shirt barely fit his chest and arms, stretching the fabric with every move. Josh grinned.

Connor pulled him off the bed by his wrists and pushed him face down on the bed, kicking his legs wide with his feet. Seconds later, he threw something on the floor—his gun belt—and put his gun on the nightstand. He leaned over Josh to grab the lube and unzipped with his other hand.

Would he?

Fuck, yes.

Strong hands grabbed his hips, his ass, and Connor pushed in, his cock slick and oh, so fucking hard. He still took it slow enough it didn't hurt, but he sure burned his way inside. Josh moaned, wanting the hot burn to last forever.

"You like that, you little greedy bottom?"

Connor didn't pull back, kept sliding deeper and deeper in till he was fully sheathed. Tears sprung in Josh's eyes. So full. So overwhelmingly full.

"Yes, Connor. More, please, I need more."

He was helpless with his arms cuffed behind his back, his body at Connor's mercy. Connor was still dressed, had merely unzipped his pants and half-dropped them. It was deeply sexy to be fucked like this, as if Connor was truly using him. Josh lifted his head, remembering they were not alone. Noah and Indy had turned on their sides, facing them. Indy's leg was on top of Noah's, keeping his ass open. Noah was still fucking him, by the looks of it gearing up for a second round. No wonder, with Josh and Connor now providing the necessary stimulation.

Connor went from zero to a hundred miles an hour in seconds, pounding Josh's ass so hard he saw stars. He closed his eyes, pushed back his ass, and welcomed every raw thrust. The force of Connor's fucking shoved him against the bed, again and again, making it hard to even keep his feet on the ground.

"You'd better not come a second time, Joshua, because there will be hell to pay if you do. And don't think I don't know you timed this on purpose, you devious sub."

Connor shoved in so hard, Josh's feet came off the floor this time. "Though I have to say you prepping yourself was a nice detail. Did you like watching them fuck?"

Josh's head was turning to mush, his thoughts disorganized and scrambled. Connor slid in deep and stayed there as he put an arm around Josh's throat, lifting his neck and head up. "I asked you a question. Answer me."

Josh opened his eyes, blinked. "Yes, Connor," he said. Was that the right answer? He hoped so.

Connor nibbled on his neck with his teeth, thrusting in as deep as he could in this position. "Is your brain shutting off already, baby? I'm sorry. I know you needed me to work you over, but I got distracted with the house and everything else. But I've got you now. Let go, baby, I'll take care of you."

Josh smiled. Connor had him. His body went pliant, and he didn't even need to work hard at not coming. An orgasm wasn't what he needed, not even what he wanted. Connor sped up, then came with a sexy growl that made Josh sigh.

He could bring his man such pleasure, and fuck knew how much Connor gave him.

Connor pulled out, smearing cum all over his crack and ass. "Ah," he said. "That was a nice start."

He smacked Josh's ass hard on both sides. "Go get the paddle."

Josh clumsily put his weight back on his feet. How was he supposed to get up without using his hands? Connor helped him by pulling on his wrists a little until he'd gained balance. "Thank you, Connor."

Connor nodded. "Hurry the fuck up. I'm still pissed at you for disobeying me, so I need to let out some aggression."

It was all part of the play, the scene. Josh understood but would Noah and Indy? He shot them a look he hoped was reassuring. He stepped into the guest bedroom where he and Connor had dedicated a drawer to all their toys. Connor had ordered a nice paddle, one that packed a serious punch. Josh loved it and hated it with equal fervor.

He frowned. How was he gonna get the damn thing out with his hands cuffed? He kneeled in front of the drawer, looked over his shoulder to position his hands correctly and pulled it open. He had to practically dislocate his shoulders to reach the paddle, but he managed to get it out without dropping it. He almost fell over when he stood up, regaining his equilibrium at the last moment. He'd done it.

Beaming with pride, he brought it to Connor, who had undressed and was waiting for him, seated in the reading chair. It was awfully close to Noah and Indy, who had switched positions. They wanted to watch, huh? Josh wasn't sure whether or not he minded. In the end, all he cared about was reaching that pain-pleasure paradise in his brain. What the fuck did he care if others watched? Master Mark observed them and that didn't bother Josh one bit.

He kneeled in front of Connor, his back toward him, so Connor could take the paddle. He did, unlocking Josh's handcuffs right after. Josh scrambled around and took his place over Connor's knee as soon as Connor gestured. The paddle came down hard before he'd even prepared himself, then once more on the other ass cheek. Fuck, that stung.

Connor rubbed his ass. "You'd better brace yourself, baby. I'm not in the mood to play nice today."

Josh relaxed, which was inexplicable considering what Connor was about to do to him. He should fear it, but instead he surrendered. He had nothing to fear. Connor knew his limits better than he knew them himself.

"Oh, Josh, you humble me with your submission," Connor said softly. His finger traveled from the top of Josh's crack to his hole, slipping inside with ease. "I love watching my cum drip out of your ass. It shows everyone who you belong to."

"You," Josh said. "I'm yours, Connor."

The finger retreated and the paddle came down again, more gently it seemed. One, two, three smacks, then Josh stopped counting. It stopped, Connor's fingers resuming their play with his hole. He rubbed Josh's buttocks again, then smacked them rapidly in succession. Another ten blows. Fingers fucking him. Rough, but gentle hands kneading his ass. More strikes with the paddle.

Noah shouted out at some point. Another orgasm. Indy, too, though quieter. Good. He was happy for them.

Pain and pleasure mixed until Josh lost all track of time. He reached that stage where everything faded away, subspace. All that was left was his body, Connor's body. Connor stopped paddling him and pushed him down on his knees. He offered him his cock and Josh took it, opening wide. He sucked until he ran out of breath, saliva dripping from his chin. When Connor pulled back, he whimpered.

"You need to breathe, baby," Connor said.

Josh obeyed, sucking in painful breaths. Almost automatically he opened his mouth again and was rewarded with Connor's cock. He rolled those big balls in his hands, reveling in the feel and weight. Connor's hand caressed his head, his hair, his ears. "You're such a good sub, Josh. You bring me such pleasure."

The peace inside him was indescribable. All thoughts ceased, the only thing remaining was obedience to Connor. He'd do everything and anything Connor told him right now.

Connor's balls pulled up in his hands and seconds later he came down Josh's throat. He slurped up every last drop, not wanting to spill even a little. Strong hands lifted him to his knees and sat him down on Connor's dick. "Open up for me, baby, I'm not done with you yet."

Josh relaxed his hole and took Connor in within seconds. He lowered himself until his ass was touching Connor's legs. His own cock was leaking with arousal, but he ignored it. Instead, he started riding Connor, rode him hard and deep until his legs gave out. Connor took over, fucking him until he came again in Josh's ass, moaning almost inhumanly.

Josh's eyes were closed as he slumped against Connor, too tired to even lift a finger. His ass hurt like a motherfucker, both the skin of his cheeks and his hole where Connor had pounded the shit out of him. He smiled, reveling in the sensation of feeling utterly used. "I love you," he whispered.

Connor lifted him up, carried him into the bathroom. Apparently, Noah and Indy had left at some point. Josh cuddled close to him as Connor bathed him tenderly, toweled him off, then rubbed cooling lotion on his ass. He carried him to the guest bedroom, lowered him on the bed.

"I'm gonna sleep for a few hours, and I want to hold you," Connor said. He crawled in bed next to Josh, putting his arm around him to draw him close. Josh draped himself all over Connor, put his head on Connor's shoulder and fell asleep within seconds.

NOAH'S BODY protested as he took it through the physical therapy exercises. He was determined to get back on his feet as soon as possible—metaphorically speaking, since he only had one foot left. He'd already had an appointment with the prosthesis specialist for a first fitting. It would take at least a few weeks before the wound was healed enough to use a prosthesis, but he wanted to get it right this time.

He went through the exercises with care, forcing his body to cooperate. It was hard but still a lot easier than after he'd gotten blown up. Aside from the amputation wound, he had no other physical limitations other than the fact that he was still way more tired than he'd been before. The whole ordeal had taken a lot out of him.

Indy had gone to Kent for a jiujitsu lesson. Noah had asked him if he needed money to pay Kent, but Indy had waved it off. "I don't need to pay. Kent does it for free to honor my professor, Matt Fox."

Noah had nodded, even though he didn't understand. Who was this Matt Fox, and what was his influence that jiujitsu schools everywhere would teach Indy for free? He'd have to ask him sometime.

It bothered Noah that Indy had to go by himself. Of

course he was more than capable of driving, and he was taking Noah's car, but Noah didn't like the idea of him being by himself. Sure, in a physical altercation he could defend himself better than Noah, Josh, and Connor combined, but still. If something happened, if he got spooked for some reason, Noah didn't want him to be on his own. Indy's flight instinct was strong, and even though he'd promised he'd stay, it wouldn't take much to make him run again. If he suspected any of them were in danger because of him, he'd take off. And the idea of facing life without Indy took Noah's breath away. Literally.

The stairs creaked, both Josh and Connor coming down after sleeping for a few hours. Josh was walking carefully, Noah noticed. No wonder, after that pounding he took. Plus, that paddle had smacked his ass raw and red. Unbelievable the guy was into that, but there was no denying he loved it. He'd completely zoned out, his eyes glazed over, and his cock rock hard.

It still blew Noah away that Connor had done it in front of him and Indy. He'd never pegged the straight-laced cop as a sexual beast and clearly an exhibitionist, but he'd been wrong. He wasn't about to bring it up, though.

"Did you catch some sleep?" he asked Connor. He knew from experience how shitty shifts were on your system.

"Yeah. About four hours, which will tide me over. Only one more night and then I'm back on days."

"Where's Indy?" Josh asked.

"Jiujitsu."

Josh looked guilty. "Fuck. I promised I'd take him."

"You were otherwise engaged," Noah said. "Don't worry about it. He should be right back."

Connor turned the TV on. "What do you want to eat,

babe?" Josh asked from the kitchen. "Want me to make an omelet?"

"Yes, please."

"For me too, please?" Noah asked. They were so lucky to have Josh, because he and Connor both sucked in the kitchen.

"Feta cheese or grated cheese?"

Noah waited for Connor to answer, but he was watching the TV with complete focus. "Oh, fuck," Connor said. "Fuck, fuck, fuck."

Noah grabbed his crutch and moved next to Connor. The TV showed images of a body being carried out of a burned-down house. His eyes trailed to the caption. "Boston District Attorney Merrick and family murdered in house fire."

His heart stopped. Merrick was dead? Holy fuck.

"What's going on?" Josh asked, stepping in from the kitchen.

"That Boston DA, Merrick, was killed. His family, too," Connor said, his voice hoarse. He turned up the volume.

Josh gasped. "Are the Fitzpatricks behind this?"

"I don't know. The guy was a DA and in a city like Boston, that puts a big fucking target on your back. But there are few criminals who would sink low enough to take out his family as well," Connor said. He reached out for Josh, Noah saw, and helped ground him.

A female reporter did a stand-up piece with the remnants of the burned home in the background. Her voice was factual and stern. "The police have confirmed the fire started around three in the morning and had multiple origins, which has led the police to treat this as a murder case. Boston District Attorney Dylan Merrick was home at the time of the fire with his wife Chantal and their two daughters Daisy and Melody, aged four and six. All have tragically perished in the fire."

Noah said, "Indy. We have to get to Indy. If he hears, he'll run."

"If he hears what?" Indy said. They'd been so caught up in the news, they hadn't even heard him come in.

Noah turned around to face him. "Don't run," he pleaded. "Please, Indy, don't. We can find a solution."

Indy's eyes focused on the TV screen, and he took a wavering step forward. His eyes widened as he took the news in. "They killed Merrick?" he whispered.

The reporter wasn't done with sharing what she knew. "Merrick was known for being tough on crime, especially organized crime. He brought many successful cases against criminals like the O'Shea crime family, and notorious drug dealer Benny 'Shady' Durant. Although the police have denied any leads as to the identity of his killers, rumor on the street is that Merrick was preparing a new case against the Fitzpatrick family. This family, known as the Boston Irish mob, has allegedly been responsible for dozens of crimes, including drug trafficking, prostitution, illegal racing and betting, rape, and more than a few murders. No felony or murder charges against the leaders have ever stuck, however. A little over a year ago, Merrick had indicted the top leaders and lieutenants of the Fitzpatricks, but had to drop the case when his star witness disappeared. To this day, no one knows the whereabouts of Stephan Moreau, but he is believed to have been killed by the Fitzpatricks. Considering Merrick's determination in bringing this crime family down, it only makes sense the police would look at them as suspects in this gruesome murder."

Noah's stomach lurched as Indy's picture was shown on the screen. His hair was a lot shorter and blonder and showed spikes instead of curls. He also looked younger, but the resemblance was undeniable. Noah wanted nothing more than to reach out to Indy, to hold him tight so he couldn't run. One look at Indy's face proved the stupidity of that plan. He'd come to recognize Indy's body language, and he was in full-on "don't touch me" mode.

"They took out his entire family," Indy whispered. "How could they murder those two little girls?"

"It's a warning," Connor said, his face grim. He was still holding on to Josh, who was leaning against him. "Nobody will dare to bring a case against them now, or that's their reasoning."

"It's a warning to me." Indy's voice was level, but his face betrayed his emotion. "They know I'm still alive. If rumors were flying around that Merrick was preparing a new case, they must've figured I'd gotten back in touch with him. This is to scare me off."

Noah wanted to console him, wished he could offer him a reassurance that it wasn't the case, but he couldn't. The exact same thought had flashed through his mind. There was one thing he could say. "This is not your fault."

Indy sighed, a sad sound. "I know. This is on them, not on me. No matter what I would've done, they still would've killed him."

"Could they've found any evidence in Merrick's home or on his person that could've led back to you?" Noah asked Connor.

"No. I used an acquaintance of mine who's a Boston cop. He had regular contact with Merrick, nothing to warrant any interest."

"And your cop friend, you're sure he's straight?" Indy asked.

"Yeah. He comes from a long line of stubborn, Italiantempered cops. They want nothing to do with the Irish on principle, let alone with the Fitzpatricks. His father works for Internal Affairs for fuck's sake, so yeah, I trust him."

Finally, Indy reached out to Noah, and his heart calmed down a bit. Indy stepped close, leaning his head back against Noah's chest. Noah's arms came around him and pulled him as tight as he could without losing his balance. "I love you," he said. He needed to say it, wanted Indy to hear it one more time.

"I love you, too." Indy was quiet for a minute or so as they all stared at the TV. The news had moved on to another story, something about a woman finding a stack of cash in a garbage bag.

"I'm gonna testify," Indy said suddenly.

Noah froze. What?

"They killed two little girls. It's enough. I'm gonna bring those motherfuckers down."

Pride and fear battled in Noah's heart. "Indy…"

"I have to. I can't keep making excuses, when all it comes down to is fear. I know it'll cost me, but it has to be worth it if it stops the violence."

He turned around and sought Noah's embrace. Noah held him, a thousand thoughts in his head but none of them sufficient for this moment.

"But who will prosecute now?" Josh asked.

Connor's mouth was grim. "This case just got bumped to the upper echelons of the FBI. That's good news for Indy, by the way, since it's a helluva lot harder to bribe Feds than it is to buy off cops. They'll offer him witness protection."

"No," Noah spoke automatically. "Not if it means breaking off all ties. He has a life here. We have a life here."

Indy leaned back, rose on his toes and kissed Noah

softly. "Not your decision to make, my bossy man. I need to think about this, all of this, okay?"

"Talk to me before you make any decisions, baby, please. We need to do this together."

Indy hesitated, then nodded. "I promise."

7

Blake barely recognized himself as he paced the living room. Where had his self-control and discipline gone? He'd never felt like this in his life. Impatient. Wanting. Needing.

He'd texted Charlie on a whim, his student with the drag queen act, and asked him if he had time to come over. Charlie had been excited, grateful to do something for Blake for once. He'd been in Aaron's room for the last two hours, doing fuck knew what. Blake had knocked once, about fifteen minutes ago, asking how long they still needed. Charlie hadn't even opened the door, had shouted at him to fuck off and be patient.

The funny thing was that Blake usually had patience. And self-control. But for some reason, both were in short supply when it came to Aaron. The man had managed to break through all of his usual defenses. As much as Blake teased him about Sexy Aaron, he couldn't deny a whole new side of himself was coming out as well.

He liked who he was with Aaron, this sexually confident guy who got to order around his pretty, cute little puppy. It scared him a little, too. He'd broken rules he'd never imagined violating, like hooking up with a student, fooling around with someone who was staying with him, and messing around in his own house.

Aaron's door opened, and Charlie stepped out. Blake shoved his hands in his pockets, unsure if he'd like how Aaron would look. What if Charlie had made him too girly? He wasn't sure if he would be into that kind of thing but vowed to be kind no matter what. Aaron needed encouragement, regardless of Blake's personal preferences.

Charlie sent him a beaming smile. He looked like he was happy with the result, at least. "Come on out, sugar," he called out to Aaron.

Seconds later, Aaron appeared. He was wearing the low-riding, tight jeans that clung to his hips, ass, and legs—and he was obviously naked underneath. He'd combined it with a short, purple ribbed top that exposed a tantalizing strip of his skin between the hem and his jeans. White Converse with pink glitter decorations finished his look. Charlie had painted Aaron's eyes in shades of pink, with purple eyeliner and black mascara and had put a hint of pink gloss on his luscious lips.

Aaron was breathtakingly gorgeous.

Blake swallowed, unable to find words. "You're perfect," he finally said.

Aaron's eyes, so hesitant and insecure before, rose to meet his. "Really?"

"Fuck, yes. You're beautiful, Aaron. Absolutely stunning."

"Turn around," Charlie told Aaron.

He did, exposing a temporary tattoo on his shoulder blade, visible underneath the racerback of his top. Pink hearts. Blake's gaze trailed lower, rested on the top of Aaron's crack, peeping out from under the jeans.

"He's completely waxed," Charlie grinned, apparently following his thoughts. "There's not a hair left on his body down there."

Blake swallowed again. When Charlie said completely, he meant completely. Smooth skin, smooth balls, smooth asshole. Hot damn, the thought alone made him want to drag Aaron back to his room and start the party right here and now.

"I'd better bring my baseball bat," he mumbled. "I'm gonna need it to keep the guys off you."

Aaron sent him a smile that was sexy and shy at the same time, like he couldn't believe Blake meant it.

"Thanks so much, Charlie. You gonna come to the club as well?" Blake asked.

"Nah. Not feeling like it today."

Blake's eyes narrowed. Something was off. He observed as Charlie carefully hugged Aaron, who returned the embrace with uncharacteristic enthusiasm. Well, it was hard not to like Charlie. He was a sweetheart.

He was also hurt, moving unnaturally stiffly.

"Who hurt you?" he asked straight out.

Charlie flinched, avoiding Blake's look.

"You're not leaving until you tell me, and you know better than to try and lie." His voice was stern, but his face kind and compassionate. He had a pretty good idea but needed Charlie to admit it.

"He didn't mean it, Blake. It's not what you think."

He stepped closer and reached out to lift Charlie's colorful shirt. He waited a beat to give Charlie the opportunity to stop him, but he didn't. A large, colorful bruise painted his ribs on his right side. A check on his back revealed more bruises, all of them recent.

He closed the distance between them, taking him gently in his arms despite the rage bubbling inside him. "This is not accidental, babe. You know better. He's hurting you."

Charlie put his head against Blake's chest. He was at least a head shorter than Blake, and a waif of a man. No match for his six foot two boyfriend, a massive asshole by the name of Zack.

"It's complicated, Blake," Charlie sighed, his voice thin and on the verge of breaking.

"I know. You deserve better, though. Stay here tonight, think it over."

"I can't impose on you like that," Charlie protested. "Besides, Aaron said you're full at the moment."

If Charlie had asked Aaron about the people staying right now, that meant he'd considered moving out. Bingo. "You can stay in Aaron's room. Aaron, move your stuff into my room for now."

For once, Aaron didn't protest or ask questions. Blake reminded himself to thank him for that later. He released Charlie, kissed him on the top of his head. "Grab a shower, get some rest. There are spare clothes in the hallway closet in various sizes. Take whatever you need. There's toiletries in the bathroom cabinet. We'll talk tomorrow, okay?"

Charlie nodded, his eyes sad. "Thanks, Blake."

"Anytime. You know that."

Charlie sighed, then seemed to regroup. "Have fun at the club."

Blake scoffed. "With Aaron looking like that? I wasn't kidding about the baseball bat."

Charlie smiled. "And yet you asked me to do his

makeup, and you offered to take him to the club. Does he realize he's got you wrapped around his little finger?"

Blake grimaced. "You're full of it," he said with more force than he felt.

"So are you, sugar. You've got it bad for him. Not that I can't see why. He's gorgeous, especially because he doesn't realize it. Keep him close tonight, Blake. Not everyone at the club is as honorable as you."

Aaron's return saved him from having to answer that one. Five minutes later they were in Blake's car, on their way. Flirt was only a twenty-minute drive, and they spent it talking about everything and nothing. Aaron was easy to talk to, Blake discovered, also because he seemed genuinely interested in what Blake was telling him, asking question after question.

Blake parked the car a block away at a parking garage that was open twenty-four seven. He didn't like the valet parking at the club, wanted to be able to leave right away when he felt like it.

"Aaron, stay close to me tonight, okay?"

"Why?"

Blake smiled. He should've seen that one coming. "Flirt is aptly named. It's a gay club with mostly male visitors, the majority of course being gay. There are many couples, but it's also the perfect place to score a hookup."

"Like you often do."

"Yes. There's an unwritten code that you don't hit on somebody else's boyfriend, so if you stay close to me you should be safe from unwanted advances."

Aaron scrunched his nose. "What if the advances are wanted?"

Blake's eyes narrowed. "What do you mean?"

He was sticking that bottom lip out again, making Blake

want to kiss him till they both ran out of breath. "I thought the whole purpose of coming here was to see if you were the best option for me. You know, to lose my virginity to. But if no one is gonna approach me when I stick close to you, how will I compare?"

Holy hell. He had him there, didn't he? He'd told Aaron to come here, to scout his opportunities, yet now he was telling him to stick close. He couldn't even think about Aaron leaving with some other guy.

"I have the perfect solution," Aaron said, his voice bubbly.

"What?" Blake snapped.

"You help me inside and get settled. After that, I'm on my own, but you keep an eye on me. That way, if something happens, you can intervene and come to my rescue."

Charlie had been so right. Aaron did have Blake wrapped around his finger.

Fifteen minutes later, Blake cursed himself for ever coming up with the harebrained idea of taking Aaron to the club. Minutes after he'd ushered them inside and had shown Aaron the basic layout of the club, Aaron had taken off. Blake had underestimated him. Even outside, when Sexy Aaron had showed up, all but demanding Blake to give him his freedom tonight, he'd figured Aaron wouldn't have the balls. Turned out, he did. Smooth, sexy balls perhaps, but he'd sure found them.

He was on the dance floor, moving that lean body of his to the beat, mesmerizing Blake. He'd never dared to imagine Aaron could move like that. There was an innate grace to him, yet he seemed oblivious to how sensual his moves were. The jeans sagged even lower on his hips as he moved and dipped, teasing with flashes of skin. He wasn't even flirting. Not deliberately, anyway. Many guys were eyeing him, but he ignored them all.

Blake wanted him with a fierceness that scared him a little. Aaron was supposed to be a fling, a cute disruption of Blake's somewhat boring litany of one-night stands. It was about doing a good deed, introducing a gay newbie to the pitfalls of gay dating and sex. Instead, Blake was caught in a web he'd never expected. What the hell did Aaron have that pushed all his buttons?

A bearded, muscular daddy approached Aaron and tapped him on the shoulder. He looked up from the trance he'd been in. The guy moved in closer, said something to Aaron. For one second Aaron's eyes flashed to Blake's, then he nodded with a soft smile. Beardy started moving with him, though he couldn't match Aaron's fluidity. Instead, he danced around Aaron, stepped in behind him, and pressed himself closer and closer until his body was plastered against Aaron's.

He was an inch or two smaller than Aaron, and it looked ridiculous, Blake scoffed. The guy's arms sneaked around Aaron's waist, were placed on his hips and chest, pulling him even closer. Aaron smiled and slowed down his moves. His hips still swayed, dipped, but now they pressed back against Beardy's crotch. Blake bet the guy had a hell of a boner from grinding against Aaron's sweet ass like that. Blake sure had one, and he was merely watching.

Beardy's hand moved to Aaron's dick, palming it over his jeans, but Aaron swatted his hand away. He tried it again, and again Aaron moved his hand. The smile on his face dimmed, and his moves lost some of their finesse. A minute or two later—Beardy had been grinding against him that whole time—the man's right hand found his way to the front again. This time, Aaron's mouth lost its smile. He tried to move away from the man, but the guy held him back. Aaron turned his head and said something, but Beardy merely smiled. Blake's eyes narrowed. The guy had about two seconds to move his hands and let Aaron go—or Blake would make him.

Aaron took matters into his own hands, however. He stepped back hard on the guy's toes and when Beardy froze in pain, he turned to escape. Beardy's hand reached out to grab him, but Aaron was faster. He turned the man's arm and clamped it tight into an arm bar that made Blake's chest swell with pride. He'd taught him that move a few days ago. Aaron said something to Beardy, who shook his head. Finally, Aaron let go, walking away from the dance floor without looking back.

Blake's eyes followed him as Aaron made his way to him, annoyance painted all over his face. He stepped close to Blake, much closer than Blake had expected. Aaron looked at him through those beautiful, long lashes with those perfect eyes.

"Dance with me, Blake."

EVERY FIBER of Indy's being screamed at him to run. He had contemplated it over and over again as Noah fell asleep next to him, then snored softly. His man was at peace in his sleep, the worry lines finally relaxed. Indy still had moments where he looked at Noah and couldn't breathe. The fact that this wonderful, gorgeous man loved him—it was too much to take in.

On his other side, Josh slept peacefully as well. No nightmares, no bad memories. His arm was half draped over Indy, with Noah claiming him from the other side. It was so telling of how Indy often felt, standing between both men. He loved them both so much.

He didn't want to run. For the first time ever, he wanted to stay. The thought of leaving Noah, of leaving behind Josh and even Connor, took away his breath. They were his family now. Besides, he'd meant what he'd told Noah. It was enough. Somebody had to take a stand and do the right thing. Merrick had tried and had paid for it with his life. If he could do it, with his family at risk, so could Indy.

He'd take his chances with the Feds. Connor was right, the probability of the Fitzpatricks having Feds in their pocket was low. He'd have to risk it.

Even after testifying, he'd never be safe. They'd come after him with all they had to take revenge. He'd never, ever be able to be free. Not outside of witness protection. It had to be on the table, considering how badly they must want to nail the Fitzpatricks to the wall, and how much Indy knew. But how could he leave Noah behind? Josh? The mere thought broke his heart with a physical pain.

"Can't sleep?" Josh whispered with a drowsy voice.

"Sorry, did I wake you?"

"It's okay. You're tense."

Indy turned on his side to face him. "My head, it won't stop spinning."

"Are you scared?" Josh asked.

"Yeah. Terrified. Were you ever scared on the battlefield?"

"All the time. Anyone who tells you they're not scared when facing enemy fire is either lying, or about to get killed. Fear is what keeps you alive."

"How do you keep the fear from paralyzing you?"

Josh reached out, pulled him close to his body. Noah's arm slipped off his shoulders, but it was okay because Josh was holding him tight. "You tell yourself that it's okay to be scared. You embrace the fear. When you do, it stops controlling you."

Indy looked at Josh in the dim light. "You know that I love you, right?"

Josh smiled. "Of course I know."

"I never meant to take Noah away from you."

"You didn't. He was never mine in the first place."

Indy bit his lip. How could he make Josh understand how much he meant to him? He was so much more than a friend, even a good friend. It was important that he knew. "I would've shared him with you...and you with him. If it had been enough for you, I would've loved you both." He wasn't sure he was even making sense.

Josh kissed him with tenderness. "I know, baby. You have the biggest heart of anyone I've ever met."

"You were my first. You'll always be my first."

Josh's face broke open in a smile. "I'll never forget it, Indy, that you trusted me with that." He kissed him again, deeper and slower this time. "You need to sleep, baby. Close your eyes."

"I can't. I'm so tense."

"I'll help you relax. Now, lie on your back, keep your eyes closed, and don't move. I need you to be selfish and take right now, okay? Take all that you need."

Indy knew what Josh was gonna do. "Connor?" he asked.

"Not your problem."

"I don't want to use you," he protested.

"Don't you get it by now, silly boy? I like being used. Close your eyes, baby. I've got you."

He did as he was told and settled down on his back with his eyes closed. Josh peppered his chest with little kisses, then nibbled his way down to Indy's cock. Indy spread his legs without being told. The bed moved. Warm hands lifted up his ass and then he was engulfed in Josh's warm mouth. He took him in completely, sucking him hard and deep. Indy bucked, and Josh let him. He let him fuck his mouth until he came hard down his throat.

Josh licked him clean, hoisted his ass higher in the air and licked his way around Indy's balls. Oh damn, he wasn't done yet, by far. Indy moaned as Josh took one of his balls in his mouth and sucked it, then the other. His tongue went lower, and he licked the hypersensitive area behind Indy's balls, teasing his way back with soft bites that made Indy's skin prickle. His cock was rock hard again.

Finally, Josh had reached his hole. He lapped around before pushing his way in. Indy's hands balled into fists as he fought to keep his moans soft enough to not wake Noah. Josh fucked his hole with his tongue until Indy was withering in pleasure on the bed, thrashing his head back and forth at the exquisite torture. Indy was so damn close to coming again, but Josh kept him teetering on the brink. He kept tonguing his hole for what felt like fifteen minutes, and Indy went crazy with the need to come.

He bucked violently, and Josh took pity on him. He released his ass and took him back in his mouth. Indy came within seconds, shooting another load down his throat. Josh swallowed, then proceeded to lick him clean. He hummed in pleasure, his nose buried between Indy's balls, and gave one last lick before he stretched out beside Indy once again. Indy snuggled close to him, needing the comfort of his touch. "Go to sleep baby, you're good now," Josh whispered.

"Thank you."

"My pleasure. Now, sleep."

Indy fell asleep with Josh wrapped around him, his mind finally at peace.

AARON LISTENED POLITELY to Blake's protests that he couldn't dance, then took his hand and pulled him toward the dance floor. Surely a guy who had mastered the most complicated jiujitsu moves could find a way to move that body to the beat.

Who would've thought he'd love dancing so much? This club was amazing. Nobody had looked at him with disgust for wearing makeup. Heck, no one had even looked surprised. And when he'd started dancing to that low, thumping beat, he'd felt free for the first time in his life.

He found a spot for them on the dance floor and turned around to face Blake, who was looking mighty uncomfortable. He laughed. It was the first time he'd seen Blake so out of his element, and it warmed his heart.

Blake yanked him close. "You laughing at me?"

He wasn't mad, not when his eyes were sparkling. Aaron shot him a smile he hoped was sexy and blinked a few times. "I wouldn't dare."

He linked his arms around Blake's neck and moved his body in as close as he could, grinding his crotch against Blake's. Blake's erection had been clearly visible before, but apparently he felt no need to hide it in here. Aaron began moving with slow, deliberate moves, pressing his body against Blake's.

After a few seconds, Blake's arms came around him. One hand found a possessive spot on his ass, the other rested on his lower back on his bare skin. Heat rolled through Aaron, weakening his knees. He put his head on Blake's shoulder, surrendering to the strength enveloping him.

Blake's hand pushed against his ass, and he rubbed his hard dick against Aaron's equally aroused member. The delicious friction made Aaron moan softly. His heart was beating fast, and sweat broke out all over his body. What was this effect that Blake had on him? When that other guy had danced with him, it had been nice. The guy had been hard, too, but it hadn't affected Aaron at all. All Blake had to do was look at him with those burning eyes and goose bumps would break out all over his skin.

Blake's finger slipped under his jeans, teased his crack. Aaron's breath caught. A flash of heat pulsed through him.

"You're so damn beautiful," Blake grunted in his ear. He pushed his finger in lower, eliciting another moan from Aaron. He widened his stance, wanting more. "And so responsive. Fuck, Aaron, you do things to me that make me lose control."

"Blake," Aaron said. His head was swarming with sensations.

Blake ground his hips against him, increasing that delicious friction that made Aaron want to keep rubbing and grinding until he came. "What is it, puppy?"

"I'm yours. Please, Blake."

"Please, what?"

"Please, Blake, I don't want anyone else but you. I'm yours."

Blake's body came to a full stop. His hand came up from Aaron's ass to gently pull his head up by his neck, so Blake could look at him. Apparently, what he saw pleased him. His mouth broke open in a smile sexier than Aaron had ever seen on him. His heart danced in his chest, recognizing Blake's approval.

Blake's hands moved to Aaron's hips, and he lifted him up with ease. Aaron's leg's circled around Blake's waist. His jeans were riding dangerously low like this, but he didn't care. Heck, even if his entire ass was exposed, he wouldn't care. Anything to be held by Blake like this.

Their mouths were so close that Blake's breath warmed his lips. "We're gonna have ourselves a little appetizer, right here, right now, and then we're going home where I'm gonna fuck you all night long, my sexy Aaron."

His eyes burned into Aaron's, but he wasn't scared, not even a little bit. Instead, he nodded. "I'm yours."

Those words seemed to do something to Blake, like they reached deep inside him on some primitive level. His eyes blazed as he spoke. "You're mine, Aaron."

He kissed him, claiming his mouth with ruthless passion until Aaron surrendered to the delicious onslaught. Blake fucked his mouth, pushing in and out with his wet tongue, exploring every place of Aaron's he could reach. Aaron opened up, his body and mind pliant in Blake's hands.

Finally, Blake set him down on his feet. He gave him one last kiss. "Come with me."

Aaron followed him without question as Blake led them to the back of the club. A short line of couples stood waiting in a hallway, most of them kissing or getting frisky. Blake took position in line, leaned against the wall and pulled Aaron close to him, his back pressed against Blake's front. "This is the line for the private bathrooms. Technically, they're bathrooms. In reality, couples come here for a quickie. Etiquette says to limit it to a few minutes." His voice was soft in Aaron's ear.

Aaron's eyes widened as realization sunk in. This line, these men, they were here to have sex, in some way. And he and Blake were in that line. What was he planning?

His confusion must have shown, because Blake chuckled. "I'm not gonna fuck you here, Aaron, don't worry. You deserve better. But you got me so fucking hard that I can't drive home like this. I need some relief 'cause you're killing me."

Aaron brought his mouth close to Blake's ear, not wanting anyone else to hear. "I could suck you off again, if you want?"

"Hell, yes, I want your sweet mouth on my cock. But only if you want to. Never feel pressured to do anything you don't want to."

Aaron turned around to face Blake, snuggling close to him. "I want to. I like it."

Blake lifted his chin with his index finger and studied him. A pleased smile spread across his lips, but he said nothing. He kissed Aaron again, lazily roaming his mouth till Aaron couldn't think at all.

They kept kissing and grinding until a bathroom opened up. The couple that stepped out were flushed and giddy. Blake dragged Aaron inside, locking the door behind them.

"Take off those dam jeans," he ordered.

Aaron pursed his lips. "I thought I got to suck you off."

"I've been driving myself crazy tonight wondering what you look like under there. Take them off."

Aaron smiled. He should feel shame or embarrassment, but all he was aware of was a deep sense of how right this was, how much he wanted it.

He turned his back toward Blake, popped his button and shimmied his jeans down, revealing his bare ass. He kicked off his shoes, managed to wrangle himself out of the ridiculously tight pants. The air teased his smooth ass, his hairless crotch and balls. It felt strange, but wonderfully sexy.

"Turn around." Blake's voice was hoarse.

He obeyed instantly, showing his erect dick.

"Oh, damn, Aaron. Look at you. You look perfect." Blake

reached out, caressed Aaron's cock, then his balls. "You're so soft, so smooth."

He pulled Aaron in, sneaking his hands around his waist to reach his ass. He trailed down Aaron's crack with his fingers, and Aaron spread his legs. "That little hole of yours is impatient, huh?" Blake teased it with his finger.

All Aaron could do was nod. More, he wanted more.

Blake pulled back his finger, and Aaron whimpered.

"Sssh, my sexy Aaron, I got you," Blake shushed him. He grabbed something from his back pocket. A little packet that he ripped open. What was it? He squeezed it onto his fingers and brought them back to Aaron's ass. Lubricant. He pushed and Aaron opened up, letting him in.

Blake's finger slowly disappeared inside him, Aaron's muscles tightening around him before he willed himself to relax. Blake moved his digit with slow, deliberate strokes. Aaron moaned, spread his legs even wider and pushed his ass back.

"You like that? You like having my finger inside you?"

"More," Aaron breathed. "Please, Blake."

The finger withdrew but came back with the middle finger next to it. Blake slid them in. Another moan rolled off Aaron's lips, and his knees buckled.

"Let me hear you. Don't hold back."

Aaron panted little sounds as Blake's fingers slid in and out of him. The friction sent ripples of pleasure through him, radiating to the tip of his toes.

Suddenly Blake moved, pulling back his fingers with an impatient curse. Aaron almost tripped as Blake lowered himself on the closed lid of the toilet seat, dragging Aaron with him. He pulled him on his lap, but planted his feet wide so Aaron's ass was wide open, immediately finding his hole again with his fingers.

Aaron let out a sigh of pleasure. The new position allowed him to go slack against Blake and concentrate on the glorious sensation of Blake fucking his ass with his fingers.

"Ugh...Blake...oh, so good...more," he babbled, the sounds flowing from his mouth without his control.

"My pretty boy," Blake whispered. "You ready for more?"

"Yes...please, yes..."

A third finger was added, his ass burning as it stretched to accommodate the extra intrusion. He moved back against Blake's hand, welcoming it.

"Look at you, riding my fingers. You were born for this, sexy. You're gonna explode when I fill you up with my cock. My big cock in your tight ass, can you imagine how that's gonna feel?"

Full. So full. Aaron could almost taste it, how perfect it would be. His balls pulled up so quickly, Aaron didn't even have time to warn Blake. With a loud shout he came, spurting his fluids all over himself and Blake.

Blake found his mouth, kissed him deeply while he kept fucking his ass till Aaron stopped shivering with the force of his release. "My sexy Aaron," Blake said when he broke off the kiss. "You came without ever touching your cock. If you needed any more proof that you're a true bottom, there you go."

Aaron looked down. Blake's black shirt was now covered in spunk, dripping down from his stomach. "I'm sorry. I didn't feel it coming." The double meaning of his words registered, and he snickered.

Blake grinned. "No worries, puppy. I'll proudly wear your cum. Now, get dressed. I want to take you home."

Aaron's face fell. He scrambled off Blake's lap, his shoulders dropping low. Had he done something to displease Blake? "Don't you want me to..."

Gentle hands pulled him back. Blake kissed him on his forehead, the most tender of kisses he'd ever given Aaron. "I'm sorry, Aaron. You deserve more than a quickie in some filthy bathroom. I shouldn't have brought you here. Yes, I want you. But not here, not like this."

Aaron's heart quieted down. "I loved what you did to me," he whispered.

"Get dressed. We'll go home, and I'll do it all over again."

8

They barely spoke during the ride home. Blake was lost in thought. He never should've taken Aaron to those bathrooms. They were known as the fuck stalls, and Blake himself had made good use of them on more than one occasion. But dammit, Aaron deserved more than that considering how new this all was to him. When Sexy Aaron came out to play, it was all too easy to forget how inexperienced he was. And how young.

Blake drove past the complex where his studio was, glancing to his left out of habit. Wait, what? He turned his eyes back to the road, took his foot off the gas, then looked left again. There it was again, a flickering light inside the studio.

It was three in the morning. Someone was breaking into his studio, for fuck's sake. He turned left on the next turn and parked the car on an adjacent lot.

"What are you doing?" Aaron asked.

"Aaron, there's a light inside the studio. I think someone is breaking in. I need you to stay here and call 911, okay?"

Aaron nodded, reaching for his phone. Blake touched

his chin and turned his face toward him. "Promise me you'll stay in the car. If anyone comes after you, floor it. I can take care of myself, but not if I have to worry about you."

Aaron's face turned white. "Be careful," he said, his voice tight with tension.

Blake kissed him quickly. "Always."

He made his way out of the car, closing the door as softly as he could. When he looked back, Aaron was already on the phone. He was an inquisitive little shit at times, but Blake trusted him to do as he was told in this case.

He stuck close to the buildings as he moved toward the studio, grateful for the black shirt, black jacket, and dark jeans he was wearing. He was barely visible in the pitch-black night, the moon covered with rainy clouds. It was probably why he'd seen the light move—a flashlight, most likely. What the hell were they looking for? It wasn't like he kept cash there, or anything else of value.

He was next door now, crouching behind the gigantic air conditioning unit of the ballet studio adjacent to his unit. The thing made a racket like you wouldn't believe in the summer, and Blake had cursed it on more than one occasion, but at this moment he was grateful for the cover it afforded him. He wasn't stupid enough to barge in without knowing how many people were inside and what the hell they wanted.

That turned out to be a smart decision because right when he decided to try and see if he could sneak a look inside, the front door of his studio opened. Blake made himself as small as he could. The door was closed with a soft click, then the lock turned. Huh, were they locking up behind them? Why the hell would they do that?

"Let's go, guys," a male voice said. "We'll come back during the day, see if we have more luck." It was soft, but the accent was thick. It tickled Blake's memory. Where had he heard that accent before?

He moved without making a sound, peeking around the corner. There were three guys, all dressed in black and with baseball caps on.

"Duncan should have never let that little shit take jiujitsu lessons," another guy said. He turned his head as he lit up a cigarette, briefly illuminating his face. Blake couldn't make out many details, but the Red Sox cap was easy to spot. He pulled back his head, not wanting to risk the guy spotting him.

"Well, let's not complain. There are only a couple of dojos near the address we have for Stephan. Even if the address was fake, chances are he's close. All we have to do is find the right dojo," the first guy said.

Blake's brain made the connection. Indy. They had to be looking for Indy. The accent was Massachusetts, Boston most likely. It was what Indy sounded like sometimes when he was too focused on winning to think about his supposed Southern drawl. It was also what the cop, O'Connor, sounded like.

The men walked away, barely making a sound. Blake watched them for as long as he could. They had a car parked around the corner, because he heard doors open and close, then watched as a red Toyota drove away.

He rose and reached for the keys inside his jacket. He knew he wouldn't find any evidence of them breaking in. These weren't amateurs. They'd probably been looking through his files to see if they could find a record of Indy taking lessons. It wasn't there, because Blake had known better than to register Indy anywhere, even with the false name he'd given him.

A quick check inside confirmed his suspicions. He

touched his computer. It was still warm. It was password protected, but that would be child's play for someone who knew what he was doing. Everything else seemed undisturbed.

As he stepped back outside, he heard cars closing in, fast. The cops were here. He raised his arms, figuring he'd better not be mistaken for the robbers. Seconds later, two cop cars pulled up, cops jumping out from both sides with weapons drawn.

"I'm the owner," Blake called out, keeping his hands visible.

"You have ID on you?" one of the cops shouted.

"Right back pocket, my wallet."

"Turn around. I need to see you reach for it. Slowly, no sudden movements."

A minute later, his identity was confirmed. Footsteps ran toward him, and he had a second to brace himself before Aaron threw himself at him. He held him tight. "It's okay, babe. Nothing happened. My boyfriend," he explained to the amused cops. It seemed easier than trying to explain the complicated thing between him and Aaron.

"Your boyfriend said you thought someone was breaking in?" one of the cops asked him. Blake increased the pressure on Aaron's wrist, signaling him to stay quiet.

"I thought I saw a flashlight, but when I checked, no one was here."

"Did you do a walk-through?" the cop asked.

"Yes, sir. Nothing is missing, nothing disturbed. I don't have any cash in there, sir, so I wouldn't even know why someone would want to break in."

"Was the front door locked?"

At least he could answer that truthfully. "Yes, I had to unlock it. I'm sorry for calling you guys."

"No problem. It's our job."

As soon as they had driven off, Blake turned to Aaron. "We need to get to your brother's house. Now."

Aaron didn't ask questions, not until they were in the car. He'd given Blake the address and told him how to get there fastest.

"Blake, what's going on? I thought you said it was nothing?"

Blake hesitated. Could he trust Aaron with this? He couldn't keep this from him, not after what they had experienced together. They weren't together but still. Plus, Aaron would find out anyway if Blake wanted to warn Indy right away. And Josh was Aaron's brother, for fuck's sake. "There were three men. They were leaving when I showed up, but I overheard them talking. I think they were looking for Indy."

"Were they from Boston?" Aaron asked.

Blake looked to his side. "Why do you ask?"

"Because Indy's real name is Stephan Moreau, and some Boston mobster is looking for him."

Aaron said it as coolly as if announcing it was gonna rain tomorrow. "How the fuck do you know this?"

"I saw the news yesterday about a Boston DA being murdered. Arson. The news said they suspected a Boston crime family, and they showed pictures of a star witness who had disappeared last year. It was Indy."

Pieces of the puzzle clicked into place. "Yes, they were from Boston. That's why we need to warn Indy. They're getting close to him."

Aaron led him to a nice suburban home with a double garage and a for sale sign in the front yard. It was not what Blake had expected. They parked in the driveway and walked up to the front door. Blake checked his watch and winced. Almost four in the morning. Not the best time, but he couldn't risk waiting. He rang the bell, waited a minute, and when nothing happened, rang it again—long this time.

Finally he heard movement inside and saw a light turning on. It was Josh who opened the door. He looked like he'd thrown on the first piece of clothing he could find, which happened to be a pair of gray sweat pants.

"What the fuck?" he said with a sleep-filled voice.

"Who is it?" a voice shouted from upstairs. Noah, Blake guessed.

"Professor Kent. And Aaron," Josh called back.

"We need to come in, Josh," Blake said. "It's about Indy."

Josh's face turned white, but he opened the door to let them in, then closed it behind them. As they stood in the hallway, Noah carefully made his way down, leaning on crutches. Indy followed him, drowning in an oversized bathrobe.

Noah gestured for them to walk into the living room, where Josh turned on the lights. Blake settled in a chair with Aaron on his left while the other three men took a seat on the couch. Noah was in the middle, Indy curling up to him on his right, and Josh clinging to his hand on the left. Where was the cop?

"Indy, three men broke into my studio tonight. I happened to overhear them when they left, and they were looking for someone. You." Indy's face became as white as Josh's. "They were from Boston," Blake added.

"Do you know who I am?" Indy asked with no trace of a Southern accent.

"Yes. I didn't find out until a few minutes ago. Aaron saw a news broadcast yesterday where they showed your picture and name."

Indy's head sagged sideways, coming to rest on Noah's

shoulder. He kissed the boy on the top of his head, then squeezed Josh's hand.

"Call Connor, Josh. He needs to come home, right now," Noah said.

Josh nodded, stood up from the couch and walked into the kitchen.

"Can we wait till Connor gets home, or does Indy need to leave right now?" Noah asked.

"We can wait. They're trying to find him through jiujitsu schools."

In the background Josh finished his call. When he walked back into the living room, his eyes widened as he took in Aaron. Aaron was still dressed in his club outfit, wearing makeup. Josh probably hadn't noticed before, in the dimly lit hallway and with all the stress of the situation.

"We went to Flirt," Aaron said, answering the question that hadn't been asked. Blake sighed inwardly. Did Aaron realize he'd outed him?

"You and Kent?" Josh asked, surprise audible.

"Blake," Aaron corrected him. "Yes."

"What's Flirt?" Indy asked. His eyes had widened when Aaron's words had sunk in, but other than that he took the news in stride.

"It's a gay club half an hour north of us. Josh and I went once, but it was too crowded for him," Noah answered.

Josh lowered himself on the couch again, shooting Noah a look. "We had fun in that bathroom, though."

Noah grinned. "I showed my prosthesis so we could skip to the front of the line, told everyone I needed Josh's assistance."

"I did assist you. Very well, I might add," Josh said with a devious smile.

"Fuck, yeah. One delicious blow job, if I remember correctly."

Blake blinked. He was not shy about sex himself, but the openness with which these two discussed their sexual encounters was on a whole different level. And all that in front of Indy, who by the looks of it was more amused than anything else. What the hell kind of relationship did these four men have?

Josh's eyes turned to Aaron. They were much like Aaron's, except more guarded, Blake noticed. His look was cool. "Is Kent fucking you?" he asked.

Blake was taken aback at his abrasiveness. There wasn't a hint of concern in Josh's voice, as Blake would have expected, just pure anger. What had happened between these two that their relationship was so chilled?

"Josh!" The outrage, unexpectedly, came from Indy.

Josh turned toward him, eyes blazing. "What?"

"Be nice, would you?"

"To him?" Josh indicated Aaron with a gesture that showed his contempt.

Blake turned his head. Aaron cringed, his shoulders stooping low. Blake's heart stumbled and fell.

"You don't know what he did."

Blake's ears perked up. What was Josh referring to? Aaron sank even lower in his chair.

"I don't give a fuck. They came in the middle of the night to warn me, so you damn well better show them some civility."

Indy was not the submissive boy he'd once thought him to be, Blake mused. The kid had a backbone of steel.

"I'm stressed, okay? You know this isn't easy for me," Josh fired back at Indy.

Indy jumped up from the couch, fists balled and body

tense as hell. "What the fuck, Josh? This is not about you, so get off your fucking PTSD high horse for a minute, would you? They're after me, you realize that? And they're close enough to make me deadly afraid... Dammit, it takes every ounce of willpower I have to not run out the door right now!"

Josh's face crumpled and he got up too, drawing Indy close. At first, the kid resisted, but then he let Josh hug him tight as Noah watched the two with approving eyes. "I'm sorry, baby. You're right." He leaned back and kissed him on his mouth as Connor stepped into the room, still dressed in his uniform.

"You kissing my man again, kiddo?" he asked.

"I am. He's such a good kisser, too," Indy quipped, clearly appeased after Josh's apology and hug.

Connor's mouth pulled up, but he disentangled Indy from Josh's arms. "Kiss your own man, this one is mine."

"That's not what he said when he sucked me off last night," Indy offered with a sexy smile.

Blake's eyes went big, but clearly this wasn't the huge revelation he'd thought it was.

"Did he now?" Connor said as Josh looked guilty and happy at the same time. Connor drew him in for a slow, deep kiss, apparently not bothered by the fact that he had an audience. "We'll have to come up with a suitable punishment, then."

Josh's eyes lit up, and Blake couldn't hold back a grin. Aaron's observation had been spot-on.

Connor lowered himself on the couch, parked Josh on his legs and shot Blake a glance. "Start talking."

Blake took them through the events of the night, making sure to mention each and every detail.

"Can you describe the three men?" Indy asked. His voice

was tight, his hand clinging to Noah until the man lifted him up and put him on his lap. Apparently, this was a very affectionate household, Blake thought.

"All about the same height. About six feet I'd guess. White. Normal build. Baseball caps, one of them a Red Sox cap. He's a smoker. They drove a red Toyota with New York plates. The two I heard talking sounded like Connor."

"Sound familiar?" Connor asked Indy.

He nodded, shivering. "Yeah. Duncan's hit team. They're nicknamed Larry, Moe, and Curly. They were with him when he..."

He didn't finish the sentence, but Blake had an idea. Once, during a grapple, Indy's shirt had pulled up, exposing a scarred back. The kid had survived something heinous, and these men had been a part of it.

"Stolen car, probably," Connor said. "Smart choice, too. One of the most common cars."

"How did they make the connection with jiujitsu?" Noah asked.

"From what I understood, they had an address for him. A false one, but they were visiting jiujitsu schools in the vicinity," Blake said.

Indy, who had been leaning back against Noah, sat up. "An address? Near here?" He frowned, then froze. "Houdini."

"What?" Connor asked.

"Houdini. He's the guy who helped me get false papers. When Noah had his surgery, I contacted him for new papers and an Ohio license. It had a Columbus address on it, though, not one near here."

"Was that license in the name of Indiana Baldwin?" Connor asked.

"No. Laura Downey. I used it when I drove south to…" Again, he stopped.

Connor's eyes indicated he understood, but Noah shot Indy a puzzled look. "When did you drive south?"

Indy looked at him until understanding dawned in Noah's eyes as well. Blake was becoming more and more intrigued. What the hell was going on?

"What?" Josh asked, looking from Connor, to Noah, to Indy, and back.

Connor kissed the top of his head. "Don't worry about it."

Josh's eyes darkened. "Don't shut me out. I can handle it."

Interestingly enough, both Noah and Indy seemed to defer to Connor. "Baby, those assholes who attacked you decided to appeal." Josh's gasp was audible, but Connor put a hand on his arm and steadied him.

Josh had been attacked? Huh, Blake wondered if Aaron knew, but judging by the puzzlement on his face, he had no idea what this was about, either.

"Indy traveled south, paid them a visit and took care of it. They've withdrawn the appeal and are back in jail," the cop said.

Josh looked to Indy. "What did you…?"

Indy smiled, a smile so full of love that it touched Blake. "I can be quite persuasive when I want to be."

Josh leaned over and grabbed Indy's head. With Noah and Connor watching, he kissed him deeply. "Thank you."

"No, Josh, no thanks needed. We're a unit, remember? We've got each other's backs."

It was so pure, this love, that it tugged at all of Blake's heartstrings. Man, he wished he'd find love like that some day. He shot a quick look at Aaron and noticed the same longing on his face.

Josh let Indy go, but Noah grabbed him, cupping his cheeks with both hands and looking him straight in the eyes. "You and I need to have a little conversation about your methods of persuasion... You took care of this yourself? What the hell, Indy?"

Noah sounded more worried than angry, Blake noted. Apparently he hadn't known about this little expedition either, though Connor obviously had.

Indy shrugged. "You were in the hospital recovering. This was something I could handle, Noah. You know I can take care of myself."

Noah kissed his forehead. "I know you can, baby. Doesn't mean I have to like it."

Indy shot him a look that was half love, half exasperation.

"How did you communicate with this Houdini?" Connor got back to business.

"Email. We have a code. I can email him see if he's compromised."

"I hate to interrupt, but is that safe?" Aaron said. "Email addresses and IP addresses are easily traceable nowadays."

Indy nodded. "I know, but mine is blocked. I have various safeguards set up to make sure I'm untraceable."

"Oh, okay."

Seconds later, Indy was back with his laptop. He fired off a quick email. "It will take an hour," he said. "It's part of the code. It still doesn't explain how they got an address in New York for me, though."

Connor leaned back, pulling Josh close. "Aaron, I hate to ask it so explicitly, but can we trust you with this? Indy's life is on the line here."

Blake frowned. What was it with these men that they were so cold toward Aaron? It had to have something to do with Josh, but what the hell had Aaron ever done to deserve this? Indy seemed to be the only one who was halfway decent toward him.

"I know," Aaron said softly. All his confidence from the club was gone. "I won't tell anyone anything."

"That would be a first," Josh mumbled.

Blake had had enough. He leaned forward. "Look, I don't know what your problem is with Aaron, but you either stop with these veiled barbs, or I'm walking away, right now. I don't owe you shit, and traumatized or not, you're being a massive asshole."

For one second, Josh looked guilty, but then his face showed anger again. "Ask him. Ask Aaron what he's done to deserve this treatment. Ask him how he has treated me."

There was such venom in the voice of this otherwise kind and gentle man that Blake turned his head. "Aaron?"

9

Aaron had always known this moment would come. The moment where Blake would discover the truth. The moment where he'd find out what Aaron was really like. The moment where he, too, would walk away, reject him. All Aaron could do was face this moment with the last bit of honor he had left.

"He's right," Aaron said. "Josh has every right to treat me like crap. It's what I did to him for years." He took a deep breath and squared his shoulders. If he was gonna go down, at least he could do it with dignity. "When he came out, my parents were horrified. Disgusted. They thought Josh a perversion, an abomination. From the day he came out till the day he enlisted, they treated him like absolute crap. They ignored him for the most part, barely talked to him."

"And so did you!" Josh lashed out. "You were my brother, and you chose their side. How could you, Aaron? How could you treat me like that? What did I ever do to you?"

Aaron's shoulders sagged. "Nothing. It was all me, Josh. I treated you horribly, and I'm so sorry."

"Why? I don't understand."

Aaron's eyes blurred from the tears that were forming. He looked down now, desperately wanting to avoid the disgust in the eyes of everyone present. "I was scared."

Josh scoffed. "What the fuck did you have to be scared about? You were the golden child."

"He was only twelve, Josh." Indy's voice was kind, steady. "He must have known he too was gay, or at least suspected it. He saw how his parents reacted to you, had discovered their love was conditional. He must have been scared out of his mind."

"He could've changed, later on, when he was older. He could have stood up for me when I got beaten up in high school for being gay."

"Josh, he wasn't even in high school back then," Noah said gently. "We were fifteen when we met, remember? Aaron was only thirteen and still in middle school. That time we met, that was the last time you got beaten up, right?"

Slowly Aaron raised his head. Josh was studying him with a mix of anger and confusion, tears dripping down his cheeks. Connor held on to him but said nothing.

"You should've heard the things he said to me, quoting the Bible and telling me how sinful I was. He was spouting the same hateful shit as them."

"No wonder, if that was all he heard. How long did it take you to get rid of your self-hate, growing up in an environment like that?" Indy asked. "It's programmed behavior, Josh. He didn't know any better. He was a child."

"He was sixteen when I enlisted. He never even said goodbye. I was going off to war, and he didn't give a shit. He was no child. Sixteen is old enough to know better."

Aaron's body shook. He'd never fully appreciated the

depth of Josh's hatred toward him. It was completely deserved, but it cut so deep he was bleeding on the inside.

Indy scooted over toward Josh and pulled him off Connor's lap to cuddle. "When I shared my story with you, you told me I was innocent, even of the things I'd done, because I was a child. I was the same age as Aaron, baby. His story and my story are different, but we were both victims of our circumstances. He didn't mean to hurt you. He just didn't see any other way. It was survival, don't you see it? Choosing your side meant losing his parents."

"I came to you," Aaron whispered. Josh turned his head to face him. Aaron swallowed, gathering his courage. "A couple of weeks before you graduated. I came to your room, wanting to talk to you. You brushed me off, told me Noah was your brother now. After that, I didn't even try. I couldn't compete with Noah. It was obvious how much you loved him. You would've followed him anywhere—and you did. You followed him into war. As far as you were concerned, you no longer had a brother." His last word ended with a sob that tore through his chest. "I'm so sorry for what I did, Josh, I swear. But I had no one. You had Noah, and I was left all alone with them."

He broke down, no longer able to look at his brother and see the pain and reproach on his face. At least Indy had tried to defend him, though it was useless. Josh would never forgive him, and he had every right not to. Aaron hid his face in his hands, closing his eyes. The idea of Blake witnessing all this—he'd never felt more ashamed in his life.

Suddenly strong hands lifted him up, picking him up as if he were a small child. Blake placed him on his lap, putting his strong arms around him. He pressed Aaron's head until he surrendered and buried it against Blake's chest. Then

Blake nuzzled his neck, kissed his forehead. "It's okay, Little Aaron," he whispered in his ear. "You're not alone anymore."

Aaron's throat was too constricted to speak. Why was Blake doing this? Hadn't he heard what Josh said? Surely he'd realized by now who Aaron really was. What he'd done to Josh, it was unforgivable.

"I didn't remember," Josh said. "I didn't remember saying that to you until you brought it up."

Aaron opened his eyes but kept his cheek resting against Blake's chest. Josh's face lacked anger for the first time that night.

"Josh, I don't know you very well, obviously," Blake said, "but is it possible that your anger toward Aaron is misdirected and is actually aimed at your parents? I don't mean to make light of how it made you feel, what he did, but aren't the real culprits your parents?"

Blake was defending him? Aaron's heart rose up, lighter than before. Blake's arm was holding him tight, his hand casually petting Aaron's cheek. For such a tough and cool MMA fighter, he sure was a cuddler.

Josh let out a shivering sigh. "I don't know. Maybe. I've been angry at him for so long that it's hard to see it in a different light."

"I get that. Trust me, I do. But try and see his side, too. He's been angry with himself forever, has pretended to be someone else all this time, and it's made him lose sight of who he is. If you think you hate him, you have no idea of the contempt he feels for himself."

Aaron blinked slowly. He felt completely exposed, naked. Blake had seen inside him, all the way to the dark depths of his soul. And yet he was still holding him, still touching him, still defending him. Did that mean that maybe there was something worthy inside him after all?

Something lovable?

He rubbed his cheek against Blake's shirt and was rewarded with another kiss on his head. For a second, he felt like the little boy he'd once been, safe on his mom's lap. How long ago that seemed. He couldn't even remember the last time he'd felt this safe, protected. Loved.

"I don't know," Josh said again. "I'll have to think about it."

"That's okay," Blake said. "Aaron isn't going anywhere."

Blake wanted him to stay. Another weight was removed from his heart. No matter what was happening between them, and even though Blake had assured him he didn't do relationships, at least he cared enough about him to want him to stay.

"You're pretty," Indy said, clearly trying to break the tension. "That makeup looks good on you."

"Thank you." He sent Indy a shy smile. He hadn't forgotten how he'd embarrassed himself with him, but maybe Indy was willing to forget about that? At least it didn't seem like he'd told Noah, or Josh for that matter.

"And where the hell did you get those jeans, because I have got to get me a pair of those."

"Hell, no. You are not putting your gorgeous ass in jeans like that. I have trouble enough keeping my hands off you as it is," Noah said.

Aaron smiled, despite his wounded heart.

Indy's laptop dinged, signaling incoming mail. He read it, frowning.

"Did he reply?" Connor asked.

"Yeah, but... Oh, damn it." His face turned white. "He's compromised. Look, Houdini has this code. He replies exactly one hour after receiving a message, no matter what time you send it. He did. He also has a code for the meeting place, which is always a Starbucks. This, too, looks legit, but there's a third element. He never, ever uses capitalization. He let me know that if he ever used a capital letter, it meant he'd written the message under duress. Look." He turned his laptop toward Connor and Josh. "I is spelled with a capital. It's not him, they got to him."

CONNOR TRUSTED Indy's assessment about Houdini. The kid had an excellent brain, plus more street smarts than anyone Connor had ever met. "What does this mean, Indy? Assuming the Fitzpatricks are behind this, what information do they have about you now?" he asked.

Indy sighed. "My current alias and my Laura Downey alias, including social security, driver's license, and maybe diplomas. Houdini set up an entire background for each, including credit card history and stuff. Maybe a previous alias, I don't know. Depends on how detailed Houdini's records are."

"Have you used those for anything that can be tracked back to you?"

Indy shook his head. "No. I'm extremely careful. I don't have bank accounts or credit cards, my phone is a burner phone, and I paid cash for my car."

"Car insurance?"

"Yeah, but registered under Laura Downey with a fake address in Columbus, Ohio."

The kid was smart. So how had they gotten so close to him? "If they're looking for you here, that means they've found your Indiana Baldwin alias. How did they know you were taking jiujitsu lessons? You never registered as a student, correct?"

"No. I have a letter from..." He suddenly turned to Blake. "You have to check in with Professor Fox."

"Matt Fox would never sell you out, Indy," Blake said.

"I'm not worried about him selling me out. I'm worried about his safety if they discovered what he did for me."

"I'll contact him," Blake said.

"No," Connor said. "Don't. If they're keeping an eye on him for some reason, a phone call from the guy owning the studio they broke into is gonna set off alarm bells. Who is this guy?"

"He's the highest ranking jiujitsu professor in the country, and he happens to live in Boston. He visited the studio where I was training at the time, and he picked me to grapple with him. He took a liking to me, I guess, offered me a private lesson. I was suspicious, figured he was some closeted gay who wanted to get into my pants, but he was the real deal. After I agreed to testify, he sent me this letter through the cops. It states that any BJJ studio in the country has to give me free lessons and protect my identity. I guess he figured I might change my mind about testifying, make a run for it. Being from Boston, he must have been familiar with the Fitzpatricks, or at least their reputation. BJJ isn't exactly a squeaky clean sport, you know. Lots of bad guys take it, too."

Connor nodded in understanding. "Who else knew about this letter?"

"Only me. And the studios I've used it at, all over the country. I've managed to get about one lesson a week in, on average, at least until I broke my arm." Indy paled. "That's it. The robbery. I had to use my Indiana Baldwin ID in the hospital after the robbery, to pay my bill. They asked for an address, so I gave them a local one. It was fake, but it was in Albany."

"If they had your driver's license number from this Houdini guy, they could have traced it back to where it had been scanned," Connor confirmed. "Still doesn't explain how they know about the jiujitsu angle."

Aaron spoke up. "I recognized Indy from the news broadcast after that DA was murdered. What if others did, too? It was national news."

"The contract," Connor said. He could have slapped himself for not thinking about it. "There's a big contract on Indy's head. You said it yourself: it's a sport that attracts criminals as well. If only two people called you in from somewhere in the country with a connection to jiujitsu, the Fitzpatricks would have figured it out."

"It doesn't even matter how they know. Fact is that they know, and they've gotten close. Both my active aliases have been compromised, so I have nowhere else to go," Indy said.

He looked so small and young, Connor thought. Too young to be dealing with all of this. When would he ever have the opportunity to live freely and fully?

"If you're sure about testifying, you'll have to connect with the FBI as soon as possible. They'll set you up in a safe house," Connor said.

"It will take them months to build a case, though, if not longer," Noah said, the anguish in his voice palpable. "With Merrick out of the picture, they have to start from scratch."

"My guess is the Merrick murder will be the whole foundation of their case," Connor said. "If they can tie the Fitzpatricks to that one, they're going down for good."

Indy shook his head. "They're not gonna get Duncan on murder, not Merrick's, anyways. He's too smart. Even if they find out who did it, it will be his men who take the fall. They'll protect him, because he'll pay them well to do so."

"No matter what, the FBI is your best bet," Connor said. "But Noah is right, it could take a while."

"And they'll sequester me somewhere for all that time," Indy realized. "Away from Noah, from you all."

"Yes."

"And they wouldn't let you visit, because that would put you in danger as well."

Connor nodded, glad the kid understood.

"So I might not see you for months, maybe even longer."

"Indy..." Noah's voice was so heartbroken, it pierced Connor's heart. Would he even survive being without Indy that long? Connor was no expert, but Noah seemed to battle his own demons, and the kid was his primary reason for keeping them at bay. Not having him close might send him in a serious downward spiral, which would affect them all, but Josh above all.

Indy climbed back on Noah's lap and wordlessly cuddled as close as he could. Noah buried his face in Indy's hair, rocking him back and forth. Connor's heart broke for them. He only had to imagine not seeing Josh for months to understand how they must feel.

The biggest problem was that there was no guarantee it would even work. Even if Indy agreed to testify, there was no certainty Duncan Fitzpatrick would be sentenced to a long jail term. Moreover, even if he was, he could still go after Indy from jail. It was personal for him, this kid who'd gotten the better of him. No, Indy would never be safe and free as long as that bastard was alive.

Connor's mind went back to the crazy-ass plan he'd come up with a few weeks earlier. It was the only thing he could think of that would make Indy truly free. He was nuts for even contemplating it, considering the danger to not only himself, but Josh as well. Yet he had to.

His guilt over not taking a stand against his family had always weighed on him, but even more so now that he'd met Indy. What they had done to that kid, it was unimaginable, and yet he'd come out not only alive, but sweet and loving. How they had not managed to break him, Connor would never understand, but he owed him. He owed him for not saving him when he could have, and then again for protecting Josh.

Indy deserved happiness and so did Noah. And honestly, Indy's happiness—or lack thereof—impacted Josh as well. Jealous as Connor had been in the beginning, he'd slowly come to understand that Indy, Noah, and Josh were connected in a unique way. What they shared, it defied all conventional notions of relationships, friendships, lovers. It was so pure, so deep, that Connor would never fully grasp it. But he did know that Indy and Noah were part of Josh's life, of his happiness and well-being, and that meant they were part of Connor's life as well. He was involved with Josh, but the reality was that there were four people in this relationship. And crazy as it was, he was okay with it.

When Indy had blurted out that Josh had sucked him off, Connor hadn't even been jealous. He'd understood it had been Josh's way of easing Indy's fear, even without Josh explaining it. It was how they rolled, how they connected. The fact that they were so open about it, not secretive at all, proved more than anything it was something they both needed. He didn't feel threatened about it anymore, had come to fully understand and believe that he had no reason to. Josh loved him, more than anything, but he loved Indy and Noah as well. Different, but equal.

If Connor needed any more reasons to execute his plan, that was it. It would demand a sacrifice of him and Josh, but it would be worth it. Josh would do it, he had no doubt. And he wasn't even worried about him, funnily enough. Not after what he'd seen of him on that paintball range. All they needed was a little time to set things up. It had to be foolproof and one hundred percent untraceable. The first step was getting Indy safe, for now.

"I'll ask my boss to contact the FBI today," he said. "His brother is a Fed. We'll see what we can arrange."

10

For the first time in forever, Blake had skipped his morning workout. It had been close to six-thirty in the morning when he and Aaron had made it home, both exhausted. Thank fuck it was Sunday, the only day the studio was closed.

He hadn't even remembered Aaron's room was occupied until they'd come home. Sex had been about the last thing on his mind, and he'd expected Aaron to be equally tired, so he'd kissed him on the head and told him to get some sleep. Aaron had looked at him sheepishly. "I think Charlie's in my room?"

So Aaron had slept with him. In his bed. Wearing only those sexy black boxers. When they went to sleep, that hadn't been an issue considering how dead tired they both had been. But Blake had woken up twenty minutes ago, a warm body plastered all over him. Aaron hadn't merely cuddled close: he was literally on top of Blake. His head was on Blake's shoulder, his arms and legs draped all over him. Everywhere he could, Aaron had made skin-to-skin contact.

He really was a little puppy, desperately wanting to be loved and held.

It was a foreign experience to Blake. He'd never slept with anyone, not in this sense. Most of his one-night stands had been at the club or at his hookup's apartment or house. He'd brought home a guy once because he'd had a roommate and they couldn't go to his place, but Blake hadn't liked the invasion of his privacy. Never, ever before had he shared his bed with anyone. Not since sharing it with his brothers as kids. They'd grown up dirt poor and sharing a bed had been the least of his problems.

By all accounts, then, having Aaron in his bed should be uncomfortable. An intrusion. And yet, it wasn't.

Blake found himself strangely at peace as he studied Aaron's face. Asleep, he looked so damn young and innocent. Well, he was in many ways. He was a full ten years younger than Blake was—though it felt like even more at times.

Blake's heart had ached for Aaron during that painful conversation with Josh. Fuck, he'd had to restrain himself from interrupting dozens of times. The only reason he'd managed was because he'd recognized Josh was honest in his convictions, no matter how unfounded they might have been. He truly believed Aaron had done him wrong—Blake had seen it in the pain on his face. He'd felt betrayed by his brother. Thank fuck Indy and Noah, at least, had tried to ascertain the truth.

Poor Aaron. Little Aaron, Blake had called him when he'd given in to the urge to hold him, comfort him. He'd looked like a little boy, scared to death, but unable to stop what was happening. Josh may have felt betrayed by his brother but so had Aaron. He'd been too young to fully understand, too young to make the choice to stand with his brother—at the cost of alienating his parents. And in the end, he'd been betrayed by his brother and his parents anyway, losing them all.

Little Aaron, peacefully asleep in Blake's arms. He'd missed out in his childhood, it seemed. He'd never had the security of parental love. Was that why he had so much difficulty in not only accepting who he was but knowing himself in the first place?

Blake's dad might have been a first-class asshole, but his mom had loved him the best she could. Her love had been flawed, coming up short at times, but she had tried. But even for Blake, it had been hard to come to terms with who he was. He still feared his father's eyes would look at him in the mirror someday, that he would see that same mix of uncontrollable rage and absolute contempt. It was one of the reasons why he was determined to keep growing in jiujitsu. It would help him foster the self-control he'd need to overcome his paternal DNA.

Aaron stirred, letting out a soft, content sigh. His left hand moved across Blake's naked chest, searching for something, it seemed, until it came to rest on his pecs.

He was so damn beautiful, even with the traces of the makeup on he hadn't bothered to wipe off before they went to sleep. His soft skin, even more so now that he'd shaved everywhere, combined with his lean body, drew Blake in. Fuck, he wanted him. Craved him. He'd been so close to yanking down those jeans and fucking him in that bathroom, right there and then.

If not for his complete surrender, those innocent moans and groans, those deliciously responsive signals from his body, Blake would have. But Aaron had trusted him with his innocence, and he deserved more.

Blake sighed. All this thinking about Aaron had gotten

him damn hard. What time was it? Hmm, almost two o'clock. Maybe he could wake Aaron up?

He let his hand trail down the boy's back, over his boxers that hid that perfect ass. He petted Aaron's butt, caressed both cheeks through the thin fabric of the boxers. Fuck, the kid was such an obvious bottom, his little hole so wanton and insatiable. He'd come like a fucking geyser from mere finger-fucking. Blake had no trouble imagining how the kid would feel with a cock inside. He'd go crazy.

Blake slipped a hand under his own boxers, scratched his balls and rearranged his cock, which was rock hard and peeking out from under his boxers. He wriggled a little, managed to slide his underwear down without waking up Aaron. That, at least, brought some relief.

He grinned. Maybe he could speed things along a little? He took Aaron's hand from his chest and placed it on his now-naked cock. With his own hand covering Aaron's, he put pressure on it. Um, nice. He ground his hips against both hands, loving the friction it created. Aaron's hand moved, and a second later his eyes opened. Blake didn't think, he just grabbed the boy by his neck and moved in for a kiss.

Aaron was still pliant from sleep and opened up immediately. Blake invaded his mouth, needing to taste him again. So sweet. So fucking addictive.

Their tongues met, danced, swirled. Aaron moaned into his mouth, signaling he was truly awake now. Blake removed his hand from Aaron's, giving him the choice to continue rubbing his cock or not. Aaron didn't miss a beat but circled his hand around him and teased the slit with his thumb. Hell, yeah, Sexy Aaron had come out to play.

Blake grabbed him by his arms and pulled him on top of

him. He brought his hands down, only to discover Aaron was still wearing underwear. He broke off their kiss.

"Take off your damn underwear. I need to feel you."

Aaron smiled, a sexy, yet shy smile. He let go of Blake's cock to drag his boxers down, creating friction with Blake's body in all kinds of delicious ways. Their naked cocks met, rubbing against each other. It sent sparks of electricity through Blake's body.

He rolled over, taking Aaron with him so Blake was on top. He brought his hips down, grinding them against Aaron's. "Do you want this, Aaron?" he whispered.

Aaron nodded.

"Words, puppy, use words. I need to know this is what you want."

"Yes. Fuck, yes."

"Well," Blake said, his mouth stretched into a devious smile, "if my little, sexy Aaron starts using swear words, I know shit is about to get real. You know I'm gonna fuck you, right?"

Aaron nodded, his cheeks growing pink.

Blake rose up on his arms, bringing even more pressure on their groins, mashing them together. "My big, fat cock is gonna bury itself in your sweet ass. I'm gonna fuck you, Aaron, hard and deep and long, until my cum is dripping out of you. You okay with that?"

"Please, Blake."

His sweet, sexy Aaron. Cheeks flushed, body tense, but ready to embrace what was coming. "You're gonna love it," he said, more gentle now. "It might hurt a bit at first, but I'll make it good."

"I know. I trust you."

Aaron's eyes, so full of trust met his. It humbled him, made him doubt whether he was doing the right thing. "Are you sure you want to do this, Aaron? I didn't mean to put pressure on you by waking you up like this. We can fool around a bit, maybe jack off together, or pleasure each other in other ways?"

Because his eyes were so fixated on Aaron's, he saw the spark of doubt and relief. Dammit, he had been going too fast, had approached this with way too much sexual aggression. He was proposing a marathon when the kid could barely run a 5k. Even if Aaron had asked Blake to fuck him, it was because he didn't know there were steps in between. Delicious steps they could take together, exploring each other's bodies.

Blake covered Aaron's lips with his, a soft and gentle kiss this time. He traced Aaron's lips with his tongue, chuckling when Aaron got impatient and kissed him back. He lowered himself on top of Aaron until their bodies were pressed together everywhere, their mouths fused in a slow, sensual kiss. When he'd taken his fill of that sweet mouth, he moved lower, peppering his soft chin and neck with kisses, scraping his teeth against his skin until Aaron was covered in goose bumps.

He went lower, spending an inordinate amount of time lavishing Aaron's nipples with attention. Like everything else on his body, they were wonderfully responsive to his touch. He flicked them, teased them with his fingers, then his tongue, sucked them until Aaron's body was writhing below his.

He licked every inch of his chest and stomach, making his way farther down. Aaron's cock was weeping precum, smearing it against Blake every time he touched it. His blow job in Macy's been hurried, but now he wanted to take his time to make Aaron feel good.

"Spread your legs," he ordered.

Aaron did as he told him, allowing Blake to settle on his stomach between Aaron's legs. Fuck, he was beautiful. His skin was so soft, so smooth under his tongue. He licked his balls, sucked them gently, which made Aaron buck his hips. By now, an endless stream of guttural sounds was flowing from his lips, his head thrashing on the mattress. Blake smiled. Look at his sexy Aaron, completely engrossed in what Blake was doing to him. So beautiful. So fucking perfect.

He licked the head of Aaron's cock, wriggling his tongue inside the foreskin to tease his sensitive crown. Aaron's fluids coated his tongue and he let them fill his mouth. He lapped his cock from top to base, and back, making sure to cover every side.

Finally, he took him in his mouth, sucked him in deep. Aaron's hips came off the mattress as he jerked deeper into Blake's mouth. It was incredibly sexy. Blake pulled back.

"Sit on your knees," he told Aaron.

The "why" he expected didn't come, though Aaron did send him a confused look. He scrambled on his knees, though. Blake pushed him back on the bed until he had enough space to lay down under him.

"Feed me your cock, Aaron. Fuck my mouth until you come."

He tilted his head back and opened wide, relaxing his throat and jaw. Aaron pushed in hesitantly. Blake pulled him closer until Aaron's balls were in his face. He encouraged Aaron with his hands to try again. This time, he went in all the way and Blake sucked. Aaron moaned and shuddered. His body knew what it wanted, because it set a rhythm, careful at first, then deeper and deeper. Blake took him in deep into his throat until he gagged, then did it all over again. His eyes watered, but he didn't give a fuck. The sounds Aaron was making were worth it.

"Oh, Blake, oh, comingcomingcoming, so close, I need to... Urgh!"

Aaron jammed his cock in till his balls hit Blake's face, unloading down his throat. Blake could barely swallow with his mouth full of cock, and some of the cum dripped out, mixed with saliva. Finally Aaron pulled out, leaving Blake gasping for breath but damn proud.

He wiped his mouth off, flexed his jaw a few times to get the tension out, then sat up. Aaron was still on his knees, watching him with big eyes, completely confused.

"What's wrong, puppy?"

Aaron swallowed, his shoulders hunched. "Did I do something wrong?"

"No! Why would you think that?"

He lowered his head and glanced at Blake from underneath his eyelashes, like he often did when he was insecure. "Because you wanted to fuck me...and then you did this. And you didn't even come, and you didn't come in Macy's or at the club. I don't understand."

Fuck, Blake was so happy he'd decided to hit the brakes. Everything Aaron had said proved Blake had been going way too fast.

He lowered himself on the bed, holding out his arms to Aaron. Without a second of doubt, he came, and Blake pulled him half on top of himself like he'd been that morning when he woke up.

"You know what you and I are going to do tonight? We're going on a date."

～

AARON HAD DRESSED CONSERVATIVELY, not knowing where Blake would take him. Gray slacks, a crisp white button-down shirt, and dress shoes. He'd even considered a tie. The clothes were all that was left of his previous life, his job. Aaron looked at himself in the mirror in Blake's room and sighed. He looked okay, he guessed. Kinda boring but respectable. Suitable for a date, at least.

He still didn't understand. Blake had told him earlier that he didn't date, didn't do romance. So why was he taking Aaron out? It made no sense. He'd wondered if Blake was tiring of him, or if maybe the sexual activities they'd engaged in so far hadn't been fulfilling for him. But even if that were true, it wouldn't explain this date. He couldn't figure it out, couldn't make sense of it. In the end, Aaron had decided to let it go and roll with it.

Blake stepped into the room, dressed in dark blue jeans and a form-fitting, short-sleeved button-down. It was black, of course, but Aaron didn't mind the guy wore black so often. It looked fantastic on him. Aaron frowned. He did seem overdressed in comparison to Blake. Had he misunderstood? Had Blake meant something other than the formal date Aaron had in mind? He bit his lip.

"You can't wear that," Blake said.

Aaron's face fell. He'd gotten it completely wrong.

"Shit, that came out wrong." Blake stepped close and lifted Aaron's chin up with his finger so he had to look at him. "This isn't you, puppy. This is the old Aaron, the stiff, uptight Aaron. You need to wear colors, something happy and pretty."

"I wasn't sure if you wanted that. It's so gay, and people might assume, you know, and I thought you didn't want everyone to know you are gay."

It wasn't the most eloquent of explanations, but he hoped Blake would understand.

Blake's eyes bore into his. "You dressed like this because you didn't want to out me?"

Aaron nodded.

Blake kissed him, soft and gentle. "That's considerate of you, and I appreciate the thought behind it. But Aaron, remember this: you shouldn't go back into the closet for anyone. Not even for me. If someone is ashamed or scared of being seen with you, walk away. You deserve more. You're worth more than being someone's shameful secret. Do you get what I'm saying?"

He nodded, even though he didn't understand the contradiction in Blake's words. If he didn't want Aaron to hide his sexuality, how would he prevent from being outed? None of this made sense, and he got tired of even trying to make heads or tails out of it.

"Get changed, puppy. Wear makeup if you like. I'll wait."

"Is Charlie still here?"

Aaron had heard him and Blake talking while he was getting dressed.

Blake sighed. "No. He decided to go back home."

Aaron's brow furrowed. "But I thought his boyfriend was abusing him?"

"He is. But Charlie doesn't see it that way. Yet. Abuse is complicated, and it's incredibly hard for victims to walk away. There's a lot of shame involved, and often victims stay for reasons that make sense to them, like what they perceive or define for themselves as expressions of love. Charlie isn't ready yet, but I have hope he will be, someday. Now, get changed."

Aaron decided on wearing the baby blue polo shirt Blake had bought him, with the first pair of tight jeans. They weren't as low cut as the other ones but still left little to the imagination. It took him three tries to put mascara on, and the tiniest hint of blue eye shadow, but he was happy with the result. He'd have to practice for a long time to get Charlie's proficiency with makeup, but he did look pretty.

When he stepped out, Blake eyed him and nodded with an approving smile. "That's my Sexy Aaron. Let's go."

Blake took him to an Italian restaurant, about twenty minutes away. It was blissfully quiet in the restaurant, probably because everyone was watching the Super Bowl—something neither of them cared about. Josh had been a football and Pats fan since he'd met Noah, but Aaron couldn't care less. He'd watch the occasional baseball game, but that was about as much sports as he could handle.

Aaron was nervous as the hostess led them to a secluded table for two in the back. He wanted to sit down, but Blake held him back, then stepped in to hold out the chair for him.

"Thank you," Aaron said automatically.

Blake sat down across from him and sent him a soft smile.

"Would you like to see our wine menu, sir?" the hostess asked Blake.

"Not for me. Would you, Aaron?"

He shook his head. "I don't drink."

She handed them their menus and walked away.

"You can drink if you want," Aaron offered. "I can drive us back."

"No, puppy, that's my job."

Aaron studied the menu.

"Do you like Italian? Sorry, little late for that question," Blake said.

"I eat everything. I'm the opposite of a picky eater,"

Aaron said. It was true. Aside from beans, which he tolerated but didn't like, there was nothing he couldn't or wouldn't eat. It made choosing hard, because everything looked good. Also, he didn't want to order something that was too expensive, and he wasn't sure if Blake wanted to do appetizers or not.

"Want me to order for you?" Blake asked.

Aaron looked up and smiled in relief. "Would you? Yes, please. I hate making decisions like this. Too much to choose from."

When their server came, Blake ordered carpaccio for them to share as a starter, which Aaron had never even heard of. For an entrée he chose seafood linguine for himself, and grilled lamb chops for Aaron.

"You're gonna love that lamb, puppy. They grill it to perfection here."

"Why do you keep calling me puppy?" Aaron asked.

Blake smiled. "You don't like it?"

"I do. I was just wondering, because you call me puppy and Little Aaron, and it's like you want to stress I'm young, or something."

"You are."

"Not that young."

"Close enough."

"Is that why you say it?"

Blake shook his head, laughed. "You're a pit bull puppy, that's for certain. Such a stubborn little shit. No, Aaron, that's not why." His face sobered. "Have you ever had a puppy?"

He shook his head. "No. My parents didn't like pets."

"My brother Brad, he found a puppy once. The owner abandoned it, probably because it was the runt of the litter. It was this tiny little fur ball, a lab mix of some sort, and from the moment Brad picked him up, Brad was his daddy. That puppy would not let him out of his sight. He followed him everywhere, even into the bathroom, and constantly wanted to be picked up by him. That little fur ball craved touch, but it was also looking at him for approval. Brad would teach him commands, like 'sit,' and he'd plop his little butt on the floor, wag his tail, and wait for Brad to say 'good boy.' Max lived for Brad, for his love and approval. He still does, by the way. Brad kept him, and Max is now fourteen. Even at the end of his life, Brad is everything to him. All Max wants to do is make Brad happy."

"What does that have to do with me?"

"When I first met you, I misjudged you. I felt you were some entitled, self-centered, arrogant kid, and boy, was I wrong. You were simply a lost little puppy, pretending to be a big dog out of survival instinct. Underneath, you were trying to find an owner who would take you in, love you, and let you please him."

Blake's words rolled around in Aaron's head. They felt big, somehow. "An owner?" Aaron whispered. "You mean as an analogy, right?"

Blake's expression changed to something so kind Aaron's breath caught. "Not entirely."

"I don't want to be owned. That's...that would make me a slave."

"That's not what I mean. Aaron, what I saw as entitlement at first, was your deep desire and expectation that someone would take care of you. You have this profound need inside of you to be cared for. You don't want independence. You want to be dependent on someone else, defer to him for decisions."

His head swirled with thoughts. "How?"

Again, Blake understood his confused question.

"You loved it when I bought clothes for you. You were immensely grateful, but not once did you offer to pay me back. It was like you were convinced that wasn't even an option—and wasn't necessary. You let me decide for you to start your jiujitsu training. You let me order food for you. Even in the club, when you went off on your own, you still wanted me to watch you. Your eyes are constantly seeking mine, as if you need to know where I am, and that we're good. When I praise you, your entire face lights up. Your body responds to every little signal from me. And even when you're asleep, you seek my presence, as if you're afraid I'd leave you alone. You are a little puppy, Aaron."

Blake had laid Aaron's soul bare, voicing what he himself had never put into words, had barely even begun to realize. Everything he said rang true, and it constricted his throat.

He was spared an immediate reaction because the server brought their appetizers. They looked perfect: thin sliced circles of meat arranged on a big platter, with arugula, roasted pine nuts, fresh shaved Parmesan cheese, and some kind of oily dressing on top.

Blake cut off a little bite and held it out on his fork to Aaron. He bit without thinking, humming as the combination of flavors hit his tongue. The meat was tender and mixed perfectly with the crunchy nuts, the dressing, the salty cheese, and the slightly bitter arugula.

"Good?" Blake asked.

Aaron nodded. Not until he'd opened his mouth to get Blake to offer him another bite did the meaning of what he'd done sink in. He wanted Blake to feed him.

"Oh," escaped from his mouth.

Blake looked at him with kindness. "Are you starting to see? It's why one-night stands will never work for you. You're loyal. You attach yourself to someone. You couldn't fuck someone, or let yourself be fucked, and walk away. It would break your heart every single time."

Aaron's eyes burned, but he pushed back the tears. "This is not normal, right?" he asked, his voice barely audible. "Is there, like, therapy or something to get this fixed?"

Blake put down his fork and knife and reached for his hand. "Aaron, you're fine. You're okay, just as you are."

He shook his head. "No. This is not normal. It can't be."

"There's no such thing as normal. We all try to figure out what works for us. Do I think this has something to do with your childhood? Yes. I think you missed out on a lot of safety and security as a teen. In some way, this may be regressive behavior. But it's not crazy, Aaron. It's not harmful to you or to others, and if it brings you the comfort you need, who cares?"

"Have you ever heard of this before?"

"Variations on it, for sure. There's the daddy/boy dynamic some couples have that can come close. Or the owner/slave role-play within the BDSM scene. There's even baby and toddler play or puppy play."

Aaron frowned. "What's that?"

"It's people behaving like a baby or toddler, or like a puppy for an agreed amount of time, and someone else will play the father or mother, or the owner."

"You mean they pretend to be an actual puppy?"

"Yup. Licking, crawling on the floor, being trained, wearing a collar, the whole nine yards."

Huh, how about that? Aaron tried to picture it, himself wearing a dog collar, sitting at Blake's feet. Blake petting his head, or his romp for being a good puppy. Instead of the sense of shame and alienation he'd expected to feel, his heart sped up. Oh, heck, no. He covered his head in his hands, too ashamed to face Blake. No matter what the man had said, he had to think Aaron was certifiably nuts.

"Did I ever tell you about my father?" Blake said.

Aaron peeked at him through his fingers. "No."

"Take your hands down, Aaron. I like looking at your face."

Hesitantly, he removed his hands. Blake held out another bite for him, and after a second of hesitation he took it.

"Good boy," Blake said.

Aaron felt the words reach deep inside him, calming him. He was so messed up.

"My father was an alcoholic who got real aggressive when he drank. I'm the oldest of four, and for as long as I can remember, my father beat my mom."

Aaron looked up, surprised.

"She would do everything she could to protect us, and for the most part, it worked. He hit us a couple of times, me mostly because I was the oldest, but not as bad as he abused her."

"Blake..." Aaron gasped. This time, he reached for Blake's hand and held it.

"My youngest brother, Benjamin, he's mentally handi-capped. I don't know what happened, but he was a crybaby when he was born. He cried all the time, and it drove my father nuts. I think he picked him up one time, shook him hard, and he sustained brain injury. I don't know for sure, but one day he was a healthy baby, and the next he had these developmental issues. But I was only seven, so I didn't realize it."

Aaron's eyes welled up with compassion. What a devas-tating tragedy. It explained why Blake was so passionate about creating a safe place for victims of domestic abuse.

"Did your mom ever leave him?" he asked, hoping it was the right thing to say.

"Once. She took us with her, but he found us. He almost killed her that time. Beat the shit out of me and my brother Burke, too, for trying to step in and protect her. I was thirteen, he was eleven. A few months later, he went on a drinking binge and killed himself in a DWI. I thanked God that day that he was dead."

"I'm so sorry, Blake. I can't even imagine. Your mom, did she ever get over it?"

He shook his head, his eyes sad and forlorn. "No. She died when I was barely eighteen. Heart attack. I think it was grief, mixed with guilt. She did her best, but she couldn't move on."

"What happened to your brothers?"

"I became the legal guardian for Burke and Brad and raised them. Benjamin, he needed more. He was adopted by a family who'd heard about our story. I fought to keep him with us, but in the end, I had to let go. They were able to offer him the care I never could. He's still with them, twenty-eight now, and he's happy."

"You did the right thing," Aaron said, squeezing his hand. "But Blake, raising your brothers, what a commitment at that age. You guys still close?"

"Yeah." He smiled, pure happiness on his face. "Brad is a middle school math teacher, and Burke runs a company that makes outdoor apparel. They both live close by, and we see each other every other week or so."

Aaron smiled, too. "That's good, that you guys have each other."

"Aaron, all three of us are single. Brad is gay, like me, but Burke isn't, yet even he has never had a long-term relationship. I wondered why that was, and for me, I know the answer. I'm scared."

That was about the last thing Aaron expected tough Blake to say. "Of what?"

"Of losing control. Of becoming my father. Of loving someone so much that you'll accept anything from them, even abuse. Of losing someone, or seeing them get hurt, because I wasn't able to protect them."

Aaron wanted to reassure him, wanted to tell Blake he was the kindest man he'd ever met, that he would never willingly hurt someone. He longed to let him know he would never stand by and let someone get hurt because he was simply too honorable. But he stayed silent. He understood.

"Aaron, if you think you're fucked up, rest assured. I am just as fucked up as you are but in a different way. I need to stay in control, call the shots. I can't allow my heart to get involved."

11

T he server came to take the entrée plate away and refill their mineral waters. All that time, Aaron looked at Blake with big eyes.

"Where does that leave us?" he finally asked, then caught himself. "Is there even an 'us'? Or is this dinner your kind way of telling me I need to find another place to live?"

Blake had considered it. Briefly. The thought of letting Aaron go had caused such tightness in his chest that he'd realized the impossibility of that option. But he couldn't treat Aaron like a one-night stand, either. The kid wasn't wired for casual sex, and that was not his fault.

"You're not going anywhere," Blake said. He waited till Aaron had found the guts to look him in the eyes. "In fact, you're moving into my room. Permanently."

"But..." Aaron sputtered.

Blake's heart constricted. Did Aaron have objections? Had Blake gotten the signals all wrong? Didn't Aaron want to be with him?

"What will the others think? It's gonna be hard to keep it a secret," Aaron said.

Phew. Blake released his breath. "I don't know and I don't care. It's my house, and I can do whatever the hell I want. And yes, there's an 'us.' If you want."

"I don't understand. Minutes ago, you told me you don't do relationships."

"I know. This is a first for me, too. I don't know what it means or what it's gonna look like between us. All I know is that the thought of letting you go scares me more than the idea of trying to make it work. So we'll experiment together. If that's what you want."

It was the second time he'd indirectly asked Aaron to confirm that hell, yes, this was what he wanted. But he didn't. Instead, he bit his bottom lip again, that adorable gesture that told Blake he was nervous.

"So you'll be my boyfriend?" he asked.

"Yes. Publicly."

"What about that puppy thing?"

"Aaron, what are you asking?"

"How am I supposed to behave as your boyfriend?"

Ah. He got it. Aaron still hadn't fully understood. "Aaron, I want you to be yourself. If you want to wear pink and put on makeup, that's fine. If you decide you'd rather wear a skirt instead of pants, go ahead. If you feel happier when you let me make decisions, works for me. If you want to see if you'd like pretending to be a puppy at times, that's okay, too. All I'm asking is that you talk to me, communicate with me. I'm pretty good at reading people, but this is new for me as well, so you'll need to use words, okay?"

Aaron nodded, his face relaxing.

The server brought their entrees, and Blake watched with delight as Aaron dug into his lamb. He'd ordered him something he figured Aaron would like. The kid was a meat-lover, Blake had discovered, and he could sure use the fat and protein to bulk up a little.

"Good?" he asked.

Aaron licked his lips. "Perfect." He chewed on his bite and swallowed. "Blake, you're truly okay with it? Me being myself? It's just that I've never felt safe enough to explore who I really am. It's scary, to show you sides of myself that I consider weird, or..." He hesitated, then pushed it out. "Or plain fucked up."

"Yes, I'm more than okay with it. I haven't seen or heard anything so far that doesn't mesh with who I am. You're so focused on yourself—and don't get me wrong, I get why—that you've overlooked how well this suits me. I like being bossy, Aaron. I need to be in control. I also relish being the caretaker. So if you want, I'll take care of you."

He held his breath, hoping this time Aaron would take the bait. Aaron's crystal blue eyes rose up to meet his. "I'd love that. Thank you, Blake."

"What the fuck are you thanking me for? I'm not doing you a service, Aaron. I need you as much as you need me."

Aaron seemed to ponder that, then his face transformed as he smiled. "So it makes you happy to take care of me?"

"Yes, puppy, it does. Now, eat your lamb, Aaron."

They talked for the rest of the meal about anything and everything. He ordered a shared dessert for them, something chocolatey that had Aaron drooling.

"Blake, can we stop by Josh's? I wanna make sure they're all okay."

"Sure thing. Do you want me to call?"

Aaron sent him a look of relief. "Would you, please?"

"That's what you have me for. Let me pay and then we'll call them, okay?"

Indy didn't sound thrilled, but he said it was okay if they

came by, as long as they were okay with watching the game with them. The Pats hadn't made it to the Super Bowl this year, but Indy and the others still wanted to watch. Blake could only imagine they needed the distraction, too.

As Blake drove, Aaron hesitantly put his hand on Blake's thigh. Blake put his own hand on top for a second and squeezed it. "You can always touch me, Aaron. Always."

Aaron let out a sigh. "I feel better when I touch you. Crazy, huh?"

Blake shrugged. "Whatever makes you feel good, puppy. I love it when you're close to me."

He drove straight to Josh's house and parked in the driveway. Indy had asked him to ring the bell a certain way so they'd know it was them. He followed instructions, and they were ushered in by Connor, who used the opportunity to quickly check the street behind them.

"Hey," Josh greeted them. He was lounging on the couch, probably against Connor before the cop had gotten up to open the door. Noah and Indy were in one of the chairs, cuddling. The TV was on low, playing a commercial.

Blake nodded to each of them and took a spot on the other chair. Before he could say anything, Aaron lowered himself on the ground at his feet. He shuffled until his back was leaning against Blake's legs. He looked up as if to ask permission if it was okay. Blake reached out and petted his hair a little before he leaned back again.

"I can get an extra chair," Connor said.

"Nah. Aaron's fine where he is," Blake said. Aaron rubbed his leg in agreement, and Blake smiled. It seemed his words had given Aaron a certain amount of freedom to explore. Blake loved seeing him experiment with who he was and what he liked.

Josh's eyebrows rose ever so slightly, and Indy shot Blake

a curious smile, but no one said anything. Blake had expected nothing else in a household where they were all fucking each other, as far as he could tell.

"We were wondering how you are all doing after the news of this morning," he said.

Connor sat down on the couch, and Josh snuggled close. It seemed the brothers shared that need for touching, Blake mused.

"We're trying to figure out what to do next," Noah said.

Blake could easily read between the lines. They were trying to find a step that wouldn't separate Indy from everyone else.

Connor said, "We've contacted the FBI through my chief. They're interested in Indy's testimony and have indicated they're willing to do anything to keep him safe."

"Witness Protection," Blake said. "I can't imagine that would include all four of you."

"No. Only Indy, and maybe if we play hardball, Noah. But he's a risk because of his prosthesis and the appointments he still needs as part of his recovery process. It makes him too easily identifiable." Connor kept it factual, but the emotions were audible in his voice.

"And you want to stay together," Blake concluded.

"Yeah. We're kind of a package deal," Connor said.

"And did they give any indication of how long it would take before the trial?"

Connor scoffed. "Anything from six months to a year. And then the trial itself could take weeks, too, if not more."

Blake sighed, understanding their conundrum. The sound of an engine shutting off made him perk his ears. He cocked his head.

Connor went on full alert at the same time. "Someone's here," he snapped.

They all listened, but there were no sounds of car doors being closed. Someone did not want to be heard. Not good.

"Indy, go!" Connor hissed. With a desperate look at Noah, Indy scrambled off his lap. He disappeared into a door, presumably leading to the basement, never turning on the light. At the same time, the doorbell rang.

Connor drew a gun Blake had never even spotted him wearing, putting it between the pillows of the couch. Much to Blake's surprise, Josh pulled a gun from his side as well and put it behind his back in his waistband, handling the gun with incredible confidence. Right, army guy.

"I'll go," Noah said. "It's my house. You're visiting," he snapped to Blake and Aaron.

Aaron trembled against Blake's leg, and Blake put his hand on the kid's shoulder. "Stay calm," he whispered.

Noah rose and made it to the front door, leaning on his crutch. Blake held his breath as Noah opened the door.

"Hi," he said. "Can I help you?"

"Good evening. We're looking for Indiana Baldwin. We were told he was staying here."

Blake recognized the voice as belonging to one of the guys who'd broken in and signaled to Connor. Oh, God.

"Who?"

"Move over, lame ass," another voice said.

"Hey!" Noah furiously called out. Rattling noises came from the hallway as Noah was knocked down, his crutch clattering on the floor.

Fucking hell, this was not good. Blake jumped up from the chair, pushed back Aaron. "Get down!"

As soon as Blake saw the first guy, his foot shot out. He nailed him with one solid kick, and the guy sagged to the floor. He got back in defensive position, ready to meet whomever came next.

"What the fuck?" a voice called out.

The second guy stepped into his vision, raising his right hand, holding a gun. If he fired that, someone would get killed. Blake jumped and attacked. He brought the guy down to the floor, slamming them both into the narrow wall between the hallway and the living room. He reached for the hand that held the gun, clamped it. It jerked and an ear-splitting bang made him dizzy for a second. Fuck, it had gone off after all. He increased the pressure on the guy's wrist, moving until he felt the bone break. The guy yelled out in pain.

He lashed out with his foot to take him out, only to discover his leg wouldn't cooperate. What the fuck? Why couldn't he move? Everything slowed down, as if someone had hit slow motion.

Someone yelling from the hallway.

Noah shouting, panicking.

Aaron screamed.

"Albany PD, drop your weapon!"

Connor.

Another gun shot.

His ears buzzed.

Shouting, but farther away.

Breaking glass. Running footsteps.

Another shot.

A fierce burn in his chest.

"Stay down!"

Josh.

Three shots in rapid succession.

Silence.

He blinked, his vision blurring.

"Clear!" Connor yelled. "I need to hear you. Josh?"

"I'm good."

"Hand me the gun, Josh. Aaron?"

"Good."

Blake let out his breath. Aaron was okay. That was all that mattered. His puppy was okay.

"Noah?"

"Okay. Blake's shot."

Blake blinked again. Shot? He was shot? Noah had to be mistaken because he didn't feel anything. He was a little dizzy at the most. Noah's face appeared above him.

"Talk to me, Blake."

One second he felt fine, the next a hundred-pound weight had been dropped on his chest.

"Not good," he managed, wheezing for breath.

"We need an ambulance!" Noah shouted.

"On it. Josh, give me your gun. I need to wipe it. Assist Noah and make sure you get as much blood on your hands as possible. Everyone, cover your ears for a second."

Three more gunshots rang out, Blake's nostrils filling with gun smoke. Why the hell was Connor shooting? And why the fuck did it hurt so much to breathe?

"His lung collapsed. Get me our first aid kit and the straw from a water bottle." Noah's hands were touching him everywhere. "Connor, tell them to hurry the fuck up! Double gun shot wound, through and through to his femur, no exit wound in his chest."

So hard to breathe.

"Aaron," he wheezed.

"I'm right here."

Soft lips on his forehead. His puppy. Thank fuck he was okay.

"Blake, your lung collapsed and I'm gonna have to re-inflate it. This is gonna hurt like hell, so hang on. Aaron, keep him calm. Let him hear you, see you, keep touching him. Josh, hold him down. If he moves, I could kill him."

In the background, Connor was yelling at something. Or someone.

Blake felt himself fade until an excruciating pain in his side woke him up. His vision black, every breath a fight, all he could do was focus on Aaron's voice. "Blake, I'm here. I'm right here."

Black spots danced around the edges of his awareness, but Aaron moved into his field of vision. He held his gaze, whispering words Blake couldn't even understand. This was not how it was supposed to be. He had to take care of Aaron, not the other way around. Tears of pain streamed down his face.

A soft hiss sounded, and it felt like a balloon inflated inside him. He drew a breath, coughed, and breathed again.

"Lung's back," Noah said. "Take it easy, Blake. Try to breathe normally. Josh, wrap a tight bandage around his thigh."

"Guys," Connor said. "Ambulance is three minutes out. Listen carefully. I shot them, okay? Not Josh, me. Switch positions for me and Josh through the whole thing. It's okay to be confused and say you don't remember."

"Indy?" Noah asked.

"Gone, I assume. He'll reconnect, Noah. He's safe."

A wave of dizziness hit Blake. "Don't feel good," he mumbled. He coughed, his chest spasming. Bitter liquid pooled in his mouth and he gagged.

Noah cursed. "Oh, dammit to hell."

Blake's eyes fluttered shut despite his efforts to focus on Aaron's pretty blue eyes.

So tired.

12

"O'Connor! What the fucking hell?"

Connor rose from the squeaky chair in the interrogation room. "Chief."

"Sit your ass down. I'm told you shot and killed three men tonight. What the fuck happened? Was this at your place?"

Connor lowered himself on the chair, forced his breathing down. He'd survived being held hostage by the Taliban. He could damn well handle a friendly interrogation by his own chief. "No, sir, it was at my boyfriend's house."

The chief didn't even blink, which meant the boyfriend part was not news to him. Connor wasn't surprised. He'd met a colleague at the hospital when Noah had been admitted for his surgery, so he must have spread the word.

"We were having friends over. The doorbell rang, Noah opened the door and immediately was attacked. One of my friends runs a jiujitsu school. He took down two assailants but got shot by a third in the process before I managed to shoot him. Two more men came in through the back door, firing shots, and I took them down. Sir."

"Who was present, aside from yourself?"

"My boyfriend, Joshua Gordon. His roommate, Noah Flint. Two friends of ours, Blake Kent, and Aaron Gordon, Josh's brother. Blake's the one who was shot twice, sir."

"And you were the only one who fired shots?"

"Yes, sir."

"Did you know these men?"

This was where it got tricky. "No, sir, not personally. But I believe they're connected to the Fitzpatricks, sir." When he'd gotten hired, he'd informed the chief about his family, figuring it'd be better to be open about it than have them find out later.

"You think this was personal, aimed at you?"

He nodded. "Yes, sir." It was the only believable explanation he'd been able to come up with without implicating Indy. Why else would five Boston gangsters attack a random house in New York?

"I thought you lived in an apartment."

"I did, sir, till recently. I moved in with Josh a few weeks ago."

"And with his roommate."

"Yes, sir."

"Who also happens to be Josh's ex."

Connor's expression soured. "Yes."

"Don't give me that, O'Connor. You know the gossip mill works fine here. I don't give a shit whether you're gay, and whether you're involved with one or both of them, you hear me?" The chief leaned forward. "You know IA will investigate this shooting, so until further notice you're on non-active duty with pay. Be smart, and contact your union rep. And O'Connor?"

"Yeah, chief?"

"If I were you, I'd come up with a reasonable explanation for two facts. The first is why you used a gun registered to Joshua Gordon to shoot these intruders, and not your own service weapon, or the private gun registered in your name. But more importantly, I'd try and explain how you managed to shoot three guys in the exact same place: straight through the heart. You're a decent shot, O'Connor, but that's pretty fucking impressive considering the chaos that had to be going on around you, wouldn't you agree?"

Connor kept his expression carefully blank. "Yes, sir."

"You know we tested you for gunshot residue, and it came back positive."

"Yes, sir."

"We did the same for the others. Aaron Gordon tested negative, but of course both Noah Flint and Joshua Gordon had scrubbed their hands squeaky clean, because they'd been elbow-deep covered in Blake Kent's blood."

"Yes, sir. Noah is a trauma physician assistant at Albany General and a former army medic. He attended to Blake right after he was shot. Blake flatlined in the ambulance, and Noah had to do another surgical procedure en route to the hospital, both with Josh assisting him. I'd imagine they wanted to wash their hands as soon as they'd arrived at the hospital."

The chief stared at him for five long seconds. "Yes, I would imagine so. They tested negative."

"Of course, sir. They were nowhere near my gun when it went off."

The chief nodded. "We've ID'd the five men who attacked you. They're all known associates from Duncan Fitzpatrick. Of course, the two who survived aren't talking."

"They never do, sir. Duncan pays them well to keep their mouths shut. It's why he's never been caught."

"Well, personally I couldn't care less that three of these

motherfuckers are dead. And the other two will go to prison for armed house robbery, because I assume that's what we're going with, correct?"

Connor nodded. "That seems smart, sir."

"What seems smart, O'Connor, is that you think carefully about your statements, and that you make sure the facts line up. As I said, IA will be interested in knowing how you suddenly developed into such a crack shot. They'd rather expect that from, say, a former army sniper. Of course, with him being treated for PTSD, it's unlikely that he would have the presence of mind in a situation like that to shoot, wouldn't you agree?"

Connor nodded. "I couldn't agree with you more, sir. Josh is fragile, especially in violent situations, which are a known trigger for him. As a matter of fact, he's considering voluntarily admitting himself to a psychiatric hospital for a complete evaluation and treatment and to prevent escalation of his symptoms due to this event."

A hint of a smile appeared on the chief's mouth. "I'm glad to hear you're taking his mental health so seriously. Go home, get some rest."

"I'm on my way to the hospital, actually, sir. Blake isn't out of surgery yet, and I'm anxious to get an update."

The chief nodded. "I hope he makes a full recovery, O'Connor. All of you."

Connor rushed to the hospital as fast as he could. Dammit, he hoped Josh was okay. He'd hated leaving him like that, but he had to follow protocol if he wanted to avoid all suspicion. He found them in the waiting room, having been told where they were by a nurse. Josh was sitting between Noah and Aaron, holding both their hands.

"Connor," Josh exhaled as soon as he spotted him. He jumped up and closed the distance between them.

Connor embraced him hard, kissing him gently after. "You okay?" He searched his blue eyes.

"Yeah. I'm good. Noah and Aaron are keeping me steady."

Aaron? Huh, there's a surprise. "How's Blake?" he asked Noah. "Any news?"

"He's still in surgery. They were able to repair his femur, but the bullet to his chest did a lot of damage. I had to open his chest in the ambulance, do a buddy transfusion."

"What's that?"

"It's a transfusion from one donor directly to the recipient. Luckily, both Josh and Aaron are O neg, meaning they're universal donors. I hooked them up to Blake to transfuse him en route since he was losing too much blood. It was a little cramped in the back of that ambulance, but we made it work."

"Noah saved his life," Josh said.

"Well, Blake pretty much saved all of ours," Noah said. "If he hadn't reacted so damn fast, they would have taken us all out. That being said, I'm gonna catch hell over this. Paramedics weren't too happy with me doing unauthorized procedures, considering I'm not a doctor. They objected every step of the way and already reported me."

"The fact that you saved his life doesn't make a difference?" Connor asked.

Noah huffed. "Hospital procedures, man. I can't imagine police procedures being much different."

He had a point there. Still, they'd cross that bridge when they got to it. At least Blake was still alive, thanks to Noah.

Connor's eyes focused on Aaron, who was motionless in his chair. He looked white as a sheet, but he was hanging in there. "You okay there, Aaron?"

"Yeah. I'm fine. I was more concerned about Josh."

Connor looked at Josh again, who shot him a guilty look. "I had trouble staying in the present," he said. "But Aaron did a good job distracting me, especially when Noah had to leave for a bit to get cleaned up."

Connor shot Aaron a grateful look. He still wasn't sure about the kid, but at least he'd proved useful on this occasion.

"Josh, can I talk to you outside for a minute? We'll be right back," he said to Noah.

Josh looked worried as he led him into an empty handicapped bathroom and closed the door behind them. There was so much he had to say, but first he needed to feel him. He yanked him close and hugged him until his arms started hurting. Josh's breathing was heavy against his neck.

"Dammit, Josh, that was too close."

"I know."

"You did so good, baby. You took them out with three clean shots. I've never seen anyone fire so fast and so damn accurate."

He finally let go.

"Is your story gonna hold?" Josh asked.

"Yeah. I think the chief knows, but he's on my side. But Josh, we have a bigger problem."

Josh nodded. "Indy. How the hell did they find us?"

"I don't know. Maybe they took a guess and trailed Blake and Aaron from the studio to see where it would lead them. It doesn't matter now. Point is, Indy was made, and we can't be sure they're not coming back."

"Connor, Noah won't survive a year without Indy," Josh said, a trace of panic in his voice.

"And neither will you, baby, I know. You guys need each other."

Josh leaned his forehead against Connor's. "What are we

gonna do? We can't disappear with the four of us. Or even six, because Blake and Aaron might be at risk, too."

Connor took a deep breath. "Josh, I have a plan. It's absolutely crazy, but I think it's the only thing that will work. But I need your help, and it's gonna be hard on us all."

Josh's eyes lit up, despite Connor's warning. "Anything. I will do anything to keep us together."

Connor looked at Josh's blue eyes, fixed on his own and so full of trust. The next few weeks, maybe even months, would be hell. It had to be worth it in the end, right? He cupped Josh's cheeks and kissed him softly.

"Josh, I need to break up with you." Josh's eyes widened in shock and his hands sought Connor's arms for stability, but he didn't say a word. "A few weeks later, but I'll let you know when, you need to let yourself be voluntarily admitted to a VA psychiatric hospital. You tell them it's because of this incident, that you're experiencing flashbacks and an increase of symptoms. Have them prescribe you antidepressants, anti-anxiety meds, and preferably antipsychotics, but don't actually take them. While you're there, I need you to have a complete breakdown. It needs to be dramatic, convincing, and well-documented."

Josh swallowed but nodded. "Okay. Why?"

"After this, Indy will have no choice but to go into protective custody with the FBI. That means he'll be safe, for now. Blake will need time to recover, with Aaron by his side, I assume. Noah isn't starting work again anytime soon, correct?"

Josh nodded. "Yeah. He has his second fitting this week. The plan was to start work next month, build up to full-time slowly." Josh's eyes narrowed. Did he suspect where this was leading? "And what will you be doing?"

"I'll be in Boston. Josh, my love, we have to end this.

What I've planned is absolutely crazy, and it's fucking dangerous, but I'm convinced it'll work."

In a few sentences, Connor explained what they would do. Josh listened and took it all in. Then he suggested a few tweaks, which was exactly why Connor wanted to go over the plan with him. As he had discovered on the paintball range, Josh was quite the strategic thinker when it came to operations like this. Connor made Josh tell him what he needed, in specific detail, repeating it until he had committed it to memory.

"Josh, baby, I'm leaving today. I have to."

Josh nodded. "I understand."

"We won't see each other for weeks, maybe more." His throat tightened unexpectedly. Fuck, this was the hardest thing he'd ever done, walking away from the man he loved more than anything or anyone else.

"It's gonna be hard, but Connor, it's worth it." Josh's eyes were moist, Connor noted. He was so brave.

Connor grabbed his head and looked him deep in his eyes. "You do what you have to do to make sure you're okay, you hear me? I don't care if you need Noah to keep you stable. You have my permission to do anything you need to, baby. You survive, and you make sure you're mentally ready, whatever you need to do to get there."

"I love you, Connor," Josh said, his voice breaking. "I promise. I can do this."

"I know you can, baby. You're the strongest man I know, well, second to Indy, probably. And I love you more than anything, Josh. Bring us back together, please."

He kissed him, first soft, then more urgent. Josh's hands came around him, pulled on his shirt, then went for his buckle.

"I need you, Connor. One last time."

He nodded, raising his hands so Josh could pull his shirt off. Their hands made fast work of their clothes and soon the bathroom floor was covered in them. They pressed up against each other, naked and on fire. It was one of those times when Connor cursed his size, because he wanted to fuck, not spend valuable time prepping.

Josh reached for his jeans on the floor, grabbed a packet of lube from his wallet. He yanked it open, smeared it on Connor's cock and put the rest in his own hole. He bent over, put his arms on the bathroom sink.

"Fuck me," he said.

"Josh, we need to prep. It will hurt."

"Fuck me, now, Connor. I want it to hurt. I want to be reminded of you in the next few days. I need the pain right now. Please, babe."

He got it. Josh needed the pain as much as Connor wanted to mark him, making sure everyone who came after him would know who Josh belonged to. But he refused to truly hurt him. He swiped some lube on his fingers and inserted one in Josh's hole, shoving it deep. Josh cried out and pushed back his ass even farther. Connor pulled back, added a second finger, rammed it in. Josh hissed, probably as much in pain as in pleasure.

"Oh, Connor. More."

He fucked him with his fingers, two, then three, until Josh was a withering mess, then pulled out and lined his cock up. He entered him in one stroke, bottoming out with his balls slapping against Josh's ass.

Josh cried out, but Connor didn't wait for him to adjust, just flexed his hips and rammed in again. And again. His vision went red, and he pounded until he came with a guttural sound, shooting his load inside Josh.

Panting, he let his head rest on Josh's back. Had Josh

even come? He honestly had no idea, until he looked past Josh in the basin, and saw Josh's fluids dripping down the drain. "You okay, babe?" he asked.

"Yeah." Josh's voice broke. "I'll miss you so much."

He pulled out, not caring about the cum dripping all over Josh's ass, and turned him around. Josh's eyes were watery. "You take care of yourself and you make us whole again, Josh. I don't care about anything else, you hear me?"

And Josh answered with the two sweetest words on the planet.

"Yes, Connor."

INDY WOKE up at five in the morning, restless, still exhausted after a night with little sleep and a lot of tossing and turning. No wonder, after what had happened.

He'd escaped from the basement as soon as he'd made it downstairs. Indy knew that he couldn't afford to wait and see who it was. If it was nothing, he'd circle back. But if it was bad news, he needed to get as big of a head start as possible.

The basement had one window that opened and was big enough for him to fit through. He'd gone over escape routes with Connor and Noah throughout the house, and Noah had pointed the window out. They had put a small box underneath for Indy to stand on and reach high enough to pull himself through the window. He'd been already outside when he'd heard the sounds of a struggle—and then that first shot had rung out.

He'd frozen, desperate to go back and find out if Noah was okay, if Josh and Connor were unharmed. That moment of freezing up had saved him because if he had moved, he would have run smack dab into the two men breaking the glass in the back door, forcing their way inside. Indy had waited till they were inside, his heart beating out of his chest. Then another shot had rung out, and he'd put his fist in his mouth to keep from screaming.

That's when he'd started running, but he'd been barely out of the yard when three more shots had sounded. His mind had filled with images of Noah, bleeding out on the floor, but he'd forced himself to move. There was no way neighbors had not heard this, and he needed to be out of sight before someone spotted him. So he'd run, staying in yards and on footpaths until he'd cleared the neighborhood.

When he'd reached a small playground, he'd stopped. He'd lowered himself on a swing and had sat there until he'd been able to think past the terrifying fear that had blazed through his body.

He'd run out with only the clothes on his back and nothing else on him, but thank fuck he'd stashed an emergency pack in a nature preserve close by. He'd wanted to have something to fall back on in case of an emergency—and this certainly qualified as one. One of the first nights he'd slept in his car there, he had explored the preserve and had discovered a fallen tree, probably struck by lightning at some point. It had formed a little shelter, not visible from the hiking trail, so last week he'd hid a Ziploc there with some cash and a pre-paid credit card. It had still been there, and so he'd made it to a motel for the night.

The problem was that he had no way of contacting Noah or anyone else to find out what had happened. If the Fitzpatricks had somehow gotten hold of Noah's phone, calling or texting him would lead them straight to Indy. He'd have to wait. Noah knew what motel he'd be staying at, if possible, so he'd send a message at some point. They'd gone over scenarios like this, just in case.

Indy turned on the TV in his motel room. Surely a shooting like this would be on the news. Indeed, it was. Images of the cordoned-off house appeared, a reporter solemnly informing viewers that three men had been killed in a shooting. Indy's heart stopped. It simply stopped, and he could only watch in stunned silence as the woman stated the police had not released any details about the victims, including their names.

"Nonononononono..." he whimpered, sucking in a painful breath.

It couldn't be, could it? Noah, Josh, Blake, and Aaron. At least one of them had survived.

He should have gone back. He should have gotten killed with them. They were dead because of him. Oh, no, if Noah had...or Josh. It couldn't be. His body spasmed, forcefully rejecting even the thought.

He turned off the TV, couldn't stomach the sight of the only home he'd ever had. He'd lost it all. Again. He would never, ever be truly safe. Or free. Not as long as Duncan was after him. And Duncan would keep coming for him until he'd found him and had tortured and killed him.

Maybe he should give up. Simply catch a ride to Boston, show up on Duncan's doorstep. Let him do whatever he wanted to do, so no more people would die. At least he'd be at peace, assuming death would be as calm and peaceful as he'd always imagined it to be. Then again, you never knew with Duncan Fitzpatrick in charge. Chances were he'd fuck even death up for Stephan.

He rolled the name on his tongue. Stephan. He hadn't called himself that in a long time, had come to like and embrace his new name. Indiana. Indiana Jones had been one badass. Fuck, he'd loved those movies. The guy was smart, scrappy, and had kicked ass. And he got the prize. Plus the girl. Would he ever find his happy ever after with Noah?

He had to stop running. If anything, yesterday had shown how impossible it was to stay out of reach of the Fitzpatricks forever. They would never stop looking, and everyone around him would be in danger. At least Noah, Josh, and Connor had known what they'd gotten into, but now Blake and Aaron had gotten sucked in as well. Hell, if either of them had gotten killed because of Indy, he'd never forgive himself.

Something rustled, and he froze. An envelope was slid under the door. He waited till he heard footsteps walk away, then went to retrieve it. His fake ID was written on the front: Alex DeWitt. It was the name he and the guys had agreed that Indy would use in an emergency. He opened the envelope. A single piece of paper fell out. He didn't recognize the handwriting, but that didn't mean anything.

"Everyone is okay. Front entrance. 8 AM. Bradford Kent. Code: Jersey number 12."

Indy's body went slack with relief, and a gulf of dizziness made him drop to the floor, sagging against the wall. They were okay. They were all okay. The code they'd agreed on proved the message was from Noah and the others.

He buried his head in his hands as hot, furious tears forced their way down his cheeks. He couldn't do this anymore. When it had been just him, running and fearing for his life, it had been one thing. But now there were so many more around him in danger. All because of him. He couldn't do this anymore, not to them, and also not to himself. The thought that he'd lost Noah, that Josh might have died because of Indy—he couldn't go through that ever again.

No, he was done. The FBI was his only option now.

He didn't eat, his stomach still too unsettled to be hungry. Instead, he lay down on the bed, eyes open, staring at the ceiling. Thinking.

Two minutes before eight he was outside, a hoodie pulled up over his head. Nobody even looked at him twice until a silver sedan pulled up. A man hastily got out, holding out his driver's license before Indy even had to ask. "I'm Brad, Blake's brother," he said.

Indy checked the license, but he had little doubt the man was who he claimed to be. First of all, the code in the letter had been correct—Tom Brady's jersey number—and second, the guy had the same olive skin and dark hair as Blake, even if he had brown eyes instead of Blake's piercing blue ones.

Indy nodded, handed him the driver's license back. "Nice to meet you, Brad. Let's go."

Brad got back into the car and drove off. Indy wasn't talkative with strangers, but now he had so many questions he didn't even know where to start. "Is everyone okay?"

"From what I understand, everyone is okay except for Blake, who got shot twice."

"Fuck, no," Indy said. "How is he?"

"He was shot in his thigh and in his chest, and he had surgery all through the night. He hasn't woken up yet, but from what I understood he's not critical anymore. But I'm taking you to the hospital now, so you can see for yourself." He shot Indy a quick look sideways. "I don't know the whole story, but Connor said to tell you the cops are guarding the hospital, and especially Blake's room."

Indy let out the breath he'd been holding. "Okay. Thank you. Also for picking me up, since you don't even know me."

"You're welcome. I didn't mind. It was better than hanging in the hospital, waiting for my brother to wake up."

He could at least be civil enough to make small talk, Indy reasoned. The guy deserved at least that for doing this. "You and Blake close?" he asked.

"Yeah," Brad said. Something sad passed over his face. "Very much so."

"I'm sorry," Indy said. What else was there to say? This was all his fault. Blake had gotten shot because of him. Fuck, he hoped the guy would be okay.

They didn't say much during the rest of the ride, but Indy didn't think it was because Brad was angry with him. It rather looked as if he was shy, an introvert.

Brad led him inside the hospital, where the entrance was indeed guarded by cops. Indy had to swallow down his fear of being recognized. He was counting on Connor to have kept him out of it, and judging by the fact they'd deemed it safe for Indy to come to the hospital, he had.

As soon as he saw Noah, Indy took off. He'd told himself to keep it cool, especially considering what he was about to do, but seeing Noah proved to be too much. Noah opened his arms wide and Indy ran, hugging him tight. With Noah's arms around him, his heart rate settled. He really was okay. Then Josh stepped in from behind, and he was once again sandwiched between the two men he loved the most.

Josh kissed his head, Noah his mouth. "So glad you're okay," Josh whispered.

Indy tore his mouth away from Noah's. "I was so scared. I heard the gunshots."

"Connor shot three of the attackers," Josh said. Something in his voice had Indy take notice. Connor's name was a little too emphasized.

Indy turned around in their arms and faced Josh. "Connor, huh?" he said so softly no one else could hear it. Josh blushed slightly, confirming Indy's suspicion. "You okay?"

Josh nodded. "I'm fine."

He stepped back, but Noah apparently wasn't quite ready to let Indy go. He hugged him from behind, and Indy leaned back against him. A few more minutes, that was it. Until he knew they were really okay, he promised himself. "How's Blake?" he asked.

"It was touch and go for a while, but the surgery went well. If he wakes up and there are no further complications, he should make a full recovery," Noah said.

Connor stepped close as well. Here they were, Indy thought. The men he'd come to trust with his life, the men he'd grown to love more than he'd thought possible.

"How you doing, kid?" Connor asked.

Looking at the faces of his men, Indy's decision was made. "Can you call the FBI, Connor? I'm turning myself in as a witness."

Connor nodded, while Noah gasped. "Indy, we need to talk about this."

Indy turned around to face him, this man he loved so much. He raised his hands to caress Noah's buzz cut, the stubble on his skin, the freckles on his nose that he hated, but Indy thought were the cutest thing ever on a man so tough and strong. Noah's beautiful green eyes grew moist. Did he realize?

"I love you, Noah." Indy's voice was strong. "I love you more than I'd ever thought possible. You gave me so much. A sense of belonging. Hope. And above all, love. I didn't know love until I met you and Josh."

He turned around, Josh still behind him, with eyes that told Indy he knew. He understood. Noah wouldn't, but Josh got it. He reached out, and Indy grabbed his hand.

"It's because I love you that I have to do this. I have to stop running. I'm so tired of being scared, not just for myself but especially for others. Merrick and his family, Houdini, and now Blake. I can't do this anymore. I can't keep putting people's lives in danger because I'm scared. So I'll put my fate in the hands of the FBI, and I'll testify against Duncan, and anyone else they want me to."

"I'll come with you," Noah said, like Indy knew he would. "We'll convince them to put us both in witness protection."

Indy took a deep breath, steeling himself. "No. I'm going alone."

Noah's eyes narrowed. "Indy, no. We do this together."

He stepped in, let go of Josh's hand, and put a hand against Noah's cheek. "It's no life for you, baby. You wouldn't be able to work, to do much of anything. You'd go stir-crazy. And I'd still have to constantly worry they'd get you, too. I'm done putting you all in danger."

"But..." Noah's face tightened. He was starting to see where this was going. "Where does that leave us?"

Indy couldn't help it. He had to taste him, one more time. He dragged Noah's head down and kissed him with all the love burning in his heart. Noah kissed him back with furious passion that coursed through Indy's veins. He broke off the kiss and stepped back.

"You have to let me go, Noah. You deserve more. I want you to live, not hide with me. I'll come back if I can."

He stopped, his throat constricted by the raw pain radiating from Noah. Indy had known it would hurt him, but he hadn't been ready for this much pain.

"Indy, please... Don't do this. Don't walk away."

His proud man begging. If anything, it showed the depth of his love for Indy. He wavered. Should he...? No, he couldn't. He couldn't keep dragging Noah into his mess. He deserved so much more.

He turned and raised to his toes to kiss Josh. "Promise me you'll take care of him."

Josh's lips were warm, soft. Gentle. Understanding. No fury here, but mere sadness. "Always. Come back to us, Indy. We need you."

He nodded. "I'll try." He didn't even bother to wipe away the tears.

Connor's face was tight with worry. "Take care of yourself, kid. Don't let your guard down."

Indy nodded and hugged him tight. "I will. Be strong for them, Connor."

Connor nodded, returning the hug. "I'll take you to the station, and we'll make the call from there."

Aaron sat forlorn on a chair, watching the whole thing. "Tell Blake I'm sorry," Indy said. "So very sorry."

"I will. But he won't be angry with you," Aaron said.

Indy nodded to Brad and another guy with a similar complexion—that had to be Blake's other brother.

As he walked out, Connor's hand protectively on his back, he heard Noah cry out. It sounded like an animal that had been deadly wounded and was fighting for his life. Blinded by tears, Indy let Connor lead him away from everything and everyone he'd ever loved.

13

Noah felt like he was slowly dying. Not literally, of course. His stump was healing well, and aside from a few bruises he had no injuries from the attack. But it had been two weeks without Indy, and Noah was shriveling on the inside. The light had been taken out of his life, leaving only darkness. And seeing Josh suffer without Connor only added to his sense of hopelessness.

What the hell was wrong with Connor that he'd walked out on Josh right now? Fuck, Noah had thought the cop had loved Josh, but he'd broken things off the same day Indy had left. Fucking unbelievable. Josh had said he'd sprouted some crap about not being able to deal with Josh being so needy all the time and that he knew he was gonna lose Josh to Noah anyway now that Indy was gone. He'd even quit his job and had moved away. Fucking asshole.

Noah was worried sick about Josh, but so far he seemed to be coping better than he himself was. Maybe Josh still harbored hope Connor would come to his senses? After all, the cop had pushed the sale of the house through. He'd not merely come up with the down payment, he'd bought the whole damn thing. It was all done and paid for. Noah and Josh had received a call from the notary, telling them to come sign the contract. It was in both of their names. Who the fuck did that and then walked away? It didn't make sense.

So yeah, maybe Josh still had hope his man would come back. Noah didn't. He knew Indy. Once he'd decided on something, he wouldn't change his mind. This was what Noah had been afraid of since he'd fallen in love with him, that Indy's sense of guilt and his deep desire to protect those he loved would make him walk away. Nothing Noah did would change that.

Not that he could even try, since Indy had gone into protective custody, and the FBI had no intention of letting Noah know where he was. Apparently, Indy had made it clear to the FBI he did not want to talk to Noah. Or Josh, because Noah had made him try, too. No, Indy had meant it when he told Noah to let him go.

He pulled his sweater over his head, then put on jeans. He rolled the pant leg back, pinning it with a few safety pins. The amputation wound was healing well, faster than expected. He had physical therapy with his new prosthesis for the first time today to test it out, see if his body could handle it. Noah was more worried about his mind. The pain in his body, he could handle. The pain in his heart...that was a different story.

Afterward, he had an appointment at the hospital. As he had expected, he was in serious shit for the procedures he'd done, both at home and the buddy transfusion in the ambulance. Owens had told him to show up for a meeting with the hospital lawyer and to bring his own lawyer. His head hurt even thinking about how that meeting was gonna go, even if he knew Owens wouldn't want to lose him. Liability weighed heavy for the hospital, as always.

Carefully, he went down the stairs on his crutches. Moving into the ranch would be a huge improvement for him and would make things a hell of a lot easier. That being said, he'd trade it in a heartbeat to have Indy back. And Connor, though Noah would beat the shit out of him for what he'd done to Josh if he ever saw him again.

In the living room, Blake was asleep on the couch. Aaron sat at his feet, of course, reading a book. The kid couldn't seem to be away from Blake, even for a little while. Fucking annoying.

"Morning," Noah said, making an effort to be friendly. "How is he?"

Aaron put his book down. "Tired. He's not sleeping well."

"He's healing, Aaron, but it'll take time."

Blake had been released from the hospital two days prior, opting to stay at Noah's place instead of his own home since Noah already had handicapped accommodations. The extra railings along the stairs and the handicapped accessible shower would make things a lot easier. Or so he'd told Noah. Noah was pretty sure they also wanted to keep an eye on him to make sure he didn't go off the rails. He appreciated it, on some level, but Aaron annoyed the fuck out of him.

Aaron got up from the couch, covering Blake again with the comforter. "I made you lunch," he told Noah.

Noah's eyebrows rose. "You didn't have to do that." Aaron meant well, probably, but he had an issue with boundaries. Josh had gone for a long run, but Noah was damn well capable of making his own lunch. He couldn't believe it didn't drive Blake mad, this constant hovering and neediness.

"There's coffee in your travel mug and a ham and egg sandwich in the fridge."

Someone had been paying attention during the few days he'd been here. It was tiresome, how he was copying his brother.

"Thank you."

"I'll do some grocery shopping today, since we're running low on a bunch of stuff. Is there anything you need?"

Noah took a sip from the coffee. Ah. At least it had the perfect temperature. "A few things. But you can wait till Josh gets back, so you don't have to leave Blake alone."

Aaron nodded. "Yeah, okay. I can help him shower, right? You said it would be okay by now? He's been dying for one."

"Yeah. His wounds are all closed, so it's fine. I wouldn't stay in too long, though. The wounds shouldn't get too soft, you know what I mean?"

"Okay."

Noah took another sip of his coffee, then grabbed the sandwich Aaron had made. It didn't look as perfect as when Josh would make it, but he had to admit it was a hell of a lot better than what he would've made himself.

Aaron jammed his hands in his pockets. "Erm, Noah, can I ask you something else?"

"Yeah."

Aaron looked at the floor, circled his left foot till it popped, then his right. Something was bothering him, but what?

"Is there anything he shouldn't do yet?" Aaron finally asked.

Noah could think of a long list of things Blake would probably be wise not to engage in. Running came to mind. Jiujitsu, for that matter. But the kid had to be talking about something else. What else would Blake—or Aaron himself —want to do that could hurt him?

Ah. Of course. He sighed.

"Hand jobs and blow jobs are fine, but he can't fuck yet. That would put too much stress on his wounds."

Aaron blushed fiercely, a trait the brothers had in common, it seemed.

"O-o-okay," he stuttered.

The relief on his face affirmed Noah had guessed right. "And Aaron," he added. "Blake is gonna be in pain for a while, as well as restricted in his physical activities. For a man like him who is so active, that's gonna be hard."

Aaron nodded, looking worried. "I know. I'm trying to do what I can, you know. I wanna take good care of Blake and help out in the house and everything."

What the fuck was so stressful about that, that he had to look so haggard? The kid had done a good job, Noah had to admit, helping with cleaning and keeping everything neat and tidy. He'd helped Josh fix some meals, which Josh had tolerated. Sort of. They were still not best buddies and probably never would be, but Josh was trying the best he could under these circumstances.

And Aaron had been there for Blake, spending the biggest part of his days in the hospital before Blake was released. Every time Noah had come to visit, Aaron had been at Blake's bedside, or even on his bed, even when Blake was sleeping. It was unnerving, as if he couldn't stand to be away from the man. Desperately clingy, was another apt description. Noah had seen Blake's brothers raise their eyebrows as well.

"I appreciate your help, Aaron. And I know you're worried about Blake, but he's recovering well. You might wanna consider backing off a little."

"What do you mean?"

"Look, Aaron, I know you're new at this and all, but you might wanna give Blake some space, okay? You're getting quite clingy, and if you want to keep him happy, I'm not sure that's the best way to go."

"Flint!" Blake called out from the living room, sounding furious.

Noah could ignore him, but that wasn't fair since the guy couldn't come to him. So he sighed and made his way to the living room, where Blake had propped himself up on the couch. His eyes were firing at Noah, and Noah cringed a little.

"What?" he snapped.

"Butt the fuck out of my relationship," Blake said, his voice frozen solid. "You don't know what the fuck you're talking about."

The intensity of his reaction surprised Noah. He looked over his shoulder. Behind him, Aaron stood with shoulders hanging low, looking like a puppy that had gotten kicked. Kind of like when Josh had gone off against him about betraying him.

"Aaron, come here," Blake said, his voice suddenly warm.

Noah was still looking at Aaron, who shook his head, biting his lip.

"Come on, puppy," Blake said. Noah turned his head at the unexpected term of endearment. Blake patted the comforter with his hand, much like you would do when you called a...puppy. He'd called him puppy. What the ever-loving fuck?

Aaron moved past him, launched himself on the couch and curled up at Blake's feet. Blake immediately put his hand on Aaron's head and rubbed him until he stopped squirming. "That's a good boy," Blake praised him.

Aaron's face relaxed, the stress leaving his body as he snuggled up to Blake's feet. Any second now, Noah expected him to stick out his tongue and start licking Blake.

Blake's eyes found Noah's, all but daring him to say something. It made Noah feel small.

"I'm sorry," he said.

Blake nodded and continued to pet Aaron's head. It was as if Noah's black glasses had been removed, and he saw it through a different lens. What he had seen as clingy and annoying had been sweet and healing, both for Blake and for Aaron.

Now that he thought about it, he'd never seen Blake react with anything other than love and endless patience toward Aaron. He'd never turned him away, had never even shown a hint of irritation. No, that had all been Noah. On the contrary, Blake seemed to love it when Aaron was close to him, touching him. If not, he wouldn't reach out for him all the time to pet him. If this was what worked for them and made them happy, who the fuck was he to judge? He'd done some pretty crazy shit himself, after all.

"I miss Indy," Noah said. It wasn't an excuse, but it was an explanation. Sort of. He could only hope Blake would accept it. Fuck, he'd been an asshole.

"Still nothing?" Blake asked. The anger on his face disappeared, making place for understanding. Thank fuck. Noah had been way out of line there.

Noah shook his head. "No. I have no idea where he is or how he's doing."

"It sucks, man. And Josh, how is he?"

"He's taking it better than I had expected, but I'm worried." He dragged a hand through his buzz cut. Blake sure was easy to talk to. "I never saw it coming, you know? Plus, the timing, it's too much at the same time."

"You had no idea Connor was unhappy?"

"No. He never said a word. It's been hard on him, I guess, trying to accept Josh's baggage."

"You mean you and Indy," Blake said.

The guy was a straight shooter, called it as he saw it. Noah could appreciate that. It sure was a hell of a lot less tiresome than beating around the bush. "Yeah. It's a lot to ask, you know?"

"Plus, maybe the guilt over his family's role in what happened to Indy?" Noah had shared the story with Blake and Aaron, figuring they had a right to know after becoming unintentionally involved. "I'm just saying, Connor seems like the type to feel responsible."

Noah's eyes narrowed as he pondered Blake's question. "Maybe. Hadn't looked at it that way."

He did have a point. Noah mulled it over on the taxi ride to physical therapy. Connor loved Josh. Truly, deeply loved him. A child could see it, the way his face lit up when Josh was even in the same room. And there was no doubt in Noah's mind that he took good care of Josh. Better than Noah had ever done, that was for sure. He'd never picked up on Josh's need for submission, had been too caught up in his own needs to see it. Selfish, he'd been selfish. Simple as that.

Josh loved Connor, too. And it was a different love than he had for Noah and Indy, though it was hard to pinpoint what was dissimilar. Maybe it was the submission thing.

Why the hell had Connor taken off? It didn't make sense. If he loved Josh and Josh loved him, why would it all be too much all of a sudden? What had changed, other than that Indy was temporarily out of the picture?

He felt so alone and unstable, as if the ground was sinking under his feet and no one was there to help him. Without Indy, his life was so damn empty. It physically hurt, being without what felt like his other hand. His heart. He envied Blake and Aaron and their weird but sweet relationship. He'd do anything, anything to be able to hold Indy again. His throat constricted, and he had to swallow hard.

"We're here," the taxi driver announced.

He handed him the money and waved off the change. It took effort to get out of the car, especially since there were spots of frozen snow here and there. If he put his crutch on one of those, things would not end well. He waited till the taxi had driven off to go inside, trying to breathe through the pain. It took a long time before he was able to go inside, and when he did, his eyes were red and swollen.

14

B lake woke up disoriented. "Aaron?"

"I'm here." The weight against his feet moved. Blake smiled. He'd grown accustomed to having Aaron sleep or cuddle at his feet. Ever since Blake had been discharged from the hospital, Aaron had seemed content to simply be near him. Sometimes he'd read a book or a magazine, but there were times when he'd lain down at his feet, waiting for Blake to wake up again. They'd spent the first week at Noah's, but had moved back into Blake's own house a week ago.

Blake stretched, careful not to put too much pressure on his wounds. Three weeks had passed since the shooting, and his injuries were healing well, but his upper body was still tender. They'd had to crack his chest open to repair the damage the bullet had caused. In the first few days, even breathing had hurt. No wonder, with the beating his lungs had taken, Noah had explained.

Blake couldn't believe he was still alive. He'd coded twice, according to Noah. If he hadn't been there, Blake would be dead. Then again, if Blake hadn't taken those two guys out, chances were someone else would be dead. All in all, Blake wasn't unhappy with the outcome.

"Oh, good. I fell asleep again."

"That's okay. Can I get you anything?"

"Are we alone?"

"Yeah. Everyone's at work."

Blake shot Aaron a sexy smile. "Good. I need to take a shower, and after that, you and I are gonna fool around a little."

Aaron swallowed. "Fool around?"

"Yeah, puppy. I've missed you horribly. I'm fucking horny, and I need to make sure you still know who you belong to."

A sweet smile spread across Aaron's face. "You," he whispered. "I'm yours."

Warmth started near Blake's heart, radiating through his entire body. "Good. Now, how about that shower?"

Blake pushed himself up and carefully swung his legs sideways. Aaron kneeled to take off his socks. Blake lifted his hips so the boy could take off his sweat pants as well. He wasn't wearing underwear, and his cock stood hard at attention. He hadn't been kidding when he'd told Aaron he was horny. Fuck, he wanted him. Badly.

But first that shower, because he stank. Since showering was such an ordeal, it had been three days since he'd showered. Sure, he couldn't get that dirty from lying in bed all day, but still.

Aaron took Blake's shirt off, moving around so he wouldn't touch Blake's wounds. "Good job, Aaron," Blake praised him. It came naturally to him, and he loved seeing what it did to Aaron. His whole face lit up whenever Blake affirmed him. It was a touching sight to witness.

"Strip, puppy. I'm gonna need your help in the shower."

Aaron nodded and stripped naked without protest. He walked into the shower, turned it on so it could warm up, then came back to help Blake. Blake leaned heavily on him as they shuffled to the bathroom, but Aaron took his weight without complaining. Blake was able to put weight on his leg, but it still hurt.

Aaron had put a stool in the shower that Blake could sit on, since standing for too long still wore him out. But Blake wanted at least to start with standing. He sighed with pleasure as the warm water hit his back.

"Fuck, yes..."

"Turn your back to me," Aaron said. He squeezed some shampoo in his hands. Blake turned and bent backward. It was a good thing Aaron was tall as well. He had no trouble reaching his head, washing his hair and giving him a delicious scalp massage.

"Lean back."

He obeyed, keeping his eyes closed as Aaron rinsed out the shampoo. Man, that already felt so much better. Aaron wasn't done yet, though. Next, he thoroughly washed every inch of Blake's body, being sweet and gentle around his wounds. He even cleaned his cock, using his hands to soap it everywhere, even between his balls.

"Don't forget my hole," Blake said, his voice hoarse with need. Damn, he wanted to bend Aaron over and take him, but he couldn't. He wouldn't.

Aaron blushed but soaped up his finger and cleaned Blake's crease, then shyly probed his hole. Blake moaned. "Push it in. Clean me deep."

Aided by the soap, Aaron's finger slipped in with ease.

"Ah..."

Blake spread his legs, leaning against the tiles. "Could

you please suck me, my sweet little Aaron? Make it good for me? I'm so horny."

Aaron sank to his knees, ignoring the water that beat down on his head. He nibbled on Blake's crown, then initiated a deliciously slow but thorough descent from the top down, down, down to Blake's balls, where he...oh, yeah. Blake moaned, letting the sound echo through the bathroom. He needed this. Fuck, he was so hard.

Aaron sucked a heavy, throbbing testicle into his mouth. His tongue did wicked things to the skin, setting it on fire everywhere. He repeated the move with Blake's other nut, sending his need higher and higher until Blake's knees buckled.

"Oh, fuck, Aaron..."

Aaron's finger slipped back into his ass, moved in and out. Blake bore down, took it in deeper. His ass craved more. Aaron seemed to sense it, as he added another finger. He shoved them both in deep, grazing Blake's prostate. He moaned again, long and deep.

Aaron's mouth moved, licking his shaft, then sucking him in deep. Blake's entire body convulsed, and he came with a roar. His hips bucked, and he shoved his cock deep into Aaron's mouth, unloading a massive load of cum down his throat. The kid couldn't swallow it all, though he bravely tried, and Blake watched with satisfaction as his cum streamed down Aaron's chin. His eyes watered, but Aaron held on, licking Blake's cock clean before releasing it.

Still on his knees, the last remnants of Blake's fluids on his mouth, he looked up at Blake with a hopeful expression. Blake's heart warmed.

"Fuck, that was so good. Your mouth is heaven, puppy. Thank you."

Aaron beamed, his shoulders relaxing. Blake petted his

head and Aaron rubbed against his hand, clearly enjoying it.

"Now, I wish that I could wash you, but I can't, so you'll have to do it yourself, okay?"

Blake sat down on the stool, the tension in his body lessening after his powerful orgasm. Aaron had sucked him off a few times since he'd been injured, but he'd had to be damn careful and it hadn't been the same. Fuck, he felt so much better already, but he was still horny. Even though Aaron did it quickly, Blake enjoyed watching him touch himself. He wanted him so much.

As soon as he was done washing himself, Aaron rinsed off, then turned off the shower. He toweled Blake off first, showing once again how much he wanted to please him, then did a half-assed job on himself. Blake leaned on him to get back into his bedroom. Aaron was probably assuming he needed to lie down again, since he'd seen before how much showering cost him. But Blake had other plans. He had every intention of helping his sweet little puppy find release as well. The poor kid hadn't been touched since the attack, aside from maybe a sloppy and fast jerking off by his own hand. Aaron's cock had been rock hard in the shower, though his erection had subsided a little now.

Aaron helped Blake lower himself to the mattress.

"Look in that drawer, Aaron," Blake told him. He scooted himself over to the headboard and leaned against it. His wounds throbbed, but it was doable. "Grab me the lube."

Aaron shyly held up a bottle and handed it to Blake.

"Good. You up for some more fooling around?"

He nodded.

"Tell me what you'd like, puppy. What do you need from me? Use words."

Aaron bit his lip, but Blake was patient. He had to allow

Aaron the time to figure out what he wanted and gather the courage to voice it. The fact that his cock had jumped to attention again as soon as Blake had mentioned fooling around, told Blake the kid was interested.

"Blake?"

"Yeah?"

"Do you think you could play with my hole a little?"

His courageous little Aaron, learning to voice his needs. It was a big step, one he intended to reward.

"On your hands and knees, facing away, straddling me. Don't put your weight on me. I want your ass as close as possible."

Aaron obeyed instantly, testament to how much he needed Blake to take care of him. Blake coated his fingers with lube, but he wanted to start with something else. He sagged a little lower on the mattress.

"Aaron, I want your ass in my face, you hear me? I can't move, so you'll have to come to me. I'm gonna fuck you with my tongue first."

Aaron moved backward, checking his position until his hole was right in front of Blake's mouth. Without shame, Aaron pushed backward. He was desperate, Blake thought. Poor puppy, he'd barely gotten any attention lately.

He dug in without waiting, first giving Aaron's crease a thorough licking, before moving deep into his hole. He tongued him, first tentative to see how he would respond, then fucking him slow and deep. Aaron moaned every time Blake's tongue went into his hole, and he kept pushing back his ass. Clearly, as much as he enjoyed this, it wasn't enough.

"Move forward a little," he told Aaron.

He slid his index finger in as soon as Aaron was in position. It bottomed out right away, with Aaron pushing back to let him in. Aaron let out a soft little whimper that shot straight to Blake's balls. He slid it back and forth a few times, added a second finger when he realized Aaron was ready. Again, that hungry little hole sucked it up with ease.

"Blake," Aaron sighed, canting his hips.

Blake moved his fingers in and out, encouraged by Aaron's wanton sighs and groans. "How's that feel?"

"More. Please, Blake."

Blake smiled. Aaron might not realize it, but his ass was made to be fucked. Blake had never encountered a bottom who adjusted with so much ease. He added a third finger and pushed back in. Aaron let out a happy little sigh and wriggled his butt, which Blake took as encouragement to go deeper. He fucked him steady with three fingers now, Aaron letting out a stream of little moans and sighs.

"Aaron, do you want more?"

The answer was swift. "Please."

"Do you want my fat cock in your hungry little hole?"

"Oh, yes. Please, Blake. I need..." He moved against Blake's fingers, restless and searching for more. This wasn't how Blake had imagined their first time, but Aaron needed it. He couldn't make him wait any longer, not when he was so obviously craving more.

"I've got you." Blake pulled out his fingers and lubed up his cock. No condom necessary, thank fuck. He couldn't even remember the last time he'd gone bareback, but with Aaron he didn't want even the thinnest layer of latex between them.

"You're gonna have to do the work, Aaron. Turn around."

Aaron scrambled around. He eyed Blake's rigid cock with pure want. Before Blake could say anything, Aaron positioned himself above his cock. Blake's hands moved to his ass to help him spread his globes and find that perfect little hole. Blake felt the head of his dick slide against moist heat. He didn't even need to push; Aaron breathed out audibly and lowered himself.

Holy fuck, he was...

"Oh!" Blake moaned as his cock was at once engulfed in a snug heat. Dammit, Aaron didn't even stop but took him in all the way at once until Blake bottomed out.

Aaron leaned back and took him in an inch deeper. With a keening wail, he came, his body spasming, spurting his load all over Blake's chest. Blake's mouth dropped open. The kid had come from merely taking him in.

A mighty shiver tore through Aaron's body, and he visibly relaxed. His eyes, which had been closed, opened and he looked at Blake.

"That was..." His face sobered as he took in the sight of his cum all over Blake's chest. "Sorry, it was... I didn't think it would... Sorry."

"Puppy, stop. Stop apologizing. Tell me how it felt, how you feel."

Interestingly enough Aaron didn't seem to feel the need to climb off, even though Blake's hard cock was still embedded in his ass. If anything, he looked relaxed, at least physically.

"I thought it would hurt, but it didn't. It feels so perfectly full, like I am complete for the first time. I loved it when you were fucking me with your tongue and with your fingers, but I still felt empty, somehow. Your cock feels perfect." Aaron exhaled after his little speech.

His perfect little bottom, hungry for cock. "Ride me, Aaron. Ride me until you come again."

Aaron's face lit up. He raised his hips, then lowered them again. It took him a few tries until he'd found the right angle and had his coordination right, but after that, Blake was treated to the sexiest thing he'd ever seen. Aaron threw back his head, closed his eyes, and rode Blake's cock. He seemed oblivious to the world, to Blake even, taking what he so desperately needed. Harder and deeper it went, hips surging up and slamming down, Blake's cock buried inside that snug heat again and again.

It was a good thing he'd come once already, otherwise Blake would have lost the battle against his impending orgasm long ago. As it was, he had to fight hard to keep himself from coming, wanting Aaron to take what he needed first.

Aaron whimpered, moaned, puffed, and murmured inaudible words, his face tight with concentration. He was so beautiful, now more than ever. So abandoned to his needs, lost to his cravings.

"Blake..." Aaron cried out, his body shaking with effort.

"I've got you, puppy. Let go. Come for me."

Aaron inhaled deeply and rammed his ass down so hard that Blake lost the battle. He tensed up, shivered, and came hard inside Aaron. Spurt after spurt jetted out of his cock, filling up Aaron's tight heat. That sensation seemed to push Aaron over the edge as well, and he shuddered violently before painting Blake's chest with more cum.

Aaron leaned forward to support himself with his arms, but he still didn't roll off Blake. Even as Blake's cock softened, he held on, until it slipped out with a wet sound. Aaron whimpered with distress, as if he'd lost something valuable. He moved off Blake, collapsing on the bed, cuddling close but still whimpering occasionally.

Blake pulled him close, dropped little kisses on his head, whispered sweet nothings until Aaron quieted down. "How are you feeling?" Blake asked.

Aaron moved even closer, though careful not to touch

Blake's wounds. Even when he was seeking comfort, he was still paying attention. "That was amazing," Aaron sighed.

"You liked having my cock in your hole?"

Aaron scoffed. "'Like' doesn't even begin to describe it. I love it. I feel so complete when you're inside me. It's like I'm empty without that."

It seemed his sweet little puppy had a serious case of anal fixation. Blake smiled. "We'll experiment with a butt plug, see if that helps."

Aaron sighed and kissed Blake's hand. "Why are you so taking such good care of me?" he asked.

"Because I like to. Because I like you. Because you deserve it, my sweet puppy."

Blake's eyes fluttered closed, his body exhausted and his mind at peace with Aaron snuggling close to him.

15

Connor hadn't been back to Boston in years. Not even the funeral of his dad had been enough to lure him back, because he'd known they would be there. His mom's family. The Fitzpatricks. He could barely say their name, even more so since he'd met Indy.

Connor had heard rumors, even when he'd been in the Marines. Rumors that Duncan had found himself a young boy. It had sickened him, but he'd wanted nothing to do with it. And now that he knew who that boy had been, he was so ashamed.

Why hadn't he done anything? Reported it? He'd been terrified of what they'd do to his parents, to himself even, if they found out he'd ratted them out. It had been fear that held him back but also a deep urge to stay away from it all. He hadn't wanted to get involved, to know details, to verify that rumor, knowing his conscience would be burdened. He'd chosen the easy way out.

If Indy ever found out, he'd never speak to Connor again. Him getting over the fact that Connor was related to the Fitzpatricks was one thing, but this? This was too much.

Maybe even for Josh. If Indy turned his back on Connor, he wasn't entirely sure what Josh would do. He loved him, Connor had no doubt, but whether Josh's love would be strong enough to weather that?

After all, Josh loved Indy and Noah nearly as much as he did Connor. He'd accepted that reality, had come to peace with it, but considering his past it was like a sword of Damocles above his head.

He nursed his beer in the corner of the dark Irish pub, waiting for his guy to show up. He was almost half an hour late, but then again criminals weren't exactly known for their time management skills. Although criminal was too big a word for this petty thief, but Connor had to start at the bottom. Plus, this guy might be low in the overall pecking order, but he had a ton of connections to others like him.

Connor knew how this particular game was played. He'd done nothing but schmooze and grease his way back in the last two weeks. This was his first big break, and fuck, he hoped it would work. The sooner he got this done, the sooner Indy would be free.

The pub was already decked out in sickening amounts of green in preparation for St. Patrick's Day. It was still over two weeks away, but here in Southie people took St. Paddy's Day as serious as the Red Sox and the Patriots. Hell, it drew more attention than the Fourth of July.

The door to the pub opened, and a skinny, shaggy man stepped in. His eyes darted around before they settled on Connor, and he made his way over after signaling the bartender for a Sam Adams. Davy Ford looked a helluva lot older than Connor—more like pushing fifty—though they had gone to school together. A hard life and a couple of years of prison showed in every tired line on the man's face.

Davy sat down across from Connor and nodded. "O'Connor."

"Ford."

They waited till Davy's beer was ready, and he picked it up from the bar with a quick nod at the bartender.

"Haven't seen you in ages. What brings you back?" Davy asked as he sat back down.

"Business."

"Heard you joined the Boys somewhere in New York," Davy said, using the Southie term for cops.

"Yeah. Had a good run for a while, but I got bagged for greasing."

"That's beat. Ya gonna try here?"

"Nah. The Boston Boys ain't what they used to be. All on the straight and narrow, man. Plus, too many Greasties," Connor said, knowing that derogatory word for East Bostonians would win him points. Like many Southies, Davy hated Easties with a passion.

"Yeah, that's mad pissa, ain't it? Fucking Greasties are taking over everything."

"You still working for big D?" Connor asked with deceptive nonchalance.

Davy shrugged, keeping his face blank. Connor knew for a fact he hated Duncan with a vengeance. "Not much. He don't like me, onna-conna my sister."

Davy's sister had the unique distinction of being the only person alive who'd ever managed to get a charge to stick against Duncan. He'd raped her, and she'd had the guts to press charges. It had ended with him taking a plea bargain, doing community service or some shit, and she'd moved away. Far, far away.

"Tough shit. You never liked him either."

Davy's eyes narrowed. "Big D's your cousin, bro. I ain't stupid enough to rattle to you."

"Didn't think you were. You're a wicked smart man, Davy. Always were. You were just shit outta luck they caught you." The man had served two years after being caught stealing a car by an off-duty cop. Since he wasn't exactly squeaky clean to begin with, he'd had to do hard time.

Davy nodded, placated. "Damn right."

"So if I asked you to mention me to a few of your mates who don't like big D either, think you could help me out?"

Davy's eyes turned sharp. "You planning mutiny?"

Connor smiled and leaned back. "That's a mighty big word, Davy. I'd like to think of it as a change in management."

Davy studied him for a second, then laughed. "Change of management. That's the balls, man."

Connor laughed with him, then turned serious. "I think you know the kind of guys I'm looking for."

Davy drained his beer and put the pint down with a thud. "Aye, Cap'n."

He walked out without saying another word. Connor leaned back, shoving his beer away from him. Three sips and he'd already had enough. This had better be fucking worth it.

THEY'D BEEN WATCHING some action movie for an hour now, but Aaron couldn't have recapped the plot if he'd been forced to. All he knew was that he was happy. For the first time in as long as he could remember, he was happy.

They were on the couch, Blake stretched out in a way that took the pressure off his leg and his chest, and Aaron curled up at his feet. He was wearing one of his new pink long sleeves and tight gray sweatpants, both courtesy of Colin. He'd assembled a great collection of clothes for Aaron, all pretty and soft and feminine.

Blake's hand was on Aaron's head, and he scratched Aaron's scalp every now and then, rubbed his neck, or caressed his hair. The constant contact was a powerful reminder of Blake's presence, his care.

His boyfriend. Blake was his boyfriend. Aaron still couldn't believe that this sexy man wanted him, had chosen him. He felt so unworthy of his attention, even though he'd done his best since Blake had gotten shot to take good care of him.

The first two weeks in the hospital, he'd barely left his side except for when the hospital staff kicked him out. If they'd thought him weird for staying by Blake's side, they'd never said it. Blake's brothers had looked at him funny a few times, but Blake had shot them an angry stare that made them keep their mouths shut. It had stressed how messed up Aaron was, though.

No matter what Blake said, Aaron wasn't buying it. That whole puppy thing, him being so frigging needy, it was not normal. The looks from Brad and Burke had made that abundantly clear. They thought he was a weirdo, and he couldn't blame them. Heck, he thought he was a weirdo, too.

The sex the day before had been so special, though. It had been life changing for Aaron. For the first time in his life, he'd felt complete, at peace. There was always this emptiness inside of him, this desperate craving he tried to ignore. Blake had filled it, had made him feel whole for the first time. He could only hope it had been good for Blake as well. He'd come, sure, but he was used to partners with more sexual experience. Partners who gave instead of took.

Aaron lifted his head when he heard a key in the front door. Two of the other people who were staying with Blake had left, and the third wasn't supposed to be home this weekend. Who was at the door, then?

"Hey, bro!"

Aaron recognized the voice. Burke.

"I'm here, too," Brad announced.

Aaron shifted his legs to sit up, but Blake pressed him down. "Stay," he said softly.

Aaron settled back down, but his heart beat wildly. He hated seeing the look of bewilderment he'd no doubt spot again in the eyes of Blake's brothers when they watched him and Blake. They had to be constantly wondering what on earth their perfect brother was doing with a guy like Aaron.

"Hi," Blake called out. "Grab a beer and a snack! We're watching a movie."

Burke and Brad rummaged around in the kitchen and made their way to the couch with chips, beer, and in Brad's case, a soda.

"Hi," Aaron said softly, peeking at them from underneath his lashes.

"Oh, hi, Aaron," Brad said. "I didn't see you."

He and Burke shared a look that made Aaron's stomach churn. His happiness was instantly gone.

"How are you feeling?" Burke asked Blake.

"Better every day. The hardest thing is not being able to exercise much. I'm really antsy from hanging around the couch all day."

"Well, maybe it would be easier to get up if Aaron wasn't glued to your feet all day," Burke said.

Aaron froze. If it was supposed to be a joke, Burke had to work on his delivery because it sure didn't feel funny to Aaron. He swallowed away the bile that rose in his throat, but the tears that sprang to his eyes weren't so easy to wipe away, not without them seeing. This time when he shifted to get off the couch, Blake let him.

"I'm gonna go to my room," Aaron whispered. "You guys hang out together."

He didn't look at them and avoided Blake's eyes. The fact that Blake said nothing as he walked away, didn't even try to stop him, said enough, didn't it?

He walked into his own old room, more by instinct than by a conscious decision and closed the door softly behind him. Aaron's shoulders dropped as he looked around the empty room. All his stuff—not that it was much, mind you—was in Blake's room, but this was where he'd gotten started with his new life. This room was where he'd dared to dream again, had begun to believe he'd find happiness one day. Now, all of that joy, that hope was gone.

He was a freak, a weirdo, and he always would be. Blake might find it amusing now, but he'd soon grow tired of it like everyone else. No one had ever wanted him the way he was. Josh had chosen Noah, and now Connor, and maybe Indy, too. His parents had only wanted him as long as he stuck to their preconceived notions of the perfect son.

And Blake... Blake couldn't really want him either. Not when he realized it would cost him the relationship with his brothers, who clearly didn't like Aaron. No, Blake would soon be done with him as well. Rightly so. Aaron didn't even want to come between him and his brothers, not after everything they'd been through. He had no right to take the first spot in Blake's life. And besides, Blake would come to the conclusion soon enough that Aaron wasn't what he wanted. He was too girly, too needy, simply too...too fucking weird.

Raised voices sounded from the living room, and Aaron clenched his fists. He did not want Blake fighting with his brothers, not over him. He wasn't worth it. No, he'd make things easy on him.

He silently opened the door again and walked into Blake's bedroom. He still had so little stuff that he'd packed it into his weekend bag in a few minutes. He left the girly clothes Blake had bought for him. Not that Blake could return them, but Aaron didn't want to take the memories with him. Besides, that part of his life had to be over. If he ever wanted to find love with somebody else…

His throat constricted as the reality of losing Blake hit him.

No, not here. Keep it together, for heaven's sake.

He clenched and unclenched his fists, breathing the pain away. It would be okay. He would be okay, someday. Maybe. For now, he had to get out of here.

He dug the key to Blake's house from his pocket and left it on the night table. He didn't make a sound as he walked into the hallway and out the front door, though Blake likely wouldn't have heard him anyways as he and his brothers were still arguing loudly. He threw his bag in his car, got in, and drove away without looking back.

He managed to hold back the tears until he was on the Northway, driving to heaven knew where. Once the tears turned out to be unstoppable, he pulled off at a rest stop, shut off the engine, and broke apart.

He was alone. Again.

BLAKE PRIDED himself on having a tight grip on his temper, but he'd never been closer to losing it than right now. Fists balled, he waited till Aaron was out of earshot, meanwhile firing deadly glares toward both his brothers.

"It was a stupid joke," Burke said. "I didn't mean anything by it."

Blake checked to see if the door to Aaron's room was closed. He'd gone into his own room, for fuck's sake, not into Blake's room, where he'd been staying all this time. God, his puppy was hurt.

He turned his head back and shot Burke a dark look. "Shut the fuck up, right now. I have never, ever been so disappointed in the two of you as I am right now. How could you? How could you hurt him like that? What has he ever done to you? This is not how you were raised, not by mom, and certainly not by me."

Both his brothers had at least the decency to look uncomfortable.

"He's weird," Brad protested weakly.

"That's rich, coming from you," Blake sneered.

"What do you mean?"

"You have quite the reputation, brother mine. Don't think that I don't know what they call you in Flirt. If you had wanted to keep me in the dark, you should have frequented another club. And I've let it go, Brad, because at the end of the day it's none of my fucking business who you fuck, or in this case who fucks you. I think you're worth more than that, but it's your life. But dammit, I expect the same courtesy. You have zero right to call Aaron weird, and I'm deeply disappointed that you would."

Brad's shoulders hunched, and he avoided Blake's look. "I didn't know you knew."

"I've known from the beginning. You can't keep shit like that secret, not in the gay community. And you," he turned toward Burke. "What the fuck do you think you're doing, passing out judgment? You don't think your long-time affair with your secretary is a secret, do you? And again, I've stayed out of it, even though I've been itching to call you a fucking idiot, but I've refrained. But you do not get to judge Aaron and me, you hear me?"

He dragged a hand through his hair in frustration. He'd better shut his mouth before he said things he'd regret later.

"We don't understand what you see in him," Brad said, his cheeks flaming red.

"We? So you and Burke have been talking about it, too, huh? Nice to know. I thought I deserved better from you."

"We're your brothers," Burke said, raising his voice.

"And that gives you the right to what, exactly? Gossip about me behind my back? Judge me? Criticize my boyfriend?"

"Yes, if we do it out of concern! For fuck's sake, Blake, he's like this constant shadow of you. He's so fucking clingy it's not even funny anymore. He's everywhere, and he never, ever fucking leaves!"

Burke's voice had reached shouting level at the end, and Blake took a deep breath to calm himself. He waited until he was sure he had full control of himself. "I like it. No, let me correct that. I love it. He needs me, and I dig it."

"How can you..." Brad's eyes widened. "You love him," he added, his tone changing.

Blake sighed. "Yeah. I do. You guys don't know him, don't understand how much rejection he's had to deal with. He's... God, he's vulnerable, and he's missed out on so much love and acceptance. His own parents rejected him for being gay. And now the two of you are doing the same thing, because he's different than what you had expected, or different than what you'd want for me. Don't you understand? That's not your choice to make. I love Aaron, and I want him in my life, more than anything. He brings me joy, a sense of purpose."

"I get that he's had it hard, and I'm sorry for him. But

he's so clingy it drives me crazy! I'd like to hang out with my brother every once in a while without him always being there," Burke snapped.

It suddenly hit Blake. "You're jealous," he said slowly. "You're jealous because you and Brad and Benjamin have been the most important people in my life forever, and you can't deal with the fact that that has changed."

Brad blushed all over again, but Burke's eyes narrowed. "You're saying Aaron is more important than your own brothers?"

Oh, holy fuck, how had he gotten himself into this impossible dilemma?

"You can't ask him that," Brad protested.

"I just did, so he can fucking answer!"

Blake slowly pushed himself up, carefully maneuvering his body off the couch until he was standing. "Burke, you know how much I love you, Brad, and Benjamin. I have sacrificed a lot for the three of you but especially for you and Brad. I could never regret making the choices that I did, raising you, and taking care of you when you needed me, but you cannot deny there was little room for me. I've focused on you two for a long time, and because of that and the whole fucked-up example of a marriage Mom and Dad had, I've never had a boyfriend. Not one. I'm thirty-four years old, man, and I've never been in a serious relationship. But I am now."

Much to his own surprise, his voice broke. "Aaron, he's the sweetest man I've ever met, and he makes me feel things I never knew I was capable of. He makes me want to try. He makes me want to grow roots, be a family. With him. And if you can't understand that, if you don't want that for me, then you are not the person I thought you were, and you don't love me the way I love you. Now, if you'll excuse me, I need to talk to Aaron."

He turned around and looked into the hallway. His eyes fell on the open door to Aaron's old room, then on his own open bedroom door. His stomach sank. It took him forever to make his way to both rooms, but he knew before he'd reached them.

Aaron was gone.

Oh, God, no.

How had he managed to sneak out without them seeing and hearing? Blake couldn't have seen him because he'd been on the couch with his back toward the hallway, and Brad had been on the chair to his side with the wall obstructing his view. But Burke…

He slowly turned around. As soon as he saw Burke's face, he knew. "Get the fuck out of my house."

Burke jammed his hands into the pockets of his jeans. "I didn't realize how much he meant to you."

Blake's grip on his temper had never been this thin. "Brad, get him the hell out before this escalates."

Brad looked from Blake to Burke with a puzzled expression. "I don't understand. What happened?"

"Aaron left, and Burke saw him leave and didn't say anything."

Brad's shocked "Burke!" was a poor balm for Blake's wounded soul. "Get the fuck out, both of you. You did this. You did this to Aaron and to me. After everything I did for you, you chased away the man I love."

Burke opened his mouth as if he wanted to say something, but Brad grabbed his arm. "Let's go."

Thank fuck. At least one of them realized he was near the end of his patience. He stood in the hallway as they left and watched them close the door behind them with a soft click.

Aaron must have left the same way, quietly, hoping no one would notice. Or had he made eye contact with Burke? Had he noticed Burke watching him and not doing a damn thing? The thought alone made Blake shiver with fear. His puppy would not survive a blow like that.

Blake needed to find him, and fast. But where the hell would Aaron go?

16

The familiar ping of his phone alerted Aaron another text message had come in. From Blake, no doubt. The man had started sending messages as soon as he'd discovered Aaron had left. Aaron had still been at that rest stop, trying to compose himself after having bawled his eyes out. His phone had dinged, and he'd looked, surprised to see a message from Blake.

Blake: Puppy, don't run. Please. Come back.

He hadn't replied, though Blake could see he'd received and read the message, since they both had an iPhone and used iMessage. What was there to say? Blake would miss him now, maybe. For a few days at most. Then he'd go back to his life and find someone who fit into his lifestyle and his family much better. Someone who didn't stand out for being weird.

So Aaron had ignored it and had started the long drive south. He'd hit the 87 all the way to New York City and had found a cheap motel in New Jersey to spend the night. He was almost out of money, but he couldn't sleep in his car. It was ten degrees at night.

Blake had texted him again.

Blake: *I'm sorry they hurt you. I've talked to them. Please, let me explain.*

Then again.

Blake: *Will you please call me?*

And once more, before Aaron had fallen asleep.

Blake: *I'm worried about you. Please be safe.*

The next day, Aaron had jumped on the 95 south and had continued driving. Traffic had been hell, first around Philadelphia, then again when he hit Baltimore. He wasn't up for facing the DC Beltway, knowing from experience that was seven lanes of hell, so he found another run-down motel.

He'd have to get a job soon. And Josh had been right, he should have accepted the first job he'd been able to get. Right now, he wasn't above waiting tables or doing the dishes, if that would earn him some cash.

Every hour, Blake had messaged him. First, it had been more pleadings.

Blake: *I miss you. Will you please call me? Talk to me?*

Blake: *I know you must be hurt, but please, let's talk.*

Aaron had reread his messages. There had been a "please" in every single one of them. What did that mean? The idea of Blake begging didn't fit. He wasn't supposed to beg. That was somehow beneath him. Yet, he did. Aaron still didn't reply, though. What was there left to say? Nothing.

Blake had apparently accepted Aaron wasn't responding and texted again.

Blake: *Puppy, I respect you're not answering my messages. Please keep reading them, so I at least know you're OK.*

Blake: *I'm gonna keep texting you, if that's okay. If you want me to stop, lmk and I will.*

The strange thing was, Aaron didn't want him to stop.

He'd never expected him to keep at it, but every waking hour, Blake sent him a new message. Sometimes it was a short "stay safe" type of thing, other times he texted a picture of himself eating or doing his physical therapy. Right before bedtime, he'd taken a picture of himself in his bed.

Blake: I miss you, puppy. My bed is empty without you and so is my heart.

The next day, Aaron braved the DC Beltway and made his way farther south, hitting Virginia, then fighting his way through North Carolina on too little sleep and a broken heart. That night, he parked his car at a rest stop, spending the night half-dozing, half-awake, scared someone would break into his car. And every hour till bedtime, Blake messaged him.

Blake: I hope you're okay, puppy. I'm worried about you.

Blake: Be safe, wherever you are.

Blake: Please know that you're always welcome to come back. I'm not angry with you.

After sleeping in his car, Aaron woke up with a horrific headache but still managed to make it farther south until he hit Georgia. He exited the 95 to get gas and spotted a "We're Hiring" sign at a motel. On impulse, he walked in. Five minutes later, he had the job.

It turned out people weren't exactly lining up for the night shift behind the reception desk of a ratty motel. No wonder, since it paid only seven bucks an hour and was off the books, but right now, he couldn't care less. He'd taken it, because it came with a room. A smelly, musty room with a shower that hadn't seen bleach in ages, but a room nonetheless. It even had a mini fridge that made one heck of a racket and a microwave that looked like it would expire any second. But he had a room and a job. It was a start.

Blake had texted again throughout the day, sending

pictures of himself, the house, his jiujitsu students. He'd started teaching again, though it was more being present in the studio than doing anything physically. Apparently, Brad and Burke were driving him back and forth, since he wasn't cleared to drive yet.

Aaron sighed, letting himself fall backward on the creaky bed as he studied Blake's face in the close-up he'd sent. He looked tired, though he'd pasted a smile on his face. Aaron could tell it was fake since his eyes weren't smiling. Besides, Blake smiled so rarely it was easy to see when he was pretending. He reread the last message.

Blake: *Even if you're mad with me, or hurt, could you please let me know you're okay?*

His fingers hesitated, then quickly tapped out the message back.

Aaron: *I'm okay. Thank you for your messages.*

The reply was almost instant.

Blake: *Oh, thank fuck you're okay. Thank you for letting me know. I miss you.*

Aaron frowned. Blake kept texting that, that he missed him. Was it an instinctual thing to say because it was expected, or did he mean it? As he was pondering this, another message came in.

Blake: *Is it okay if I keep sending you messages?*

He sighed. Wouldn't it be better for Blake to stop, to give up? He would at some point, anyway? But maybe he hadn't reached that point yet. And to be honest, Aaron did feel better Blake was texting him. It made it feel like he had at least some human connection left because Josh probably hadn't even noticed he was gone. Things had gotten a bit better between them after the shooting, but he still wasn't reaching out to Aaron. Not even when he had to be going through a heck of a hard time with Connor gone.

Aaron stared at his phone, trying to decide if he should tell Blake to stop or not. He might as well let it run its course. That way, no one could accuse him of not giving it a chance.

Aaron: *Yes.*

He put his phone in his pocket and went downstairs to the office to report for his first shift behind the desk.

NOAH WOKE UP GRUMPY, as had been the case ever since Indy had been gone. He slept like crap, tossing and turning in his bed without that little, tight body draped all over him. Even Josh's presence hadn't managed to calm him, but that might be because he was hurting as much as Noah was.

Next to him, Josh stirred and slowly opened his eyes. "Hey," he said with a sleepy voice.

"Hi," Noah responded.

It was eerily familiar, the two of them back together again, even if the ranch they had moved into last week still smelled new. No Indy, no Connor. Just him and Josh.

"Did you sleep?" Josh asked.

He shrugged. "Not much."

"You're starting work again, Noah. You need sleep. Take a pill if you have to tonight."

"No. I'm too scared I'll become addicted to them."

Josh relented, probably knowing Noah was right. "How you feeling about going back to work?"

Noah sighed. He'd gotten a severe reprimand from the hospital and was now under probation for an entire year. If he fucked up again, he'd be out on his ass. "I don't want to, to be honest. I like the idea of feeling useful again, but even thinking about that constant stress and adrenaline makes me tired before setting foot inside the door."

Josh's answer was swift. "So quit."

Noah grimaced. "You sound like Indy." He swallowed as memories flooded him. "He told me I should quit too, go back to college to get my psychology degree."

Josh smiled. "He called that one right."

"He usually did. He wasn't wrong often, you know."

"So what's keeping you?"

"I hate to say it, Josh, because I don't want you to feel guilty, but what will we live off of?"

Josh slowly sat up on the bed. "This house is paid for, Noah, and we have the profits from the sale of the house. We can live off that, combined with our mutual savings. And it's not much, my disability benefits, but it's a little. In time, I can find a job."

"Do you really want to stay here, live in the house Connor bought for you?" Noah asked. "Wouldn't that remind you every day of him, of what you've lost?"

He hadn't dared to ask Josh before, not even when they were moving into this place. It was a beautiful ranch and incredibly practical for Noah, but he couldn't imagine staying here if he were Josh.

"No. It will remind me of being loved. I love this place, Noah, and it's so much easier for you to navigate."

Noah pushed himself up as well, leaning against the headboard. Was he really considering it? The thought of not having to go back to the hospital opened up something in his chest. Relief.

"I can't just up and leave."

Josh smiled slowly. "Why the hell not? Come on, don't you think Owens sees this coming? He knows how hard this job is on you mentally and physically. He'll handwrite you a letter of recommendation. You know he never wanted you suspended or fired."

Noah's face broke open as well. It was the first time he'd smiled since Indy had left. "Are we really doing this?"

Josh scooted over, leaning his head against Noah's shoulder. "No, you are. You are doing this, Noah."

Noah's smile faltered. He swallowed. "Do you think he'll ever come back?"

"I have no doubt. He loves you so much."

"Us. He loves us."

"Yeah, he does. He'll come back as soon as he can. I know he will."

"It hurts so fucking much," Noah said, his voice breaking. "And the truth is that I can't even be mad at him. He did it to protect me, to protect us. I get that and I can't argue with it. But I miss him so much. It's like somebody turned off the light, and all that's left is empty darkness."

He buried his head in his hands, fighting to keep the tears at bay. Crying was senseless, and it didn't make him feel better. Nothing made him feel better anymore.

Josh pulled him close and Noah surrendered, putting his head on Josh's lap, only a sheet between them. He wrapped his arms around Josh's waist, finding comfort in the familiar feel and smell of his best friend. Josh softly stroked his hair while Noah snuggled close, calmed down his erratic breathing. It took a few minutes before the sensation of the hardening cock under him registered.

He turned his head, seeking Josh's eyes. "Josh," he said.

"I can't help it," Josh said, but there was no apology in his eyes, nor his voice. "My body is still programmed to respond to you, Noah."

Noah turned his head back and rubbed his cheek

against Josh's cock, the sheet still between them. "Do you still want me?" he asked hoarsely.

"I don't think I will ever stop wanting you."

Noah rested his hand on Josh's cock, which grew harder and harder. "What about Connor?" he asked, putting pressure on his hand.

Josh lifted his hips ever so slightly, pushing against Noah's hand. "You know the rule, Noah: you have to ask. What are you asking me?"

He wanted to feel better, if only for a minute. But he could never go back to the egotistical asshole he'd been with Josh before. He didn't want to use him. It had to be equal, this time. No guilt. No pressure. Simply two best friends, loving each other the best they could.

"Will you let me fuck you, Josh?"

It HAD BEEN inevitable they'd end up this way. Him and Noah, together again. Connor had known too, otherwise he would've never given Josh permission so explicitly. It freed him from guilt, knowing that he could say yes without fearing Connor's anger. But he wasn't the same Josh he'd been when Noah and he had started this. He needed more. Deserved more.

He met Noah's eyes, knew Noah could read him like a book. "Will you make it good for me too, Noah? Give me what I need?"

"Tell me what to do, Josh. We'll take care of each other, as we always have."

He needed it, the pain, the pleasure, the release. The tension in his body and mind had been slowly increasing. He'd fought it hard, but he'd almost reached his limits. And when that call came, he needed to be ready. Plus, Noah had reached his limits, too. Josh had never seen him so dark, so lifeless. He'd do anything to keep him from sinking in deeper.

"I need you to use me. You've seen what Connor does. I need that. Boss me around. Don't ask, take. Fuck me as hard as you can, as many times as you can, and order me not to come until you're done."

"I can't read you like Connor can. How will I know when you've reached your limit?"

Hmm, he had a good point. Connor had this instinctive knowledge of Josh's needs and limits but Noah didn't. Besides, he wasn't the natural Dom Connor was.

"We'll use a safe word. Red Sox. That's our safe word, Red Sox."

Noah nodded. "Okay, that will work." He furrowed his brow. "Do you want me to spank you?"

Josh smiled, touched that Noah had offered. "Could you? It would help me, but I know it's not your thing."

"No, but it's yours. If that's what you need, I'll do it."

"Use your hand, not the paddle. I'll use the safe word if it gets too much. And Noah, remember that for me, that's not pain. It's pleasure, release. You're not hurting me, okay?"

"Okay."

They looked at each other, and Josh grinned. "Things have changed, huh?"

Noah smiled back. "We're sure as fuck not in Kansas anymore. You ready for this?"

"Fuck, yeah. Bring it on."

Noah seemed to hesitate for a second on how to progress, and Josh couldn't blame him. They couldn't fall back on their previous pattern of Josh taking care of Noah and Noah making sure Josh came first. No, they were equals now, Josh needing Noah as much as the other way around.

Noah sat up against the headboard and whipped the sheets off of him to reveal his hard cock. His hand shot out, grabbing Josh's head, pulling him down. A rush of adrenaline hummed through Josh's veins. Fuck, yes.

"I've missed your sweet mouth on my cock, Josh, so why don't you start by sucking me off?"

Noah pulled him down on his cock, not too gently—which was exactly what Josh had hoped for. He gave an experimental lick over Noah's crown. Familiar salty sensations tickled his tongue as Noah moaned. Josh turned to his stomach and nibbled his way down Noah's cock till he reached the base. He teased with his tongue, lapping Noah's balls, sucking gently.

Noah had one advantage over Connor. Because his cock was smaller, Josh could take him in way deeper. And since he'd been practicing with Connor's beast, he was pretty damn sure he'd be able to take Noah in all the way. He shifted till he had the right angle, teasing Noah with soft kisses and little nips.

Noah moved, undoubtedly getting impatient. Noah's hands came around his head, pulling him down. Josh opened his mouth and took him in as deep as he could, then relaxed his throat and took him deeper still. Noah's hips bucked, and his balls hit Josh's chin.

"Uhhhh," Noah groaned. "Fucking hell, you're so damn good at this."

He kept still, but Josh wanted him to move. He brought his hands to Noah's hips, pulled until Noah got the hint and thrust into his mouth. Josh relaxed around his cock, sucking as hard as he could.

"You like that huh?" Noah said, his voice low. "You like

me fucking your mouth. Look at you, your whole mouth stuffed with cock."

Josh's eyes watered, and Noah pulled back to allow him to breathe and swallow. His eyes were focused on Josh, and as soon as Josh had breathed a few times, he shoved his cock right back in. Josh gagged, but Noah didn't pull back, simply waited till he'd relaxed again.

"I'm close to coming, and you damn well better not spill a drop. If I spot one drip of cum outside your mouth, I'll have to punish you."

Josh almost smiled, except his mouth was full of cock. Noah still needed a reason to spank him, whereas Connor would simply do it, knowing Josh craved it. Josh would make sure to spill. He couldn't wait to feel Noah's hands on his ass.

Noah fucked his mouth hard, unrelentingly, and Josh loved every second of it. This sensation of being used, being taken—there was nothing like it. Noah grunted and tensed up. He gave one last hard thrust, then came hard down Josh's throat. Josh swallowed the first load but let the second stream dribble out of his mouth where it dripped down his chin onto the sheets. He released Noah's cock and licked his lips.

"Oops," he said, smiling deviously.

Noah grinned. "Oops, my ass," he said. "You're gonna regret this, Joshua."

He yanked him down by his arm, splayed him across his legs and his hand came down hard before Josh could even utter a word. Fucking hell, that stung. The second slap brought tears to his eyes. He'd underestimated the strength Noah had in his upper body and especially his hands. If he continued like this, Josh wouldn't be able to sit tomorrow. Noah smacked him again, the sound echoing through the bedroom.

Josh gasped, breathing away the burning sensation in his ass. Thank fuck Noah stopped for a little bit, moving underneath him to reach for something... What was he getting? Josh barely had time to wonder, because seconds later cold lube drizzled in his crack, followed by two fingers that shoved in unceremoniously. His initial curse transitioned into a moan as those fingers started sliding in and out. He pushed his ass back and was rewarded with a vicious slap to his right butt cheek. Dammit, had the fucker taken lessons from Connor?

Noah's fingers resumed their rhythm until they were in as far as they could be. Noah's middle finger curled, finding that spot inside of him that made him want to beg to be fucked. He managed to hold himself in check for all of three seconds before his body moved all by itself. This time, he knew what was coming and braced himself. Yup, his left cheek got the same treatment.

"Fuck, Josh, your ass is fiery red. That has got to sting."

Damn right, it did. It throbbed every time Noah moved his fingers. Josh canted his hips, seeking friction for his cock that was pressed against Noah's leg. Two slaps convinced him that was not a good idea. Noah meant business. Thank fuck.

A third finger was added, creating a burn inside his ass in addition to the heat coming off his cheeks. He hoped this meant Noah was getting him ready to be fucked, because he needed it. He wanted nothing more than cock up his ass, and since the Beast was unavailable, Noah would have to do.

The fingers pulled out. Josh exhaled, braced himself for being flipped, because Noah couldn't fuck him in this position. Instead, a cold rubber hardness pushed against his ass and he opened up by instinct.

Huh. A massager. A small one, by the feel of it. Why the

fuck would Noah use that? Maybe he wanted to tease him a little?

"You know the rules, Josh. Don't you dare come."

He wanted to answer there was no chance in hell he'd come with that tiny thing up his ass, unless Noah aimed it directly at his prostate. Before he could open his mouth, Noah turned it on. Josh figured it'd be polite to let him at least try, so he swallowed back his comment. It was...pleasant, this nice little buzz in his ass. Not overwhelming, but nice.

Noah slapped his ass again, softer this time. Then again. And again. Josh shifted as his ass started to hum. Hmm, this felt good. Noah adjusted the setting on the vibrator, letting it vibrate a tad stronger. His slaps came down steadily now, not so hard Josh couldn't take it, but enough to get his attention. His body responded, hummed and throbbed, wanting more. Josh shifted again, his cock hard as granite.

Sweat pearled on his forehead as the tension in his body started to build. His balls tightened, weighing heavy. No, he couldn't come. Not yet. Not until Noah told him he could.

Noah moved underneath him, changing position. His right hand pulled out the vibrator and shoved it back in, while the left kept spanking Josh in a steady rhythm. He was gonna wear him down. Dammit, this assault on multiple levels was getting to him, the pain and pleasure entwining till he was gasping for breath. Josh fought back the wave of desire rolling through him, but a moan slipped through his lips.

Noah chuckled. "Hang in there, Josh. I'm not done yet. Ready for the next phase?"

The massager was yanked out of him, eliciting a groan of protest. This time, Noah's hands did lift him up and turned him. "On your hands and knees."

He scrambled up. Noah's hands dug into his hips as he slammed deep in one powerful stroke, bottoming out so hard his balls slapped against Josh's ass.

"Fuck," Josh grunted through clenched teeth.

"I'm about to," Noah quipped.

He pulled out and surged back, clutching Josh's hips. Damn, Noah's cock was hard as steel, pulsing inside him. Josh lowered his arms and pushed his ass back in a wordless invitation. More. Harder.

Noah thrust in again with even more force, making Josh fist the bed to keep himself from moving. His breath whooshed out every time Noah plunged into him. He cried out when Noah hit his prostate, which only seemed to encourage him more.

He'd never fucked Josh this hard, this deep, this raw. Josh's body was completely alive, throbbing, burning, wanting. He was so close to reaching that high, he could touch it. All he needed was...

Noah let out a roar, unloading in his ass. Tears sprang to Josh's eyes. Dammit, he'd been so close, almost there. There was no way Noah would have the stamina for a third round. Josh would come if Noah ordered him to, but it wasn't the orgasm he craved. It was the pain-pleasure high, that state that made him forget everything. He'd been so fucking close.

Noah kept moving, however, creating obscene slick sounds as he fucked the cum out of Josh's ass till it dripped down his legs. He thrust in deep and stopped. Josh felt him moving. What was he doing? Then the pressure on his ass increased as something else demanded to be let in. Wait, what? Was he...?

He bore down, and Noah slid in the dildo next to his own cock. Josh bit down hard as the burning in his ass was tripled. Aided by his own cum and the slick dildo, Noah buried the thing in Josh's ass, snug against his own cock. Josh grunted. So full. Oh, fuck. It was even more than the Beast. Harder. Tighter. It stretched and burned until his inner canal adjusted.

Then Noah started fucking, his cock and the dildo moving at the same time. Their moans mingled, became one. Josh panted, moaned again, then surrendered to his body, the pain and pleasure lifting him higher and higher. Noah impaled him on his monster cock, fucking him over and over till nothing else existed but the pleasure building inside Josh.

His knees gave out, but Noah dragged him up, holding him with a bruising grip as he kept on hammering hard and deep. Every muscle tightened and small electric shocks danced over his skin. He opened up completely, gave up the last bit of fight he had left in him. He was Noah's, to do with as he pleased. Time stood still as Noah fucked and fucked—finally coming with an inhuman cry of relief.

Josh still hadn't come, his body and mind waiting for the words that would allow him to let go.

"Dammit, Joshua, come for me."

17

It had been the longest car ride of Indy's life. Albany to Buffalo. Change cars. Buffalo to Columbus. Hotel. Change cars. Columbus to St. Louis. Change cars. St. Louis to Kansas City. Hotel. Change cars. Then they'd traveled to some bumfuck town—if you could even call it that—smack dab in the middle of nowhere, Kansas. Welcome home.

Home was an old farm, bright red amidst endless fields. Some had been harvested, others stood brown and decaying. It had been wheat, or corn, maybe? Indy knew shit about farming.

The house was so isolated you could spot visitors from far away, which was good, Indy supposed. There was only one road leading to and from the farm. The farm itself consisted of several buildings. The main house had five bedrooms and Indy's was on the second floor. Then there was a horse barn, minus the horses, another barn that housed all kinds of farming equipment and tools, several sheds and storage barns, and even a huge former chicken coop. Close to the farm was a water tower overlooking a natural pond. It was as idyllic as could be, yet Indy was going absolutely stir-crazy.

He'd barely spoken a word during the ride, too tired to even bother trying to make conversation. Too hurt as well. His heart had been aching, knowing every mile was bringing him farther away from Noah and Josh. Besides, why would he try and be polite? They'd already told him these agents weren't gonna stay anyways. The agents who had traveled with him had left the day after arriving, leaving in place four agents to guard Indy twenty-four seven. Three men, one woman.

Leticia Nunez, the woman, was nice enough. She was spunky and had a great sense of humor. Plus, the woman could cook. In the almost six weeks that Indy had been there, she'd whipped up more than one Mexican dish that had made Indy's mouth water.

Then there was Jim Crouch, an older guy, who was the lead agent on this operation. Aloof but professional, Crouch tolerated Indy's presence but made little effort to get to know him.

Robin Fisher was agent number three: a cocky, Ivy League educated asshole that felt a Boston lowlife like Stephan Moreau was way beneath his dignity. Or maybe he objected to the fact that Indy was gay, who the fuck knew. Fact was, Fisher was not happy about this assignment, and it showed. Indy had flat-out refused to answer when Fisher called him Stephan, until the guy had gotten the message.

Even then, Fisher had needed a little persuading from the last agent on the job: Miles Hampton. Indy sighed as he thought of Miles. Tall, fit, and as masculine as they came, he reminded Indy of Noah. Same stubbornness, equal amounts of bossiness and arrogance. Plus, he simply wouldn't leave Indy alone.

The big difference between Noah and Miles was that Miles was one hundred percent gay. Openly, brazenly gay. Which pissed off Fisher but seemed to amuse Nunez and Crouch. He was one of the first openly gay agents, Miles had told Indy, and he was determined not to take any crap for it. Good for him, Indy supposed. It couldn't be easy in an alpha job like that to put yourself out there.

He'd explored every building on the farm, wanting to know where he could hide, in case it became necessary. Call him paranoid, but he didn't think the Fitzpatricks were done looking for him. If they found out he was gonna testify, he'd become their number one enemy. That contract on his head? It would change to dead or alive. Preferably dead.

So he'd taken his precautions, had done what he could in case disaster ever came knocking. Knowing his luck so far, it would at some point. At least he'd have several escape routes and options.

Today, Indy had found a spot on a dilapidated wooden bench against the back side of the main house, enjoying the sunshine and being outside. He hadn't had much of that in the previous months, too scared of being recognized. It was bright and sunny, if still chilly with the temperature hovering in the high forties, which Indy had found out was normal for mid-March. Kansas didn't get the massive snow dumps he'd become accustomed to in Boston.

He'd never thought he'd miss Boston, but he did. St. Patrick's Day had come and gone two days ago, and he'd missed the crazy green antics it brought. The parade, most of all, but also the outrageous outfits and the celebrations. Would there ever come a day when it would be safe for him to return home? Home to Noah and Josh, but also home to Boston?

He raised his head to the sun, closing his eyes. It was nice out, if you were sheltered from the wind.

"What are you doing?" Miles' voice interrupted Indy's thoughts.

"Nothing. Soaking up some sunlight," Indy said.

Miles sat down next to him and Indy sighed. The agent shot him a grin. "Two seconds and you're already sighing. Must be a record."

Indy rolled his eyes. "You could ask, you know, if I wanted company."

"True. But asking means risking the chance of you saying no. Plus, why would you not want to spend time with me? I'm awesome, you know."

This, in a nutshell, was the problem with Miles Hampton. As hard as you tried, you could not get angry with him. He had a confidence and a happiness that was pretty damn irresistible. The constant joy he exuded was another huge difference between him and Noah.

"You're so full of it," Indy said, but there was no anger behind his words.

"You love me, and you know it," Miles joked. His arm shot out for a playful bump, but Indy's body reacted faster than his brain could process it was not an attack. He blocked Miles' hand, twisted it until the agent had to bend with the move to prevent his arm from being broken. He cried out, more in surprise than pain, but it registered with Indy, and he let go.

"Don't touch me," Indy said lamely, cringing.

Miles rubbed his hand and sat up again. "That's some fast reflexes you've got there," he said. There was no anger in his voice, and Indy let out a breath he'd been holding.

"I don't like to be touched," Indy said.

"I know. I'm sorry. I wasn't thinking."

Indy turned his head, looked at him sideways. "You know?"

"Sure. Wasn't hard to spot. Every time I even come close to you your defenses go up. I'm sorry, I didn't mean to startle you."

He was so open about it that Indy had no doubt he meant it. "It's okay."

"Where'd you learn to move like that?" Miles asked.

Indy shrugged. "Jiujitsu."

Miles eyebrows went up. "Really? Cool. I practice jiujitsu, too. Are you any good?"

Indy smiled. "I'm fairly decent. Why?"

"I've been dying for a good grapple. Wanna try if you can take me down?" Indy bit back his laugh. The guy had no idea what he was getting into.

Five minutes later, they were outside on the pathetic excuse for grass, dressed in training pants and T-shirts. Miles had spray-painted a circle on the grass. Even Nunez and Fisher had come outside to watch. Crouch was still asleep, having done the night shift last night.

"I'll take it easy on you," Miles said.

Indy sent him a cocky grin. "Don't."

It took him less than ten seconds in the first round. Miles was flat on his back before he realized what had happened, Indy's knee on his throat.

"What the fuck?" the agent sputtered.

Indy rose and extended a hand to pull him up. "Wanna try again?"

Embarrassment colored Miles' cheeks. "Damn right." His eyes narrowed. "Fairly decent, huh?"

Indy shrugged. "Let's go."

To his credit, Miles went all-in this time, trying much

harder than the first round. That was the reason it took Indy almost thirty seconds to pin him.

Nunez laughed and applauded. "This is entertaining."

Indy got up again, smiling in quiet triumph as he pulled Miles to his feet. The guy towered over him. He had to be at least two inches taller than Noah was. His smile faded. Fuck, he missed him.

"One faggot kicking another faggot's ass," Fisher sneered.

Miles' eyes narrowed, and Indy caught a flash of anger before he composed himself again. "Yeah, and both of these faggots can kick your ass," he said.

Indy admired that in him. He had self-control where it concerned Fisher and his nasty homophobic remarks. Indy would've smacked him black and blue by now, but Miles kept his temper in check.

"Pff," Fisher said. "Sure, in a match like this one, where you have to follow the rules of some silly sport. In real life, neither of you would stand a chance."

Indy put a hand on Miles' arm, the first time he'd touched him of his own volition. I got this, he signaled. Miles seemed to jolt in surprise at Indy's touch. Was he averse to being touched as well? Indy shook his head mentally and refocused on Fisher.

"You sure about that?" Indy asked him, the challenge clear. Fuck, he was itching to take this asshole down a peg or two. Preferably all the way down to the bottom where he belonged.

"Kid, I wouldn't do that to you. I boxed at Harvard, you know. It wouldn't be fair."

"I don't mind," Indy said.

"You're half my size."

"Don't worry about me. I can take it."

"You're our protectée. It wouldn't be right to cause any damage."

"You have my permission. Besides, Nunez can be the ref, call it off when she thinks it's getting out of hand."

Nunez hesitated for a second, then nodded.

"No rules, except we stay inside the circle," Fisher stated.

"No rules," Indy agreed amicably. This fucker was so going down. "Get changed."

Fisher walked off, a nasty smile on his face. As soon as he was gone, Miles turned to Indy, concern painting his face. "Are you sure about this? He wasn't kidding about boxing. Apparently, he was quite good at it."

Indy smiled. "Boxing is all rules. Even if he excelled at kickboxing, it would still be limited to the moves he learned there. Besides, he's arrogant as shit, convinced he'll win. That alone will make him lose."

"How fairly decent are you at this?"

"Brown belt. One exam away from black." Miles whistled through his teeth. "Trust me, Miles. I got this."

Nunez stepped close. "Indy, one thing. Don't make the same mistake Fisher is. He's not only arrogant, he's also a mean, cheating son of a bitch. He'll do whatever he has to in order to win."

Indy nodded. She was right. He shouldn't be overconfident.

Fisher came back, changed into shorts and a shirt. Indy took his place opposite him in the circle, crouching low, arms in front of his face. As soon as Nunez gave the signal, Fisher's foot shot out. Indy barely managed to evade it. Kickboxing it was, then.

He pivoted, ducked when Fisher's foot came at him again. The guy had the advantage of height. And speed. Fuck, he was fast, dancing around Indy. Indy spun around and half-blocked the fist coming at him. It still hit his cheek, stunning him for a second. Dammit, that hurt.

Fisher kept coming at him with punches and kicks. Indy blocked, but a few slipped through. He took a kick to his ribs that made him gasp.

Down. He had to take this to the floor, where Fisher couldn't move.

The next time Fisher kicked, Indy was ready. He caught his foot, twisted it, and dropped himself on top of Fisher with force. The agent went down with a grunt, wildly kicking with arms and legs. But this was what Indy knew, where he was at his best. This was where size and weight didn't mean shit. Fisher shoved his hand in Indy's face, but he grabbed it and pinned it down. He clamped the guys' legs with his own, blocking his moves.

The agent headbutted him, but that was a move Indy saw coming, since his head was the only thing the guy could still move. So he released him suddenly, causing him to lose his balance and topple over. Now he had his back turned toward Indy. Big mistake. Indy was on his back in a flash, clamping him like a little monkey. A monkey who had him in a chokehold.

"You have about five seconds till you lose consciousness," Indy snapped at him. "Do you call defeat?"

Fisher clawed at his face, but Indy ducked, pinned one of his arms down with his free arm.

"Three more seconds."

He jerked and attempted to move his legs, but they were pinned by Indy's legs.

"Defeat." Fisher's voice was barely audible.

Indy released the pressure on his throat but waited to let go of the man's arms and legs until he was completely still. When he felt Fisher's body relax, he let go.

He inched back as Fisher turned on his back, panting. Indy's eyes never left the man, remembering Nunez's warning. He felt more than he saw Fisher tighten again, whipping out a foot that would have broken his jaw, had he not been ready. He caught it in a blinding fast move, shot out his own foot and connected with Fisher's groin.

The man wailed in pain, curling up into a ball.

"Fucker," Indy mumbled. He touched his throbbing lip, coming away with blood on his fingers. "Shoulda choked him when I had the chance."

A hand reached out, and he almost kicked it away but realized in time it was Miles, offering to help him up. He grabbed it, wincing as he put pressure on his ribs. Fisher had gotten a good kick in there.

"You okay?" Nunez asked, concern dripping from her voice.

"Yeah. You were right. He is a cheating son of a bitch."

"Well, he got what was coming to him," Nunez said. "I'll get some ice for your face."

"I'll do it," Miles said. "You'd better stay with Fisher. If you leave me here, he's bound to get another kick in his nuts. Or his ribs. Fucking asshole. Come on, Indy."

Indy followed him inside. Miles went into his own room, and Indy hesitated. "Come on in," Miles called out. "I've got a first aid kit here, including an ice pack."

Indy stepped inside the room, which looked like a bomb had gone off. Clothes were thrown everywhere, mixed in with empty chip bags, candy wrappers, and whatnot.

"Yeah. Sorry. I'm a slob," Miles said, wincing. He swiped a heap of clothes off his bed, ruthlessly sending them to the floor. "Here, sit down."

Indy lowered himself to the bed, grimacing as another stab of pain radiated from his ribs. It wasn't as bad as when he'd taken down Josh during the robbery, but it would be tender for a few days, that much was certain. Miles walked into the bathroom and came back with a wet wash cloth.

He reached out to Indy, then stopped. "Can I touch you?"

The similarities to Noah were eerie. Indy nodded. Miles cleaned his lip, the washcloth turning red with blood. He broke a cooling gel pack, making it freeze. "Here, put that on your lip."

Indy obeyed, sighing as the cold pack took away some of the throbbing.

"Can I check your ribs?" Miles asked.

"You a doctor?" Indy asked, half-joking.

"My degree is in psychology, but I'm a certified EMT. Worked as an EMT all through college and grad school."

Hot damn. Now Indy had no reason to refuse, did he? Other than that it made him uncomfortable, it was way too intimate, and he fucking wanted Noah. Noah should be here to check him out and take care of him. He closed his eyes, fighting back the sadness.

"Indy?"

"Yeah. Whatever. Don't touch me, though."

He pulled up his shirt, making sure Miles could only see the front. There was no way he was showing him the scars on his back. "There's a visible red spot where he kicked you. I'd need to touch you to feel if it's broken."

"It's not," Indy said. "And your hands aren't getting anywhere near me." He pulled down his shirt again.

"How would you know? You a doctor?" Miles mocked him.

Indy's eyes rose to meet his. "No, but my boyfriend is. Now, fuck off. I'm fine."

He got up, wavering as a spell of dizziness hit him. Miles

shot to his side, keeping him from toppling over. Indy froze as he was pressed against a hard body.

Hard. It registered immediately. Miles was sporting a fucking boner.

Indy pushed him away, stumbling and almost falling again. "What the hell?"

Miles winced. "It's not what you think."

Indy's eyes flashed. "Are you fucking hard?" He pointed to Miles' crotch. "Then it's exactly what I think."

Miles stepped back, his face flushed. "I'm sorry. But I swear, not for the reason you think."

"Don't ever fucking touch me again," Indy snapped.

He walked out, straight into his own room, locking the door behind him. Hot damn, even here he wasn't safe. He laid down on his bed, closing his eyes when hot tears threatened to escape. How was he supposed to do this for months, a year even? He was so fucking alone. He wanted Noah, needed to feel safe and loved. Instead, he got a cheating, homophobic asshole and a horny fucker who thought it was okay to hit on him.

Though, technically, Miles hadn't hit on him. He'd sought out Indy's company since they'd arrived here, but he'd never touched him. In fact, if he hadn't held up Indy and inadvertently given himself away, Indy would have never found out. Still, it was awkward as fuck, right?

Indy guessed the agent to be in his early thirties, which made him at least ten, twelve years older than Indy was. That alone should make Indy off-limits—though Noah and Josh were older than him as well. Objectively speaking, Miles was good looking. He was from California, and he still had that blond, tanned surfer look. His hair was a tad too long, giving him that careless attitude that fit him well. Still,

Indy wasn't interested. At all. Which Miles should have respected.

What the hell had he meant when he said it wasn't what it looked like? A boner could only mean one thing, couldn't it? Indy bit his lip. If it was so obvious, why had Miles insisted it was something else?

Oh, fuck it. He'd give the man a chance to explain. If he didn't like it, he could still kick his ass.

Indy went back to Miles' room and walked in without knocking. Miles wasn't in his room, and Indy was about to leave when he heard a noise from the bathroom. It took him a few seconds to identify it. Miles was jerking off. Frantically, judging by the sounds. Definitely not something Indy wanted to hear. The sounds stopped, and Indy heard Miles moan.

Okay, then. Talk about awkward.

In the bathroom, Miles cursed. Seconds later it sounded like he hit the wall. Hard. What the hell was going on? Despite every urge to run, Indy stayed. The faucet ran inside the bathroom. At least he was strict on hygiene, Indy thought wryly.

The bathroom door opened, and Miles walked back into the room, tucking his cock in his pants, his face tight with anger. When he spotted Indy, that anger transformed into deep embarrassment. He released his hands.

"Fuck, Indy... I guess you heard me... Yeah, sorry. Again."

Something was off. This was about more than having a hard-on for a guy you weren't supposed to be attracted to.

Indy took the ice pack off his lip for a second. "You said it wasn't what it looked like. Explain."

Miles studied him. "Can I trust you?" he finally said.

Indy harrumphed. "You're talking to the guy who's never trusted another soul in his life, until recently."

Miles gestured. "Mind if I close the door? This is not something I want to share with the others."

"Yeah. But keep your distance."

Miles nodded and closed the door. Indy sat down on the bed, in the cleared-out spot he'd been in earlier. Miles kept his word, taking position against the wall. "I apologize in advance for any embarrassment this may cause you," he said.

Indy raised his eyebrows. "Dude, I lived with Boston's biggest crime boss for years. Nothing embarrasses me. Trust me, I've seen it all."

Miles seemed to be comforted by that. "I have a condition," he said softly. "I have an unusual libido. For some reason, my body responds to every little stimulus. I'm hard half the time."

Indy's eyes dropped down, eyeing Miles' crotch.

"Yes, I'm hard right now. And I jerked off not two minutes ago, as you heard. That was my fourth orgasm of today, by the way. As I said, it's embarrassing."

Indy forced himself to look at Miles' eyes. He was watching Indy warily as if he expected him to walk out any second now. "Sounds like a fucking nuisance," Indy said.

"Yes. Hell, yes. It is." Relief at Indy's reaction colored Miles' voice.

"What helps?" Indy asked, genuinely curious.

Miles sighed. "Fucking. Actual, hard fucking. That holds me off for a few hours at least. But that's kinda impossible when I'm on the job. One-night stands aren't doable on an assignment like this, and as a federal agent I have to be extra careful."

"Why?"

"People who know I'm an agent could try to use a one-night stand to get leverage against me. Blackmail," he added, when Indy frowned.

That made sense. "No boyfriend for you, then?" Indy asked.

"I've tried. Turns out, the novelty of having a constantly horny boyfriend wears off fast. He broke up with me."

"Aren't there any meds?"

"None that come without serious side effects. Taking hormones could help, but they affect more than your libido."

"Damn," Indy said.

"Yeah, well, now you know. It's nothing personal, Indy, and I hope you're not offended. It's been a long month, and I'm really fucking horny, and you're not exactly ugly, so, yeah."

Indy snickered. "You're such a smooth talker, Miles. Seriously. I wonder how anyone could resist you."

Miles sent out a hesitant smile. "You're not angry?"

"No. I appreciate you explaining. But Miles, I'm dead serious when I say I'm not interested. You're a nice guy and all, but I have a boyfriend."

"I know. Two, if the file on you is correct."

Indy grinned. "You guys keeping tabs on my love life now?"

"It did make for salacious reading material," Miles joked. "Is it true?"

"What, that I have two boyfriends? No, it's not true. Noah is my boyfriend, Josh is... I don't know what he is. A friend with benefits, maybe? Whatever. He's like my best friend and soul mate, with a sexual spark thrown in. But he has a boyfriend, too."

"Had."

Indy frowned. What was Miles talking about? "What do

you mean, had? We're talking about O'Connor, right? The Albany PD cop?"

Miles looked uncomfortable now. "Shit. I shouldn't have said anything. Pretty sure you weren't supposed to know."

Indy rose. "You'd better start talking right now. What the hell happened?"

"He broke up with Josh, according to our intel. Same day you left. Quit his job and moved back to Boston."

Indy's eyes went big. "Boston? No fucking way."

"Yeah. We kept an eye on him for the first two weeks, but he told us to get lost. Said he was fine, didn't want protection anymore. A police informant told the Boston PD he's recruiting."

"Recruiting? For what?"

"They don't know. Some kind of job. Indy, I hate to say it, but are you sure he wasn't behind the attack? He is a Fitzpatrick."

Indy clamped down hard to prevent himself from blurting out what he knew about Connor and his family. He might like Miles, but he didn't trust him. There was no way that Connor had broken up with Josh, and even less chance he'd gone bad. Connor's love for Josh was real and pure, his devotion to Josh so complete he'd even been willing to accept Noah's and Indy's more-than-casual relationship with the love of his life.

If Connor was in Boston—and considering the FBI's resources, Indy was willing to accept the truth of that— there was a reason for it. A reason that undoubtedly had everything to do with the Fitzpatricks but not in the way Miles was suggesting. Whatever Connor had planned, he did not need the FBI fucking things up.

"I know nothing anymore. I've wondered how they knew

to find me, but I never could figure it out. If it was Connor, it would explain a lot."

What else did the FBI know? Miles looked like he knew more, but he wasn't saying anything. Indy could make an educated guess, though. Probably something about Noah and Josh. Together. A fact that Miles expected Indy to be devastated over, but he wasn't.

He'd known they would gravitate toward each other, had only hoped Connor would allow it. Josh wouldn't be able to stand seeing Noah down and depressed, would've stepped in to make him feel better. Apparently, with Connor gone for whatever reason, he had. It didn't make Indy mad or even jealous. It only made him sad, because he would give anything to be with them right now. Anything.

18

His puppy had proven to be a hell of a lot more stubborn than Blake had given him credit for. He'd been gone for three weeks now, and he wasn't showing any signs of coming back. Blake sighed as he reread Aaron's last message.

Aaron: *I've been working so I'm good on money but thank you. How's the PT going?*

He'd offered Aaron money—again. But Aaron had turned it down—again. He'd expected no differently, but at least this time Aaron had volunteered he had a job, so Blake considered that progress. He still messaged him at least once every hour, and while Aaron had read his messages almost immediately at first, he'd rarely replied. The last few days Aaron had started to respond to things, which Blake considered a good sign.

Blake: *Good. I'm cleared for light exercise. No BJJ yet, obviously.*

Aaron: *Oh, good. That must make you happy. Be careful.*

Blake: *I will, puppy. Are you getting any exercise in?*

Aaron: *I run every other day, 5k at least.*

Blake frowned. If he was getting runs in, he wasn't anywhere near the northeast. They'd gotten slammed with a nor'easter a few days ago, and the sidewalks still weren't cleared. He'd been worried about Aaron, but Aaron hadn't responded to specific questions about the weather. But if it was good enough to run, he had to have gone south. South of Maryland at least, since the whole northeastern coast had gotten hit.

Blake: *I'm so proud of you! God, I miss you.*

He made sure to text that at least once a day, but usually more often. It wasn't a lie. He'd never expected to become so attached to someone he'd known for such a short time, but he was. His arms, his bed, his life felt empty and cold without Aaron. He hadn't fully appreciated the joy and contentment Aaron's presence brought until he was gone. He sighed, an all-too-familiar ache spreading from his heart throughout his body. *I didn't know how much of my heart you'd conquered, puppy.*

His phone dinged in his hand. A new text from Aaron.

Aaron: *I miss you too.*

Blake's heart jumped up. Aaron missed him. It was the first time Aaron had shown any emotion in his texts, and a warm feeling radiated from his belly. Thank fuck.

He almost dropped his phone when it rang. Huh. What could Josh want?

"Hi, Josh," he answered.

"Hey. I was trying to reach Aaron, but he's not answering his phone."

Blake fought back a swell of irritation. Josh didn't even know Aaron had left. "Listen, I understand things must be hard for you with Connor and Indy gone, but if you had bothered to show any interest in your brother, you would have known he's gone."

Okay, so his tone wasn't exactly friendly, but this was the best he could do right now.

"You don't under... What do you mean, he's gone?"

Was that honest-to-God worry in Josh's voice? "He left me. He's gone south, I think."

"You think? Are you telling me you don't even know where he is?"

Yup, definitely worry. "He won't tell me. He's not taking my calls either, but he's responding to texts."

"What the fuck happened?"

"I guess he got tired of people treating him like crap. My brothers, they didn't exactly warm up to him, and I didn't do enough to stop it. That's on me. But what you and Noah did, that sure as hell didn't help, either. Dammit, Josh, he was waiting for you to call him, to lean on him. He wanted to be there for you, but you didn't let him. He's so fucking lost, and we failed him."

It took a while before Josh answered. "I know. Fuck, I know, Blake. It's just... I've been hating him for so long that it's hard to switch it off. I haven't figured it all out, and with everything that's happened I can't find the mental peace to work through it."

"He needs you, Josh. He needs to know that you want in him in your life. He feels like nobody truly wants him, not even me."

"God, Blake...I'm... I was calling him to tell him I'm not gonna be here for a few weeks. I'm being admitted to a VA mental facility. The shooting has triggered my PTSD, and I'm not doing well."

Fucking hell. Now Blake felt like a total asshole for going off against Josh. "I'm sorry, man. And I'm sorry for getting angry with you when you clearly have enough on your plate."

Josh sighed. "No, you were right. I should've reached out to him."

"Can he visit you?"

"No. I'm going to a closed ward. No outside contact."

There was an edge to his voice, and Blake didn't need to ask what Josh was worried about. "I can check in on Noah, if you want me to. And if he'll let me."

"I feel like a total asshole asking you that, after what you told me about Aaron. But Noah is not doing well. He's... depressed. Dark. He's putting up a front for me because he's worried sick I'll crack, but he's not good. He quit his job to go get a degree in psychology, but he's home a lot since it's a low-residency program, and it's not good for him."

"Will he allow me to be there for him?"

Josh sighed. "Probably not. Dammit. I don't know what else to do."

Blake's head was racing with thoughts. What could he do to make Noah accept help? It had to look like he was helping someone instead of the other way around. Noah had a strong urge to jump in and help people in need, much like Blake himself.

Suddenly he had an idea. "Josh, what about someone temporarily moving in with him? My brother Brad is renting a duplex, but the owner just told him he has to move out for at least three weeks because of a leaking roof. They wanna do some remodeling while they fix the roof. He has nowhere to go since my house is full at the moment. What if he moves in with Noah temporarily? He works, but he's a teacher, so relatively short days. He could be there for him. He would bring his dog, though, but we're talking about a sweet, old Lab mix who spends most of his days sleeping on Brad's bed."

"That could work," Josh said slowly. "If I present it to

him as Brad having nowhere else to go. The dog certainly wouldn't be an issue. But Blake, and I mean no offense, you need to tell Brad to keep his hands off Noah."

Oh, God. Talk about embarrassing. Blake clenched his jaw. "I see his reputation has preceded him."

"I'm not judging. Not at all." Josh let out a short laugh. "I wouldn't have any right to. But Noah is fragile, and Brad can't mess with him."

Blake sighed. "I understand, and I'll be sure to tell him in no uncertain terms, but I don't think you have to worry. Brad has a strict no-cheating rule, and he considers Noah taken. Let me talk to my brother first. He fucking owes me, so I don't think he'll protest. Plus, despite what you may have heard, he's a good guy, Josh. He is. Just...messed up."

"Aren't we all? As I said, I'm not judging him, Blake. Honestly. I wanna look out for Noah, that's all."

"I understand. And Josh, could you maybe text Aaron? Ask him to call you so you can tell him yourself you're leaving? I think it would mean a lot to him."

"Yeah, I will. I promise. And thank you, Blake. You looking out for Noah after the way we treated your... Man, it's way more than you owed us."

He'd barely hung up with Josh, when his phone rang again. *Brad. Huh.* He must've felt Blake wanted to talk to him. He'd sort of patched things up with Brad, but his relationship with Burke was still strained.

"What's up?" he answered.

"Blake, it's Charlie. He needs a place to stay."

"What happened?"

"Zack, his asshole boyfriend, that's what happened. He beat the shit out of him. And I can't let him stay with me because that's the first place that bastard will look, and you're the second."

Oh, dammit. The hits just kept coming at the moment, didn't they? "How bad is it? Does he need a hospital?"

"He should, but he doesn't want to go. He showed up at my doorstep this morning, and he's black and blue. I don't know what to do."

Blake swallowed. "Was he...violated?" he had to ask, because that would change things considerably. If Charlie was raped, they'd have to talk to him about getting a rape kit done as soon as possible.

"No. Thank fuck for that. But he's beaten up badly, and I'm worried about his injuries."

The puzzle pieces clicked. "I know exactly what we're gonna do. Put him in a car, and drive over to Noah's. I'll text you the address in a sec. He can stay there for a few days, and Noah can check him out."

Brad hummed his approval. "But Blake, I'm not sure he'll feel comfortable staying with Noah and Josh by himself."

Blake almost smiled. Almost, because it was incredibly sad, and yet perfect timing. "It's only Noah right now. Josh is about to leave, since he's being admitted to a facility for his PTSD. I'll talk to Noah, but I'm sure you can stay with Charlie. He's got the space, and you need to stay out of your house for a while, right?"

"Yeah, but are you sure Noah would be okay with the two of us getting sprung on him like this? And I'd have to take Max with me as well. Noah's probably not in the mood for visitors right now."

No, he wouldn't be, but it would be the perfect distraction for him, Blake thought. "I'll call him, but I'm pretty sure it'll be fine. Start loading up your car, before Zack comes looking for him. And Brad, if he does, keep your hands off him. Stay calm and do not engage him. He'll fucking press charges, and you know he'll win."

Brad sighed loudly. "I know, I know. I want to, though. No, actually, I want to sic you on him and have you beat him to a pulp. Is that wrong of me, to wish actual, physical pain on someone?"

With anyone else, it might have been a rhetorical question, but not with Brad. His brother tended to consider things like this deeply. "No. Wishing it isn't. Doing it would lower you to his level, and you can't do that. Tell Charlie I love him, will you? I gotta call Noah, set things up."

He hung up and immediately called Noah. As he had expected, as soon as Noah heard Charlie was hurt, he went from reluctant to completely welcoming. The guy couldn't help it. Taking care of people was in his blood. It was how he was wired, much like Blake.

He sighed with relief after he'd hung up. Charlie was safe, Brad had a place to stay, and Noah would not be alone. Not bad for an hour's work. Now all he needed was his puppy in his arms, and he'd be good. He reached for his phone again.

Blake: *I'm so sorry, puppy. I should have protected you better. I miss you so much.*

NOAH HEARD the car pull up in the driveway and walked outside, Josh on his heels. Brad had pulled the backseat down, and the car was stuffed to the max with boxes and clothes, with a black lab sitting in between the boxes, his tongue lolling out of his mouth. In the front seat, Noah spotted a pale, slender guy, sitting with his eyes closed.

Brad got out as soon as he'd shut off the engine.

"Hey," Noah greeted him.

"Hi. Thank you. For taking us in, I mean."

Noah nodded. "You're more than welcome."

Brad opened the passenger door. "We're here, honey."

Noah kneeled as best as he could with his leg, so Charlie could see him.

"Hey, Charlie. I'm Noah, and this is Josh. You're gonna be safe here, okay?"

Charlie nodded, a wince passing over his face. Noah kept his face neutral, but his stomach lurched when he took in Charlie's injuries. Somebody had done a number on him.

Charlie bravely tried to push himself up, but it seemed his arms wouldn't hold his weight. "I've got you," Brad said, stepping in. He unbuckled the seatbelt and turned Charlie sideways.

"Can you walk, or do you need help to get inside?" Brad asked. Noah loved that he didn't assume but let Charlie make his own choices. It saved what little dignity Charlie had left.

"I need help."

"Do you want me to carry you, honey?" Brad asked.

"Please."

"I'll get the dog out, if that's okay," Josh said.

"Yeah, please. His name is Max, and he's a total sweetheart. He'd cuddle you to death if you let him," Brad answered.

Josh smiled. "Good, 'cause I love cuddles."

Brad turned back to Charlie and plucked him off the seat, wrapped in the blanket, cradling him in his arms as Noah led the way inside. It was a good thing Charlie was a featherweight, because Brad shared his brother's lean, toned build and wasn't as strong as Noah himself, or Connor. If

Charlie had been bigger, Brad might not have been able to hold him the way he did.

Noah would examine Charlie on the huge kitchen table, which Josh had covered with a couple of fluffy bath towels. A bed would have been more comfortable for Charlie but way less practical for Noah. This way, he had easier access. He'd put out some medical supplies and his stethoscope, wanting to be ready.

Brad lowered Charlie onto the kitchen table. The poor kid was shivering despite the blankets around him from a combination of cold and stress, and he was clinging to Brad's hand. Noah stepped into Charlie's line of vision—well, as far as he could see with his eye swollen shut. "Hey, Charlie, are you okay with me checking you out?"

Charlie nodded hesitantly.

"I know you're scared and hurting." Noah's voice was kind and warm. "I promise I'll be careful with you, and this is between you and me, okay? No one else needs to see unless you want them to."

"Okay," Charlie gave in.

"Do you want Brad to stay?" Noah asked.

"Please." His voice was soft but definitive.

"Okay. Josh will stay out of the kitchen, okay?"

He put on some gloves while visually examining Charlie's body. From what he could see, his face and torso had taken the most impact. He was a little waif, maybe a hundred-thirty pounds soaking wet. He wouldn't have stood a chance against a bigger man. Fuck, what an asshole to take his anger out on a guy so much smaller. Noah pushed down the anger inside. That would not help Charlie right now.

The body he was examining was frail, but the mental state of the man inside the battered body was even more fragile. Charlie was retreating into his mind and while Noah understood, he needed him to be present to answer questions.

"Do you want to tell me what happened?"

Charlie's eye glazed over, his other too swollen to open. "I got beaten up," he said.

"Yeah, you did," Noah said. He'd affirm whatever truth Charlie said, hopefully empowering him enough to share the whole story. "Is it okay if I cut your shirt off to check your upper body?"

Maybe if he started easy, Charlie would trust him to see the rest as well. He reminded Noah a bit of Indy when he'd first come in, so distrusting and hurt, both on the outside and on the inside.

"Yeah."

With the big kitchen scissors, Noah cut off the pale pink shirt Charlie was wearing. His upper body was bruised, but at least there was no blood visible. Noah checked both his arms first, causing Brad to let go of Charlie's hand. They showed some bruising, defensive wounds most likely, but nothing seemed broken.

"Are you comfortable with me touching your chest and belly, Charlie?"

After a slight hesitation, he nodded.

Noah let his gloved fingers follow the collarbones first—not broken, thank fuck. That was always an easy one to break if you were slammed down the wrong way. He checked his ribs, which were painful in some areas but not so much they seemed broken.

"I need to press on your belly, okay? Wanna make sure everything inside is okay."

Charlie didn't respond, so Noah waited. As long as a patient was not critical, he'd value consent over anything else.

"Sweetie," Brad said, his voice tender as if they were making out. He took Charlie's hand again and kissed it with deep affection. Noah was seeing a whole new side of him. Noah had gotten to know him from when Blake had stayed with him and Josh, and Brad was quiet, somewhat surly even, but he was a sweetheart for Charlie. "You can do this. I'm right here."

Thank fuck Charlie had someone he let in. He could not, should not go through this alone.

"You can touch me," Charlie said to Noah, his face brave.

"Charlie, would it be okay if I took pictures throughout? That way, you still have evidence of what was done to you." Noah kept his voice light.

"No." Charlie's answer was swift. "I don't want to... No."

"Sweetie, let him take pictures. You don't need to decide now what you want to do with them. It's just in case, okay? No pressure."

Noah was grateful Brad had come to his help. He could understand why Charlie was reluctant in his current state, but he might regret it later.

"I'll save them on my computer, and you can decide later what you want to do with them," he added.

"Okay." Charlie's voice was a breath, barely audible.

"Thank you. You're doing the smart thing," Noah said. He got his phone from his pocket and snapped a few pictures of Charlie's face and upper body. He put the phone down and palpated his abdomen to make sure it was soft. No internal bleeding as far as he could tell. He did have bruised ribs, from the looks of it.

"Were you hit or kicked in your belly at any point?" he asked, double-checking.

"No. My face, mostly. He slammed my head against the edge of the bed."

It was the first detail he'd offered. Noah gave him an encouraging smile. "I'm gonna test your pupil reflexes, okay?"

He shone the light in his pupils, which showed normal reflexes.

"Track the light with your eyes only."

Noah was satisfied with his reactions so far. There was no indication of major head trauma.

"Can I examine your head?"

"Yeah."

His head exam revealed a large bump on the back of his head, which was tender to the touch. Looked like he might have a minor concussion but probably nothing more than that. Thank fuck.

Now they were getting to the hard part. "Charlie, I'm sorry I need to ask you this, but did he violate you?"

Charlie's answer was swift. "No. But he did..." He swallowed. "Could you maybe check my balls?"

Noah nodded. "Sure. Did he hurt you there?"

"Yeah." He looked like he wanted to say more, but instead he turned toward Brad. "Distract me," he said. "Tell me a sexy story."

Brad's eyes sought Noah's, and he nodded. It wouldn't bother him.

"I let this furry bear fuck me last night, and oh my God, it was amazing. We literally didn't even say a word. He just fucked me raw, and then he left."

Charlie's giggle was carefree, and Noah loved hearing it. Brad looked at Noah while he was sharing some more details as if waiting for him to comment, but Noah had no intention of doing so. Anything that would help Charlie cope with this trauma was more than fine with him. Besides, why the fuck would he care how Brad got off? If it was consensual, it was all fine with him.

He cut off Charlie's jeans and underwear, not wanting to hurt the man more by dragging them down his legs. A quick look in his underwear showed it was clean. Thank fuck. It looked like Charlie had been telling the truth, as there were no stains of either semen or blood.

"I'm gonna examine your penis and testicles now, okay?"

Charlie's penis looked normal aside from one large scratch, but his balls were bruised and tender to the touch.

"Sorry to interrupt, but Charlie, do you want to tell me what happened to your balls?"

Charlie sighed. "He likes to squeeze them when he fucks me. Today, he..." He stopped.

Brad leaned over and kissed him gently on his swollen lips. "Tell him, sweetie. Noah is an honest-to-God good guy."

Whether Charlie was surrendering to the inevitability of sharing his story or whether Brad's glowing appraisal of Noah had done the trick, Noah didn't know, but the man started talking. Noah inconspicuously turned the camera on his phone on, letting it record what Charlie said.

"He came in early this morning from the night shift, grumpy as usual. I was still asleep. It's Sunday, you know? Figured I could sleep in, since I'd done a show yesterday at Flirt and didn't get home till five."

"He does an awesome drag show," Brad said.

"Cool," Noah said, figuring his job was to be supportive of whatever was coming out of Charlie's mouth.

"He woke me up, wanted me to suck him off. I didn't feel like it but figured it would be easier to go along. Once he'd come, he'd pass out, and I could go back to sleep as well. He's always rough with blow jobs but this time even more so. He was stuffing me with his dick, and I was running out of air, and in panicking, I nicked him with my teeth. It was a scratch, not even bleeding, but he was furious and slapped me right across the cheek."

He brought his hand up to his right cheek as if reliving the moment. Brad's face flashed over with rage, but Noah watched him push it down. Good man.

"He's hit me before, but this time I got mad for some reason. I was tired, and it felt so fucking unfair since I hadn't done it on purpose, so I told him to stop. He wanted to hit me again, but I blocked him. Jiujitsu training, you know? God, he was so furious after that. I swear, I could see the red haze covering his eyes. He's fucking tall and heavy, and he pinned me down on the bed, knocked my head around till I was bleeding and dizzy. I fought back, but he grabbed me by my balls, squeezed so hard I thought I was gonna throw up, then slammed the back of my head on the edge of the bed. He knocked me out cold, and when I came to, he was all apologetic, as usual. I waited till he fell asleep, and then I took a cab to Brad's."

His voice broke. "He beat the shit out of me. God damn him, he beat me unconscious." A violent tremor tore through his body, and he clung to Brad's hand as if it was his lifeline, preventing him from drowning. "Why would he do that?"

Brad must have been as tempted as Noah was to answer that question but he didn't. As Charlie's body trembled and shook, Brad held his hand, whispered sweet words of love and encouragement and was a shining example of what to do in a situation like this.

Noah turned the video mode off but took some pictures of Charlie's balls, which were swollen and turning blue. It was cumbersome because he had to keep taking gloves off and putting them back on afterward, but it was worth it.

Plus, he wouldn't ask Brad to take pictures. His job was to be there for Charlie, and he was doing a damn fine job of that.

"I fucking hate him," Charlie said. "Fucking, egotistical, lying, cheating son of a bitch."

He was moving into the anger phase, good. It beat the hell out of the closed-off Charlie who was locked into his own head.

Charlie's testicles were bruised, but nothing was torn that Noah could see. If he'd been in the hospital, he would've done an ultrasound, but with someone merely squeezing his balls the chances of severe injuries weren't that big. Still, Charlie would feel them for a while. Noah checked Charlie's legs, which seemed unharmed. All done. He took off his gloves and threw them in the trash.

"Okay," he said. "Looks like you may have a minor concussion, a few bruised ribs, and bruised testicles. I recommend plenty of rest, especially napping. I can tape up your ribs so they'll be supported. For your testicles the recommended course of action is cooling with an ice pack when they throb and wearing a jockstrap under your normal underwear, as this will support them better. You'll be hitting the painkillers hard the next few days. You'd be better off with some prescription painkillers, but I can't prescribe them, so you'd have to ask your family doctor."

Charlie let out a relieved sigh. "That's not too bad, right?'

"No. But Charlie, please keep in mind that I've only done a physical exam as far as possible. If we'd been in the ER, I would've ordered an ultrasound of your testicles and probably a head CT to rule out head trauma. Also, I'm not a doctor, you know that, right?"

"I know, and I understand, but I can't go to the hospital. Zack would find out."

"Hospital records are sealed," Noah said.

A look passed between Brad and Charlie. "Zack's a cop," Brad said, his voice ice cold. "He's got a long reach."

A cop had done this to his partner? Unbelievable. No wonder Charlie was so scared. "I understand. I just wanted you to know."

"Thanks, Noah, for doing this. We really appreciate it," Brad said.

"You're welcome, though I'm so sorry for the circumstances. Know that you can stay as long as you need to, both of you. Josh has made up two guest bedrooms, so feel free to bring your stuff in, Brad."

Brad nodded, but Charlie bit his already bruised lip. "Brad, would it be okay if I stay with you? In the same room, I mean? I don't wanna be alone right now."

Brad smiled, another one of those tender smiles that seemed to be reserved for Charlie. "I'd love that, sweetie."

Fuck, Noah felt for the kid. "Do you want to take a shower?" he offered. "Brad could help you, and you could borrow some clean clothes from my...boyfriend, Indy. He's closest to your size."

Even mentioning Indy inspired a gulf of pain rolling through him, but he ignored it.

"God, yes. I feel so dirty," Charlie said. "I wanna wash his stench off."

Minutes later, Brad and Charlie had taken up residence in the biggest guest bedroom, and Noah heard the shower turn on. Poor Charlie, he thought while cleaning up the stuff he used in the kitchen. He couldn't believe a cop had done this. Damn, that guy should be fired from his job immediately. Still, he could understand why Charlie would be hesitant to press charges. Cops were known to protect each other's backs, even against accusations like domestic abuse.

"How is he?" Josh asked, walking in from wherever he'd been staying during the examination, Brad's dog on his heels.

"Bruised and battered, but it could be worse. I think he'll be okay, but I'm keeping a close eye on him."

Josh sighed. "Poor kid."

Noah put the box of gloves back in the cabinet and checked to make sure he'd tidied up everything.

"Noah."

He heard it in Josh's voice. His name was spoken with so much love and pain at the same time, that he knew. "You're leaving now."

He slowly turned around and faced Josh, who looked at him with worry.

"Yeah. It's time."

"I know."

Josh stepped closer, cupped Noah's cheek with his right hand. "Do you know I never asked you for a promise in all these years?"

Noah processed that statement. Huh, Josh was right. He hadn't.

"It's because I know you're a man who does what he says, so there's no need for a formal promise. But I'm asking you for one now. I need you to promise me you'll take care of yourself. I need to do this, for me and for us, but I can't leave without knowing you'll be okay. So promise me, Noah. Promise me you'll be okay. Promise me you'll take good care of yourself. Promise me that when I come back, you'll be healthy."

Noah's throat was so constricted, even breathing hurt. Everything in him screamed to refuse. How could he promise he'd be okay when he wasn't? He was dying inside. Losing Indy had left him in the dark, but losing Josh as well was like losing the very foundation under his feet. Yet he could not deny Josh this, not when he'd given so much and had asked for so little in return.

"I promise."

Josh closed the distance between them and hugged him tighter than he ever had before. "You'll be okay, Noah. We'll be okay, I promise. Hang in there. Indy will come back to you, to us."

Noah held him. He loved that Josh had so much faith in a happy end, that his belief in Indy's return was unwavering. Noah couldn't see it, couldn't make himself look past the big, gaping hole Indy's absence had created. "You take good care of you, Josh. Get better."

When he watched Josh walk out the door, it felt like the last little bit of light in his life was fading.

19

He'd been gone four weeks now. Aaron sighed as he finalized the registration screen for the guest he'd checked in. He leaned back in the creaky desk chair, careful to not tip it over again, like he'd done the second day on the job.

Dang, he missed Blake.

He'd thought it would lessen, this physical pain in his body whenever he thought of him, but it didn't. If anything, it only got worse. Blake was still texting him at least once an hour throughout the day, and Aaron kept rereading his messages.

I miss you so much, puppy. You brought me such joy.

I'll wait for you to come back as long as it takes.

I'm cleared to drive again. Can I meet you somewhere to talk? I want to see you so badly.

He also texted pictures of himself, what his wounds looked like now, of his students. Aaron had figured Blake would give up after a week or so, but he hadn't. Four weeks later, Blake showed no sign of giving up, though he never demanded or put pressure on Aaron. He merely let him know in every single text how much he...

Aaron's breath caught, and a tingle danced over his spine. Blake loved him.

These texts, the words he wrote, this was not disappointment over a friend leaving. This was not someone being miffed something hadn't worked out the way he'd hoped. Blake was showing in every text how much he missed Aaron, how much he...loved him.

He hadn't used those exact words, but suddenly it was crystal clear. Aaron had no idea how and why, but somewhere along the way, Blake had fallen in love with him. There was no other explanation for how Blake was feeling now that Aaron had left.

Blake loved him.

It took him five minutes to quit his job, five more to persuade his former boss to buy Aaron's car for a ridiculously low price, and another five to use that money to book the first plane ticket home.

Home. To Blake.

He persuaded his ex-boss to drop him off at the airport. He couldn't stop smiling during the flight or the taxi ride home, which ate up his last cash. He spotted Blake's car in the driveway when the taxi dropped him off, and his stomach rolled with excitement. He was flat broke and dead tired, yet he'd never felt happier.

He'd left his key, so he had to ring the bell. When the door opened, Blake's tired face filled his vision. He'd lost weight, and judging by the bags under his eyes, he wasn't sleeping too well. But all that was forgotten when Blake's face broke open in a smile that brought tears to Aaron's eyes.

He smiled back through his tears. "I'm home."

Blake's hand reached out to touch his face, his hair, then grabbed his neck and pulled him in for a bone-crushing hug. "Oh, God, Aaron...I missed you so much."

More tears fell from Aaron's eyes as he reveled in the sensation of those two strong arms around him again. He breathed in Blake's smell, rubbing his cheek against Blake's shirt. A sob escaped from his lips, and Blake pushed him back to study his face. Much to Aaron's surprise, Blake's eyes were teary, too.

"You love me," Aaron said in wonder.

"You have no idea how much. I need you, puppy. You make me whole."

Aaron lifted his hand, let it slide through Blake's silky dark hair. "Tell me again. Please."

Blake cupped his cheeks and focused those piercing blue eyes on him. "I love you, Aaron. You fulfill me, complete me."

"I didn't realize it until today," Aaron said.

"I don't think I fully grasped it until you were gone, and my life was so empty and bleak without you. I'm so sorry, puppy. I fucked up royally by not supporting you against my brothers."

They were still outside in the chilly April wind, and Aaron shivered in Blake's arms. "Can we go inside?"

Blake looked at him for a few seconds as if searching for something, then let go. "Yeah. Please."

Aaron breathed in deeply as he stepped inside. Home. This was truly his home. He didn't even think, just rolled his suitcase right into Blake's room. Their room.

He turned around to find Blake watching him with a guarded expression. "If you want to, there's also a guest room free," he said.

Aaron raised his eyebrows. "Why would I prefer that?"

Blake shrugged, jamming his hands into the pockets of his jeans. "I just wanted to let you know you have options. You're welcome to stay even if you choose to stay in a different room."

Blake's sudden aloofness puzzled Aaron. Blake had been so happy Aaron was back, and now he wanted them to sleep in different rooms? Aaron didn't understand what had happened. His shoulders dropped. Had he misunderstood? Fucked up again, somehow? "Don't you want me to stay with you?" he asked softly, avoiding Blake's eyes.

"Fuck, yes. I want nothing more. But you have a choice, and I'd understand if you needed some time to...I don't know, adjust."

It wasn't making any sense, the way Blake was talking. Aaron had thought he'd be over the moon and he had been, until...until Blake had declared his love and Aaron hadn't said it back. Blake had apologized and Aaron had asked to go inside. He was such an idiot.

He'd tell him back, but first, he had to do something else. He had to finish what they'd started, together.

Aaron dug in his pocket until he found the thing he wanted to give to Blake. "Remember when you asked me to make that list of five things I didn't want to be and five things I wanted? It took me a long time, but I finally made it." He handed Blake a folded sheet of paper. "Read them out loud."

Blake looked insecure, and it made Aaron's heart clench.

"Five things I don't want to be: masculine, boring, empty, independent, and alone," Blake read. He looked up from the paper. "Oh, puppy, you don't—"

"Read the rest," Aaron interrupted him.

Blake hesitated for a second before he looked down at the paper again. "Five things I want to be: feminine, pretty, cared for, loved, owned by..." His voice broke, and when he looked up there were tears in his eyes again.

"Owned by Blake," Aaron said, filled with a sudden calm and peace. He met Blake's eyes. "I love you," he said simply.

He watched the words register with Blake, saw the look of relief and joy spread over his face. "You're mine."

Aaron nodded. "I'm yours. Blake, I hated being by myself, hated being independent. You were right. I want someone to take care of me. I want that more than anything, and I want it to be you, because you get me. I love you and I need you. Will you please be my owner and take care of me?"

"I want nothing more. I love you, puppy, and I promise I'll be and do whatever you need to be happy."

Blake closed the distance between them with three big steps and crushed his mouth to Aaron's. He opened up immediately, needing Blake so fiercely it bordered on painful. Blake ravished his mouth, invading every cell of his being. Aaron sighed, then moaned. He needed more.

Blake broke off the kiss and stared deep into Aaron's eyes, breaths coming out in pants. "I bought you a present. Give me one sec."

Aaron watched as Blake walked over to his nightstand and took out a small box. He turned around and handed it to Aaron.

It was light. A soft smile played around Blake's lips, which encouraged Aaron to open the package. Inside the plain brown box was a smaller box, and he ripped off the tape sealing it. He upended it, and out came something pink and shiny. He turned it in his hands. What the heck was that?

A collar. A beautiful pink collar with rhinestones, looking like it was big enough to fit him. And the box held a leash as well, in the same style. Blake had bought him a collar and leash.

He raised his eyes to look at Blake. "You bought this for me without knowing I'd come back?"

"I hoped you'd realize how much I love you. Bow your head, Aaron."

He couldn't disobey that voice even if he wanted to, which he didn't. Blake fit the collar around his neck, clicked it close and pulled it so it fit snugly, without restricting him.

"Beautiful." Aaron looked up. Blake looked at him with tenderness radiating from his eyes. "My beautiful puppy."

He reached up to feel his collar. It was so pretty, so perfect, and it showed how much Blake loved him exactly the way he was. He wouldn't have to change himself, be more masculine, or less needy, or more independent. Blake loved him the way he was. A weight lifted off him, like a heavy blanket that had been draped over his heart.

"You like it?" Blake asked, his voice soft and kind.

"I love it. I love you."

"You're beautiful with my collar around your neck. I love you, puppy."

Aaron's heart and mind were at peace but his body wasn't. He needed. Badly. "Blake?"

"Yes, puppy."

"Will you please fuck me?"

Blake smiled. "That's the first time you've said 'fuck' without stuttering. I'm so proud of you for voicing what you need." His eyes darkened. "I'm gonna fuck you hard and deep. I know what you need, Aaron. I'll take care of you."

Aaron whimpered with impatient need. "Please, Blake. I need you so much."

"Strip."

The order was firm, yet kind, and Aaron didn't waste a

second before obeying. He was naked within seconds, his clothes in a heap on the floor. Blake needed a little more time, and Aaron helped him drag down his jeans, then pulled off his socks. Blake's cock was standing at attention, and Aaron gave it a quick lick when it almost poked him in the face.

He'd blow Blake some other time because he wanted to feel his cock in his mouth again, wanted to taste him, but right now he needed something else first. He climbed on the bed in eager anticipation, his cock already straining. The mere thought of Blake filling him up again made his hole quiver and his cock leak. He needed him so much, to the point that his brain was shutting down.

Blake climbed on the bed, lube in his hand, immediately reaching out for Aaron. "Want me to skip the foreplay for now?"

Aaron let out a happy sigh that Blake was so tuned in to him. "Would that be okay?"

"Anything that makes you happy is okay. I want to take care of you. Am I right that you need me to fill you?"

Aaron nodded, unable to form words anymore. His body was shaking. Blake squeezed lube on his fingers, lubed up his cock first and then coated his fingers. "Lie on your back for me, sweetheart," he said. "Yes, like that. Good boy. Open your legs wide, put them on my shoulders. Look at your pretty little hole, all eager for my touch."

He breached his entrance without delay, pushing his middle finger in. Aaron moaned, taking him in with ease.

"Did you miss this, puppy? Miss me?"

"So much. I'm so empty without you."

Blake added a second finger and started fucking him in a steady rhythm. "Shhh, puppy, no more worries, okay? I'm right here."

Aaron shuddered, shifted his ass, tried to push back. "Feels so good."

Blake seemed to sense he couldn't wait anymore. He pulled out his fingers and lined up his slick cock. Aaron breathed out as it demanded entry, welcoming the burn. Blake was careful, sliding in inch by delicious inch, Aaron panting and moaning at every move.

"Blakeblakeblakeblake..." Aaron babbled, thrashing his head with eyes closed. So close.

Blake pushed in all the way, filling him to the max. Aaron cried out, his cock jerking as he orgasmed. Like the first time, the mere sensation of Blake inside him was enough for him to come.

"Oh, puppy, I love how you respond to me. I'll never grow tired of watching you come," Blake said.

"I love you," Aaron said again. It was as if he couldn't hold back the words now that he'd said them once. He opened his eyes, meeting Blake's blue eyes that were completely focused on him.

"I love you too." Blake smiled, still embedded inside Aaron.He looked at him with so much love it made Aaron's insides melt. "One of these days I'll explain in excruciating detail why you are perfect for me, but right now we have other priorities. You need a second orgasm, and I have a desperate need to pound your ass."

He angled his hips and slowly withdrew, only to surge back in. Aaron's skin tingled. Blake repeated his move, with more force this time.

"Uhhhh..." Aaron moaned.

"The first time we made love, you had to do all the work. But now that I'm almost fully recovered, I want you to feel what it can be like. I'm gonna fuck you hard and deep,

Aaron. I haven't come in days, and I'm gonna fill you up with my cum."

Those words. They rolled around in his head, triggering all kinds of sexy images. He could picture it, Blake's fat cock breaching him, fucking him. The dirty words made him feel so good, so sexy.

He scrambled off Blake's cock, ignoring his surprised face, planting himself on his hands and knees, his head low. Shamelessly, he pushed his ass backward, looking over his shoulder. "I'm yours, Blake. Claim me."

Which he did. Over and over again, until Aaron's hole was, indeed, overflowing with cum. They showered, fell into each other's arms as soon as they hit the bed, Aaron touching Blake wherever he could.

I'm finally home.

20

J osh rammed the vibrator in his ass with one final thrust. His cock exploded, his balls emptying almost painfully as he spurted thick ropes of cum onto the sheets. Fuck, he'd needed that. He should have done it sooner, but the therapy had him too busy and too fucking tired afterward. He let out a shuddering sigh of relief as the stress was leaving his body. Well, some of it at least.

He pulled the toy out and threw it on the sheets. Good thing his room was due for fresh linens today. And no, he didn't give a shit what the household staff would think of the stains. Any guess they'd make would probably be correct, and why the fuck would he care? He was a man, he had needs, and since he was on his own, he had to get creative.

Damn, he missed Connor. He missed the sex, of course, and the intimacy. But he especially missed the emotional connection. The being known, being seen. The freedom to completely be himself. Even with Noah he'd had to hold back out of fear Noah would reject him. And with Indy, he'd had to be careful as well—though for different reasons. Indy was fragile in a sense, and Josh would do anything to keep from hurting him.

But Connor, Connor was different. Connor could take him as he was, with all his strength, with all his emotional hang-ups, and even with his mental and physical needs. Connor was his equal in every aspect, and he'd never felt more at peace than when he was with him. The man was a miracle Josh had never even dreamed of finding.

And this plan of Connor's, the cop had been so right. It was absolutely fucking crazy, but it was the only chance they had to give Indy the freedom he deserved. No cost would be too high to achieve that, though Josh had felt like shit for deceiving Noah. When he'd told Noah he wanted to be admitted, it had taken everything to not tell him the truth. God, Noah had been so broken already from losing Indy, and now he had to face living without Josh for a while as well. Noah had looked so forlorn but had supported Josh completely, as Josh had known he would. Noah had his back, even now.

They'd fucked one more time the evening before he'd left, a hard and furious round of fucking for Noah, and a serious walloping for Josh. His ass had hurt for days after, but it had been necessary. It would be worth it, Josh kept telling himself. In the end, Noah would understand. If he ever found out. At least he had Brad and Charlie to keep an eye on him.

He finally got up from the bed, taking the dildo with him into the shower to clean it. He'd throw it in one of his drawers, not caring if a maid found it. The water was brutally hot, to the point of scalding—exactly the way he liked it. He scrubbed himself clean, toweled off hard, and shaved. It was funny how even being in the strict discipline of a military clinic brought back some of his old habits. He'd even gotten a haircut the first week—but that was also because he wanted to do everything he could to get back into the groove.

He got dressed, chose dark blue cargo pants, a tight white shirt, and boots that resembled military boots. It felt slightly off, but more comfortable than jeans, and since he was not on active duty, he wasn't allowed to wear a uniform.

The rhythm in the hospital was basic: rise, shower, breakfast, therapy, physical exercise, lunch, group therapy, creative session, yoga and relaxation exercises, dinner, and socializing. The last part of the schedule was his absolute nightmare. Playing Ticket to Ride with complete strangers with whom he had little in common except a diagnosis—somebody sedate him, please. That part of the ten days he'd been staying here had been hell.

Halfway through his breakfast, his name was called out. He jumped up.

"Yes, Corporal."

He didn't recognize the face of the corporal in front of him, but he sure as hell recognized the rank.

"We're doing simulations today as part of your therapy, Gordon. Follow me."

"Yes, sir."

He didn't touch the rest of his breakfast, trusting someone else would clean that up after him. The corporal led him into a hallway, then another one, around a corner, then into a room, which surprisingly had a door that led directly outside. Josh blinked against the sudden light but didn't miss a beat.

He was led into a van, the doors closing quickly behind him. He'd expected something like this when he'd told Connor he needed at least one day of practice. Connor had called in favors everywhere, fuck knew how, but it seemed to have worked. He'd told Josh he had connections that he couldn't talk about but that could arrange for a practice time. And he'd get him out without anyone noticing on Freedom Day. That's what he and Connor had called it, Operation Freedom.

The van drove off immediately, even before he realized he wasn't alone in the back. A thirty-something muscular man studied him with dark eyes. Snapes, his nametag read. Panic flashed, but Josh pushed it down. Connor was counting on him, and he would not let him down.

He was handed a uniform, boots, and dog tags. "Put this on. You're posing as Sergeant Gable, first name Brody. Don't draw any attention to yourself. They're expecting a sharp-shooter, so don't fuck up."

Josh stripped, not caring about the guy watching. Modesty was not an admired quality in the army. He quickly got dressed, reveling in how familiar the uniform still felt. "Trust me, I have no intention of fucking up."

"Considering we picked you up from a psych ward, I'd thought I'd mention it."

Josh finished lacing his boots, then drilled the guy with an icy stare. "Subtle."

He didn't say a word until they were at the base. Snapes led him to the armory, where he was introduced to the master-at-arms.

"What's your weapon of choice today, Sarge?"

"Sniper rifle, please." It was the colloquial term for the army-issued 20" HK417 A2. It definitely had its flaws—like the limited ammunition capacity—but considering the job he had to do, it was the best option. It had great penetrating power, even over long distances. Plus, it was the rifle he was most familiar with, one he knew every trick, flaw, and strength of. She would not let him down.

After doing the required safety check, he was handed the rifle with several boxes of ammunition. Snape escorted him to the shooting range—or the practice fields, more precisely. Considering what he wanted to practice for, shooting at a target a few hundred feet away wouldn't do the trick. He needed long range, moving targets.

For the next hours, as he took shot after shot—not missing even once—all time ceased to exist. There was no hunger, no thirst, no panic, or even a hint of PTSD. He was one with his rifle, getting reacquainted, all but making love to her. She could be fickle, but in Josh's hands she was perfect.

He hadn't held a rifle in well over a year. Hadn't had the rush of seeking out his target through his telescope, of calculating wind speed and direction, angles. He'd missed it. If that made him a sick fuck, well, so be it. The power of holding a weapon so powerful, so deadly, rushed through his veins with an all-too-familiar hum.

He was ready.

Now, all he had to do was have a breakdown. And he'd better make it damn good.

21

Indy hadn't caught a full night's sleep since he arrived at the farm. Even ten weeks in, he still woke up multiple times each night. Sometimes it was because of nightmares, but most of the time the cause was that he didn't allow himself to sink too deep into sleep. Four agents on his detail, but he didn't trust them to protect him. Not because of them or lack of skills on their part but because of the tenacity and the depravity of the Fitzpatricks. There was nothing they wouldn't do to get to him.

He shifted in the queen-size bed. The metal frame squeaked every time he did that, which drove him nuts. That didn't help with sleeping either, and neither did the fact that he always slept dressed. He missed the super-comfy king-size bed in Noah's room. He missed Noah, period. And Josh. Even Connor.

For the first time he understood why it was called heart-break. It physically hurt. The mere act of thinking of Noah caused his heart to contract painfully and his throat to become all constricted, every breath agony.

Had he made a mistake, going into protective custody

without him? Noah would have gone crazy here. The lack of privacy for one—it was kinda hard to have a sex life here, even if the two of them had been together. Letting Josh and Connor hear, or watch, was one thing, but not complete strangers. Not even Miles with his super sex drive.

Aside from that, Noah would have gone nuts from not being able to do anything. Even Indy struggled. He did some courses online, fake ID and logins courtesy of the FBI. He was taking a few free college courses in various subjects to see what he liked.

A low thud made him open his eyes. He checked his watch. Three o'clock. Was it a shift change? They did it at irregular hours to avoid setting any kind of pattern. Miles had said the change was at seven in the morning, though. Maybe one of the agents had bumped into something in the dark?

He held his breath, focused on any sounds. The Kansas prairie was so fucking quiet, you could hear every little noise. The only things you heard during the day were birds and the occasional plane. At night it was completely quiet, though he'd heard what sounded like a coyote once.

Nothing.

He relaxed again, closed his eyes and imagined he was home, lying between Noah and Josh. Noah would spoon him from the back as he so often did, making him feel safe and protected with those big, strong arms around him. He'd be naked, his cock brushing up against Indy's ass every now and then.

Josh would hug him from the front, his limbs all inter-twined with Indy's. Josh was such a hugger and cuddler, way more than Noah. He'd kiss Indy, one of those sweet, sexy kisses that made heat pool in his belly until his cock was rock hard and his hole quivering to be filled. Damn, the guy could kiss.

A high-pitched scream pierced the night and Indy's eyes flew open, his heart stopping.

"Run!"

Agent Nunez.

Fuck, no.

Indy slid out of bed, not even considering running into the hallway. Sounds of a struggle were drifting up from downstairs. His door was locked from the inside, and he'd barricaded it with a dresser, like he did every night. The floor had better not squeak now. He didn't want anyone to know he'd woken up. He grabbed the backpack that always sat ready next to his bed.

He stepped over the floorboard he knew would make noise. Soundlessly, he went into his bathroom and lifted the window frame out of the sockets. The screws had been taken out since the day they'd installed him here, as an emergency exit had been his number one priority. He'd even practiced taking out the window a few times.

He lowered it to the floor without making a sound. The window was big enough for him to fit through but not with his backpack on. He stuck his head out and listened. Muffled noises were coming from downstairs. Outside, everything was dark and quiet. For now.

Indy slid his backpack out and followed suit. He wasn't wearing shoes, too scared of making a noise, but he had a pair in his backpack, which had been ready from the day he'd arrived here. Thank fuck there was a sliver of a moon tonight—enough to light the way outside.

The cold roof tiles hurt his bare feet, but he ignored it. With some effort, he crawled to the side of the house where the barns were. Thank fuck for his jiujitsu training which had helped him develop excellent coordination. He lowered himself off the roof, had to jump the last few feet to the ground. His bare feet landed on gravel, tiny stones digging into the soft skin of his feet. Indy winced but forced himself to stand still and listen.

The house had gone quiet. Not good. At least nobody was outside. Yet.

He crossed the short path between the house and the hay barn as he called it, slipped in and closed the door gently behind him. Shit, it was pitch-black inside—too dark to see anything, let alone find the hatch to the cellar. The barn didn't have any windows. He'd have to use his phone and hope that light wouldn't spill to the outside. Indy grabbed his phone, turned on the screen but dimmed the intensity so he could see where he was going.

The attic was still filled with hay, but the barn itself held various farming equipment and tools, including a huge, rusty John Deere tractor that would never run again. The walls were lined with racks and hooks, holding all kinds of tools Indy didn't even recognize.

He shoved his backpack under the John Deere first, then crawled underneath it on his belly. The thing was massive, with double tires front and back. Touching with his fingers, Indy felt around until he'd found the iron ring. He'd discovered on an exploring expedition a few days before that he could lift the hatch high enough to slip inside. His backpack went first, landing on the horse blankets he'd piled underneath when he'd discovered the cellar.

He'd better cover his tracks. There was hay everywhere on the barn floor, but sliding under the tractor might have left a trail that would lead them straight to him. He turned with his legs toward the hatch. In the distance, a door squeaked.

Shouting voices could be heard. They'd discovered he was gone.

Fuck.

He crawled backward, sweeping the hay in front of him as he went, then stepped down the wooden stairs underneath the hatch, making sure not to misstep. The voices were close now. Too close for comfort. He threw some last hay around him, then closed the hatch as softly as he could and stepped off the last two steps to the floor. Standing still, he turned his phone off. Listened. He could still hear voices, but they weren't in the barn. Yet.

Shoes. He needed shoes. If he had to run, he'd better not do it barefoot. Shit, this was no easy feat in the pitch-black. He located his backpack by touch and opened it by feeling around until he'd found his shoes. Tying your laces in the dark was hard, Indy found out. It took him a few tries until both shoes were tied tight.

Above his head, something rattled. The beam of a flashlight was visible through the cracks in the rustic boarded floor above his head. Someone was walking there, sending slivers of hay down between the cracks. He couldn't see them, but he felt them rain down on his skin. Indy sat motionless. They had no reason to suspect he was down there, so any movement could only alert them to his presence.

Indy forced his erratic breathing to slow down. If he panicked now, he too was dead. He sat down, eyes closed, relaxing every muscle from his neck down to his toes, until his breathing was slow and steady.

Someone was searching the barn, kicking over empty buckets and pushing hay bales aside. Another set of footsteps joined in.

Should he stay or try and make a run for it? Indy hadn't

had enough time to discover where the storm cellar led to. He'd seen a dark tunnel leading somewhere, but wasn't sure where. When he'd discovered the hatch and the cellar, he'd known that it was his best hiding option, should the shit ever hit the fan. And it had, hadn't it? Nunez would not have screamed like that if it hadn't been dire.

"He's not here. There's nowhere to hide in here," a voice said.

"I checked the horse barn. No one there, either."

"Get that agent in here."

Indy's eyebrows rose. What agent were they talking about? Was Nunez still alive?

More footsteps, something being dragged. Whines and whimpers as someone was kicked, beaten probably.

"Where the hell is he?"

"I don't know." Indy's stomach soured. Miles. They had Miles.

"Did you discuss escape routes with him? An evacuation plan?"

Silence, then more sounds of Miles being hit.

"Listen, asshole, the kid fucking barricaded his door, so you must have talked with him about this. Tell us now, or we'll discover how much pain it will take before you talk."

A gulf of bile rose in Indy's mouth. He didn't recognize the voices and their accents were not Bostonian, but that didn't mean shit. They could be thugs for hire, guys lured in by the contract on his head. They would not hesitate to torture and kill an FBI agent, but damn if Indy was gonna sit there and listen to them while they did it.

Miles was not talking, merely groaning in what Indy assumed was pain.

More hits, kicks.

Miles cursing.

The barn door opened again. "He talking yet?" a new voice asked. He sounded like he was in charge.

"No. Nothing, and we hit him pretty hard." That was the guy who'd been asking Miles questions.

"What the hell, man? You said he would know."

"I'm sorry..." another voice said. Fucking hell, Indy knew that voice, and his stomach sank. They had an inside man. "I don't know what else to tell you. The kid was upstairs in his room last time I checked. I don't know how he got away... Please, I've done everything you asked."

Agent Crouch. Hot damn, he was in on this. But he didn't sound like he was doing this willingly. What did they have on him?

"We don't have time for this," the leader said. "We would've heard a car, so he must've taken off on foot. He won't get far in the dark. We'll spread out. Danny, you take the north, Wes will take the south, Brian east and I'll do west. We'll find him. Call in when you see something. If not, we reconvene here in an hour. Crouch, you're coming with me."

"What do we do with him?" one of the others asked.

"Tie him up, leave him here. If we find the kid, we'll finish him. If we don't find him, we can try to make him talk again."

Rustling sounds, then the thump of a body being dropped on the floor.

"Crouch, how long do we have until relief shows up?"

"At least four hours. Shift change is at seven. I need to check in every hour on the hour, though."

The men departed, leaving silence behind. Indy left out a shuddering breath.

Fucking hell.

22

Indy sat shivering in the storm cellar. What should he do now? If he took off and they didn't find him, they'd take it out on Miles. Nunez and Fisher were probably dead already. Even if they weren't, he couldn't save them. Crouch was beyond his control as well. Whatever they had on him, it was enough to make him cooperate. That wouldn't change if Indy tried to reason with him—provided he'd even get the chance.

But Miles was a different story. Too many people had died because of Indy already. He couldn't bear the thought of another victim on his conscience.

But what could he do? Assuming he'd even be able to drag Miles down here, where would that leave them? They'd know Indy was close because he wouldn't be able to take Miles far. They'd search and find the cellar. No, he had to make sure they wouldn't find a trace. But how?

Hay. The whole barn was filled with hay. What if he...?

No, that was crazy. If he didn't get out in time, they'd both burn alive. Plus, the smoke would get into the cellar.

Yeah, but smoke rises, he thought. It would take a while before it would seep down through the floor into the cellar. By that time he and Miles would be gone. Provided the tunnel he'd spotted before did actually lead somewhere. It had to, right? These were tornado shelters, built in the fucking middle of tornado alley. These folks would not shit around with stuff like that. He'd have to follow the tunnel, see where it would lead.

And run the risk of meeting someone who'd followed it from the other side. He'd hear them, probably, but even if he did, where the fuck would he go? All he could do was hope there was another way out, and that he'd get there before anyone else.

He couldn't wait anymore. They could be back any moment for Miles, and then it would be too late. He had to risk it. Crouching, he reached out in front of him until he'd located the steps leading up. He took a step, listened, and repeated the process until he'd lifted the hatch. Inside the barn it was pitch black. What if they'd tricked him and this was an attempt to lure him out? No, that didn't make sense. If they knew he was in the cellar, they would've come after him.

He turned his phone back on and shone it around until he spotted a dark form on the floor. Miles. He wasn't moving. Please, be breathing, Indy thought. He hurried toward him, shining the weak light of his phone on his body, then his face. They'd tied him with tie wraps, taped his mouth shut with duct tape. Underneath, his lip looked swollen and bloody. His entire face was swelling, and he sported what looked like a broken nose.

Indy put his fingers against Miles' throat. Yes! He was breathing. Thank fuck. Anything else would have to wait. Now came the hard part.

He clamped his phone between his teeth so he could see something, then grabbed Miles by his arms and started pulling. Hot damn, why did the guy have to be so fucking heavy? Thank fuck the floor was covered in hay. It rustled, but it didn't make too much noise. Miles groaned, luckily muted by the tape on his mouth. Indy wanted to reassure him but couldn't talk with that phone in his mouth. Dammit, dragging dead weight was impossible. Finally, he reached the tractor.

He pushed Miles under first, then crawled in himself from the other side. He couldn't very well push Miles down the steps. The guy might break even more bones. No, Indy would have to step down first and drag him down the stairs. Fuck, he hoped it wouldn't make too much noise. Above all, speed counted, though.

He took the phone out of his mouth for a second, wiped his mouth and swallowed. Then he put it back in, stepped down the stairs, and reached for Miles' arms. Once he had a solid grip on his wrists, he pulled. Holy mother of all. Sweat pearled on his forehead and broke out all over his body.

Up till now he'd dragged, but now he had to carry Miles' entire dead weight down the steps. He managed to step down, almost falling backward when Miles' legs swiped in. Indy groaned with effort, then cursed himself. Quiet. He had to stay quiet. If they heard him now, they were both dead.

Finally, Miles was inside the cellar, and Indy lowered him unceremoniously to the floor. He had to get back up and execute the second phase of his plan. The front pocket of his backpack held a box of old-fashioned matches. He'd thrown them in when he'd spotted them in the kitchen on his second day here, figuring they might come in handy. Hello, perfect timing.

He took his phone in his hand, hastening up the steps back into the barn. Thankfully all was quiet outside. Where should he start the fire? If he started in the loft, they might have time to discover the hatch. No, the whole barn had to go up at once. He looked around, illuminating with his phone. Was that a... Yes, it was. Thank you, lucky stars.

He emptied the gas canister onto the floor near the door. It had been maybe a third full, but it would do the job. The hay on the floor would spread the fire fast enough, Indy reckoned. OK, now all he needed was one match and his fastest sprint ever. He opened the box of matches, took one out.

Please, let this work.

He lit the match and threw it on the floor.

Whoosh.

Oh yeah, it worked all right. The floor was on fire in seconds.

Indy sprinted back and launched himself on his belly under the tractor. He almost fell down the hatch face first but stopped himself just in time. He crawled down the steps. The barn was on fire. They'd come running any second now. He closed the hatch, swiping his phone to create more light and turned around.

Miles' eyes were wide open, his face terrified. Indy kneeled beside him.

"It's okay," he whispered. "We're gonna get out of here."

He took the tape off his mouth first. Even though he did it as gentle as he could, Miles' lip started bleeding again.

"Fire," was the first thing out of Miles' mouth.

"I started it as a distraction. This tunnel leads somewhere, presumably to another storm cellar, and then outside. We'll follow it."

The plain kitchen knife he'd swiped two weeks ago

wasn't ideal for cutting through tie wraps, but it would have to do. He started working on Miles' feet. The guy wasn't even wearing shoes. They'd dragged him straight out of bed, judging by his PJ bottoms and shirt.

"Crouch," Miles said, swallowing.

"I know. They got something on him, probably. You need some water?"

Miles nodded, then winced. His head had to hurt like a motherfucker. Indy grabbed a bottled water from his backpack, screwed off the cap and held it out to Miles' mouth. Miles rinsed his mouth with the first sip, spit it out to the side, then took a few big gulps.

"Better. Thank you."

Indy went back to cutting through the tie wraps. The smell of the fire was unmistakable now, and the noise was increasing. They had to get out of here.

"Finally," Indy breathed as the tie around Miles' legs snapped. "Can you stand up?"

He helped Miles get to his feet. The agent staggered, probably dizzy from the beating he took.

"Shit," he said, before turning his head to the side and throwing up.

Indy held out the bottle of water again to his lips, and he drank a few sips.

"Anything broken?"

"My nose. Few bruised ribs, but I don't think they're broken. Bruised and battered all over and I took a few severe kicks to my stomach, but there's nothing we can do about that now. Let's go."

"Your hands are still tied."

"We'll get to that later. We need to get out of here before the whole barn collapses on top of us."

Indy nodded. Good point. He grabbed his backpack,

threw a few more water bottles in that were stacked against the wall, and put it on.

"I'll lead," he said, holding out his phone to illuminate the way.

Above them the fire roared, and the first smoke was seeping through the cracks. Indy walked into the tunnel, and the noise lessened. It got cooler, too. They had to be under the gravel driveway that connected all the farm buildings.

The wall curved and their soft footsteps sounded hollower. Another chamber, similar to the one under the hay barn. Was this the horse barn? It was empty, of course, but Indy hadn't had much time to explore it, since it was farther out from the main house. It would make sense, though.

Indy kept following the tunnel, sighing with relief as it continued around a bend. The air turned even colder. His body hurt as if he'd run a marathon—at least, that's what he imagined his body would feel like after completing such a brutal distance. Dragging Miles had taken a toll out of him. Still, compared to Miles he was peachy. The guy was walking this tunnel barefoot. That alone had to hurt like a motherfucker, let alone all his injuries.

"Where the hell does this thing lead?" Miles asked, keeping his voice low. He was panting behind Indy.

"I don't know. I'm glad it's leading us out of there, though."

They walked on. Indy's hand touched the wall. Moisture. The wall was wet. He stopped, tried to picture the farm's layout in his mind. If you drew a straight line from the hay barn to the horse barn and then farther out, what was next? There was a water tower, situated near a small pond. That could explain the moisture, access water from a well, or the pond. Fuck, he hoped whoever had built this tunnel had known his shit. If this thing collapsed, they'd be dead.

"I think we're near the water tower," he said.

"That makes sense."

They kept walking, the wall turning dry again, then colder and colder. A draft circled around his arms, making him shiver. It meant there was a connection with the outside, somewhere. But where the hell were they?

They hit another chamber and this time the wall circled around. This was the end of the tunnel. In the middle of the chamber, wooden steps led up to another hatch with three huge metal bolts—all unlocked. Which made sense, because you wanted them locked from the inside once you were inside. That meant they'd have to be able to crawl out, but where would they end up? How visible was this storm shelter?

Indy couldn't hear anything except for Miles' labored breaths. The air felt fresher, less stale. No smells of hay or horses. He was certain they'd walked at least half a mile, maybe more, so they were somewhere outside the direct line of the farm buildings. Hell, the water tower and pond were already on the edge. Maybe somewhere at the end of the fields? It would make sense to build a shelter there, in case you were working on the land and saw a twister coming. You wouldn't have enough time to make it back to the farm.

He shone the light around. Ah. A few wooden shelves with more bottles of water and some food. This was an active storm shelter, then. He took three bottles, put them in his backpack. This was Kansas, so these people would have more than mere water down here. Storms could last and he was right in the middle of tornado alley, so it made sense this cellar was stocked.

"Take the candy bars," Miles said, his voice tight. The guy had to be in excruciating pain.

"They're way past the expiration date," Indy said.

"Yeah, somehow I don't think that's our biggest problem right now," Miles said.

He had a point there. Indy grabbed a handful of the bars and stuffed them in his backpack. At least they'd have something to eat, even if it tasted like crap and gave them explosive diarrhea.

"Now what?" he asked Miles.

"Can you try and untie my hands? I'm losing circulation."

Indy put his phone between Miles' hands so he'd have light, took the knife from his backpack, and worked on the tie wraps. "How are you doing?" he asked.

"Pretty shitty," Miles said. That was probably a gross understatement. Indy looked up at him. Even in the dim light, it was clear Miles looked like death warmed over.

Indy swallowed. "You're not gonna keel over, I hope?"

"I don't intend to. But Indy, if I do, you get out of here, you hear me? I can't believe you dragged me out of that barn in the first place. You shoulda run."

Indy shook his head, continuing to saw at the tie wrap. "Enough people have died for me."

The tie wrap gave, and Miles' hands sprung free. Indy took his phone back as Miles rubbed his wrists.

"Wait, listen," Indy said.

Miles stopped rubbing. They both angled their heads.

"Sirens," Indy said. "Fire trucks are coming."

"And cops," Miles said. He looked at Indy. "What do you want to do?"

Indy scoffed. "You're asking me? You're the hotshot FBI agent."

A look of pain passed over the agent's face. "We failed you. Again. Dammit, Indy, if you hadn't made what looks like at least three back-up plans, you'd be dead. And me too."

Indy's face softened. "I know. It's not your fault."

"I gotta sit down," Miles said.

Indy watched with rising worry as Miles lowered himself to the floor, his breaths irregular and his face covered with sweat. "What's wrong?"

"What do you want to do, Indy?" Miles ignored his question.

Indy bit his bottom lip. "I don't know. You're in no condition to go far. I think you need medical help."

Miles reached for his pocket and drew out his phone with uncoordinated moves. He pressed his thumb on the screen to unlock it, then held it out with a trembling hand. "Remember what I said, Indy. Get the fuck out of here."

Indy took the phone as Miles blinked. Oh no. He was gonna keel over. "Miles, stay with me," Indy said. He dropped to the floor beside him and reached out to steady him. Miles let out a loud groan, then went slack. Indy barely had time to catch him and ease him to the floor while holding Miles' phone. Now what?

What the hell was wrong with the agent? Was it the concussion? He was so fucking pale. Sweaty.

It had to be something else. But how bad was it? He was not losing him, but he didn't want to call in the cavalry if the guy had merely fainted from pain. He needed advice. Medical advice.

His own phone was nothing but a shell. The FBI had taken out his SIM card first thing. That made sense since he'd be traceable with it. But Miles had handed him his phone, had unlocked it, so that meant this thing had to be safe, right? He'd wanted Indy to use it. He wasted no time, called the only number he could think of.

One, two, three rings. Then that sweet, sweet voice.

"Yeah?"

He sounded sleepy. Indy checked his watch. No wonder, it was just after four in the morning, though an hour later in New York. "Noah," he said.

"Indy! Are you okay?"

Indy's eyes filled. "No. I need your help. There's an agent with me, Miles. He's wounded, and he passed out a minute ago, and I need to know what to do."

"Okay, baby. Describe his condition to me. Start with what you know happened to him, then describe what you see on his body, from top to bottom."

Indy nodded. Thank fuck Noah knew what to do. "He's beaten up. Kicked too, I think, 'cause I see footprints on his belly. He threw up earlier. His nose is broken and his face is bloody. Split lip."

"Was he lucid at first? Did he talk to you?"

"Yeah. He was in pain, but we walked about half a mile, maybe more. He said he had to sit down, and he was pale and sweaty."

"Check his upper body," Noah said. "Can you see anything?"

Indy held the phone with one hand while he lifted Miles' gray T-shirt up. "Damn, he's got big bruises all over. They hit him hard."

"Feel his belly. Does it feel bloated? Extended?"

Indy placed a hesitant hand on Miles' abdomen and pushed gently. He didn't feel the solid muscles he'd expected. Instead, it was hard, but swollen. "It's hard, but like he's blown up inside," he reported.

"It sounds like he's got internal bleeding. His spleen, most likely, or maybe his kidneys. Depending on how big the bleed is, you don't have much time. He needs surgery as soon as possible."

"Okay," Indy said, but his heart sank. Surgery. That meant calling an ambulance. How the fuck would he pull that off without endangering them both?

"Babe, are you okay?"

"I am. I love you, Noah. So much. I'm so sorry. I gotta go."

He hung up before he could change his mind. Miles needed him. Indy took off the agent's FBI badge, held it close to the phone so he could read the number on it.

He dialed the all-too-familiar number, taking a deep breath. He had to pull this off if he wanted to save Miles.

"911, what is your emergency?"

"This is Special Agent Miles Hampton, FBI, badge number 9529537. I need an ambulance under police escort at the Kensington Farm."

"Okay. Fire trucks and law enforcement is already at the scene, and they've reported finding two bodies. Where are you located? And can you tell us what is going on?"

They were dead. Nunez and Fisher were indeed dead. Indy swallowed. Fuck, he had no idea where he was. Now what? "I'm at an undisclosed location close to the farm. Send the ambulance and I'll let you know where to meet me."

"Ambulance is en route."

"I also need immediate backup from all available law enforcement personnel in the area. Please be advised Special Agent James Crouch is compromised, and the FBI team at the farm was attacked by at least four assailants, identities unknown. Please contact the FBI headquarters and refer to the Stephan Moreau case for further information. I'll call you back in two minutes with my location."

He hung up before the operator could ask anything else. Had he managed to convince her he was Miles? He'd tried to sound professional, but he could only copy what he'd seen in movies and TV series. Fuck knew how agents talked in real life.

Miles was still unconscious, but at least he was still breathing. To get him to a hospital, Indy needed to know where they were first.

Fuck, he hoped the hinges of the hatch had been oiled. Indy walked up the stairs till he was right below the hatch, then stowed away his phone. Too risky to use now. The light could spill and alert others to their presence.

He pushed it open. Damn, that thing was heavy. No wonder, if it was located outside and had to withstand an F5 tornado. He pushed his weight into it and felt it budge. It slowly opened, not making a sound until it was almost at ninety degrees. Then it let out a tired squeak, and Indy froze.

No one called out in the blackness surrounding him. A breeze touched his cheeks. He was definitely outside. He pushed it completely open and stepped outside, stumbling over a small metal rail he hadn't seen and landing on his hands and feet. Still nothing.

He had no trouble orienting himself because a huge orange glow lit up the sky where the farm was, accentuated by many flashing lights from fire trucks and police cars. He'd been right, he was somewhere out in the fields. A few hundred yards down, he spotted the road leading to the farm.

His one big gamble was his assumption that Crouch and his men were long gone by now. They had to be, with emergency personnel flooding the farm. The operator had said they'd already discovered two bodies, so the cops had to be searching the area. No, the attackers had to be gone.

Indy hurried back down into the cellar. Was it even safe to carry Miles up the steps? He had to, otherwise he'd never get him to the surface where he could be found. Maybe he shouldn't put pressure on his belly. This time, he lifted him under his armpits and dragged him up the steps, inch by inch. So damn heavy.

By the time he had him out on the field, Indy was panting like crazy. That could come in handy. He grabbed Miles' phone and redialed.

"911, what is your…"

"Special Agent Hampton again."

"Your ambulance is two minutes out. We need your location."

"Flare. I'm shooting a flare." Indy panted and loudly groaned. "I'm hurt. Internal bleeding, hurry the fuck up. Not feeling well."

"We're on our way. Stay on the line."

Indy disconnected and dumped the phone on Miles' body, then ran back down for one last trip. He'd spotted the flare gun amongst the emergency stuff in the storm cellar. He waited till he saw flashlights coming down the road and shot the flare gun, then put it next to Miles.

"Don't die on me, Miles. Not after all this," he whispered.

He knew the cops would find his fingerprints on the flare gun and on Miles' phone, but he'd be long gone by then. On the road, police cars came to a screeching halt.

Right, his exit cue.

He took off, headed for the fields with wheat or what-ever the fuck it was. The stalks were tall enough to hide him, so he slipped between them and started running as fast as he could without making noise. He had no idea where he was heading, but anywhere but here was fine with him.

23

Noah was frantic. Indy had hung up on him, and he couldn't call back because the number had been blocked. Fuck knew where he was calling from and under what circumstances. Fact was that something had happened. An agent had been wounded. Miles, Indy had called him. That meant they had been attacked at their safe location. Did the FBI know this? Should he call it in?

Fuck, he wished Josh was here, or that he could at least call him. Aside from the fact that it was five in the morning, it was not an option. A nurse from the clinic had called him a week earlier, informing him Josh had suffered a severe breakdown and would be admitted to the closed ward again for at least two weeks. Since Noah was still his health care proxy, they'd asked for his permission to provide Josh with various anti-depressants and anti-psychotics. Noah was worried sick about him, even more so because Josh wasn't allowed any contact while there.

"Noah, is everything okay?" Brad's voice called out from

outside his bedroom. He must've woken up from the phone ringing or Noah talking to Indy.

"Yeah. No," Noah corrected himself. Brad. He could ask Brad. It wasn't his first choice, but he'd shown to be a good man and a perfect roommate who cleaned up after himself, and he took great care of Charlie. Plus, he was smart. Much smarter than he let on, Noah had discovered.

"Can you come in?" he asked. It would be faster than him getting up.

"Erm, yeah, sure... Hold on a sec, I gotta get dressed."

Noah frowned. Get dressed? Was the guy sleeping naked or something? That seemed unlikely, with Charlie in the same room. A minute later, there was a knock at his door.

"Yeah, come in already," Noah called out, impatient.

Brad stepped in, dressed in jeans and a sweater, though still barefoot. "What's wrong?" he asked.

"Indy called," Noah said.

"Is he okay?" The worry in Brad's voice was palpable, and it reinforced Noah's decision to ask Brad for his opinion.

"I don't know. Sit down, and I'll explain."

Brad shuffled his feet. "Could you maybe put on a shirt or something?"

What the hell? Noah looked at his bare chest, then at Brad again, narrowing his eyes. "Why?"

Brad stared at the floor. It took a long time for him to answer. "Because I promised Blake I'd stay away from you and I'm in your bedroom, you're only wearing boxers, and I don't want things to get misinterpreted. I don't want to fuck this up, so please, can you put on some clothes?"

"Brad, you're not making any sense. I know you're gay, but I also know you're not in the least attracted to me. And what do you mean, you promised to stay away from me? What, Blake thought you'd pity-fuck me?"

Brad's head shot up. "Can you do as I fucking asked you and stop fucking analyzing this and me? I don't owe you a fucking explanation, and we should focus on what's important instead of wasting our fucking energy on nothing."

Wow. This was a side of Brad he hadn't observed before. The sweet, introverted man he'd witnessed with Charlie had transformed into someone with a serious temper and an affinity for the f-bomb. He did have a point, however.

Noah grabbed his hoodie from where he'd dropped it on the floor and dragged it over his head, then wiggled himself into a pair of sweatpants, while Brad stood waiting with his back turned to Noah. "Better?"

Brad turned around. "Yes. Now talk."

Bossy much? No, Brad wasn't bossy, Noah thought. More like teenager-defiant. He was right, though. They had more important things to focus on.

"As I said, Indy called." He recapped the conversation for Brad. "What should I do?"

"Call the FBI," Brad said. "They have to know something is up. Call them, but don't volunteer too much info before you know what's going on."

Noah nodded. Brad had confirmed his own gut feeling. He still had the card Connor had given him before he'd taken off, and he took it from his wallet. It was the agent Connor had contacted through his boss—his chief's brother, if Noah remembered correctly. Special Agent Tobias Wells, the card read.

With trembling hands he made the call.

Wells answered on the second ring, which told Noah he'd been awake already. "Wells."

"Agent Wells, this is Noah Flint. I'm…"

"I know who you are. What do you know?"

"Excuse me?"

"It's just past five and shit is going down. What have you heard?"

Noah took the jump. "Indy called me maybe fifteen minutes ago, seeking medical advice. He told me he was with an agent named Miles. From what he described, this guy had been beaten severely, and I suspected internal bleeding. I told him he needed surgery, and he hung up shortly after. Please, sir, what's going on?"

Wells cursed, using some colorful words even Noah hadn't heard before. "Noah, listen. You have to trust me. I will tell you everything you need to know, but right now, time is of the essence. Is Indy safe as far as you know?"

"Yes. I asked him if he was okay, and he confirmed it. Do you know where he is?"

"No, not at this time. I need to make some calls, but I will send an agent to your house to pick you up, okay? Stay tight. Call me if you hear from Indy."

Wells hung up without saying anything else, but Noah could hardly blame him. If something had gone this wrong, the guy had better things to do than chat to an anxious boyfriend. Noah had been in this position many times and had always prioritized patient care over updating the family. They could wait, the patient couldn't. So he'd get ready, as Wells had asked, and wait for news.

"They're sending someone to pick me up."

"And go where?" Brad asked.

"I have no idea. Will you and Charlie be okay here by yourself?"

"Yeah, absolutely. Do whatever you have to do. We'll man the fort here in your absence."

"How's Charlie?" Noah asked, while hooking up his prosthesis.

"Better. His headache is gone, but he's still sore everywhere."

"His balls?" Noah hated to ask something so personal, but he wanted to make sure before he left to go wherever the FBI was taking him.

"Still blue and tender, but getting better."

"OK, good. Keep a close eye on him, okay? Call me if you see anything you don't trust, like fever, or changes in his behavior, or whatever."

Brad nodded. "Thanks again for letting us stay here, especially now."

"No problem. I'm glad you've been here. Charlie has been a good distraction for me, and I like the company."

He grabbed some things he thought would come in handy, threw them in a backpack. Clean clothes, a book, his phone, some snacks and a couple of bottles of water. It could take hours before they updated him on whatever was going on.

He explained a few things to Brad about the heating system and showed him where everything was that he'd need. Max followed Brad wherever they walked. Noah had to admit, he'd never met a sweeter dog than Max. He was a big ole cuddler, and Noah had found himself lounging on the couch with Max at his feet more than once. When Josh got back, they really had to look into getting a dog, he thought.

By the time he was done packing and explaining stuff, two men walked up to his front door, both dressed in suits. He didn't think anyone else would show up at this hour, but still asked to see their IDs. As far as he could tell they were legit.

"Mr. Flint, Special Agent Wells has asked us to escort you to Albany Airport, where we have a flight waiting to take you to DC."

DC? Wells wasn't kidding around. "Okay," he said.

"Are you carrying any weapons?"

"No."

"Mind if we check? Search your bag?"

He lifted the strap off his shoulder and held it out. "Be my guest."

One agent took his bag while the other stepped in to pat him down. Noah casually raised his pant leg. "Careful there, I'm already a leg short," he said.

Much to his surprise, the agent looked up at him, eyes narrowing when he spotted his dog tags. "Thank you for your service," he said.

As always, Noah had no idea what to say to that. In this case, even more so, because the guy was a federal agent, for fuck's sake. Not the easiest job either, and if anything, today proved it came at a helluva risk. The agent patted him down gently while the other searched his bag.

"Okay, thank you. We're good to go."

He waved goodbye to Brad, who locked the front door behind them.

The car ride to the airport was done in silence, the agents driving way over the speed limit. The flashing blue light on the roof of their car made the early morning traffic move over so they could pass. They parked in front of the main entrance and walked him straight inside.

Badges were flashed left and right, orders were given, and it took only minutes before Noah was rushing through the airport, seated on one of those golf carts, both agents flanking him. They boarded a commercial flight and were seated in the first row. Being an FBI agent had its perks.

Again, both agents stayed silent during the flight. No wonder, it wasn't like they had any privacy to talk. Noah closed his eyes and tried to nap, even though he knew it was useless. How could he sleep when Indy was in danger? What the fuck had happened? He didn't even know where Indy was, what state. Was he even still in the US? They could have flown him to Germany, for all Noah knew. It would explain the hour of the call. The phone number had come up blocked, so he had no way of knowing.

At least Indy was okay. He'd sounded okay, if panicked. That was understandable if he had a wounded agent at his side. Knowing Indy, he'd feel responsible. It was what had driven him to testify in the first place, the deep desire to stop the Fitzpatricks from killing more people, especially those connected in some way to Indy. He had such a big, tender heart, which was nothing short of amazing considering his past. How the hell had he managed to turn out so kind and soft with a mother who'd sold him and a drug dealer as a boyfriend?

If Indy ever came back to him, Noah would spend the rest of his life taking care of him. He'd worship the very ground the man walked on—even more than he already did. His heart was a big, gaping, Indy-shaped hole right now. He needed him.

After this new debacle, whatever the hell had happened, the chances of Indy returning were even less, however. If he couldn't even trust the FBI to protect him, what alternatives did that leave him? With the price on his head, it would only be a matter of time before someone found him. Again.

Noah took a deep breath, pushed down the hopeless-ness that threatened to choke him. It wouldn't help anybody if he broke down, least of all himself.

The pilot announced their descent, and Noah looked out

the window. In the distance the Washington Monument rose, a gray shape against the early morning sun. A new dawn, a new day. Please, let it be a good one.

Clearing the airport in DC took a little more time, as did the heavy morning traffic, but it still didn't take too long to arrive at their destination. Noah was ushered inside and brought into a waiting area where he was offered coffee—which he politely declined—and a breakfast sandwich, which he accepted. He'd barely finished it, when a gray-haired man stepped in.

"Noah, I'm Special Agent Tobias Wells." They shook hands, the agent's hand a strong grip. "Follow me."

They walked half a mile of hallways and corridors, Wells checking every now and then to make sure Noah could keep up, before Wells knocked on a door. The plaque beside it read "Assistant Director Joseph L. Holmes." Noah bit back a smile. In his experience, people who needed a middle initial to look more important lacked the balls to get respect any other way.

Wells led the way into a huge corner office, where another silver-haired man was seated behind a large desk.

"Sir, Noah Flint," Wells said.

Holmes rose. "Yes, grab a seat," he said, pointing toward a conference table against the wall.

Noah lowered himself into one of the chairs. Holmes waited till Noah sat down, then walked up to shake his hand, towering over him. Noah didn't react, meeting his inquisitive gaze head-on.

"Thank you for coming in," Holmes said. He sat down across from Noah, next to Wells, folding his hands in one of the most calculated gestures Noah had ever seen. If this was playing games at assistant director level, the guy still had a lot to learn.

"You're welcome," Noah said pleasantly. "Let's talk."

"Special Agent Wells told me Stephan called you this morning?"

"Indy," Noah corrected him. "His name is Indy now."

"Legally, his name is Stephan Moreau."

The man didn't like to be corrected, that much was clear. "Practically, his name is Indy Baldwin," Noah fired back.

"Regardless, what was the call about?"

Noah leaned back. He wasn't about to tell them shit before they'd shared what they knew. "I already shared this with Special Agent Wells. Tell me what's going on."

"I'd appreciate it if you told me."

"And I'd appreciate it if you shared some information first." He kept his tone light and his posture nonchalant, but Holmes had to know he wasn't fucking around.

Holmes leaned back in his chair and sighed. "The FBI team assigned to Stephan's...Indy's protective detail has been compromised. We discovered two of our agents dead at the house, and one in critical condition. Indy is missing, as is one of our other agents."

Fuck. They'd lost two other agents. Miles had to be the one in critical condition.

Noah inhaled deeply, forcing himself to stay calm. "What is your theory?"

"I can't share that with you," Holmes said. "That's classified, as it concerns a high-level security FBI operation."

"In that case, I'm not sharing either."

"Noah, we need to know what Indy told you, in as much detail as possible. This could be crucial in our efforts to find out what happened to our agents and to find Indy."

Sweet fuck, could the guy be any more condescending? Noah leaned forward. "Maybe he doesn't want to be found."

"Because he killed those agents?"

Noah blinked. Was he serious? Hell, yes, he looked like he was. "Indy is no killer," he snapped.

"From what I've been told, he's highly skilled in one of the most effective and deadly martial arts."

"A defensive martial art," Noah bit back. "And you have got to be fucking kidding me about Indy killing them. You and I both know he saved that agent's life."

It was pure intimidation, Noah realized. Holmes was trying to scare him or bully him into doing what he wanted. Well, he didn't give a shit after spending years standing up to his dad.

"Noah, you need to tell us what you know."

Noah leaned back and crossed his arms. "I don't need to do anything."

"Don't you want Stephan to be found? The Fitzpatricks might be looking for him at this very moment."

"Indy. His name is Indy. And I'm gonna take a wild guess here. The fact that two of your agents are dead and one is in critical condition, yet a fourth one is missing, seems highly suspicious to me. Surely, if that agent had somehow managed to escape the attack with Indy, he would have contacted you by now. Plus, we both know Indy was with Miles at some point, and concerned enough about him to call me for medical advice. My guess is he called an ambulance for him and took off himself. Also, they were supposed to be at a secret location. This tells me that you have a snitch, and the process of elimination leads me to your fourth agent. The fact that you are certain Indy is missing tells me you have reason to believe he was not taken by this agent, or by any possible others who aided him in the attack. Because the only ones with reason to take him are the Fitzpatricks, and if they had him, they wouldn't be looking for him. No, you must have a credible reason to believe Indy made it out of there alive and is on the run, probably on his own. Now, if all that is true, why the fuck would I want to help you find him? Seems to me he's safer on his own. How am I doing so far?"

24

T*he zone.* It was what he called it when he'd found complete inner silence and heard and saw nothing else but his target. Once he was in the zone, he could stay that way for hours, never moving. He didn't eat, didn't drink, would barely blink until he'd taken out his target. After that, he'd crash.

They'd found the perfect spot for him in an apartment building three blocks down that provided an unobstructed view and an excellent angle. Getting into the apartment had been easy with the help of John—whose name was something else entirely, of course, just like he'd never been called Mike before. Apparently, whoever lived here worked during the day, so he had till five to get the fuck out—or until the cops figured out where the shots came from. He'd be long gone before then.

He'd found a spot in the bedroom of the apartment, which offered the best view. He'd counted on having to smash a window but had been pleasantly surprised to be able to slide it open, allowing the freezing air in. Boston in the winter, now that was a different sight than what he'd seen through his telescope so far.

They'd gotten slammed with snow a couple days before, despite it being early April already, the snow piles still shoveled high into parking lots. Dump trucks were picking up snow banks everywhere, transporting them outside the city to be dumped on snow fields. His glasses protected his eyes from the blinding glare of the sun on the snow and ice. On his part, everything that could reflect had been covered—a practice perfected by having been in warmer climates so much.

Aside from the snow, only his clothes were different. He missed the sensation of his uniform, his boots, even his helmet. Taking up position while wearing full battle rattle was different than installing himself here, dressed in a crisp light blue shirt and dark blue pinstripe pants. It was so much lighter and yet felt strangely off. Then again, everything had been off ever since the assault. This was the closest he'd been to feeling himself again.

He perfected his position, already knowing the wind speed and direction. He'd practiced shooting in cold weather in Norway, learning how the cold affected the bullet's trajectory. He adjusted the telescope slightly, aligning it perfectly with his weapon. Breathed in, out, in, out, until he felt nothing else but his breaths. The targets were clearly visible. Arrogant idiots, meeting in a hotel room with windows, the blinds drawn open. Never suspecting a thing.

He'd wait for the signal. The three men in the hotel room were bored, by the looks of it. One was flicking through channels, the other two sitting at a table, nursing a beer. Their body postures were relaxed, despite the guns they had laid out on the table.

One of the men switched off the TV and walked toward the door. *Show time.*

He lay motionless, even when he saw the fourth person enter the room after being thoroughly patted down. He was in the zone, saw nothing else but the targets. The fourth person shook hands, then took a seat at the table with the other three, taking the position farthest away from the window.

They talked for minutes, but his eyes purely watched body language. The second they became aggressive he'd take them out. The fourth person slowly reached for his pocket, clearly explaining what he was doing, because although there was more alertness, they didn't respond with force. He took out a red envelope and put it on the table.

Three seconds. He started counting. One...Two...Three.

He squeezed the trigger on target one. The fourth person dove to the ground. Target two, clean shot as the guy reached for the gun on the table. Target three was smarter, going for the floor instantly. He was awfully close to the fourth person, but it didn't matter. He took the shot, hitting him in the chest before he reached the ground. He watched through his telescope as the fourth person got up, shaking ever so slightly, and picked up the red envelope from the table. He never even looked at the window as he put his coat back on and exited the room as fast as he could.

He exhaled. Done. It was done. Operation Freedom was a success.

He pulled back his rifle, closed the window. He disassembled the rifle in seconds, put it in his five-hundred-dollar black leather lawyer briefcase. Collected the three shell cases. Sprayed the window and window stiles with special cleaning spray, wiped them down, even though he'd been wearing gloves the entire time. Put everything in his briefcase, checked to see he had left nothing behind.

He waited till he was at the front door to put on a thick, dark gray overcoat that screamed money. A beanie in the same color—few people were venturing outside without head covering as the temperature was hovering in the low twenties—complemented his business attire. No one seeing him would suspect he had just killed three men. And had enjoyed every fucking second of it.

Payback, it really was a bitch.

25

H olmes' face had grown redder with every word Noah had spoken. The steam was about to blow from his ears. "Son, you need to start cooperating with us, or we will charge you with obstruction of justice."

"I'm not your son. You wanna know whose son I am? General Flint's. You charge me, and you better believe my first call will be to my dad. Do you want to take a bet on who will win that pissing match? You cannot intimidate me or bully me into saying anything because I'm immune to it after spending years with my dad and in the army."

"It's not our intention to intimidate you, Noah," Wells spoke up for the first time. A little tic near his eye told Noah he wasn't entirely comfortable with the way things were going. That made two of them.

"Sure you were. This is a good cop/bad cop routine. I'm more than familiar with it, trust me. If you want me to cooperate, change tactics. Share openly with me and I'll do the same."

"We need Indy to put away the Fitzpatricks for good,

Noah. Surely you realize there's a bigger picture here," Wells said.

"I need Indy to stay alive. After what happened, you can't blame me for not taking my chances with the FBI. I hate to say this, but you got a serious security issue."

"We lost two agents today, Noah. You don't need to convince us we have a problem."

For the first time, Holmes sounded sincere, and Noah experienced a flash of guilt about keeping information from the FBI. Assuming the agents who had died were the good ones, they had been murdered protecting Indy. "I am truly sorry for your loss. I know that sounds like a meaningless cliché, but it's the truth. Doesn't mean I'm willing to risk my boyfriend's life, though."

Holmes placed his fingers against each other in a move that looked so studied, Noah had to bite back a grin. "So, Stephan is your boyfriend? Rumors are, he's not the only one. What exactly is your relationship to Joshua Gordon and Ignatius O'Connor?"

Noah laughed. He flat-out laughed. "Seriously? You think I'm gonna be embarrassed? I don't give a flying fuck what you've heard, or what you think. I don't owe you any explanation, and even if I did fuck all of them, and God knows who else, it still wouldn't be any of your business. This still is a free country, and Josh, Connor, and I have sacrificed a lot to keep it that way. Now, are you done with this bullshit or not?"

Holmes balled his fists, then forcibly relaxed. He shot Wells a look, who cleared his throat.

"Right. Just after four in the morning local time, emergency dispatchers received a call from a man identifying himself as Special Agent Miles Hampton. He is one of the agents assigned to Indy's protective detail. We have reason to believe it wasn't Hampton who made the call, however, but Indy. Listen to this."

Wells hit a few buttons on the laptop in front of him, and a file started to play. Noah recognized Indy's voice right away, even if he'd tried to lower it. He sounded so calm, his brave man. He had to have been so scared. He played it smart, kept up the pretense until he hung up.

Noah fought hard to keep his face blank when Indy mentioned this agent Crouch being compromised. So the FBI did have a traitor on their hands, and yet they'd tried to make Noah believe Indy had killed those agents. Fucking assholes.

"What makes you think this was Indy?" Noah asked when the recording ended, keeping his voice neutral.

Wells smiled. "It's not Hampton's voice, but even the dispatcher suspected at the time of the call. The caller didn't use the right language, but it was close enough that the dispatcher sent what he asked for anyway."

Noah nodded. He didn't see the harm in confirming what they already knew. "It's Indy."

"He called back a few minutes later. This is the second recording."

Noah's stomach turned as he heard Indy pant and groan. Had he been injured after all? Or was he pretending to be, so they'd believe he was the FBI agent?

"Emergency services discovered Special Agent Miles Hampton near a storm cellar. He was transported to the hospital where his spleen was operated on. He's out of surgery but still in serious condition with multiple fractured ribs, a broken nose, a concussion, and a slew of minor issues."

"Indy said they beat him up," Noah offered.

"Did he say who? Mention any names?"

"No. The call was focused on the agent's medical issues. He hung up as soon as I told him he needed to get him to a hospital."

"The team was staying at a Kansas farm, which was discovered on fire even before Indy made that call. We believe Indy started the fire as a distraction, then escaped with Agent Hampton through a storm cellar leading into a tunnel."

"You mentioned two dead agents?"

Wells' face tightened. "Yes. A neighbor called in the fire, which would have been visible from miles away. When cops arrived at the scene, they discovered the bodies of two agents in the farm house. They were shot multiple times and both were found in their respective bedrooms. Indy's room was found empty, a window in his bathroom lifted from the frame. We assume that's how he escaped. He must have climbed over the roof and managed to get into a barn. We're not entirely sure how he discovered Agent Hampton was still alive. Marks on Hampton's wrists and ankles suggest he'd been tied up, so Indy must have freed him."

Noah couldn't resist it. "So much for your absurd theory where Indy is the killer."

Holmes merely shot him a dark look but ignored the barb. Unfortunately.

"Our fourth agent is missing."

"Crouch," Noah said, allowing his anger to shine through. "The man Indy identified as being compromised, and yet you wanted me to believe Indy had something to do with this."

Wells let out a sigh. Noah suspected he hadn't been happy with the way his boss had handled that. At all. "We're allowed to lie to try and get people to cooperate," he said diplomatically.

"The fact that you're legally allowed doesn't make it morally justified," Noah snapped. "Especially when you have information that proves the opposite, like in this case. Indy had nothing to do with this attack, can we at least agree on that?"

Wells nodded. "It doesn't seem likely, no."

Noah realized he'd have to take that answer as the best outcome. This was the FBI. They wouldn't rule out anything until they had cold, hard proof.

"Look, Noah, based on the information we have right now it looks like Crouch played a role in the attack, but we have no concrete intel as to what, or how and why. He was the lead agent on the detail and a long-time FBI veteran, so it's hard to imagine him doing this."

"Do you know who the attackers were?" Noah asked.

Wells shook his head. "No. We suspect they're linked to the Fitzpatricks, obviously, but we have no leads. They escaped on foot, stole a car from a neighboring farm, then another one at a truck stop. That's where we lost them—if they're even still together at this point."

Noah leaned forward. "What do you want to know from me?"

"What can you tell us about Indy's state of mind? What will he do in a situation like this?"

Noah's answer came fast. "Run."

CONNOR GLANCED around the room to make sure he wasn't forgetting anything. When he was satisfied, he put his jacket back on, then his gloves. He'd been careful not to touch any smooth surfaces with his bare hands. It was freezing outside, so no one would notice anything weird about him wearing leather gloves, even inside the hotel. His jacket would conceal the blood splatters and brain matter on his shirt.

He took off his shoes before he opened the door so he wouldn't track any bloodstains back to his room and peeked into the hallway to make sure no one was there yet. He then hurried into the staircase, listened again to make sure no one was in there yet. Noise from below him traveled up, but it was nowhere near his floor. With his shoes in his hand, he took the stairs two floors up. He'd picked a room right next to the staircases, so the chances of him running into someone were small, and he swiped his key card to get inside, making sure to stay on the plastic tarp he'd put on the floor before leaving his room.

When he closed the door behind him, he noticed his hands were shaking slightly. No wonder. That had been damn close. Connor knew the shooter wouldn't miss, but still. Seeing someone's brains get blown out a few feet away from you would make even a seasoned Marine shake in his boots. He exhaled slowly, his mind still completely alert.

He put the bolt on the door, took his shoes off and dropped all his clothes on the tarp. He put everything he'd been wearing in a trash bag he'd placed there before he'd left and tied it securely. The bag went into a suitcase, along with the tarp he now took off the floor.

First, he needed to set the second part of the plan in motion. He fired off a message that would send a detailed list of Fitzpatrick properties and what could be found there to his contact at the Boston Police Department. His former classmate Davy Ford had more than come through, connecting him with a slew of low-level criminals who were sick and tired of the Fitzpatricks' iron-fisted reign. Connor had collected names, dates, evidence, and had given the

BPD a heads-up through an informant they trusted to prepare for a big raid. He'd delivered them everything on a fucking silver platter, so now he could only hope the boys in blue wouldn't fuck it up.

Either way, Duncan Fitzpatrick was dead, and Connor had never been happier to see a man die than to watch that asshole's brains get blown to bits. His only regret was that he hadn't been able to do it himself.

Duncan and his father Brian, Connor's uncle, had been so fucking careless about meeting Connor, even when they'd known he'd been a cop. All Connor had to do was tell them he wanted in the family business and that he could deliver dirty cops to them. They'd jumped on his proposal to meet in the hotel, had even brought Duncan's brother Alan along, who was as much as asshole as the rest of his family.

And now they were all dead. The only one left was Connor's grandfather Jeremy, the patriarch of the Fitz-patricks, but he was in hospice about to die from lung cancer. When he died, they would all be gone, and Connor only felt relief.

Satisfied he'd left no visible traces behind, Connor walked into the bathroom and ran a shower. The water was scalding hot, and he cleaned himself meticulously. He packed up his towel in another plastic sheet and folded it as well to place it in the suitcase. Then he cleaned the bathroom with bleach, making sure as little as possible remained of his DNA.

He'd rented the room under a different name, of course, and he hadn't slept in the bed—though he had messed it up to make it look like he'd used it, just like he left some soap and shower gel splatters in the bathroom after cleaning it to make it look dirty. Wetted towels were carelessly thrown on the floor, like the housekeeping ladies would expect from any guest. With a satisfied look he concluded no one would see anything suspect about this room.

If the crime scene investigators did their job, they'd soon discover there had been a fourth man in that hotel room. He'd absorbed blood spatters and brain matter that would have otherwise fallen on the floor, so they'd know there was someone else. They would have no idea who, however, and he intended to keep it that way. The hotel had security cameras, but he'd paid a guy handsomely to disable the recording, and with the reputation this man had, Connor had no doubt there wouldn't be a digital trace of him anywhere.

He walked out of the room, leaving the key card in his room, since he'd already checked out and paid earlier that morning. With his suitcase rolling behind him he made his way over to the elevator, where two other men were waiting.

"Did you hear?" one of the men asked as soon as he was within earshot. "Someone got shot two floors below us."

"They shot him from outside, through the window," his companion added.

Connor's eyebrows rose. "For real?" he asked. His New York accent wasn't as good as Indy's would have been, but he could fool these two who were obviously not from Boston. Or New York, judging by their Australian accents. "That's terrible!"

Both men nodded, clearly happy they had someone they could share their knowledge with. "It's all over the telly. Apparently, there are multiple victims, all belonging to some crime family. Good riddance, I say," the first man said.

"Well, if it's criminals killing criminals, then I'm all for it. Easy solution, right?" Connor played along.

"Exactly. Saves the US government a lot of bloody

trouble arresting and prosecuting them," the second man chimed in.

They kept talking about it on the elevator ride down, Connor agreeing amicably with everything they said. Downstairs, the lobby was crawling with cops, but Connor wasn't worried. They had no reason to suspect anyone inside the hotel yet, since it had clearly been a shooter from outside. They'd focus on the building the shooter had used and on processing the room the victims were in. By the time they concluded there had been another person in the room, he'd be long gone. Besides, no one would ever recognize him with his scruff and his hair longer than he'd ever had it. And according to the VA facility records, he was visiting Josh right now.

He kept his head straight and his strides purposeful as he made his way to the exit. Two cops were guarding the exit, and they gave him a quick once-over, then let him pass.

It was done.

26

Noah had tried to answer their questions as best as he could. No, he had not heard from Indy since that morning. No, as far as he knew Indy had no friends or acquaintances in Kansas. No, Indy did not have a working phone. They told him he'd used Miles' phone to call him, which didn't surprise Noah. The blocked number had been a giveaway.

Then Wells had started asking questions about how Indy had managed to stay under the radar for so long, and that's when Noah had stopped talking. Apparently, Indy hadn't told the FBI about dressing as a woman—and Noah wasn't about to blow the lid on that one. It was clear to him Indy didn't want to be found right now, and as hard as it was to accept that, he'd damn well try.

When it had become clear Noah was done cooperating, they'd brought him to some kind of waiting area. It was a room with a few comfortable chairs and a supply of ancient magazines, telling him Brad and Angelina were splitting up. Duh.

In the corner of the room a TV screen showed the news

with the volume set to blissfully low. Noah looked up every now and then when he caught something that piqued his attention, but he ignored it for the most part. Not that the book he was attempting to read could really hold his attention, but news would only depress him further, so what was the point?

He slouched lower in his seat and yawned. As he stretched, his eye caught the news again. He froze, watching completely stunned as images showed a cordoned-off hotel, then bodies being carried outside in body bags and lifted into police vans. *What the...?*

The name "Fitzpatricks" finally set him in motion. He jumped up, yanked the remote from the coffee table and turned up the volume.

"Investigators have no clue as to how the three men have been shot but confirmed they were targeted from outside, through the hotel window. The police have identified the three victims as Brian Fitzpatrick, age fifty-two, and his sons Duncan, age twenty-eight, and Alan, age twenty-two. Police have confirmed the three were known top leaders in the infamous Fitzpatrick organization, the Irish mob that has been terrorizing the Boston South Side for the last two decades. A spokesperson for the Boston PD said he had little doubt the murders were connected to these men leading a life of crime that had caught up to them, though confirmed the police were still working the case and had no concrete information on the shooter or shooters at this time. The police requests everyone with information to contact them, anonymously, if need be.

"Later today, police raided several houses and locations on the South Side believed to be connected to the Fitzpatricks. The police spokesman declined to comment on these raids, stating that they were part of an ongoing investigation. Our crime reporter Jack Donovan is on the scene and has more details. Jack?"

"Our sources confirm that the police seem to have taken advantage of the total chaos in the Fitzpatrick organization after three of their top leaders were taken out this morning. Police were busy the entire afternoon arresting individuals known or suspected to have ties to the Fitzpatricks, as well as loading up dozens of vans with evidence. The raids were so coordinated, sources informed me, that many of the suspects were taken by surprise, resulting in much incriminating evidence being taken by the police. One source speculated the police may have been tipped off about the killings beforehand, though not the specific date, time, and location, allowing them to prepare these raids ahead of time. The police declined to comment, but we will, of course, follow this case closely. It's no secret law enforcement has been after the Fitzpatricks for years. This included Boston District Attorney Donovan Merrick who was killed in a fire two months ago with his family—a brutal act of murder that has been attributed to the Fitzpatricks as well. And of course, police are still speculating about the fate of Stephan Moreau, the former lover of Duncan Fitzpatrick who turned state witness after surviving a brutal attack on his life. He disappeared into thin air before the trial, however, and is suspected to have died at the hands of the Fitzpatricks. With today's murders and the subsequent raids, it seems at least that the Fitzpatrick clan has been dealt a devastating, if not deadly, blow it will likely not recover from."

Noah slowly lowered his hand, which had flown to his mouth in disbelief at watching the news. How the fuck was this possible?

"Did you know about this?"

Noah turned around, startled by Wells' voice. "What?"

Wells pointed toward the TV. "Did you know about this?"

Noah frowned. "How the fuck would I have known?"

Wells seemed to study him for a bit before he shrugged. "I dunno, but it seems mighty convenient that you're here when that went down. It's the perfect alibi."

Did he really think Noah had something to do with this? Those assholes were shot from...

He stopped mid-track in his thoughts. Could it be? No, he was in the closed ward of a psych hospital. There was no way. Was there?

"You invited me here, remember? And it was about what happened in Kansas, not about this. I'm only now seeing this."

Wells gestured for him to sit down and took a seat across from him. "This means freedom for Indy," he said. "The three guys killed were the only ones with a motive to go after him. Jeremy Fitzpatrick, the old guy, is dying. He has days at most. They've arrested all lower-level lieutenants. If Indy testifies against them, he'll bring them all down."

Noah's head was about to explode with all the thoughts assaulting him at the same time. "What about the contract on his head?"

Wells shook his head. "That was guaranteed by Duncan. Now that he's gone, there's no one to pay out. The lieutenants don't have access to the funds. These guys, they're in it for the money. They'll stop looking for him, I guarantee you."

"Holy fuck, he's free," Noah said. A gulf of emotion rolled over him, making it hard to breathe. "He's finally free."

~

INDY HAD RUN for hours until he was too exhausted to move anymore. He'd made his way across fields, following dirt tracks and country roads, heading south. That little compass in his backpack had sure come in handy.

His usual strategy was to head for a big city and get lost amongst the masses, but this was Kansas. There were no big cities, not for miles, anyways. Dodge City had to be closest, since he'd seen signs when they drove him in, but even that had to be tens of miles away. He wouldn't be able to reach it before sunset, and he was sure as hell not spending a night outside here. Fuck knew what kind of animals roamed these fields. No, he had to think of a way to make it to Dodge City, one that didn't involve walking.

Fuck, he wished he had his female clothes. He felt too exposed without them, especially after that broadcast. Then again, this was a long way from Boston. Would they even have shown that on the news here? Plus, by now that was months ago. No one would remember, most likely. The only people who were looking for him were Duncan's men, the guys who had attacked the farm. And the odds of running into them in broad daylight on a country road somewhere in the southwest of Kansas were small. No, they'd still be hiding, knowing law enforcement was hunting them down.

He'd have to take his chances. He had no money, no ID, and food and water that would last him a couple of days at best. If he didn't find a solution soon, he would be fucked. Maybe in Dodge City he could find a way to contact Noah.

Even the thought of him made Indy's heart contract painfully. Fuck, he missed him so damn much. He pushed back the thought. Thinking of Noah was a luxury he couldn't afford right now. He had to get the fuck out of there.

A truck appeared on the horizon, and he made his decision. When he raised his thumb in the universal hitchhiking gesture, the truck came to a slow stop. The driver, a fifty-something guy with a long, brown beard, gestured for him to get in. He pulled himself up, opened the door and climbed in.

"Howdy, son," the driver said with a friendly smile. "Whatcha doing here by yourself?"

Indy's eyes fell on the small pictures taped to his dashboard. School pictures of two girls and a boy. The man was a dad. He could work with that.

"My stepfather kicked me out, sir," Indy lied. He let his shoulders hunch. "He didn't like my momma giving me attention, I guess. She's a wonderful mom, but she can't see him for the monster he is."

The man gave him a sympathetic look. "That's a tough situation to be in, son. You got a place to go?"

Indy nodded. "Yes, sir. I have family in Dodge City. I woulda called my aunt, but my stepdad took my phone. And all my money. But my aunt Jenny will take me in, I'm sure."

His eyes fell on the large tattoo on the driver's right arm, depicting a curled-up snake with familiar words written underneath. Don't tread on me. Now there was something he could definitely use.

He lowered his voice, putting some sadness in it. "She's my late dad's sister, my aunt Jenny. He was a marine, my dad. Killed in action in Iraq."

"I'm sorry for your loss, son, but you should be proud of your dad and the sacrifice he made for this country."

"I am, sir. My dad is my hero."

The driver reached out with his meaty hand. "I'm Stan, and I'd be happy to drop you off anywhere in Dodge City."

Indy shook his hand. "Thank you so much. I'm Alex."

Seconds later, they were on their way, and he sighed

with relief. It was almost four in the afternoon, and he was exhausted. The muscles in his legs were trembling with fatigue and overexertion, and his feet were killing him.

Stan made small talk with the radio playing in the background, and Indy forced himself to respond, sticking to the persona he'd created.

"I'm gonna listen to the news for a minute," Stan announced. He turned up the radio.

Indy's stomach twisted. Would the attack be on the news? It was damn local, but surely the FBI would have tried to keep it under wraps, right? His hands got clammy as the news reader announced the first story, which was something about the president, thank fuck.

"The Boston Police Department is still not coming forth with any information about the identity of the sniper who shot three men through a hotel window this morning. The three victims were top leaders in the notorious Fitzpatrick crime family and have been identified as Brian Fitzpatrick and his two sons Duncan and Alan. A police spokesperson stated the shooting is most likely related to the many crimes of this Boston mob family but refused to speculate about the identity of the shooter."

Blood rushed out of Indy's head, and he wavered in his seat. Duncan was dead. Holy motherfucking hell, he was dead.

Shot.

By a sniper.

Duncan was dead.

"Stan, can you please... I'm sick..."

Stan stopped the truck immediately, shooting Indy a worried look, but Indy was out of the cabin before the truck had even fully stopped. His stomach heaved violently, and he threw up on the shoulder. A tremor tore through his body as his stomach revolted again, and he deposited more on the side of the road.

Indy wiped his mouth with the back of his hand as his stomach settled down. Duncan was dead. That son of a bitch was finally dead. Unbelievable.

His lightheadedness lifted, and instead, a sense of euphoria rushed through his veins, even as tears started falling down his cheeks.

He was free. For the first time since his mom had sold him to Duncan, he was free.

Indy breathed in deeply, wiped the tears from his eyes, and straightened himself. A massive wave of longing hit him.

Home.

He was about to go home, to the one true home he'd ever had, with Noah and Josh and hopefully Connor.

Finally.

(To be continued in No Shame)

MEET NORA PHOENIX

Would you like the long or the short version of my bio?

The short? You got it.

I write steamy gay romance books and I love it. I also love reading books. Books are everything.

How was that?

A little more detail? Gotcha.

I started writing my first stories when I was a teen...on a freaking typewriter. I still have these, and they're adorably romantic. And bad, haha. Fear of failing kept me from following my dream to become a romance author, so you can imagine how proud and ecstatic I am that I finally over-came my fears and self doubt and did it. I adore my genre because I love writing and reading about flawed, strong men who are just a tad broken..but find their happy ever after anyway.

My favorite books to read are pretty much all MM/gay romances as long as it has a happy end. Kink is a plus... Aside from that, I also read a lot of nonfiction and not just books on writing. Popular psychology is a favorite topic of mine and so are self help and sociology.

Hobbies? Ain't nobody got time for that. Just kidding. I love traveling, spending time near the ocean, and hiking. But I love books more.

Come hang out with me in my Facebook Group Nora's Nook where I share previews, sneak peeks, freebies, fun stuff, and much more:

   https://www.facebook.com/groups/norasnook/

Wanna get first dibs on freebies, updates, sales, and more? Sign up for my newsletter (no spamming your inbox full... promise!) here:

   http://www.noraphoenix.com/newsletter/

You can also stalk me on Twitter: @NoraFromBHR
   On Instagram:
   https://www.instagram.com/nora.phoenix/
   On Bookbub:
   https://www.bookbub.com/profile/nora-phoenix

ACKNOWLEDGMENTS

Three down, one to go. In hindsight, it may have been a little ambitious to publish four books back-to-back, but the support of so many people around made it possible.

A first huge thanks to my readers, who constantly encourage me with their messages and emails. Every time I post a teaser, you guys go all "Gimme, gimme," on me, and I love it. You make me feel special, and it's the best feeling in the world.

Sloan, I love this cover. Thanks for your hard work on this.

Courtney, your editing rocks, both because of your smart advice and because of your hilarious remarks along the way.

Kyleen, Michele, Amanda, and Tania: thanks for beta reading this book. I loved your feedback, and it helped make the book so much better. Tania, your scene-by-scene comments while you were reading were so awesome. I loved reading the book through your eyes!

Last but not least, a big thanks to my ARC readers for reading and reviewing my book. Reviews matter SO much to self-published authors like me, so thanks for taking the time to leave a review.

NO SHAME

Don't miss the last installment in the No Shame Series! In No Shame, we'll follow Miles, Brad, and Charlie on their journey to love:

Brad feels nothing but shame about himself. Shame about his sexual needs, about his reputation, about his medical problem no one knows about. No one, except his best friend Charlie, but no matter what feelings Brad may have for him, he's not going there. Charlie deserves so much better, and Brad desperately needs something not even Charlie can provide.

Charlie has loved Brad forever, but he's never acted on his feelings, unsure of where he stood. Plus, there was the complication of his boyfriend. But when his boyfriend's abuse gets too much for Charlie, it's Brad who helps him escape and recover.

Miles ends up severely wounded in the line of duty as an FBI agent. He's floored when the man he was protecting, Indy, opens his home to him so he can recover. Indy also sets him up with Brad, who turns out to be a perfect solution for Miles' sexual issues...until Miles wants more than sex from him, and a developing friendship between Miles and Charlie complicates things even more.

Bit by bit Charlie and Miles break through Brad's defenses, until they come crumbling down. Miles will have to prove he can provide what Brad needs, and Charlie's sweet love will be put to the test. But when Brad finally finds the courage to break free of his shame, will the fragile love that has blossomed between the three of them survive?

Order No Shame now on Amazon

(Turn the page from a sneak peek at No Shame)

ALSO BY NORA PHOENIX

No Shame Series:

No Filter

No Limits

No Fear

No Shame

No Angel

No Shame: The Complete Series

(With Bonus Materials and Deleted Scenes)

Irresistible Omegas Series (mpreg):

Alpha's Sacrifice

Alpha's Submission

Beta's Surrender

Alpha's Pride

Beta's Strength

Ignite Series (dystopian/sci-fi):

Ignite

Stand Alones:

The Time of My Life

Kissing the Teacher

Ballsy Boys Series (with K.M. Neuhold):

Ballsy (free prequel)

Rebel

Tank

Heart

Campy

Printed in Poland
by Amazon Fulfillment
Poland Sp. z o.o., Wrocław